I0565438

"Will you tell how you did it or shall I?"

Jacques Futrelle *The Scarlet Thread—p. 70*

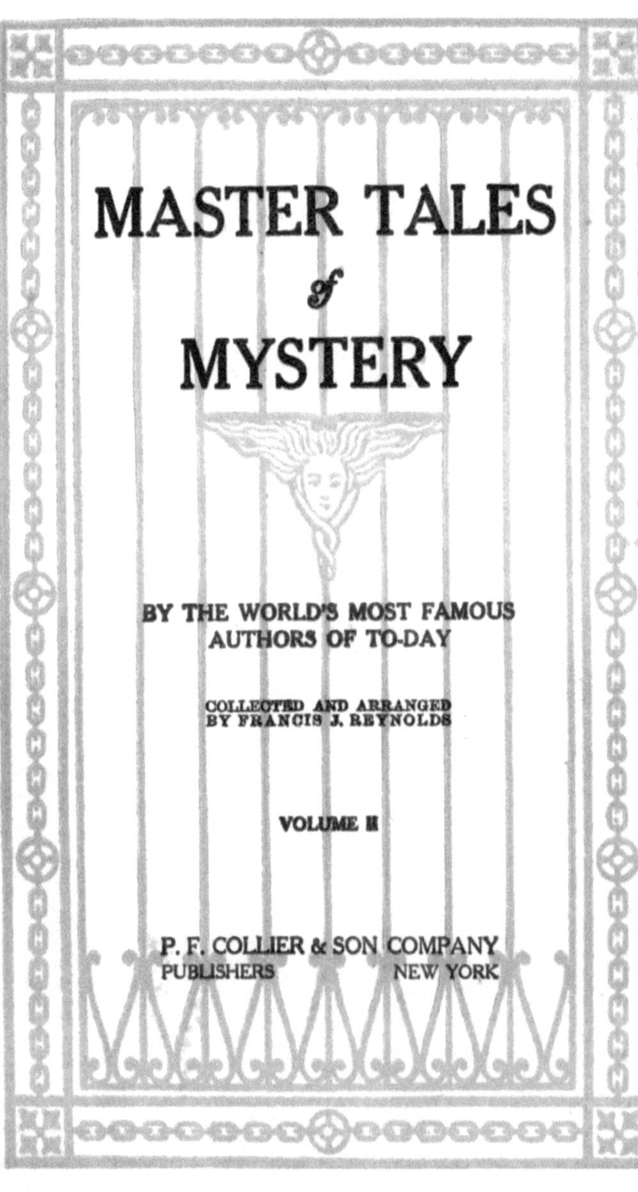

MASTER TALES
of
MYSTERY

BY THE WORLD'S MOST FAMOUS AUTHORS OF TO-DAY

COLLECTED AND ARRANGED BY FRANCIS J. REYNOLDS

VOLUME II

P. F. COLLIER & SON COMPANY
PUBLISHERS NEW YORK

Contents

The Problem of Cell 13

BY JACQUES FUTRELLE

The Problem of Cell 13

BY JACQUES FUTRELLE

I

PRACTICALLY all those letters remaining in the alphabet after Augustus S. F. X. Van Dusen was named were afterward acquired by that gentleman in the course of a brilliant scientific career, and, being honorably acquired, were tacked on to the other end. His name, therefore, taken with all that belonged to it, was a wonderfully imposing structure. He was a Ph. D., an LL. D., an F. R. S., an M. D., and an M. D. S. He was also some other things—just what he himself couldn't say—through recognition of his ability by various foreign educational and scientific institutions.

In appearance he was no less striking than in nomenclature. He was slender with the droop of the student in his thin shoulders and the pallor of a close, sedentary life on his clean-shaven face. His eyes wore a perpetual, forbidding squint—of a man who studies little things—and when they could be seen at all through his thick spectacles, were mere slits of watery blue. But above his eyes was his most striking feature. This was a tall, broad brow, almost abnormal in height and width, crowned by a heavy shock of bushy, yellow hair. All these things conspired to give him a peculiar, almost grotesque, personality.

Professor Van Dusen was remotely German. For generations his ancestors had been noted in the sciences; he was the logical result, the master mind. First and above all he was a logician. At least thirty-five years of the half-century or so of his existence had been devoted exclusively to proving that two and two always equal four, except in unusual cases, where they equal three or five, as the case may be. He stood broadly on the general proposition that all things that start must go somewhere, and was able to bring the concentrated mental force of his forefathers to bear on a given problem. Incidentally it may be remarked that Professor Van Dusen wore a No. 8 hat.

The world at large had heard vaguely of Professor Van Dusen as The Thinking Machine. It was a newspaper catch-phrase applied to him at the time of a remarkable exhibition at chess; he had demonstrated then that a stranger to the game might, by the force of inevitable logic, defeat a champion who had devoted a lifetime to its study. The Thinking Machine! Perhaps that more nearly described him than all his honorary initials, for he spent week after week, month after month, in the seclusion of his small laboratory from which had gone forth thoughts that staggered scientific associates and deeply stirred the world at large.

It was only occasionally that The Thinking Machine had visitors, and these were usually men who, themselves high in the sciences, dropped in to argue a point and perhaps convince themselves. Two of these men, Dr. Charles Ransome and Alfred Fielding, called one evening to discuss some theory which is not of consequence here.

"Such a thing is impossible," declared Dr. Ransome emphatically, in the course of the conversation.

"Nothing is impossible," declared The Thinking Machine with equal emphasis. He always spoke petulantly. "The mind is master of all things. When science fully recognizes that fact a great advance will have been made."

"How about the airship?" asked Dr. Ransome.

"That's not impossible at all," asserted The Thinking Machine. "It will be invented some time. I'd do it myself, but I'm busy."

Dr. Ransome laughed tolerantly.

"I've heard you say such things before," he said. "But they mean nothing. Mind may be master of matter, but it hasn't yet found a way to apply itself. There are some things that can't be *thought* out of existence, or rather which would not yield to any amount of thinking."

"What, for instance?" demanded The Thinking Machine.

Dr. Ransome was thoughtful for a moment as he smoked.

"Well, say prison walls," he replied. "No man can *think*

himself out of a cell. If he could, there would be no prisoners."

"A man can so apply his brain and ingenuity that he can leave a cell, which is the same thing," snapped The Thinking Machine.

Dr. Ransome was slightly amused.

"Let's suppose a case," he said, after a moment. "Take a cell where prisoners under sentence of death are confined—men who are desperate and, maddened by fear, would take any chance to escape—suppose you were locked in such a cell. Could you escape?"

"Certainly," declared The Thinking Machine.

"Of course," said Mr. Fielding, who entered the conversation for the first time, "you might wreck the cell with an explosive—but inside, a prisoner, you couldn't have that."

"There would be nothing of that kind," said The Thinking Machine. "You might treat me precisely as you treated prisoners under sentence of death, and I would leave the cell."

"Not unless you entered it with tools prepared to get out," said Dr. Ransome.

The Thinking Machine was visibly annoyed and his blue eyes snapped.

"Lock me in any cell in any prison anywhere at any time, wearing only what is necessary, and I'll escape in a week," he declared, sharply.

Dr. Ransome sat up straight in the chair, interested. Mr. Fielding lighted a new cigar.

"You mean you could actually *think* yourself out?" asked Dr. Ransome.

"I would get out," was the response.

"Are you serious?"

"Certainly I am serious."

Dr. Ransome and Mr. Fielding were silent for a long time.

"Would you be willing to try it?" asked Mr. Fielding, finally.

"Certainly," said Professor Van Dusen, and there was a trace of irony in his voice. "I have done more asinine things than that to convince other men of less important truths."

The tone was offensive and there was an undercurrent

THE PROBLEM OF CELL 13

strongly resembling anger on both sides. Of course it was an absurd thing, but Professor Van Dusen reiterated his willingness to undertake the escape and it was decided upon.

"To begin now," added Dr. Ransome.

"I'd prefer that it begin to-morrow," said The Thinking Machine, "because—"

"No, now," said Mr. Fielding, flatly. "You are arrested, figuratively, of course, without any warning locked in a cell with no chance to communicate with friends, and left there with identically the same care and attention that would be given to a man under sentence of death. Are you willing?"

"All right, now, then," said The Thinking Machine, and he arose.

"Say, the death-cell in Chisholm Prison."

"The death-cell in Chisholm Prison."

"And what will you wear?"

"As little as possible," said The Thinking Machine. "Shoes, stocking, trousers and a shirt."

"You will permit yourself to be searched, of course?"

"I am to be treated precisely as all prisoners are treated," said The Thinking Machine. "No more attention and no less."

There were some preliminaries to be arranged in the matter of obtaining permission for the test, but all three were influential men and everything was done satisfactorily by telephone, albeit the prison commissioners, to whom the experiment was explained on purely scientific grounds, were sadly bewildered. Professor Van Dusen would be the most distinguished prisoner they had ever entertained.

When The Thinking Machine had donned those things which he was to wear during his incarceration he called the little old woman who was his housekeeper, cook and maid servant all in one.

"Martha," he said, "it is now twenty-seven minutes past nine o'clock. I am going away. One week from to-night, at half-past nine, these gentlemen and one, possibly two, others will take supper with me here. Remember Dr. Ransome is very fond of artichokes."

The three men were driven to Chisholm Prison, where the warden was awaiting them, having been informed of the matter by telephone. He understood merely that the eminent Professor Van Dusen was to be his prisoner, if he could keep him, for one week; that he had committed no crime, but that he was to be treated as all other prisoners were treated.

"Search him," instructed Dr. Ransome.

The Thinking Machine was searched. Nothing was found on him; the pockets of the trousers were empty; the white, stiff-bosomed shirt had no pocket. The shoes and stockings were removed, examined, then replaced. As he watched all these preliminaries—the rigid search and noted the pitiful, childlike physical weakness of the man, the colorless face, and the thin, white hands—Dr. Ransome almost regretted his part in the affair.

"Are you sure you want to do this?" he asked.

"Would you be convinced if I did not?" inquired The Thinking Machine in turn.

"No."

"All right. I'll do it."

What sympathy Dr. Ransome had was dissipated by the tone. It nettled him, and he resolved to see the experiment to the end; it would be a stinging reproof to egotism.

"It will be impossible for him to communicate with anyone outside?" he asked.

"Absolutely impossible," replied the warden. "He will not be permitted writing materials of any sort."

"And your jailers, would they deliver a message from him?"

"Not one word, directly or indirectly," said the warden. "You may rest assured of that. They will report anything he might say or turn over to me anything he might give them."

"That seems entirely satisfactory," said Mr. Fielding, who was frankly interested in the problem.

"Of course, in the event he fails," said Dr. Ransome, "and asks for his liberty, you understand you are to set him free?"

"I understand," replied the warden.

The Thinking Machine stood listening, but had nothing to say until this was all ended, then:

"I should like to make three small requests. You may grant them or not, as you wish."

"No special favors, now," warned Mr. Fielding.

"I am asking none," was the stiff response. "I would like to have some tooth powder—buy it yourself to see that it is tooth powder—and I should like to have one five-dollar and two ten-dollar bills."

Dr. Ransome, Mr. Fielding and the warden exchanged astonished glances. They were not surprised at the request for tooth powder, but were at the request for money.

"Is there any man with whom our friend would come in contact that he could bribe with twenty-five dollars?" asked Dr. Ransome of the warden.

"Not for twenty-five hundred dollars," was the positive reply.

"Well, let him have them," said Mr. Fielding. "I think they are harmless enough."

"And what is the third request?" asked Dr. Ransome.

"I should like to have my shoes polished."

Again the astonished glances were exchanged. This last request was the height of absurdity, so they agreed to it. These things all being attended to, The Thinking Machine was led back into the prison from which he had undertaken to escape.

"Here is Cell 13," said the warden, stopping three doors down the steel corridor. "This is where we keep condemned murderers. No one can leave it without my permission; and no one in it can communicate with the outside. I'll stake my reputation on that. It's only three doors back of my office and I can readily hear any unusual noise."

"Will this cell do, gentlemen?" asked The Thinking Machine. There was a touch of irony in his voice.

"Admirably," was the reply.

The heavy steel door was thrown open, there was a great scurrying and scampering of tiny feet, and The Thinking Machine passed into the gloom of the cell. Then the door was closed and double locked by the warden.

"What is that noise in there?" asked Dr. Ransome, through the bars.

"Rats—dozens of them," replied The Thinking Machine, tersely.

The three men, with final good-nights, were turning away when The Thinking Machine called:

"What time is it exactly, warden?"

"Eleven seventeen," replied the warden.

"Thanks. I will join you gentlemen in your office at half-past eight o'clock one week from to-night," said The Thinking Machine.

"And if you do not?"

"There is no 'if' about it."

II

Chisholm Prison was a great, spreading structure of granite, four stories in all, which stood in the center of acres of open space. It was surrounded by a wall of solid masonry eighteen feet high, and so smoothly finished inside and out as to offer no foothold to a climber, no matter how expert. Atop of this fence, as a further precaution, was a five-foot fence of steel rods, each terminating in a keen point. This fence in itself marked an absolute deadline between freedom and imprisonment, for, even if a man escaped from his cell, it would seem impossible for him to pass the wall.

The yard, which on all sides of the prison building was twenty-five feet wide, that being the distance from the building to the wall, was by day an exercise ground for those prisoners to whom was granted the boon of occasional semi-liberty. But that was not for those in Cell 13.

At all times of the day there were armed guards in the yard, four of them, one patrolling each side of the prison building.

By night the yard was almost as brilliantly lighted as by day. On each of the four sides was a great arc light which rose above the prison wall and gave to the guards a clear sight. The lights, too, brightly illuminated the spiked top of the wall. The wires which fed the arc lights ran up the side of the prison building on insulators and from the top story led out to the poles supporting the arc lights.

All these things were seen and comprehended by The Thinking Machine, who was only enabled to see out his closely barred cell window by standing on his bed. This was on the morning following his incarceration. He gathered, too, that the river lay over there beyond the wall somewhere, because he heard faintly the pulsation of a motor boat and high up in the air saw a river bird. From that same direction came the shouts of boys at play and the occasional crack of a batted ball. He knew then that between the prison wall and the river was an open space, a playground.

Chisholm Prison was regarded as absolutely safe. No man had ever escaped from it. The Thinking Machine, from his perch on the bed, seeing what he saw, could readily understand why. The walls of the cell, though built he judged twenty years before, were perfectly solid, and the window bars of new iron had not a shadow of rust on them. The window itself, even with the bars out, would be a difficult mode of egress because it was small.

Yet, seeing these things, The Thinking Machine was not discouraged. Instead, he thoughtfully squinted at the great arc light—there was bright sunlight now—and traced with his eyes the wire which led from it to the building. That electric wire, he reasoned, must come down the side of the building not a great distance from his cell. That might be worth knowing.

Cell 13 was on the same floor with the offices of the prison—that is, not in the basement, nor yet upstairs. There were only four steps up to the office floor, therefore the level of the floor must be only three or four feet above the ground. He couldn't see the ground directly beneath his window, but he could see it further out toward the wall. It would be an easy drop from the window. Well and good.

Then The Thinking Machine fell to remembering how he had come to the cell. First, there was the outside guard's booth, a part of the wall. There were two heavily barred gates there, both of steel. At this gate was one man always on guard. He admitted persons to the prison after much clanking of keys and locks, and let them out when ordered to do so. The warden's office was in the prison building, and in order to reach that official from the prison yard one had to pass a gate of solid steel with only a peep-hole in it. Then coming from that inner office to Cell 13, where he was now, one must pass a heavy wooden door and two steel doors into the corridors of the prison; and always there was the double-locked door of Cell 13 to reckon with.

There were then, The Thinking Machine recalled, seven doors to be overcome before one could pass from Cell 13 into the outer world, a free man. But against this was the fact that he was rarely interrupted. A jailer appeared at his cell door at six in the morning with a breakfast of prison fare; he would come again at noon, and again at six in the afternoon. At nine o'clock at night would come the inspection tour. That would be all.

"It's admirably arranged, this prison system," was the mental tribute paid by The Thinking Machine. "I'll have to study it a little when I get out. I had no idea there was such great care exercised in the prisons."

There was nothing, positively nothing, in his cell, except his iron bed, so firmly put together that no man could tear it to pieces save with sledges or a file. He had neither of these. There was not even a chair, or a small table, or a bit of tin or crockery. Nothing! The jailer stood by when he ate, then took away the wooden spoon and bowl which he had used.

One by one these things sank into the brain of The Thinking Machine. When the last possibility had been considered he began an examination of his cell. From the roof, down the walls on all sides, he examined the stones and the cement between them. He stamped over the floor carefully time after time, but it was cement, perfectly solid. After the examination he sat on the edge of the iron bed and was lost in thought for a long time. For Professor Augustus S. F. X. Van Dusen, The Thinking Machine, had something to think about.

He was disturbed by a rat, which ran across his foot, then scampered away into a dark corner of the cell, frightened at its own daring. After a while The Thinking Machine, squinting steadily into the darkness of the corner where the rat had gone, was able to make out in the gloom many little beady eyes staring at him. He counted six pair, and there were perhaps others; he didn't see very well.

Then The Thinking Machine, from his seat on the bed, noticed for the first time the bottom of his cell door. There was an opening there of two inches between the steel bar and the floor. Still looking steadily at this opening, The Thinking Machine backed suddenly into the corner where he had seen the beady eyes. There was a great scampering of tiny feet, several squeaks of frightened rodents, and then silence.

None of the rats had gone out the door, yet there were none in the cell. Therefore there must be another way out of the cell, however small. The Thinking Machine, on hands and knees, started a search for this spot, feeling in the darkness with his long, slender fingers.

At last his search was rewarded. He came upon a small opening in the floor, level with the cement. It was perfectly round and somewhat larger than a silver dollar. This was the way the rats had gone. He put his fingers deep into the opening; it seemed to be a disused drainage pipe and was dry and dusty.

Having satisfied himself on this point, he sat on the bed again for an hour, then made another inspection of his surroundings through the small cell window. One of the outside guards stood directly opposite, beside the wall, and happened to be looking at the window of Cell 13 when the head of The Thinking Machine appeared. But the scientist didn't notice the guard.

Noon came and the jailer appeared with the prison dinner of repulsively plain food. At home The Thinking Machine merely ate to live; here he took what was offered without comment. Occasionally he spoke to the jailer who stood outside the door watching him.

"Any improvements made here in the last few years?" he asked.

"Nothing particularly," replied the jailer. "New wall was built four years ago."

"Anything done to the prison proper?"

"Painted the woodwork outside, and I believe about seven years ago a new system of plumbing was put in."

"Ah!" said the prisoner. "How far is the river over there?"

"About three hundred feet. The boys have a baseball ground between the wall and the river."

The Thinking Machine had nothing further to say just then, but when the jailer was ready to go he asked for some water.

"I get very thirsty here," he explained. "Would it be possible for you to leave a little water in a bowl for me?"

"I'll ask the warden," replied the jailer, and he went away.

Half an hour later he returned with water in a small earthen bowl.

"The warden says you may keep this bowl," he informed the prisoner. "But you must show it to me when I ask for it. If it is broken, it will be the last."

"Thank you," said The Thinking Machine. "I shan't break it."

The jailer went on about his duties. For just the fraction of a second it seemed that The Thinking Machine wanted to ask a question, but he didn't.

Two hours later this same jailer, in passing the door of Cell No. 13, heard a noise inside and stopped. The Thinking Machine was down on his hands and knees in a corner of the cell, and from that same corner came several frightened squeaks. The jailer looked on interestedly.

"Ah, I've got you," he heard the prisoner say.

"Got what?" he asked, sharply.

"One of these rats," was the reply. "See?" And between the scientist's long fingers the jailer saw a small gray rat struggling. The prisoner brought it over to the light and looked at it closely. "It's a water rat," he said.

"Ain't you got anything better to do than to catch rats?" asked the jailer.

"It's disgraceful that they should be here at all," was the irritated reply. "Take this one away and kill it. There are dozens more where it came from."

The jailer took the wriggling, squirmy rodent and flung it down on the floor violently. It gave one squeak and lay still. Later he reported the incident to the warden, who only smiled.

Still later that afternoon the outside armed guard on Cell 13 side of the prison looked up again at the window and saw the prisoner looking out. He saw a hand raised to the barred window and then something white fluttered to the ground, directly under the window of Cell 13. It was a little roll of linen, evidently of white shirting material, and tied around it was a five-dollar bill. The guard looked up at the window again, but the face had disappeared.

With a grim smile he took the little linen roll and the five-dollar bill to the warden's office. There together they deciphered something which was written on it with a queer sort of ink, frequently blurred. On the outside was this:

"Finder of this please deliver to Dr. Charles Ransome."

"Ah," said the warden, with a chuckle. "Plan of escape number one has gone wrong." Then, as an afterthought: "But why did he address it to Dr. Ransome?"

"And where did he get the pen and ink to write with?" asked the guard.

The warden looked at the guard and the guard looked at the warden. There was no apparent solution of that mystery. The warden studied the writing carefully, then shook his head.

"Well, let's see what he was going to say to Dr. Ransome," he said at length, still puzzled, and he unrolled the inner piece of linen.

"Well, if that—what—what do you think of that?" he asked, dazed.

The guard took the bit of linen and read this:

"Epa cseot d'net niiy awe htto n'si sih. "T."

III

The warden spent an hour wondering what sort of a cipher it was, and half an hour wondering why his prisoner should attempt to communicate with Dr. Ransome, who was the cause of him being there. After this the warden devoted some thought to the question of where the prisoner got writing materials, and what sort of writing materials he had With the idea of illuminating this point, he examined the linen again. It was a torn part of a white shirt and had ragged edges.

Now it was possible to account for the linen, but what the

prisoner had used to write with was another matter. The warden knew it would have been impossible for him to have either pen or pencil, and, besides, neither pen nor pencil had been used in this writing What, then? The warden decided to personally investigate. The Thinking Machine was his prisoner; he had orders to hold his prisoners; if this one sought to escape by sending cipher messages to persons outside, he would stop it, as he would have stopped it in the case of any other priscner.

The warden went back to Cell 13 and found The Thinking Machine on his hands and knees on the floor, engaged in nothing more alarming than catching rats. The prisoner heard the warden's step and turned to him quickly.

"It's disgraceful," he snapped, "these rats. There are scores of them."

"Other men have been able to stand them," said the warden. "Here is another shirt for you—let me have the one you have on."

"Why?" demanded The Thinking Machine, quickly. His tone was hardly natural, his manner suggested actual perturbation.

"You have attempted to communicate with Dr. Ransome," said the warden severely. "As my prisoner, it is my duty to put a stop to it."

The Thinking Machine was silent for a moment.

"All right," he said, finally. "Do your duty."

The warden smiled grimly. The prisoner arose from the floor and removed the white shirt, putting on instead a striped convict shirt the warden had brought. The warden took the white shirt eagerly, and then and there compared the pieces of linen on which was written the cipher with certain torn places in the shirt. The Thinking Machine looked on curiously.

"The guard brought *you* those, then?" he asked.

"He certainly did," replied the warden triumphantly. 'And that ends your first attempt to escape."

The Thinking Machine watched the warden as he, by comparison, established to his own satisfaction that only two pieces of linen had been torn from the white shirt.

"What did you write this with?" demanded the warden.

"I should think it a part of your duty to find out," said The Thinking Machine, irritably.

The warden started to say some harsh things, then restrained himself and made a minute search of the cell and of the prisoner instead. He found absolutely nothing; not even a match or toothpick which might have been used for a pen. The same mystery surrounded the fluid with which the cipher had been written. Although the warden left Cell 13 visibly annoyed, he took the torn shirt in triumph.

"Well, writing notes on a shirt won't get him out, that's certain," he told himself with some complacency. He put the linen scraps into his desk to await developments. "If that man escapes from that cell I'll—hang it—I'll resign."

On the third day of his incarceration The Thinking Machine openly attempted to bribe his way out. The jailer had brought his dinner and was leaning against the barred door, waiting, when The Thinking Machine began the conversation.

"The drainage pipes of the prison lead to the river, don't they?" he asked.

"Yes," said the jailer.

"I suppose they are very small?"

"Too small to crawl through, if that's what you're thinking about," was the grinning response.

There was silence until The Thinking Machine finished his meal. Then:

"You know I'm not a criminal, don't you?"

"Yes."

"And that I've a perfect right to be freed if I demand it?"

"Yes."

"Well, I came here believing that I could make my escape," said the prisoner, and his squint eyes studied the face of the jailer. "Would you consider a financial reward for aiding me to escape?"

The jailer, who happened to be an honest man, looked at the slender, weak figure of the prisoner, at the large head with its mass of yellow hair, and was almost sorry.

"I guess prisons like these were not built for the likes of you to get out of," he said, at last.

"But would you consider a proposition to help me get out?" the prisoner insisted, almost beseechingly.

"No," said the jailer, shortly.

"Five hundred dollars," urged The Thinking Machine. "I am not a criminal."

"No," said the jailer.

"A thousand?"

"No," again said the jailer, and he started away hurriedly to escape further temptation. Then he turned back. "If you should give me ten thousand dollars I couldn't get you out. You'd have to pass through seven doors, and I only have the keys to two."

Then he told the warden all about it.

"Plan number two fails," said the warden, smiling grimly. "First a cipher, then bribery."

When the jailer was on his way to Cell 13 at six o'clock, again bearing food to The Thinking Machine, he paused, startled by the unmistakable scrape, scrape of steel against steel. It stopped at the sound of his steps, then craftily the jailer, who was beyond the prisoner's range of vision, resumed his tramping, the sound being apparently that of a man going away from Cell 13. As a matter of fact he was in the same spot.

After a moment there came again the steady scrape, scrape, and the jailer crept cautiously on tiptoes to the door and peered between the bars. The Thinking Machine was standing on the iron bed working at the bars of the little window. He was using a file, judging from the backward and forward swing of his arms.

Cautiously the jailer crept back to the office, summoned the warden in person, and they returned to Cell 13 on tiptoes. The steady scrape was still audible. The warden listened to satisfy himself and then suddenly appeared at the door.

"Well?" he demanded, and there was a smile on his face.

The Thinking Machine glanced back from his perch on the bed and leaped suddenly to the floor, making frantic efforts to hide something. The warden went in, with hand extended.

"Give it up," he said.

"No," said the prisoner, sharply.

"Come, give it up," urged the warden. "I don't want to have to search you again."

"No," repeated the prisoner.

"What was it, a file?" asked the warden.

The Thinking Machine was silent and stood squinting at the warden with something very nearly approaching disappointment on his face—nearly, but not quite. The warden was almost sympathetic.

"Plan number three fails, eh?" he asked, good-naturedly. "Too bad, isn't it?"

The prisoner didn't say.

"Search him," instructed the warden.

The jailer searched the prisoner carefully. At last, artfully concealed in the waist band of the trousers, he found a piece of steel about two inches long, with one side curved like a half moon.

"Ah," said the warden, as he received it from the jailer. "From your shoe heel," and he smiled pleasantly.

The jailer continued his search and on the other side of the trousers waist band another piece of steel identical with the first. The edges showed where they had been worn against the bars of the window.

"You couldn't saw a way through those bars with these," said the warden.

"I could have," said The Thinking Machine firmly.

"In six months, perhaps," said the warden, good-naturedly.

The warden shook his head slowly as he gazed into the slightly flushed face of his prisoner.

"Ready to give it up?" he asked.

"I haven't started yet," was the prompt reply.

Then came another exhaustive search of the cell. Carefully the two men went over it, finally turning out the bed and searching that. Nothing. The warden in person climbed upon the bed and examined the bars of the window where the prisoner had been sawing. When he looked he was amused.

"Just made it a little bright by hard rubbing," he said to the prisoner, who stood looking on with a somewhat crestfallen air. The warden grasped the iron bars in his strong hands and tried to shake them. They were immovable, set firmly in the solid granite. He examined each in turn and found them all satisfactory. Finally he climbed down from the bed.

"Give it up, professor," he advised.

The Thinking Machine shook his head and the warden and jailer passed on again. As they disappeared down the corridor The Thinking Machine sat on the edge of the bed with his head in his hands.

"He's crazy to try to get out of that cell," commented the jailer.

"Of course he can't get out," said the warden. "But he's clever. I would like to know what he wrote that cipher with."

. . . .

It was four o'clock next morning when an awful, heart-racking shriek of terror resounded through the great prison. It came from a cell, somewhere about the center, and its tone told a tale of horror, agony, terrible fear. The warden heard and with three of his men rushed into the long corridor leading to Cell 13.

IV

As they ran there came again that awful cry. It died away in a sort of wail. The white faces of prisoners appeared at cell doors upstairs and down, staring out wonderingly, frightened.

"It's that fool in Cell 13," grumbled the warden.

He stopped and stared in as one of the jailers flashed a lantern. "That fool in Cell 13" lay comfortably on his cot, flat on his back with his mouth open, snoring. Even as they looked there came again the piercing cry, from somewhere above. The warden's face blanched a little as he started up the stairs. There on the top floor he found a man in Cell 43, directly above Cell 13, but two floors higher, cowering in a corner of his cell.

"What's the matter?" demanded the warden.

"Thank God you've come," exclaimed the prisoner, and he cast himself against the bars of his cell.

"What is it?" demanded the warden again.

He threw open the door and went in. The prisoner dropped on his knees and clasped the warden about the body. His face was white with terror, his eyes were widely distended, and he was shuddering. His hands, icy cold, clutched at the warden's.

"Take me out of this cell, please take me out," he pleaded.

"What's the matter with you, anyhow?" insisted the warden, impatiently.

"I heard something—something," said the prisoner, and his eyes roved nervously around the cell.

"What did you hear?"

"I—I can't tell you," stammered the prisoner. Then, in a sudden burst of terror: "Take me out of this cell—put me anywhere—but take me out of here."

The warden and the three jailers exchanged glances.

"Who is this fellow? What's he accused of?" asked the warden.

"Joseph Ballard," said one of the jailers. "He's accused of throwing acid in a woman's face. She died from it."

"But they can't prove it," gasped the prisoner. "They can't prove it. Please put me in some other cell."

He was still clinging to the warden, and that official threw his arms off roughly. Then for a time he stood looking at the cowering wretch, who seemed possessed of all the wild, unreasoning terror of a child.

"Look here, Ballard," said the warden, finally, "if you heard anything, I want to know what it was. Now tell me."

"I can't, I can't," was the reply. He was sobbing.

"Where did it come from?"

"I don't know. Everywhere—nowhere. I just heard it."

"What was it—a voice?"

"Please don't make me answer," pleaded the prisoner.

"You must answer," said the warden, sharply.

"It was a voice—but—but it wasn't human," was the sobbing reply.

"Voice, but not human?" repeated the warden, puzzled.

"It sounded muffled and—and far away—and ghostly," explained the man.

"Did it come from inside or outside the prison?"

"It didn't seem to come from anywhere—it was just here, here, everywhere. I heard it. I heard it."

For an hour the warden tried to get the story, but Ballard had become suddenly obstinate and would say nothing—only pleaded to be placed in another cell, or to have one of the jailers remain near him until daylight. These requests were gruffly refused.

"And see here," said the warden, in conclusion, "if there's any more of this screaming I'll put you in the padded cell."

Then the warden went his way, a sadly puzzled man. Ballard sat at his cell door until daylight, his face, drawn and white with terror, pressed against the bars, and looked out into the prison with wide, staring eyes.

That day, the fourth since the incarceration of The Thinking Machine, was enlivened considerably by the volunteer prisoner, who spent most of his time at the little window of his cell. He began proceedings by throwing another piece of linen down to the guard, who picked it up dutifully and took it to the warden. On it was written:

"Only three days more."

The warden was in no way surprised at what he read; he understood that The Thinking Machine meant only three days more of his imprisonment, and he regarded the note as a boast. But how was the thing written? Where had The Thinking Machine found this new piece of linen? Where? How? He carefully examined the linen. It was white, of fine texture, shirting material. He took the shirt which he had taken and carefully fitted the two original pieces of the linen to the torn places. This third piece was entirely superfluous; it didn't fit anywhere, and yet it was unmistakably the same goods.

"And where—where does he get anything to write with?" demanded the warden of the world at large.

Still later on the fourth day The Thinking Machine, through the window of his cell, spoke to the armed guard outside.

"What day of the month is it?" he asked.

"The fifteenth," was the answer.

The Thinking Machine made a mental astronomical calculation and satisfied himself that the moon would not rise until after nine o'clock that night. Then he asked another question:

"Who attends to those arc lights?"

"Man from the company."

"You have no electricians in the building?"

"No."

"I should think you could save money if you had your own man."

"None of my business," replied the guard.

The guard noticed The Thinking Machine at the cell window frequently during that day, but always the face seemed listless and there was a certain wistfulness in the squint eyes behind the glasses. After a while he accepted the presence of the leonine head as a matter of course. He had seen other prisoners do the same thing; it was the longing for the outside world.

That afternoon, just before the day guard was relieved, the head appeared at the window again, and The Thinking Machine's hand held something out between the bars. It fluttered to the ground and the guard picked it up. It was a five-dollar bill.

"That's for you," called the prisoner.

As usual, the guard took it to the warden. That gentleman looked at it suspiciously; he looked at everything that came from Cell 13 with suspicion.

"He said it was for me," explained the guard.

"It's a sort of a tip, I suppose," said the warden. "I see no particular reason why you shouldn't accept—"

Suddenly he stopped. He had remembered that The Thinking Machine had gone into Cell 13 with one five-dollar bill and two ten-dollar bills; twenty-five dollars in all. Now a five-dollar bill had been tied around the first pieces of linen that came from the cell. The warden still had it, and to convince himself he took it out and looked at it. It was five dollars; yet here was another five dollars, and The Thinking Machine had only had ten-dollar bills.

"Perhaps somebody changed one of the bills for him," he thought at last, with a sigh of relief.

But then and there he made up his mind. He would search Cell 13 as a cell was never before searched in this world.

When a man could write at will, and change money, and do other wholly inexplicable things, there was something radically wrong with his prison. He planned to enter the cell at night—three o'clock would be an excellent time. The Thinking Machine must do all the weird things he did sometime. Night seemed the most reasonable.

Thus it happened that the warden stealthily descended upon Cell 13 that night at three o'clock. He paused at the door and listened. There was no sound save the steady, regular breathing of the prisoner. The keys unfastened the double locks with scarcely a clank, and the warden entered, locking the door behind him. Suddenly he flashed his dark-lantern in the face of the recumbent figure.

If the warden had planned to startle The Thinking Machine he was mistaken, for that individual merely opened his eyes quietly, reached for his glasses and inquired, in a most matter-of-fact tone:

"Who is it?"

It would be useless to describe the search that the warden made. It was minute. Not one inch of the cell or the bed was overlooked. He found the round hole in the floor, and with a flash of inspiration thrust his thick fingers into it. After a moment of fumbling there he drew up something and looked at it in the light of his lantern.

"Ugh!" he exclaimed.

The thing he had taken out was a rat—a dead rat. His inspiration fled as a mist before the sun. But he continued the search.

The Thinking Machine, without a word, arose and kicked the rat out of the cell into the corridor.

The warden climbed on the bed and tried the steel bars in the tiny window. They were perfectly rigid; every bar of the door was the same.

Then the warden searched the prisoner's clothing, beginning at the shoes. Nothing hidden in them! Then the trousers waist band. Still nothing! Then the pockets of the trousers. From one side he drew out some paper money and examined it.

"Five one-dollar bills," he gasped.

"That's right," said the prisoner.

"But the—you had two tens and a five—what the—how do you do it?"

"That's my business," said The Thinking Machine.

"Did any of my men change this money for you—on your word of honor?"

The Thinking Machine paused just a fraction of a second.

"No," he said.

"Well, do you make it?" asked the warden. He was prepared to believe anything.

"That's my business," again said the prisoner.

The warden glared at the eminent scientist fiercely. He felt—he knew—that this man was making a fool of him, yet he didn't know how. If he were a real prisoner he would get the truth—but, then, perhaps, those inexplicable things which had happened would not have been brought before him so sharply. Neither of the men spoke for a long time, then suddenly the warden turned fiercely and left the cell, slamming the door behind him. He didn't dare to speak, then.

He glanced at the clock. It was ten minutes to four. He had hardly settled himself in bed when again came that heart-breaking shriek through the prison. With a few muttered words, which, while not elegant, were highly expressive, he relighted his lantern and rushed through the prison again to the cell on the upper floor.

Again Ballard was crushing himself against the steel door, shrieking, shrieking at the top of his voice. He stopped only when the warden flashed his lamp in the cell.

"Take me out, take me out," he screamed. "I did it, I did it, I killed her. Take it away."

"Take what away?" asked the warden.

"I threw the acid in her face—I did it—I confess. Take me out of here."

Ballard's condition was pitiable; it was only an act of mercy to let him out into the corridor. There he crouched in a corner, like an animal at bay, and clasped his hands to his ears. It took half an hour to calm him sufficiently for him to speak. Then he told incoherently what had happened. On the night before at four o'clock he had heard a voice—a sepulchral voice, muffled and wailing in tone.

"What did it say?" asked the warden, curiously.

"Acid—acid—acid!" gasped the prisoner. "It accused me. Acid! I threw the acid, and the woman died. Oh!" It was a long, shuddering wail of terror.

"Acid?" echoed the warden, puzzled. The case was beyond him.

"Acid. That's all I heard—that one word, repeated several times. There were other things, too, but I didn't hear them."

"That was last night, eh?" asked the warden. "What happened to-night—what frightened you just now?"

"It was the same thing," gasped the prisoner. "Acid—acid—acid." He covered his face with his hands and sat shivering. "It was acid I used on her, but I didn't mean to kill her. I just heard the words. It was something accusing me—accusing me." He mumbled, and was silent.

"Did you hear anything else?"

"Yes—but I couldn't understand—only a little bit—just a word or two."

"Well, what was it?"

"I heard 'acid' three times, then I heard a long, moaning sound, then—then—I heard 'No. 8 hat.' I heard that voice."

"No. 8 hat," repeated the warden. "What the devil—No. 8 hat? Accusing voices of conscience have never talked about No. 8 hats, so far as I ever heard."

"He's insane," said one of the jailers, with an air of finality.

"I believe you," said the warden. "He must be. He probably heard something and got frightened. He's trembling now. No. 8 hat! What the—"

V

When the fifth day of The Thinking Machine's imprisonment rolled around the warden was wearing a hunted look. He was anxious for the end of the thing. He could not help but feel that his distinguished prisoner had been amusing himself. And if this were so, The Thinking Machine had lost none of his sense of humor. For on this fifth day he flung down another linen note to the outside guard, bearing the words: "Only two days more." Also he flung down half a dollar.

Now the warden knew—he *knew*—that the man in Cell 13 didn't have any half dollars—he *couldn't* have any half dollars, no more than he could have pen and ink and linen, and yet he did have them. It was a condition, not a theory; that is one reason why the warden was wearing a hunted look.

That ghastly, uncanny thing, too, about "Acid" and "No 8 hat" clung to him tenaciously. They didn't mean anything, of course, merely the ravings of an insane murderer who had been driven by fear to confess his crime, still there were so many things that "didn't mean anything" happening in the prison now since The Thinking Machine was there.

On the sixth day the warden received a postal stating that Dr. Ransome and Mr. Fielding would be at Chisholm Prison on the following evening, Thursday, and in the event Professor Van Dusen had not yet escaped—and they presumed he had not because they had not heard from him—they would meet him there.

"In the event he had not yet escaped!" The warden smiled grimly. Escaped!

The Thinking Machine enlivened this day for the warden with three notes. They were on the usual linen and bore generally on the appointment at half-past eight o'clock Thursday night, which appointment the scientist had made at the time of his imprisonment.

On the afternoon of the seventh day the warden passed Cell 13 and glanced in. The Thinking Machine was lying on the iron bed, apparently sleeping lightly. The cell appeared precisely as it always did from a casual glance. The warden would swear that no man was going to leave it between that hour—it was then four o'clock—and half-past eight o'clock that evening.

On his way back past the cell the warden heard the steady breathing again, and coming close to the door looked in. He wouldn't have done so if The Thinking Machine had been looking, but now—well, it was different.

A ray of light came through the high window and fell on

the face of the sleeping man. It occurred to the warden for the first time that his prisoner appeared haggard and weary. Just then The Thinking Machine stirred slightly and the warden hurried on up the corridor guiltily. That evening after six o'clock he saw the jailer.

"Everything all right in Cell 13?" he asked.

"Yes, sir," replied the jailer. "He didn't eat much, though."

It was with a feeling of having done his duty that the warden received Dr. Ransome and Mr. Fielding shortly after seven o'clock. He intended to show them the linen notes and lay before them the full story of his woes, which was a long one. But before this came to pass the guard from the river side of the prison yard entered the office.

"The arc light in my side of the yard won't light," he informed the warden.

"Confound it, that man's a hoodoo," thundered the official. "Everything has happened since he's been here."

The guard went back to his post in the darkness, and the warden 'phoned to the electric light company.

"This is Chisholm Prison," he said through the 'phone. "Send three or four men down here quick, to fix an arc light."

The reply was evidently satisfactory, for the warden hung up the receiver and passed out into the yard. While Dr. Ransome and Mr. Fielding sat waiting the guard at the outer gate came in with a special delivery letter. Dr. Ransome happened to notice the address, and, when the guard went out, looked at the letter more closely.

"By George!" he exclaimed.

"What is it?" asked Mr. Fielding.

Silently the doctor offered the letter. Mr. Fielding examined it closely.

"Coincidence," he said. "It must be."

It was nearly eight o'clock when the warden returned to his office. The electricians had arrived in a wagon, and were now at work. The warden pressed the buzz-button communicating with the man at the outer gate in the wall.

"How many electricians came in?" he asked, over the

short 'phone. "Four? Three workmen in jumpers and overalls and the manager? Frock coat and silk hat? All right. Be certain that only four go out. That's all."

He turned to Dr. Ransome and Mr. Fielding. "We have to be careful here—particularly," and there was broad sarcasm in his tone, "since we have scientists locked up."

The warden picked up the special delivery letter carelessly, and then began to open it.

"When I read this I want to tell you gentlemen something about how— Great Cæsar!" he ended, suddenly, as he glanced at the letter. He sat with mouth open, motionless, from astonishment.

"What is it?" asked Mr. Fielding.

"A special delivery letter from Cell 13," gasped the warden. "An invitation to supper."

"What?" and the two others arose, unanimously.

The warden sat dazed, staring at the letter for a moment, then called sharply to a guard outside in the corridor.

"Run down to Cell 13 and see if that man's in there."

The guard went as directed, while Dr. Ransome and Mr. Fielding examined the letter.

"It's Van Dusen's handwriting; there's no question of that," said Dr. Ransome. "I've seen too much of it."

Just then the buzz on the telphone from the outer gate sounded, and the warden, in a semi-trance, picked up the receiver.

"Hello! Two reporters, eh? Let 'em come in." He turned suddenly to the doctor and Mr. Fielding. "Why, the man *can't* be out. He must be in his cell."

Just at that moment the guard returned.

"He's still in his cell, sir," he reported. "I saw him. He's lying down."

"There, I told you so," said the warden, and he breathed freely again. "But how did he mail that letter?"

There was a rap on the steel door which led from the jail yard into the warden's office.

"It's the reporters," said the warden. "Let them in," he instructed the guard; then to the two other gentlemen: "Don't say anything about this before them, because I'd never hear the last of it."

The door opened, and the two men from the front gate entered.

"Good-evening, gentlemen," said one. That was Hutchinson Hatch; the warden knew him well.

"Well?" demanded the other, irritably. "I'm here."

That was The Thinking Machine.

He squinted belligerently at the warden, who sat with mouth agape. For the moment that official had nothing to say. Dr. Ransome and Mr. Fielding were amazed, but they didn't know what the warden knew. They were only amazed; he was paralyzed. Hutchinson Hatch, the reporter, took in the scene with greedy eyes.

"How—how—how did you do it?" gasped the warden, finally.

"Come back to the cell," said The Thinking Machine, in the irritated voice which his scientific associates knew so well.

The warden, still in a condition bordering on trance, led the way.

"Flash your light in there," directed The Thinking Machine.

The warden did so. There was nothing unusual in the appearance of the cell, and there—there on the bed lay the figure of The Thinking Machine. Certainly! There was the yellow hair! Again the warden looked at the man beside him and wondered at the strangeness of his own dreams.

With trembling hands he unlocked the cell door and The Thinking Machine passed inside.

"See here," he said.

He kicked at the steel bars in the bottom of the cell door and three of them were pushed out of place. A fourth broke off and rolled away in the corridor.

"And here, too," directed the erstwhile prisoner as he stood on the bed to reach the small window. He swept his hand across the opening and every bar came out.

"What's this in the bed?" demanded the warden, who was slowly recovering.

"A wig," was the reply. "Turn down the cover."

The warden did so. Beneath it lay a large coil of strong rope, thirty feet or more, a dagger, three files, ten feet of electric wire, a thin, powerful pair of steel pliers, a small tack hammer with its handle, and—and a Derringer pistol.

"How did you do it?" demanded the warden.

"You gentlemen have an engagement to supper with me at half-past nine o'clock," said The Thinking Machine. "Come on, or we shall be late."

"But how did you do it?" insisted the warden.

"Don't ever think you can hold any man who can use his brain," said The Thinking Machine. "Come on; we shall be late."

VI

It was an impatient supper party in the rooms of Professor Van Dusen and a somewhat silent one. The guests were Dr. Ransome, Albert Fielding, the warden, and Hutchinson Hatch, reporter. The meal was served to the minute, in accordance with Professor Van Dusen's instructions of one week before; Dr. Ransome found the artichokes delicious. At last the supper was finished and The Thinking Machine turned full on Dr. Ransome and squinted at him fiercely.

"Do you believe it now?" he demanded.

"I do," replied Dr. Ransome.

"Do you admit that it was a fair test?"

"I do."

With the others, particularly the warden, he was waiting anxiously for the explanation.

"Suppose you tell us how—" began Mr. Fielding.

"Yes, tell us how," said the warden.

The Thinking Machine readjusted his glasses, took a couple of preparatory squints at his audience, and began the story. He told it from the beginning logically; and no man ever talked to more interested listeners.

"My agreement was," he began, "to go into a cell, carrying nothing except what was necessary to wear, and to leave that cell within a week. I had never seen Chisholm Prison. When I went into the cell I asked for tooth powder, two ten and one five-dollar bills, and also to have my shoes blacked. Even if these requests had been refused it would not have mattered seriously. But you agreed to them.

"I knew there would be nothing in the cell which you thought I might use to advantage. So when the warden locked the door on me I was apparently helpless, unless I could turn three seemingly innocent things to use. They were things which would have been permitted any prisoner under sentence of death, were they not, warden?"

"Tooth powder and polished shoes, yes, but not money," replied the warden.

"Anything is dangerous in the hands of a man who knows how to use it," went on The Thinking Machine. "I did nothing that first night but sleep and chase rats." He glared at the warden. "When the matter was broached I knew I could do nothing that night, so suggested next day. You gentlemen thought I wanted time to arrange an escape with outside assistance, but this was not true. I knew I could communicate with whom I pleased, when I pleased."

The warden stared at him a moment, then went on smoking solemnly.

"I was aroused next morning at six o'clock by the jailer with my breakfast," continued the scientist. "He told me dinner was at twelve and supper at six. Between these times, I gathered, I would be pretty much to myself. So immediately after breakfast I examined my outside surroundings from my cell window. One look told me it would be useless to try to scale the wall, even should I decide to leave my cell by the window, for my purpose was to leave not only the cell, but the prison. Of course, I could have gone over the wall, but it would have taken me longer to lay my plans that way. Therefore, for the moment, I dismissed all idea of that.

"From this first observation I knew the river was on that side of the prison, and that there was also a playground there. Subsequently these surmises were verified by a keeper. I knew then one important thing—that anyone might approach the prison wall from that side if necessary without attracting any particular attention. That was well to remember. I remembered it.

"But the outside thing which most attracted my attention was the feed wire to the arc light which ran within a few feet—probably three or four—of my cell window. I knew that would be valuable in the event I found it necessary to cut off that arc light."

"Oh, you shut it off to-night, then?" asked the warden.

"Having learned all I could from that window," resumed The Thinking Machine, without heeding the interruption, "I considered the idea of escaping through the prison proper. I recalled just how I had come into the cell, which I knew would be the only way. Seven doors lay between me and the outside. So, also for the time being, I gave up the idea of escaping that way. And I couldn't go through the solid granite walls of the cell."

The Thinking Machine paused for a moment and Dr. Ransome lighted a new cigar. For several minutes there was silence, then the scientific jail-breaker went on:

"While I was thinking about these things a rat ran across my foot. It suggested a new line of thought. There were at least half a dozen rats in the cell—I could see their beady eyes. Yet I had noticed none come under the cell door. I frightened them purposely and watched the cell door to see if they went out that way. They did not, but they were gone. Obviously they went another way. Another way meant another opening.

"I searched for this opening and found it. It was an old drain pipe, long unused and partly choked with dirt and dust. But this was the way the rats had come. They came from somewhere. Where? Drain pipes usually lead outside prison grounds. This one probably led to the river, or near it. The rats must therefore come from that direction. If they came a part of the way, I reasoned that they came all the way, because it was extremely unlikely that a solid iron or lead pipe would have any hole in it except at the exit.

"When the jailer came with my luncheon he told me two important things, although he didn't know it. One was that a new system of plumbing had been put in the prison seven years before; another that the river was only three hundred feet away. Then I knew positively that the pipe was a part of an old system; I knew, too, that it slanted generally toward the river. But did the pipe end in the water or on land?

"This was the next question to be decided. I decided it

by catching several of the rats in the cell. My jailer was surprised to see me engaged in this work. I examined at least a dozen of them. They were perfectly dry; they had come through the pipe, and, most important of all, they were *not house rats, but field rats.* The other end of the pipe was on land, then, outside the prison walls. So far, so good.

"Then, I knew that if I worked freely from this point I must attract the warden's attention in another direction. You see, by telling the warden that I had come there to escape you made the test more severe, because I had to trick him by false scents."

The warden looked up with a sad expression in his eyes.

"The first thing was to make him think I was trying to communicate with you, Dr. Ransome. So I wrote a note on a piece of linen I tore from my shirt, addressed it to Dr. Ransome, tied a five-dollar bill around it and threw it out the window. I knew the guard would take it to the warden, but I rather hoped the warden would send it as addressed. Have you that first linen note, warden?"

The warden produced the cipher.

"What the deuce does it mean, anyhow?" he asked.

"Read it backward, beginning with the 'T' signature and disregard the division into words," instructed The Thinking Machine.

The warden did so.

"T-h-i-s, this," he spelled, studied it a moment, then read it off, grinning:

"This is not the way I intend to escape."

"Well, now what do you think o' that?" he demanded, still grinning.

"I knew that would attract your attention, just as it did," said The Thinking Machine, "and if you really found out what it was it would be a sort of gentle rebuke."

"What did you write it with?" asked Dr. Ransome, after he had examined the linen and passed it to Mr. Fielding.

"This," said the erstwhile prisoner, and he extended his foot. On it was the shoe he had worn in prison, though the polish was gone—scraped off clean. "The shoe blacking, moistened with water, was my ink; the metal tip of the shoe lace made a fairly good pen."

The warden looked up and suddenly burst into a laugh, half of relief, half of amusement.

"You're a wonder," he said, admiringly. "Go on."

"That precipitated a search of my cell by the warden, as I had intended," continued The Thinking Machine. "I was anxious to get the warden into the habit of searching my cell, so that finally, constantly finding nothing, he would get disgusted and quit. This at last happened, practically."

The warden blushed.

"He then took my white shirt away and gave me a prison shirt. He was satisfied that those two pieces of the shirt were all that was missing. But while he was searching my cell I had another piece of that same shirt, about nine inches square, rolled into a small ball in my mouth."

"Nine inches of that shirt?" demanded the warden. "Where did it come from?"

"The bosoms of all stiff white shirts are of triple thickness," was the explanation. "I tore out the inside thickness. leaving the bosom only two thicknesses. I knew you wouldn't see it. So much for that."

There was a little pause, and the warden looked from one to another of the men with a sheepish grin.

"Having disposed of the warden for the time being by giving him something else to think about, I took my first serious step toward freedom," said Professor Van Dusen. "I knew, within reason, that the pipe led somewhere to the playground outside; I knew a great many boys played there; I knew that rats came into my cell from out there. Could I communicate with some one outside with these things at hand?

"First was necessary, I saw, a long and fairly reliable thread, so—but here," he pulled up his trousers legs and showed that the tops of both stockings, of fine, strong lisle, were gone. "I unraveled those—after I got them started it wasn't difficult—and I had easily a quarter of a mile of thread that I could depend on.

"Then on half of my remaining linen I wrote, laboriously enough I assure you, a letter explaining my situation to this gentleman here," and he indicated Hutchinson Hatch. "I knew he would assist me—for the value of the newspaper story. I tied firmly to this linen letter a ten-dollar bill—there is no surer way of attracting the eye of anyone—and wrote on the linen: 'Finder of this deliver to Hutchinson Hatch, *Daily American,* who will give another ten dollars for the information.'

"The next thing was to get this note outside on that playground where a boy might find it. There were two ways, but I chose the best. I took one of the rats—I became adept in catching them—tied the linen and money firmly to one leg, fastened my lisle thread to another, and turned him loose in the drain pipe. I reasoned that the natural fright of the rodent would make him run until he was outside the pipe and then out on earth he would probably stop to gnaw off the linen and money.

"From the moment the rat disappeared into that dusty pipe I became anxious. I was taking so many chances. The rat might gnaw the string, of which I held one end; other rats might gnaw it; the rat might run out of the pipe and leave the linen and money where they would never be found; a thousand other things might have happened. So began some nervous hours, but the fact that the rat ran on until only a few feet of the string remained in my cell made me think he was outside the pipe. I had carefully instructed Mr. Hatch what to do in case the note reached him. The question was: Would it reach him?

"This done, I could only wait and make other plans in case this one failed. I openly attempted to bribe my jailer, and learned from him that he held the keys to only two of seven doors between me and freedom. Then I did something else to make the warden nervous. I took the steel supports out of the heels of my shoes and made a pretense of sawing the bars of my cell window. The warden raised a pretty row about that. He developed, too, the habit of shaking the bars of my cell window to see if they were solid. They were—then."

Again the warden grinned. He had ceased being astonished.

"With this one plan I had done all I could and could only wait to see what happened," the scientist went on. "I couldn't know whether my note had been delivered or even found, or whether the mouse had gnawed it up. And I didn't dare to draw back through the pipe that one slender thread which connected me with the outside.

"When I went to bed that night I didn't sleep, for fear there would come the slight signal twitch at the thread which was to tell me that Mr. Hatch had received the note. At half-past three o'clock, I judge, I felt this twitch, and no prisoner actually under sentence of death ever welcomed a thing more heartily."

The Thinking Machine stopped and turned to the reporter.

"You'd better explain just what you did," he said.

"The linen note was brought to me by a small boy who had been playing baseball," said Mr. Hatch. "I immediately saw a big story in it, so I gave the boy another ten dollars, and got several spools of silk, some twine, and a roll of light, pliable wire. The professor's note suggested that I have the finder of the note show me just where it was picked up, and told me to make my search from there, beginning at two o'clock in the morning. If I found the other end of the thread I was to twitch it gently three times, then a fourth.

"I began the search with a small bulb electric light. It was an hour and twenty minutes before I found the end of the drain pipe, half hidden in weeds. The pipe was very large there, say twelve inches across. Then I found the end of the lisle thread, twitched it as directed and immediately I got an answering twitch.

"Then I fastened the silk to this and Professor Van Dusen began to pull it into his cell. I nearly had heart disease for fear the string would break. To the end of the silk I fastened the twine, and when that had been pulled in I tied on the wire. Then that was drawn into the pipe and we had a substantial line, which rats couldn't gnaw, from the mouth of the drain into the cell."

The Thinking Machine raised his hand and Hatch stopped.

"All this was done in absolute silence," said the scientist. "But when the wire reached my hand I could have shouted. Then we tried another experiment, which Mr. Hatch was prepared for. I tested the pipe as a speaking tube. Neither of us could hear very clearly, but I dared not speak loud for fear of attracting attention in the prison. At last I made him understand what I wanted immediately. He seemed to have great difficulty in understanding when I asked for nitric acid, and I repeated the word 'acid' several times.

"Then I heard a shriek from a cell above me. I knew instantly that some one had overheard, and when I heard you coming, Mr. Warden, I feigned sleep. If you had entered my cell at that moment that whole plan of escape would have ended there. But you passed on. That was the nearest I ever came to being caught.

"Having established this improvised trolley it is easy to see how I got things in the cell and made them disappear at will. I merely dropped them back into the pipe. You, Mr. Warden, could not have reached the connecting wire with your fingers; they are too large. My fingers, you see, are longer and more slender. In addition I guarded the top of that pipe with a rat—you remember how."

"I remember," said the warden, with a grimace.

"I thought that if any one were tempted to investigate that hole the rat would dampen his ardor. Mr. Hatch could not send me anything useful through the pipe until next night, although he did send me change for ten dollars as a test, so I proceeded with other parts of my plan. Then I evolved the method of escape, which I finally employed.

"In order to carry this out successfully it was necessary for the guard in the yard to get accustomed to seeing me at the cell window. I arranged this by dropping linen notes to him, boastful in tone, to make the warden believe, if possible, one of his assistants was communicating with the outside for me. I would stand at my window for hours gazing out, so the guard could see, and occasionally I spoke to him. In that way I learned that the prison had no electricians of its own, but was dependent upon the lighting company if anything should go wrong.

"That cleared the way to freedom perfectly. Early in the evening of the last day of my imprisonment, when it was dark, I planned to cut the feed wire which was only a few feet from my window, reaching it with an acid-tipped wire I had. That would make that side of the prison perfectly dark while the electricians were searching for the break. That would also bring Mr. Hatch into the prison yard.

"There was only one more thing to do before I actually began the work of setting myself free. This was to arrange final details with Mr. Hatch through our speaking tube. I did this within half an hour after the warden left my cell on the fourth night of my imprisonment. Mr. Hatch again had serious difficulty in understanding me, and I repeated the word 'acid' to him several times, and later the words: 'Number eight hat'—that's my size—and these were the things which made a prisoner upstairs confess to murder, so one of the jailers told me next day. This prisoner heard our voices, confused of course, through the pipe, which also went to his cell. The cell directly over me was not occupied, hence no one else heard.

"Of course the actual work of cutting the steel bars out of the window and door was comparatively easy with nitric acid, which I got through the pipe in thin bottles, but it took time. Hour after hour on the fifth and sixth and seventh days the guard below was looking at me as I worked on the bars of the window with the acid on a piece of wire. I used the tooth powder to prevent the acid spreading. I looked away abstractedly as I worked and each minute the acid cut deeper into the metal. I noticed that the jailers always tried the door by shaking the upper part, never the lower bars, therefore I cut the lower bars, leaving them hanging in place by thin strips of metal. But that was a bit of daredeviltry. I could not have gone that way so easily."

The Thinking Machine sat silent for several minutes.

"I think that makes everything clear," he went on. "Whatever points I have not explained were merely to confuse the warden and jailers. These things in my bed I brought in to please Mr. Hatch, who wanted to improve the story. Of course, the wig was necessary in my plan. The special delivery letter I wrote and directed in my cell with Mr. Hatch's fountain pen, then sent it out to him and he mailed it. That's all, I think."

"But your actually leaving the prison grounds and then coming in through the outer gate to my office?" asked the warden.

"Perfectly simple," said the scientist. "I cut the electric light wire with acid, as I said, when the current was off.

Therefore when the current was turned on the arc didn't light. I knew it would take some time to find out what was the matter and make repairs. When the guard went to report to you the yard was dark. I crept out the window—it was a tight fit, too—replaced the bars by standing on a narrow ledge and remained in a shadow until the force of electricians arrived. Mr. Hatch was one of them.

"When I saw him I spoke and he handed me a cap, a jumper and overalls, which I put on within ten feet of you, Mr. Warden, while you were in the yard. Later Mr. Hatch called me, presumably as a workman, and together we went out the gate to get something out of the wagon. The gate guard let us pass out readily as two workmen who had just passed in. We changed our clothing and reappeared, asking to see you. We saw you. That's all."

There was silence for several minutes. Dr. Ransome was first to speak.

"Wonderful!" he exclaimed. "Perfectly amazing."

"How did Mr. Hatch happen to come with the electricians?" asked Mr. Fielding.

"His father is manager of the company," replied The Thinking Machine.

"But what if there had been no Mr. Hatch outside to help?"

"Every prisoner has one friend outside who would help him escape if he could."

"Suppose—just suppose—there had been no old plumbing system there?" asked the warden, curiously.

"There were two other ways out," said The Thinking Machine, enigmatically.

Ten minutes later the telephone bell rang. It was a request for the warden.

"Light all right, eh?" the warden asked, through the 'phone. "Good. Wire cut beside Cell 13? Yes, I know. One electrician too many? What's that? Two came out?"

The warden turned to the others with a puzzled expression.

"He only let in four electricians, he has let out two and says there are three left."

"I was the odd one," said The Thinking Machine.

"Oh," said the warden. "I see." Then through the 'phone: "Let the fifth man go. He's all right."

The Scarlet Thread

BY JACQUES FUTRELLE

The Scarlet Thread

BY JACQUES FUTRELLE

I

THE THINKING MACHINE—Professor Augustus S. F. X. Van Dusen, Ph. D., LL. D., F. R. S., M. D., etc., scientist and logician—listened intently and without comment to a weird, seemingly inexplicable story. Hutchinson Hatch, reporter, was telling it. The bowed figure of the savant lay at ease in a large chair. The enormous head with its bushy yellow hair was thrown back, the thin, white fingers were pressed tip to tip and the blue eyes, narrowed to mere slits, squinted aggressively upward. The scientist was in a receptive mood.

"From the beginning, every fact you know," he had requested.

"It's all out in the Back Bay," the reporter explained. "There is a big apartment house there, a fashionable establishment, in a side street, just off Commonwealth Avenue. It is five stories in all, and is cut up into small suites, of two and three rooms with bath. These suites are handsomely, even luxuriously furnished, and are occupied by people who can afford to pay big rents. Generally these are young unmarried men, although in several cases they are husband and wife. It is a house of every modern improvement, elevator service, hall boys, liveried door men, spacious corridors and all that. It has both the gas and electric systems of lighting. Tenants are at liberty to use either or both.

"A young broker, Weldon Henley, occupies one of the handsomest of these suites, being on the second floor, in front. He has met with considerable success in the Street. He is a bachelor and lives there alone. There is no personal servant. He dabbles in photography as a hobby, and is said to be remarkably expert.

"Recently there was a report that he was to be married this Winter to a beautiful Virginia girl who has been visiting Boston from time to time, a Miss Lipscomb—Charlotte Lipscomb, of Richmond. Henley has never denied or affirmed this rumor, although he has been asked about it often. Miss Lipscomb is impossible of access even when she visits Boston. Now she is in Virginia, I understand, but will return to Boston later in the season."

The reporter paused, lighted a cigarette and leaned forward in his chair, gazing steadily into the inscrutable eyes of the scientist.

"When Henley took the suite he requested that all the electric lighting apparatus be removed from his apartments," he went on. "He had taken a long lease of the place, and this was done. Therefore he uses only gas for lighting purposes, and he usually keeps one of his gas jets burning low all night."

"Bad, bad for his health," commented the scientist.

"Now comes the mystery of the affair," the reporter went on. "It was five weeks or so ago Henley retired as usual—about midnight. He locked his door on the inside—he is positive of that—and awoke about four o'clock in the morning nearly asphyxiated by gas. He was barely able to get up and open the window to let in the fresh air. The gas jet he had left burning was out, and the suite was full of gas."

"Accident, possibly," said The Thinking Machine. "A draught through the apartments; a slight diminution of gas pressure; a hundred possibilities."

"So it was presumed," said the reporter. "Of course it would have been impossible for—"

"Nothing is impossible," said the other, tartly. "Don't say that. It annoys me exceedingly."

"Well, then, it seems highly improbable that the door had been opened or that anyone came into the room and did this deliberately," the newspaper man went on, with a slight smile. "So Henley said nothing about this; attributed it to accident. The next night he lighted his gas as usual, but he left it burning a little brighter. The same thing happened again."

"Ah," and The Thinking Machine changed his position a little. "The second time."

"And again he awoke just in time to save himself," said Hatch. "Still he attributed the affair to accident, and determined to avoid a recurrence of the affair by doing away with the gas at night. Then he got a small night lamp and used this for a week or more."

"Why does he have a light at all?" asked the scientist, testily.

"I can hardly answer that," replied Hatch. "I may say, however, that he is of a very nervous temperament, and gets up frequently during the night. He reads occasionally when he can't sleep. In addition to that he has slept with a light going all his life; it's a habit."

"Go on."

"One night he looked for the night lamp, but it had disappeared—at least he couldn't find it—so he lighted the gas again. The fact of the gas having twice before gone out had been dismissed as a serious possibility. Next morning at five o'clock a bell boy, passing through the hall, smelled gas and made a quick investigation. He decided it came from Henley's place, and rapped on the door. There was no answer. It ultimately developed that it was necessary to smash in the door. There on the bed they found Henley unconscious with the gas pouring into the room from the jet which he had left lighted. He was revived in the air, but for several hours was deathly sick."

"Why was the door smashed in?" asked The Thinking Machine. "Why not unlocked?"

"It was done because Henley had firmly barred it," Hatch explained. "He had become suspicious, I suppose, and after the second time he always barred his door and fastened every window before he went to sleep. There may have been a fear that some one used a key to enter."

"Well?" asked the scientist. "After that?"

"Three weeks or so elapsed, bringing the affair down to this morning," Hatch went on. "Then the same thing happened a little differently. For instance, after the third time the gas went out Henley decided to find out for himself what caused it, and so expressed himself to a few friends who knew of the mystery. Then, night after night, he lighted the gas as usual and kept watch. It was never disturbed during all that time, burning steadily all night. What sleep he got was in daytime.

"Last night Henley lay awake for a time; then, exhausted and tired, fell asleep. This morning early he awoke; the room was filled with gas again. In some way my city editor heard of it and asked me to look into the mystery."

That was all. The two men were silent for a long time, and finally The Thinking Machine turned to the reporter.

"Does anyone else in the house keep gas going all night?" he asked.

"I don't know," was the reply. "Most of them, I know, use electricity."

"Nobody else has been overcome as he has been?"

"No. Plumbers have minutely examined the lighting system all over the house and found nothing wrong."

"Does the gas in the house all come through the same meter?"

"Yes, so the manager told me. This meter, a big one, is just off the engine room. I supposed it possible that some one shut it off there on these nights long enough to extinguish the lights all over the house, then turned it on again. That is, presuming that it was done purposely. Do you think it was an attempt to kill Henley?"

"It might be," was the reply. "Find out for me just who in the house uses gas; also if anyone else leaves a light burning all night; also what opportunity anyone would have to get at the meter, and then something about Henley's love affair with Miss Lipscomb. Is there anyone else? If so, who? Where does he live? When you find out these things come back here."

. . . .

That afternoon at one o'clock Hatch returned to the apartments of The Thinking Machine, with excitement plainly apparent on his face.

"Well?" asked the scientist.

"A French girl, Louise Regnier, employed as a maid by Mrs. Standing in the house, was found dead in her room on the third floor to-day at noon," Hatch explained quickly. "It looks like suicide."

"How?" asked The Thinking Machine.

"The people who employed her—husband and wife—have been away for a couple of days," Hatch rushed on. "She was in the suite alone. This noon she had not appeared, there was an odor of gas and the door was broken in. Then she was found dead."

"With the gas turned on?"

"With the gas turned on. She was asphyxiated."

"Dear me, dear me," exclaimed the scientist. He arose and took up his hat. "Let's go see what this is all about."

II

When Professor Van Dusen and Hatch arrived at the apartment house they had been preceded by the Medical Examiner and the police. Detective Mallory, whom both knew, was moving about in the apartment where the girl had been found dead. The body had been removed and a telegram sent to her employers in New York.

"Too late," said Mallory, as they entered.

"What was it, Mr. Mallory?" asked the scientist.

"Suicide," was the reply. "No question of it. It happened in this room," and he led the way into the third room of the suite. "The maid, Miss Regnier, occupied this, and was here alone last night. Mr. and Mrs. Standing, her employers, have gone to New York for a few days. She was left alone, and killed herself."

Without further questioning The Thinking Machine went over to the bed, from which the girl's body had been taken, and, stooping beside it, picked up a book. It was a novel by "The Duchess." He examined this critically, then, standing on a chair, he examined the gas jet. This done, he stepped down and went to the window of the little room. Finally The Thinking Machine turned to the detective.

"Just how much was the gas turned on?" he asked.

"Turned on full," was the reply.

"Were both the doors of the room closed?"

"Both, yes."

"Any cotton, or cloth, or anything of the sort stuffed in the cracks of the window?"

"No. It's a tight-fitting window, anyway. Are you trying to make a mystery out of this?"

"Cracks in the doors stuffed?" The Thinking Machine went on.

"No." There was a smile about the detective's lips.

The Thinking Machine, on his knees, examined the bottom of one of the doors, that which led into the hall. The lock of this door had been broken when employees burst into the room. Having satisfied himself here and at the bottom of the other door, which connected with the bedroom adjoining, The Thinking Machine again climbed on a chair and examined the doors at the top.

"Both transoms closed, I suppose?" he asked.

"Yes," was the reply. "You can't make anything but suicide out of it," explained the detective. "The Medical Examiner has given that as his opinion—and everything I find indicates it."

"All right," broke in The Thinking Machine abruptly. "Don't let us keep you."

After a while Detective Mallory went away. Hatch and the scientist went down to the office floor, where they saw the manager. He seemed to be greatly distressed, but was willing to do anything he could in the matter.

"Is your night engineer perfectly trustworthy?" asked The Thinking Machine.

"Perfectly," was the reply. "One of the best and most reliable men I ever met. Alert and wide-awake."

"Can I see him a moment? The night man, I mean?"

"Certainly," was the reply. "He's downstairs. He sleeps there. He's probably up by this time. He sleeps usually till one o'clock in the daytime, being up all night."

"Do you supply gas for your tenants?"

"Both gas and electricity are included in the rent of the suites. Tenants may use one or both."

"And the gas all comes through one meter?"

"Yes, one meter. It's just off the engine room."

"I suppose there's no way of telling just who in the house uses gas?"

"No. Some do and some don't. I don't know."

This was what Hatch had told the scientist. Now together

they went to the basement, and there met the night engineer, Charles Burlingame, a tall, powerful, clean-cut man, of alert manner and positive speech. He gazed with a little amusement at the slender, almost childish figure of The Thinking Machine and the grotesquely large head.

"You are in the engine room or near it all night every night?" began The Thinking Machine.

"I haven't missed a night in four years," was the reply.

"Anybody ever come here to see you at night?"

"Never. It's against the rules."

"The manager or a hall boy?"

"Never."

"In the last two months?" The Thinking Machine persisted.

"Not in the last two years," was the positive reply. "I go on duty every night at seven o'clock, and I am on duty until seven in the morning. I don't believe I've seen anybody in the basement here with me between those hours for a year at least."

The Thinking Machine was squinting steadily into the eyes of the engineer, and for a time both were silent. Hatch moved about the scrupulously clean engine room and nodded to the day engineer, who sat leaning back against the wall. Directly in front of him was the steam gauge.

"Have you a fireman?" was The Thinking Machine's next question.

"No. I fire myself," said the night man. "Here's the coal," and he indicated a bin within half a dozen feet of the mouth of the boiler.

"I don't suppose you ever had occasion to handle the gas meter?" insisted The Thinking Machine.

"Never touched it in my life," said the other. "I don't know anything about meters, anyway."

"And you never drop off to sleep at night for a few minutes when you get lonely? Doze, I mean?"

The engineer grinned good-naturedly.

"Never had any desire to, and besides I wouldn't have the chance," he explained. "There's a time check here"—and he indicated it. "I have to punch that every half hour all night to prove that I have been awake."

"Dear me, dear me," exclaimed The Thinking Machine, irritably. He went over and examined the time check—a revolving paper disk with hours marked on it, made to move by the action of a clock, the face of which showed in the middle.

"Besides there's the steam gauge to watch," went on the engineer. "No engineer would dare go to sleep. There might be an explosion."

"Do you know Mr. Weldon Henley?" suddenly asked The Thinking Machine.

"Who?" asked Burlingame.

"Weldon Henley?"

"No-o," was the slow response. "Never heard of him. Who is he?"

"One of the tenants, on the second floor, I think."

"Lord, I don't know any of the tenants. What about him?"

"When does the inspector come here to read the meter?"

"I never saw him. I presume in daytime, eh Bill?" and he turned to the day engineer.

"Always in daytime—usually about noon," said Bill from his corner.

"Any other entrance to the basement except this way—and you could see anyone coming here this way I suppose?"

"Sure I could see 'em. There's no other entrance to the cellar except the coal hole in the sidewalk in front."

"Two big electric lights in front of the building, aren't there?"

"Yes. They go all night."

A slightly puzzled expression crept into the eyes of The Thinking Machine. Hatch knew from the persistency of the questions that he was not satisfied; yet he was not able to fathom or to understand all the queries. In some way they had to do with the possibility of some one having access to the meter.

"Where do you usually sit at night here?" was the next question.

"Over there where Bill's sitting. I always sit there."

The Thinking Machine crossed the room to Bill, a typical, grimy-handed man of his class.

"May I sit there a moment?" he asked.

Bill arose lazily, and The Thinking Machine sank down into the chair. From this point he could see plainly through the opening into the basement proper—there was no door—the gas meter of enormous proportions through which all the gas in the house passed. An electric light in the door made it bright as daylight. The Thinking Machine noted these things, arose, nodded his thanks to the two men and, still with the puzzled expression on his face, led the way up stairs. There the manager was still in his office.

"I presume you examine and know that the time check in the engineer's room is properly punched every half-hour during the night?" he asked.

"Yes. I examine the dial every day—have them here, in fact, each with the date on it."

"May I see them?"

Now the manager was puzzled. He produced the cards, one for each day, and for half an hour The Thinking Machine studied them minutely. At the end of that time, when he arose and Hatch looked at him inquiringly, he saw still the perplexed expression.

After urgent solicitation, the manager admitted them to the apartments of Weldon Henley. Mr. Henley himself had gone to his office in State Street. Here The Thinking Machine did several things which aroused the curiosity of the manager, one of which was to minutely study the gas jets. Then The Thinking Machine opened one of the front windows and glanced out into the street. Below fifteen feet was the sidewalk; above was the solid front of the building, broken only by a flagpole which, properly roped, extended from the hall window of the next floor above out over the sidewalk a distance of twelve feet or so.

"Ever use that flagpole?" he asked the manager.

"Rarely," said the manager. "On holidays sometimes—Fourth of July and such times. We have a big flag for it."

From the apartments The Thinking Machine led the way to the hall, up the stairs and to the flagpole. Leaning out of this window, he looked down toward the window of the apartments he had just left. Then he inspected the rope of the flagpole, drawing it through his slender hands slowly and carefully. At last he picked off a slender thread of scarlet and examined it.

"Ah," he exclaimed. Then to Hatch: "Let's go, Mr. Hatch. Thank you," this last to the manager, who had been a puzzled witness.

Once on the street, side by side with The Thinking Machine, Hatch was bursting with questions, but he didn't ask them. He knew it would be useless. At last The Thinking Machine broke the silence.

"That girl, Miss Regnier, *was murdered,*" he said suddenly, positively. "There have been four attempts to murder Henley."

"How?" asked Hatch, startled.

"By a scheme so simple that neither you nor I nor the police have ever heard of it being employed," was the astonishing reply. *"It is perfectly horrible in its simplicity."*

"What was it?" Hatch insisted, eagerly.

"It would be futile to discuss that now," was the rejoinder. "There has been murder. We know how. Now the question is—who? What person would have a motive to kill Henley?"

III

There was a pause as they walked on.

"Where are we going?" asked Hatch finally.

"Come up to my place and let's consider this matter a bit further," replied The Thinking Machine.

Not another word was spoken by either until half an hour later, in the small laboratory. For a long time the scientist was thoughtful—deeply thoughtful. Once he took down a volume from a shelf and Hatch glanced at the title. It was "Gases: Their Properties." After a while he returned this to the shelf and took down another, on which the reporter caught the title, "Anatomy."

"Now, Mr. Hatch," said The Thinking Machine in his perpetually crabbed voice, "we have a most remarkable riddle. It gains this remarkable aspect from its very simplicity. It is not, however, necessary to go into that now. I will make it clear to you when we know the motives.

"As a general rule, the greatest crimes never come to light because the greatest criminals, their perpetrators, are too clever to be caught. Here we have what I might call a great crime committed with a subtle simplicity that is wholly disarming, and a greater crime even than this was planned. This was to murder Weldon Henley. The first thing for you to do is to see Mr. Henley and warn him of his danger. Asphyxiation will not be attempted again, but there is a possibility of poison, a pistol shot, a knife, anything almost. As a matter of fact, he is in great peril.

"Superficially, the death of Miss Regnier, the maid, looks to be suicide. Instead it is the fruition of a plan which has been tried time and again against Henley. There is a possibility that Miss Regnier was not an intentional victim of the plot, but the fact remains that she was murdered. Why? Find the motive for the plot to murder Mr. Henley and you will know why."

The Thinking Machine reached over to the shelf, took a book, looked at it a moment, then went on:

"The first question to determine positively is: Who hated Weldon Henley sufficiently to desire his death? You say he is a successful man in the Street. Therefore there is a possibility that some enemy there is at the bottom of the affair, yet it seems hardly probable. If by his operations Mr. Henley ever happened to wreck another man's fortune find this man and find out all about him. He may be the man. There will be innumerable questions arising from this line of inquiry to a man of your resources. Leave none of them unanswered.

"On the other hand there is Henley's love affair. Had he a rival who might desire his death? Had he any rival? If so, find out all about him. He may be the man who planned all this. Here, too, there will be questions arising which demand answers. Answer them—all of them—fully and clearly before you see me again.

"Was Henley ever a party to a liaison of any kind? Find that out, too. A vengeful woman or a discarded sweetheart of a vengeful woman, you know, will go to any extreme. The rumor of his engagement to Miss—Miss—"

"Miss Lipscomb," Hatch supplied.

"The rumor of his engagement to Miss Lipscomb might have caused a woman whom he had once been interested in or who was once interested in him to attempt his life. The subtler murders—that is, the ones which are most attractive as problems—are nearly always the work of a cunning woman. I know nothing about women myself," he hastened to explain; "but Lombroso has taken that attitude. Therefore, see if there is a woman."

Most of these points Hatch had previously seen—seen with the unerring eye of a clever newspaper reporter—yet there were several which had not occurred to him. He nodded his understanding.

"Now the center of the affair, of course," The Thinking Machine continued, "is the apartment house where Henley lives. The person who attempted his life either lives there or has ready access to the place, and frequently spends the night there. This is a vital question for you to answer. I am leaving all this to you because you know better how to do these things than I do. That's all, I think. When these things are all learned come back to me."

The Thinking Machine arose as if the interview were at an end, and Hatch also arose, reluctantly. An idea was beginning to dawn in his mind.

"Does it occur to you that there is any connection whatever between Henley and Miss Regnier?" he asked.

"It is possible," was the reply. "I had thought of that. If there is a connection it is not apparent yet."

"Then how—how was it she—she was killed, or killed herself, whichever may be true, and—"

"The attempt to kill Henly killed her. That's all I can say now."

"That all?" asked Hatch, after a pause.

"No. Warn Mr. Henley immediately that he is in grave danger. Remember the person who has planned this will probably go to any extreme. I don't know Mr. Henley, of course, but from the fact that he always had a light at night I gather that he is a timid sort of man—not necessarily a coward, but a man lacking in stamina—therefore, one who might better disappear for a week or so until the mystery is cleared up. Above all, impress upon him the importance of the warning."

The Thinking Machine opened his pocketbook and took from it the scarlet thread which he had picked from the rope of the flagpole.

"Here, I believe, is the real clew to the problem," he explained to Hatch. "What does it seem to be?"

Hatch examined it closely.

"I should say a strand from a Turkish bath robe," was his final judgment.

"Possibly. Ask some cloth expert what he makes of it, then if it sounds promising look into it. Find out if by any possibility it can be any part of any garment worn by any person in the apartment house."

"But it's so slight—" Hatch began.

"I know," the other interrupted, tartly. "It's slight, but I believe it is a part of the wearing apparel of the person, man or woman, who has four times attempted to kill Mr. Henley and who did kill the girl. Therefore, it is important."

Hatch looked at him quickly.

"Well, how—in what manner—did it come where you found it?"

"Simple enough," said the scientist. "It is a wonder that there were not more pieces of it—that's all."

Perplexed by his instructions, but confident of results, Hatch left The Thinking Machine. What possible connection could this tiny bit of scarlet thread, found on a flagpole, have with some one shutting off the gas in Henley's rooms? How did any one go into Henley's rooms to shut off the gas? How was it Miss Regnier was dead? What was the manner of her death?

A cloth expert in a great department store turned his knowledge on the tiny bit of scarlet for the illumination of Hatch, but he could go no further than to say that it seemed to be part of a Turkish bath robe.

"Man or woman's?" asked Hatch.

"The material from which bath robes are made is the same for both men and women," was the reply. "I can say nothing else. Of course there's not enough of it to even guess at the pattern of the robe."

Then Hatch went to the financial district and was ushered into the office of Weldon Henley, a slender, handsome man of thirty-two or three years, pallid of face and nervous in manner. He still showed the effect of the gas poisoning, and there was even a trace of a furtive fear—fear of something, he himself didn't know what—in his actions.

Henley talked freely to the newspaper man of certain things, but of other things was resentfully reticent. He admitted his engagement to Miss Lipscomb, and finally even admitted that Miss Lipscomb's hand had been sought by another man, Regnault Cabell, formerly of Virginia.

"Could you give me his address?" asked Hatch.

"He lives in the same apartment house with me—two floors above," was the reply.

Hatch was startled; startled more than he would have cared to admit.

"Are you on friendly terms with him?" he asked.

"Certainly," said Henley. "I won't say anything further about this matter. It would be unwise for obvious reasons."

"I suppose you consider that this turning on of the gas was an attempt on your life?"

"I can't suppose anything else."

Hatch studied the pallid face closely as he asked the next question.

"Do you know Miss Regnier was found dead to-day?"

"Dead?" exclaimed the other, and he arose. "Who—what—who is she?"

It seemed a distinct effort for him to regain control of himself.

The reporter detailed then the circumstances of the finding of the girl's body, and the broker listened without comment. From that time forward all the reporter's questions were either parried or else met with a flat refusal to answer. Finally Hatch repeated to him the warning which he had from The Thinking Machine, and feeling that he had accomplished little went away.

At eight o'clock that night—a night of complete darkness—Henley was found unconscious, lying in a little used walk in the Common. There was a bullet hole through his left shoulder, and he was bleeding profusely. He was removed to the hospital, where he regained consciousness for just a moment.

"Who shot you?" he was asked.

"None of your business," he replied, and lapsed into unconsciousness.

IV

Entirely unaware of this latest attempt on the life of the broker, Hutchinson Hatch steadily pursued his investigations. They finally led him to an intimate friend of Regnault Cabell. The young Southerner had apartments on the fourth floor of the big house off Commonwealth Avenue, directly over those Henley occupied, but two flights higher up. This friend was a figure in the social set of the Back Bay. He talked to Hatch freely of Cabell.

"He's a good fellow," he explained, "one of the best I ever met, and comes of one of the best families Virginia ever had—a true F. F. V. He's pretty quick tempered and all that, but an excellent chap, and everywhere he has gone here he has made friends."

"He used to be in love with Miss Lipscomb of Virginia, didn't he?" asked Hatch, casually.

"Used to be?" the other repeated with a laugh. "He *is* in love with her. But recently he understood that she was engaged to Weldon Henley, a broker—you may have heard of him?—and that, I suppose, has dampened his ardor considerably. As a matter of fact, Cabell took the thing to heart. He used to know Miss Lipscomb in Virginia—she comes from another famous family there—and he seemed to think he had a prior claim on her."

Hatch heard all these things as any man might listen to gossip, but each additional fact was sinking into his mind, and each additional fact led his suspicions on deeper into the channel they had chosen.

"Cabell is pretty well to do," his informant went on, "not rich as we count riches in the North, but pretty well to do, and I believe he came to Boston because Miss Lipscomb spent so much of her time here. She is a beautiful young woman of twenty-two and extremely popular in the social world everywhere, particularly in Boston. Then there was the additional fact that Henley was here."

"No chance at all for Cabell?" Hatch suggested.

"Not the slightest," was the reply. "Yet despite the heartbreak he had, he was the first to congratulate Henley on winning her love. And he meant it, too."

"What's his attitude toward Henley now?" asked Hatch. His voice was calm, but there was an underlying tense note imperceptible to the other.

"They meet and speak and move in the same set. There's no love lost on either side, I don't suppose, but there is no trace of any ill feeling."

"Cabell doesn't happen to be a vindictive sort of man?"

"Vindictive?" and the other laughed. "No. He's like a big boy, forgiving, and all that; hot-tempered, though. I could imagine him in a fit of anger making a personal matter of it with Henley, but I don't think he ever did."

The mind of the newspaper man was rapidly focusing on one point; the rush of thoughts, questions and doubts silenced him for a moment. Then:

"How long has Cabell been in Boston?"

"Seven or eight months—that is, he has had apartments here for that long—but he has made several visits South. I suppose it's South. He has a trick of dropping out of sight occasionally. I understand that he intends to go South for good very soon. If I'm not mistaken, he is trying now to rent his suite."

Hatch looked suddenly at his informant; an idea of seeing Cabell and having a legitimate excuse for talking to him had occurred to him.

"I'm looking for a suite," he volunteered at last. "I wonder if you would give me a card of introduction to him? We might get together on it."

Thus it happened that half an hour later, about ten minutes past nine o'clock, Hatch was on his way to the big apartment house. In the office he saw the manager."

"Heard the news?" asked the manager.

"No," Hatch replied. "What is it?"

"Somebody's shot Mr. Henley as he was passing through the Common early to-night."

Hatch whistled his amazement.

"Is he dead?"

"No, but he is unconscious. The hospital doctors say it is a nasty wound, but not necessarily dangerous."

"Who shot him? Do they know?"

"He knows, but he won't say."

Amazed and alarmed by this latest development, an accurate fulfillment of The Thinking Machine's prophecy, Hatch stood thoughtful for a moment, then recovering his composure a little asked for Cabell.

"I don't think there's much chance of seeing him," said the manager. "He's going away on the midnight train—going South, to Virginia."

"Going away to-night?" Hatch gasped.

"Yes; it seems to have been rather a sudden determination. He was talking to me here half an hour or so ago, and said something about going away. While he was here the telephone boy told me that Henley had been shot; they had 'phoned from the hospital to inform us. Then Cabell seemed greatly agitated. He said he was going away to-night, if he could catch the midnight train, and now he's packing."

"I suppose the shooting of Henley upset him considerably?" the reporter suggested.

"Yes, I guess it did," was the reply. "They moved in the same set and belonged to the same clubs."

The manager sent Hatch's card of introduction to Cabell's apartments. Hatch went up and was ushered into a suite identical with that of Henley's in every respect save in minor details of furnishings. Cabell stood in the middle of the floor, with his personal belongings scattered about the room; his valet, evidently a Frenchman, was busily esgaged in packing.

Cabell's greeting was perfunctorily cordial; he seemed agitated. His face was flushed and from time to time he ran his fingers through his long, brown hair. He stared at Hatch in a preoccupied fashion, then they fell into conversation about the rent of the apartments.

"I'll take almost anything reasonable," Cabell said hurriedly. "You see, I am going away to-night, rather more suddenly than I had intended, and I am anxious to get the lease off my hands. I pay two hundred dollars a month for these just as they are."

"May I look them over?" asked Hatch.

He passed from the front room into the next. Here, on a bed, was piled a huge lot of clothing, and the valet, with deft fingers, was brushing and folding, preparatory to packing. Cabell was directly behind him.

"Quite comfortable, you see," he explained. "There's room enough if you are alone. Are you?"

"Oh, yes," Hatch replied.

"This other room here," Cabell explained, "is not in very tidy shape now. I have been out of the city for several weeks, and— What's the matter?" he demanded suddenly.

Hatch had turned quickly at the words and stared at him, then recovered himself with a start.

"I beg your pardon," he stammered. "I rather thought I saw you in town here a week or so ago—of course I didn't know you—and I was wondering if I could have been mistaken."

"Must have been," said the other easily. "During the time I was away a Miss ——, a friend of my sister's, occupied the suite. I'm afraid some of her things are here. She hasn't sent for them as yet. She occupied this room, I think; when I came back a few days ago she took another place and all her things haven't been removed."

"I see," remarked Hatch, casually. "I don't suppose there's any chance of her returning here unexpectedly if I should happen to take her apartments?"

"Not the slightest. She knows I am back, and thinks I am to remain. She was to send for these things."

Hatch gazed about the room ostentatiously. Across a trunk lay a Turkish bath robe with a scarlet stripe in it. He was anxious to get hold of it, to examine it closely. But he didn't dare to, then. Together they returned to the front room.

"I rather like the place," he said, after a pause, "but the price is—"

"Just a moment," Cabell interrupted. "Jean, before you finish packing that suit case be sure to put my bath robe in it. It's in the far room."

Then one question was settled for Hatch. After a moment the valet returned with the bath robe, which had been in the far room. It was Cabell's bath robe. As Jean passed the reporter an end of the robe caught on a corner of the trunk, and, stopping, the reporter unfastened it. A tiny strand of thread clung to the metal; Hatch detached it and stood idly twirling it in his fingers.

"As I was saying," he resumed, "I rather like the place, but the price is too much. Suppose you leave it in the hands of the manager of the house—"

"I had intended doing that," the Southerner interrupted.

"Well, I'll see him about it later," Hatch added.

With a cordial, albeit pre-occupied, handshake, Cabell ushered him out. Hatch went down in the elevator with a feeling of elation; a feeling that he had accomplished something. The manager was waiting to get into the lift.

"Do you happen to remember the name of the young lady who occupied Mr. Cabell's suite while he was away?" he asked.

"Miss Austin," said the manager, "but she's not young. She was about forty-five years old, I should judge."

"Did Mr. Cabell have his servant Jean with him?"

"Oh, no," said the manager. "The valet gave up the suite to Miss Austin entirely, and until Mr. Cabell returned occupied a room in the quarters we have for our own employees."

"Was Miss Austin ailing any way?" asked Hatch. "I saw a large number of medicine bottles upstairs."

"I don't know what was the matter with her," replied the manager, with a little puzzled frown. "She certainly was not a woman of sound mental balance—that is, she was eccentric, and all that. I think rather it was an act of charity for Mr. Cabell to let her have the suite in his absence. Certainly we didn't want her."

Hatch passed out and burst in eagerly upon The Thinking Machine in his laboratory.

"Here," he said, and triumphantly he extended the tiny scarlet strand which he had received from The Thinking Machine, and the other of the identical color which came from Cabell's bath robe. "Is that the same?"

The Thinking Machine placed them under the microscope and examined them immediately. Later he submitted them to a chemical test.

"It is the same," he said, finally.

"Then the mystery is solved," said Hatch, conclusively.

V

The Thinking Machine stared steadily into the eager, exultant eyes of the newspaper man until Hatch at last began to fear that he had been precipitate. After awhile, under close scrutiny, the reporter began to feel convinced that he had made a mistake—he didn't quite see where, but it must be there, and the exultant manner passed. The voice of The Thinking Machine was like a cold shower.

"Remember, Mr. Hatch," he said, critically, "that unless every possible question has been considered one cannot boast of a solution. Is there any possible question lingering yet in your mind?"

The reporter silently considered that for a moment, then:

"Well, I have the main facts, anyway. There may be one or two minor questions left, but the principal ones are answered."

"Then tell me, to the minutest detail, what you have learned, what has happened."

Professor Van Dusen sank back in his old, familiar pose in the large arm chair and Hatch related what he had learned and what he surmised. He related, too, the peculiar circumstances surrounding the wounding of Henley, and right on down to the beginning and end of the interview with Cabell in the latter's apartments. The Thinking Machine was silent for a time, then there came a host of questions.

"Do you know where the woman—Miss Austin—is now?" was the first.

"No," Hatch had to admit.

"Or her precise mental condition?"

"No."

"Or her exact relationship to Cabell?"

"No."

"Do you know, then, what the valet, Jean, knows of the affair?"

"No, not that," said the reporter, and his face flushed under the close questioning. "He was out of the suite every night."

"Therefore might have been the very one who turned on the gas," the other put in testily.

"So far as I can learn, nobody could have gone into that room and turned on the gas," said the reporter, somewhat aggressively. "Henley barred the doors and windows and kept watch, night after night."

"Yet the moment he was exhausted and fell asleep the gas was turned on to kill him," said The Thinking Machine; "thus we see that *he was watched more closely than he watched.*"

"I see what you mean now," said Hatch, after a long pause.

"I should like to know what Henley and Cabell and the valet knew of the girl who was found dead," The Thinking Machine suggested. "Further, I should like to know if there was a good-sized mirror—not one set in a bureau or dresser—either in Henley's room or the apartments where the girl was found. Find out this for me and—never mind. I'll go with you."

The scientist left the room. When he returned he wore his coat and hat. Hatch arose mechanically to follow. For a block or more they walked along, neither speaking. The Thinking Machine was the first to break the silence:

"You believe Cabell is the man who attempted to kill Henley?"

"Frankly, yes," replied the newspaper man.

"Why?"

"Because he had the motive—disappointed love."

"How?"

"I don't know," Hatch confessed. "The doors of the Henley suite were closed. I don't see how anybody passed them."

"And the girl? Who killed her? How? Why?"

Disconsolately Hatch shook his head as he walked on. The Thinking Machine interpreted his silence aright.

"Don't jump at conclusions," he advised sharply. "You

are confident Cabell was to blame for this—and he might have been, I don't know yet—but you can suggest nothing to show how he did it. I have told you before that imagination is half of logic."

At last the lights of the big apartment house where Henley lived came in sight. Hatch shrugged his shoulders. He had grave doubts—based on what he knew—whether The Thinking Machine would be able to see Cabell. It was nearly eleven o'clock and Cabell was to leave for the South at midnight.

"Is Mr. Cabell here?" asked the scientist of the elevator boy.

"Yes, just about to go, though. He won't see anyone."

"Hand him this note," instructed The Thinking Machine, and he scribbled something on a piece of paper. "He'll see us."

The boy took the paper and the elevator shot up to the fourth floor. After a while he returned.

"He'll see you," he said.

"Is he unpacking?"

"After he read your note twice he told his valet to unpack," the boy replied.

"Ah, I thought so," said The Thinking Machine.

With Hatch, mystified and puzzled, following, The Thinking Machine entered the elevator to step out a second or so later on the fourth floor. As they left the car they saw the door of Cabell's apartment standing open; Cabell was in the door. Hatch traced a glimmer of anxiety in the eyes of the young man.

"Professor Van Dusen?" Cabell inquired.

"Yes," said the scientist. "It was of the utmost importance that I should see you, otherwise I should not have come at this time of night."

With a wave of his hand Cabell passed that detail.

"I was anxious to get away at midnight," he explained, "but, of course, now I shan't go, in view of your note. I have ordered my valet to unpack my things, at least until tomorrow."

The reporter and the scientist passed into the luxuriously furnished apartments. Jean, the valet, was bending over a suit case as they entered, removing some things he had been carefully placing there. He didn't look back or pay the least attention to the visitors.

"This is your valet?" asked The Thinking Machine.

"Yes," said the young man.

"French, isn't he?"

"Yes."

"Speak English at all?"

"Very badly," said Cabell. "I use French when I talk to him."

"Does he know that you are accused of murder?" asked The Thinking Machine, in a quiet, conversational tone.

The effect of the remark on Cabell was startling. He staggered back a step or so as if he had been struck in the face, and a crimson flush overspread his brow. Jean, the valet, straightened up suddenly and looked around. There was a queer expression, too, in his eyes; an expression which Hatch could not fathom.

"Murder?" gasped Cabell, at last.

"Yes, he speaks English all right," remarked The Thinking Machine. "Now, Mr. Cabell, will you please tell me just who Miss Austin is, and where she is, and her mental condition? Believe me, it may save you a great deal of trouble. What I said in the note is not exaggerated."

The young man turned suddenly and began to pace back and forth across the room. After a few minutes he paused before The Thinking Machine, who stood impatiently waiting for an answer.

"I'll tell you, yes," said Cabell, firmly. "Miss Austin is a middle-aged woman whom my sister befriended several times—was, in fact, my sister's governess when she was a child. Of late years she has not been wholly right mentally, and has suffered a great deal of privation. I had about concluded arrangements to put her in a private sanitarium. I permitted her to remain in these rooms in my absence, South. I did not take Jean—he lived in the quarters of the other employees of the place, and gave the apartment entirely to Miss Austin. It was simply an act of charity."

"What was the cause of your sudden determination to go South to-night?" asked the scientist.

"I won't answer that question," was the sullen reply.

There was a long, tense silence. Jean, the valet, came and went several times.

"How long has Miss Austin known Mr. Henley?"

"Presumably since she has been in these apartments," was the reply.

"Are you sure *you* are not Miss Austin?" demanded the scientist.

The question was almost staggering, not only to Cabell, but to Hatch. Suddenly, with flaming face, the young Southerner leaped forward as if to strike down The Thinking Machine.

"That won't do any good," said the scientist, coldly. "Are you sure you are not Miss Austin?" he repeated.

"Certainly I am not Miss Austin," responded Cabell, fiercely.

"Have you a mirror in these apartments about twelve inches by twelve inches?" asked The Thinking Machine, irrelevantly.

"I—I don't know," stammered the young man. "I—have we, Jean?"

"Oui," replied the valet.

"Yes," snapped The Thinking Machine. "Talk English, please. May I see it?"

The valet, without a word but with a sullen glance at the questioner, turned and left the room. He returned after a moment with the mirror. The Thinking Machine carefully examined the frame, top and bottom and on both sides. At last he looked up; again the valet was bending over a suit case.

"Do you use gas in these apartments?" the scientist asked suddenly.

"No," was the bewildered response. "What is all this, anyway?"

Without answering, The Thinking Machine drew a chair up under the chandelier where the gas and electric fixtures were and began to finger the gas tips. After a while he climbed down and passed into the next room, with Hatch and Cabell, both hopelessly mystified, following. There the scientist went through the same process of fingering the gas jets. Finally, one of the gas tips came out in his hand.

"Ah," he exclaimed, suddenly, and Hatch knew the note of triumph in it. The jet from which the tip came was just on a level with his shoulder, set between a dressing table and a window. He leaned over and squinted at the gas pipe closely. Then he returned to the room where the valet was.

"Now, Jean," he began, in an even, calm voice, "please tell me *if you did or did not kill Miss Regnier purposely?*"

"I don't know what you mean," said the servant sullenly, angrily, as he turned on the scientist.

"You speak very good English now," was The Thinking Machine's terse comment. "Mr. Hatch, lock the door and use this 'phone to call the police."

Hatch turned to do as he was bid and saw a flash of steel in young Cabell's hand, which was drawn suddenly from a hip pocket. It was a revolver. The weapon glittered in the light, and Hatch flung himself forward. There was a sharp report, and a bullet was buried in the floor.

VI

Then came a fierce, hard fight for possession of the revolver. It ended with the weapon in Hatch's hand, and both he and Cabell blowing from the effort they had expended. Jean, the valet, had turned at the sound of the shot and started toward the door leading into the hall. The Thinking Machine had stepped in front of him, and now stood there with his back to the door. Physically he would have been a child in the hands of the valet, yet there was a look in his eyes which stopped him.

"Now, Mr. Hatch," said the scientist quietly, a touch of irony in his voice, "hand me the revolver, then 'phone for Detective Mallory to come here immediately. Tell him we have a murderer—and if he can't come at once get some other detective whom you know."

"Murderer!" gasped Cabell.

Uncontrollable rage was blazing in the eyes of the valet, and he made as if to throw The Thinking Machine aside, despite the revolver, when Hatch was at the telephone. As Jean started forward, however, Cabell stopped him with a quick, stern gesture. Suddenly the young Southerner turned on The Thinking Machine; but it was with a question.

"What does it all mean?" he asked, bewildered.

"It means that that man there," and The Thinking Machine indicated the valet by a nod of his head, "is a murderer—that he killed Louise Regnier; that he shot Weldon Henley on Boston Common, and that, with the aid of Miss Regnier, he had four times previously attempted to kill Mr. Henley. Is he coming, Mr. Hatch?"

"Yes," was the reply. "He says he'll be here directly."

"Do you deny it?" demanded The Thinking Machine of the valet.

"I've done nothing," said the valet sullenly. "I'm going out of here."

Like an infuriated animal he rushed forward. Hatch and Cabell seized him and bore him to the floor. There, after a frantic struggle, he was bound and the other three men sat down to wait for Detective Mallory. Cabell sank back in his chair with a perplexed frown on his face. From time to time he glanced at Jean. The flush of anger which had been on the valet's face was gone now; instead there was the pallor of fear.

"Won't you tell us?" pleaded Cabell impatiently.

"When Detective Mallory comes and takes his prisoner," said The Thinking Machine.

Ten minutes later they heard a quick step in the hall outside and Hatch opened the door. Detective Mallory entered and looked from one to another inquiringly.

"That's your prisoner, Mr. Mallory," said the scientist, coldly. "I charge him with the murder of Miss Regnier, whom you were so confident committed suicide; I charge him with five attempts on the life of Weldon Henley, four times by gas poisoning, in which Miss Regnier was his accomplice, and once by shooting. He is the man who shot Mr. Henley."

The Thinking Machine arose and walked over to the prostrate man, handing the revolver to Hatch. He glared down at Jean fiercely.

"Will you tell how you did it or shall I?" he demanded.

His answer was a sullen, defiant glare. He turned and picked up the square mirror which the valet had produced previously.

"That's where the screw was, isn't it?" he asked, as he indicated a small hole in the frame of the mirror. Jean stared at it and his head sank forward hopelessly. "And this is the bath robe you wore, isn't it?" he demanded again, and from the suit case he pulled out the garment with the scarlet stripe.

"I guess you got me all right," was the sullen reply.

"It might be better for you if you told the story then?" suggested The Thinking Machine.

"You know so much about it, tell it yourself."

"Very well," was the calm rejoinder. "I will. If I make any mistake you will correct me."

For a long time no one spoke. The Thinking Machine had dropped back into a chair and was staring through his thick glasses at the ceiling; his finger tips were pressed tightly together. At last he began:

"There are certain trivial gaps which only the imagination can supply until the matter is gone into more fully. I should have supplied these myself, but the arrest of this man, Jean, was precipitated by the attempted hurried departure of Mr. Cabell for the South to-night, and I did not have time to go into the case to the fullest extent.

"Thus, we begin with the fact that there were several clever attempts made to murder Mr. Henley. This was by putting out the gas which he habitually left burning in his room. It happened four times in all; thus proving that it was an attempt to kill him. If it had been only once it might have been accident, even twice it might have been accident, but the same accident does not happen four times at the same time of night.

"Mr. Henley finally grew to regard the strange extinguishing of the gas as an effort to kill him, and carefully locked and barred his door and windows each night. He believed that some one came into his apartments and put out the light, leaving the gas flow. This, of course, was not true. Yet the gas was put out. How? My first idea, a natural one, was that it was turned off for an instant at the meter, when the light would go out, then turned on again. This, I convinced myself, was not true. Therefore still the question—how?

"It is a fact—I don't know how widely known it is—but it is a fact that every gas light in this house might be extinguished at the same time from this room without leaving it. How? Simply by removing the gas jet tip and blowing into the gas pipe. It would not leave a jet in the building burning. It is due to the fact that the lung power is greater than the pressure of the gas in the pipes, and forces it out.

"Thus we have the method employed to extinguish the light in Mr. Henley's rooms, and all the barred and locked doors and windows would not stop it. At the same time it threatened the life of every other person in the house—that is, every other person who used gas. It was probably for this reason that the attempt was always made late at night, I should say three or four o'clock. That's when it was done, isn't it?" he asked suddenly of the valet.

Staring at The Thinking Machine in open-mouthed astonishment the valet nodded his acquiescence before he was fully aware of it.

"Yes, that's right," The Thinking Machine resumed complacently. "This was easily found out—comparatively. The next question was how was a watch kept on Mr. Henley? It would have done no good to extinguish the gas before he was asleep, or to have turned it on when he was not in his rooms. It might have led to a speedy discovery of just how the thing was done.

"There's a spring lock on the door of Mr. Henley's apartment. Therefore it would have been impossible for anyone to peep through the keyhole. There are no cracks through which one might see. How was this watch kept? How was the plotter to satisfy himself positively of the time when Mr. Henley was asleep? How was it the gas was put out at no time of the score or more nights Mr. Henley himself kept watch? Obviously he was watched through a window.

"No one could climb out on the window ledge and look into Mr. Henley's apartments. No one could see into that apartment from the street—that is, could see whether Mr. Henley was asleep or even in bed. They could see the light. Watch was kept with the aid offered by the flagpole, supplemented with a mirror—this mirror. A screw was driven into the frame—it has been removed now—it was swung on the flagpole rope and pulled out to the end of the pole, facing the building. To a man standing in the hall window of the third floor it offered precisely the angle necessary to reflect the interior of Mr. Henley's suite, possibly even showed him in bed through a narrow opening in the curtain. There is no shade on the windows of that suite; heavy curtains instead. Is that right?"

Again the prisoner was surprised into a mute acquiescence.

"I saw the possibility of these things, and I saw, too, that at three or four o'clock in the morning it would be perfectly possible for a person to move about the upper halls of this house without being seen. If he wore a heavy bath robe, with a hood, say, no one would recognize him even if he were seen, and besides the garb would not cause suspicion. This bath robe has a hood.

"Now, in working the mirror back and forth on the flagpole at night a tiny scarlet thread was pulled out of the robe and clung to the rope. I found this thread; later Mr. Hatch found an identical thread in these apartments. Both came from that bath robe. Plain logic shows that the person who blew down the gas pipes worked the mirror trick; the person who worked the mirror trick left the thread; the thread comes back to the bath robe—that bath robe there," he pointed dramatically. "Thus the person who desired Henley's death was in these apartments, or had easy access to them."

He paused a moment and there was a tense silence. A great light was coming to Hatch, slowly but surely. The brain that had followed all this was unlimited in possibilities.

"Even before we traced the origin of the crime to this room," went on the scientist, quietly now, "attention had been attraced here, particularly to you, Mr. Cabell. It was through the love affair, of which Miss Lipscomb was the center. Mr. Hatch learned that you and Henley had been rivals for her hand. It was that, even before this scarlet thread was found, which indicated that you might have some knowledge of the affair, directly or indirectly.

"You are not a malicious or revengeful man, Mr. Cabell. But you are hot-tempered—extremely so. You demonstrated that just now, when, angry and not understanding, but feeling that your honor was at stake, you shot a hole in the floor."

"What?" asked Detective Mallory.

"A little accident," explained The Thinking Machine quickly. "Not being a malicious or revengeful man, you are not the man to deliberately go ahead and make elaborate plans for the murder of Henley. In a moment of passion you might have killed him—but never deliberately as the result of premeditation. Besides you were out of town. Who was then in these apartments? Who had access to these apartments? Who might have used your bath robe? Your valet, possibly Miss Austin. Which? Now, let's see how we reached this conclusion which led to the valet.

"Miss Regnier was found dead. It was not suicide. How did I know? Because she had been reading with the gas light at its full. If she had been reading by the gas light, how was it then that it went out and suffocated her before she could arise and shut it off? Obviously she must have fallen asleep over her book and left the light burning.

"If she was in this plot to kill Henley, why did she light the jet in her room? There might have been some slight defect in the electric bulb in her room which she had just discovered. Therefore she lighted the gas, intending to extinguish it—turn it off entirely—later. But she fell asleep. Therefore when the valet here blew into the pipe, intending to kill Mr. Henley, he unwittingly killed the woman he loved—Miss Regnier. It was perfectly possible, meanwhile, that she did not know of the attempt to be made that particular night, although she had participated in the others, knowing that Henley had night after night sat up to watch the light in his rooms.

"The facts, as I knew them, showed no connection between Miss Regnier and this man at that time—nor any connection between Miss Regnier and Henley. It might have been that the person who blew the gas out of the pipe from these rooms knew nothing whatever of Miss Regnier, just as he didn't know who else he might have killed in the building.

"But I had her death and the manner of it. I had eliminated you, Mr. Cabell. Therefore there remained Miss Austin and the valet. Miss Austin was eccentric—insane, if you will. Would she have any motive for killing Henley? I could imagine none. Love? Probably not. Money? They had nothing in common on that ground. What? Nothing that I could see. Therefore, for the moment, I passed Miss Austin by, after asking you, Mr. Cabell, if you were Miss Austin.

"What remained? The valet. Motive? Several possible ones, one or two probable. He is French, or says he is. Miss Regnier is French. Therefore I had arrived at the conclusion that they knew each other as people of the same nationality will in a house of this sort. And remember, I had passed by Mr. Cabell and Miss Austin, so the valet was the only one left; he could use the bath robe.

"Well, the motive. Frankly that was the only difficult point in the entire problem—difficult because there were so many possibilities. And each possibility that suggested itself suggested also a woman. Jealousy? There must be a woman. Hate? Probably a woman. Attempted extortion? With the aid of a woman. No other motive which would lead to so elaborate a plot of murder would come forward. Who was the woman? Miss Regnier.

"Did Miss Regnier know Henley? Mr. Hatch had reason to believe he knew her because of his actions when informed of her death. Knew her how? People of such relatively different planes of life can know each other—or do know each other—only on one plane. Henley is a typical young man, fast, I dare say, and liberal. Perhaps, then, there had been a liaison. When I saw this possibility I had my motives—all of them—jealousy, hate and possibly attempted extortion as well.

"What was more possible than Mr. Henley and Miss Regnier had been acquainted? All liaisons are secret ones Suppose she had been cast off because of the engagement to a young woman of Henley's own level? Suppose she had confided in the valet here? Do you see? Motives enough for any crime, however diabolical. The attempts on Henley's life possibly followed an attempted extortion of money. The shot which wounded Henley was fired by this man, Jean. Why? Because the woman who had cause to hate Henley was dead. Then the man? He was alive and vindictive.

Henley knew who shot him, and knew why, but he'll never say it publicly. He can't afford to. It would ruin him. I think probably that's all. Do you want to add anything?" he asked of the valet.

"No," was the fierce reply. "I'm sorry I didn't kill him, that's all. It was all about as you said, though God knows how you found it out," he added, desperately.

"Are you a Frenchman?"

"I was born in New York, but lived in France for eleven years. I first knew Louise there."

Silence fell upon the little group. Then Hatch asked a question:

"You told me, Professor, that there would be no other attempt to kill Henley by extinguishing the gas. How did you know that?"

"Because one person—the wrong person—had been killed that way," was the reply. "For this reason it was hardly likely that another attempt of that sort would be made. You had no intention of killing Louise Regnier, had you, Jean?"

"No, God help me, no."

"It was all done in these apartments," The Thinking Machine added, turning to Cabell, "at the gas jet from which I took the tip. It had been only loosely replaced and the metal was tarnished where the lips had dampened it."

"It must take great lung power to do a thing like that," remarked Detective Mallory.

"You would be amazed to know how easily it is done," said the scientist. "Try it some time."

The Thinking Machine arose and picked up his hat; Hatch did the same. Then the reporter turned to Cabell.

"Would you mind telling me why you were so anxious to get away to-night?" he asked.

"Well, no," Cabell explained, and there was a rush of red to his face. "It's because I received a telegram from Virginia—Miss Lipscomb, in fact. Some of Henley's past had come to her knowledge and the telegram told me that the engagement was broken. On top of this came the information that Henley had been shot and—I was considerably agitated."

THE SCARLET THREAD

The Thinking Machine and Hatch were walking along the street.

"What did you write in the note you sent to Cabell that made him start to unpack?" asked the reporter, curiously.

"There are some things that it wouldn't be well for everyone to know," was the enigmatic response. "Perhaps it would be just as well for you to overlook this little omission."

"Of course, of course," replied the reporter, wonderingly.

The Man Who Was Lost

BY JACQUES FUTRELLE

The Man Who Was Lost

BY JACQUES FUTRELLE

I

HERE are the facts in the case as they were known in the beginning to Professor Augustus S. F. X. Van Dusen, scientist and logician. After hearing a statement of the problem from the lips of its principal he declared it to be one of the most engaging that had ever come to his attention, and—

But let me begin at the beginning:

. . . .

The Thinking Machine was in the small laboratory of his modest apartments at two o'clock in the afternoon. Martha, the scientist's only servant, appeared at the door with a puzzled expression on her wrinkled face.

"A gentleman to see you, sir," she said.

"Name?" inquired The Thinking Machine, without turning.

"He—he didn't give it, sir," she stammered.

"I have told you always, Martha, to ask names of callers."

"I did ask his name, sir, and—and he said he didn't know it."

The Thinking Machine was never surprised, yet now he turned on Martha in perplexity and squinted at her fiercely through his thick glasses.

"Don't know his own name?" he repeated. "Dear me! How careless! Show the gentleman into the reception room immediately."

With no more introduction to the problem than this, therefore, The Thinking Machine passed into the other room. A stranger arose and came forward. He was tall, of apparently thirty-five years, clean shaven and had the keen, alert face of a man of affairs. He would have been handsome had it not been for dark rings under the eyes and the unusual white of his face. He was immaculately dressed from top to toe; altogether a man who would attract attention.

For a moment he regarded the scientist curiously; perhaps there was a trace of well-bred astonishment in his manner. He gazed curiously at the enormous head, with its shock of yellow hair, and noted, too, the droop in the thin shoulders. Thus for a moment they stood, face to face, the tall stranger making The Thinking Machine dwarf-like by comparison.

"Well?" asked the scientist.

The stranger turned as if to pace back and forth across the room, then instead dropped into a chair which the scientist indicated.

"I have heard a great deal about you, Professor," he began, in a well-modulated voice, "and at last it occurred to me to come to you for advice. I am in a most remarkable position —and I'm not insane. Don't think that, please. But unless I see some way out of this amazing predicament I shall be. As it is now, my nerves have gone; I am not myself."

"Your story? What is it? How can I help you?"

"I am lost, hopelessly lost," the stranger resumed. "I know neither my home, my business, nor even my name. I know nothing whatever of myself or my life; what it was or what it might have been previous to four weeks ago. I am seeking light on my identity. Now, if there is any fee—"

"Never mind that," the scientist put in, and he squinted steadily into the eyes of the visitor. "What *do* you know? From the time you remember things tell me all of it."

He sank back into his chair, squinting steadily upward. The stranger arose, paced back and forth across the room several times and then dropped into his chair again.

"It's perfectly incomprehensible," he said. "It's precisely as if I, full grown, had been born into a world of which I knew nothing except its language. The ordinary things, chairs, tables and such things, are perfectly familiar, but who I am, where I came from, why I came—of these I have no idea. I will tell you just as my impressions came to me when I awoke one morning, four weeks ago.

THE MAN WHO WAS LOST

"It was eight or nine o'clock, I suppose. I was in a room. I knew instantly it was a hotel, but had not the faintest idea of how I got there, or of ever having seen the room before. I didn't even know my own clothing when I started to dress. I glanced out of my window; the scene was wholly strange to me.

"For half an hour or so I remained in my room, dressing and wondering what it meant. Then, suddenly, in the midst of my other worries, it came home to me that I didn't know my own name, the place where I lived nor anything about myself. I didn't know what hotel I was in. In terror I looked into a mirror. The face reflected at me was not one I knew. It didn't seem to be the face of a stranger; it was merely not a face that I knew.

"The thing was unbelievable. Then I began a search of my clothing for some trace of my identity. I found nothing whatever that would enlighten me—not a scrap of paper of any kind, no personal or business card."

"Have a watch?" asked The Thinking Machine.

"No."

"Any money?"

"Yes, money," said the stranger. "There was a bundle of more than ten thousand dollars in my pocket, in one-hundred-dollar bills. Whose it is or where it came from I don't know. I have been living on it since, and shall continue to do so, but I don't know if it is mine. I knew it was money when I saw it, but did not recollect ever having seen any previously."

"Any jewelry?"

"These cuff buttons," and the stranger exhibited a pair which he drew from his pocket.

"Go on."

"I finally finished dressing and went down to the office. It was my purpose to find out the name of the hotel and who I was. I knew I could learn some of this from the hotel register without attracting any attention or making anyone think I was insane. I had noted the number of my room. It was twenty-seven.

"I looked over the hotel register casually. I saw I was at the Hotel Yarmouth in Boston. I looked carefully down the pages until I came to the number of my room. Opposite this number was a name—John Doane, but where the name of the city should have been there was only a dash."

"You realize that it is perfectly possible that John Doane is your name?" asked The Thinking Machine.

"Certainly," was the reply. "But I have no recollection of ever having heard it before. This register showed that I had arrived at the hotel the night before—or rather that John Doane had arrived and been assigned to Room 27, and I was the John Doane, presumably. From that moment to this the hotel people have known me as John Doane, as have other people whom I have met during the four weeks since I awoke."

"Did the handwriting recall nothing?"

"Nothing whatever."

"Is it anything like the handwriting you write now?"

"Identical, so far as I can see."

"Did you have any baggage or checks for baggage?"

"No. All I had was the money and this clothing I stand in. Of course, since then I have bought necessities."

Both were silent for a long time and finally the stranger—Doane—arose and began pacing nervously again.

"That a tailor-made suit?" asked the scientist.

"Yes," said Doane, quickly. "I know what you mean. Tailor-made garments have linen strips sewed inside the pockets on which are the names of the manufacturers and the name of the man for whom the clothes were made, together with the date. I looked for those. They had been removed, cut out."

"Ah!" exclaimed The Thinking Machine suddenly. "No laundry marks on your linen either, I suppose?"

"No. It was all perfectly new."

"Name of the maker on it?"

"No. That had been cut out, too."

Doane was pacing back and forth across the reception room; the scientist lay back in his chair.

"Do you know the circumstances of your arrival at the hotel?" he asked at last.

"Yes. I asked, guardedly enough, you may be sure, hinting to the clerk that I had been drunk so as not to make him think I was insane. He said I came in about eleven o'clock at night, without any baggage, paid for my room with a one-hundred-dollar bill, which he changed, registered and went upstairs. I said nothing that he recalls beyond making a request for a room."

"The name Doane is not familiar to you?"

"No."

"You can't recall a wife or children?"

"No."

"Do you speak any foreign language?"

"No."

"Is your mind clear now? Do you remember things?"

"I remember perfectly every incident since I awoke in the hotel," said Doane. "I seem to remember with remarkable clearness, and somehow I attach the gravest importance to the most trivial incidents."

The Thinking Machine arose and motioned to Doane to sit down. He dropped back into a seat wearily. Then the scientist's long, slender fingers ran lightly, deftly through the abundant black hair of his visitor. Finally they passed down from the hair and along the firm jaws; thence they went to the arms, where they pressed upon good, substantial muscles. At last the hands, well shaped and white, were examined minutely. A magnifying glass was used to facilitate this examination. Finally The Thinking Machine stared into the quick-moving, nervous eyes of the stranger.

"Any marks at all on your body?" he asked at last.

"No," Doane responded. "I had thought of that and sought for an hour for some sort of mark. There's nothing—nothing." The eyes glittered a little and finally, in a burst of nervousness, he struggled to his feet. "My God!" he exclaimed. "Is there nothing you can do? What is it all, anyway?"

"Seems to be a remarkable form of aphasia," replied The Thinking Machine. "That's not an uncommon disease among people whose minds and nerves are overwrought. You've simply lost yourself—lost your identity. If it is aphasia, you will recover in time. When, I don't know."

"And meantime?"

"Let me see the money you found."

With trembling hands Doane produced a large roll of bills,

principally hundreds, many of them perfectly new. The Thinking Machine examined them minutely, and finally made some memoranda on a slip of paper. The money was then returned to Doane.

"Now, what shall I do?" asked the latter.

"Don't worry," advised the scientist. "I'll do what I can."

"And—tell me who and what I am?"

"Oh, I can find that out all right," remarked The Thinking Machine. "But there's a possibility that you wouldn't recall even if I told you all about yourself."

II

When John Doane of Nowhere—to all practical purposes—left the home of The Thinking Machine he bore instructions of divers kinds. First he was to get a large map of the United States and study it closely, reading over and pronouncing aloud the name of every city, town and village he found. After an hour of this he was to take a city directory and read over the names, pronouncing them aloud as he did so. Then he was to make out a list of the various professions and higher commercial pursuits, and pronounce these. All these things were calculated, obviously, to arouse the sleeping brain. After Doane had gone The Thinking Machine called up Hutchinson Hatch, reporter, on the 'phone.

"Come up immediately," he requested. "There's something that will interest you."

"A mystery?" Hatch inquired, eagerly.

"One of the most engaging problems that has ever come to my attention," replied the scientist.

It was only a question of a few minutes before Hatch was ushered in. He was a living interrogation point, and repressed a rush of questions with a distinct effort. The Thinking Machine finally told what he knew.

"Now it seems to be," said The Thinking Machine, and he emphasized the "seems," "it seems to be a case of aphasia. You know, of course, what that is. The man simply doesn't know himself. I examined him closely. I went over his head for a sign of a possible depression, or abnormality. It didn't appear. I examined his muscles. He has biceps of great power, is evidently now or has been athletic. His hands are white, well cared for and have no marks on them. They are not the hands of a man who has ever done physical work. The money in his pocket tends to confirm the fact that he is not of that sphere.

"Then what is he? Lawyer? Banker? Financier? What? He might be either, yet he impressed me as being rather of the business than the professional school. He has a good, square-cut jaw—the jaw of a fighting man—and his poise gives one the impression that whatever he has been doing he has been foremost in it. Being foremost in it, he would naturally drift to a city, a big city. He is typically a city man.

"Now, please, to aid me, communicate with your correspondents in the large cities and find if such a name as John Doane appears in any directory. Is he at home now? Has he a family? All about him."

"Do you believe that John Doane is his name?" asked the reporter.

"No reason why it shouldn't be," said The Thinking Machine. "Yet it might not be."

"How about inquiries in this city?"

"He can't well be a local man," was the reply. "He has been wandering about the streets for four weeks, and if he had lived here he would have met some one who knew him."

"But the money?"

"I'll probably be able to locate him through that," said The Thinking Machine. "The matter is not at all clear to me now, but it occurs to me that he is a man of consequence, and that it was possibly necessary for some one to get rid of him for a time."

"Well, if it's plain aphasia, as you say," the reporter put in, "it seems rather difficult to imagine that the attack came at a moment when it was necessary to get rid of him."

"I say it *seems* like aphasia," said the scientist, crustily. "There are known drugs which will produce the identical effect if properly administered."

"Oh," said Hatch. He was beginning to see.

"There is one drug particularly, made in India, and not

unlike hasheesh. In a case of this kind anything is possible. To-morrow I shall ask you to take Mr. Doane down through the financial district, as an experiment. When you go there I want you particularly to get him to the sound of the 'ticker.' It will be an interesting experiment."

The reporter went away and The Thinking Machine sent a telegram to the Blank National Bank of Butte, Montana:

"To whom did you issue hundred-dollar bills, series B, numbering 846380 to 846395 inclusive? Please answer."

It was ten o'clock next day when Hatch called on The Thinking Machine. There he was introduced to John Doane, the man who was lost. The Thinking Machine was asking questions of Mr. Doane when Hatch was ushered in.

"Did the map recall nothing?"

"Nothing."

"Montana, Montana, Montana," the scientist repeated monotonously; "think of it. Butte, Montana."

Doane shook his head hopelessly, sadly.

"Cowboy, cowboy. Did you ever see a cowboy?"

Again the head shake.

"Coyote—something like a wolf—coyote. Don't you recall ever having seen one?"

"I'm afraid it's hopeless," remarked the other.

There was a note of more than ordinary irritation in The Thinking Machine's voice when he turned to Hatch.

"Mr. Hatch, will you walk through the financial district with Mr. Doane?" he asked. "Please go to the places I suggested."

So it came to pass that the reporter and Doane went out together, walking through the crowded, hurrying, bustling financial distict. The first place visited was a private room where market quotations were displayed on a blackboard. Mr. Doane was interested, but the scene seemed to suggest nothing. He looked upon it all as any stranger might have done. After a time they passed out. Suddenly a man came running toward them—evidently a broker.

"What's the matter?" asked another.

Montana copper's gone to smash," was the reply.

Copper! Copper!" gasped Doane suddenly.

Hatch looked around quickly at his companion. Doane's face was a study. On it was half realization and a deep perplexed wrinkle, a glimmer even of excitement.

"Copper!" he repeated.

"Does the word mean anything to you?" asked Hatch quickly. "Copper—metal, you know."

"Copper, copper, copper," the other repeated. Then, as Hatch looked, the queer expression faded; there came again utter hopelessness.

There are many men with powerful names who operate in the Street—some of them in copper. Hatch led Doane straight to the office of one of these men and there introduced him to a partner in the business.

"We want to talk about copper a little," Hatch explained, still eying his companion.

"Do you want to buy or sell?" asked the broker.

"Sell," said Doane suddenly. "Sell, sell, sell copper. That's it—copper."

He turned to Hatch, stared at him dully a moment, a deathly pallor came over his face, then, with upraised hands, fell senseless.

III

Still unconscious, the man of mystery was removed to the home of The Thinking Machine and there stretched out on a sofa. The Thinking Machine was bending over him, this time in his capacity of physician, making an examination. Hatch stood by, looking on curiously.

"I never saw anything like it," Hatch remarked. "He just threw up his hands and collapsed. He hasn't been conscious since."

"It may be that when he comes to he will have recovered his memory, and in that event he will have absolutely no recollection whatever of you and me," explained The Thinking Machine.

Doane moved a little at last, and under a stimulant the color began to creep back into his pallid face.

"Just what was said, Mr. Hatch, before he collapsed?" asked the scientist.

Hatch explained, repeating the conversation as he remembered it.

"And he said 'sell,'" mused The Thinking Machine. "In other words, he thinks—or imagines he knows—that copper is to drop. I believe the first remark he heard was that copper had gone to smash—down, I presume that means?"

"Yes," the reporter replied.

Half an hour later John Doane sat up on the couch and looked about the room.

"Ah, Professor," he remarked. "I fainted, didn't I?"

The Thinking Machine was disappointed because his patient had not recovered memory with consciousness. The remark showed that he was still in the same mental condition—the man who was lost.

"Sell copper, sell, sell, sell," repeated The Thinking Machine, commandingly.

"Yes, yes, sell," was the reply.

The reflection of some great mental struggle was on Doane's face; he was seeking to recall something which persistently eluded him.

"Copper, copper," the scientist repeated, and he exhibited a penny.

"Yes, copper," said Doane. "I know. A penny."

"Why did you say sell copper?"

"I don't know," was the weary reply. "It seemed to be an unconscious act entirely. I don't know."

He clasped and unclasped his hands nervously and sat for a long time dully staring at the floor. The fight for memory was a dramatic one.

"It seemed to me," Doane explained after awhile, "that the word copper touched some responsive chord in my memory, then it was lost again. Some time in the past, I think, I must have had something to do with copper."

"Yes," said The Thinking Machine, and he rubbed his slender fingers briskly. "Now you are coming around again."

His remarks were interrupted by the appearance of Martha at the door with a telegram. The Thinking Machine opened it hastily. What he saw perplexed him again.

"Dear me! Most extraordinary!" he exclaimed.

"What is it?" asked Hatch, curiously.

The scientist turned to Doane again.

"Do you happen to remember Preston Bell?" he demanded, emphasizing the name explosively.

"Preston Bell?" the other repeated, and again the mental struggle was apparent on his face. "Preston Bell!"

"Cashier of the Blank National Bank of Butte, Montana?" urged the other, still in an emphatic tone. "Cashier Bell?"

He leaned forward eagerly and watched the face of his patient; Hatch unconsciously did the same. Once there was almost realization, and seeing it The Thinking Machine sought to bring back full memory.

"Bell, cashier, copper," he repeated, time after time.

The flash of realization which had been on Doane's face passed, and there came infinite weariness—the weariness of one who is ill.

"I don't remember," he said at last. "I'm very tired."

"Stretch out there on the couch and go to sleep," advised The Thinking Machine, and he arose to arrange a pillow. "Sleep will do you more good than anything else right now. But before you lie down, let me have, please, a few of those hundred-dollar bills you found."

Doane extended the roll of money, and then slept like a child. It was uncanny to Hatch, who had been a deeply interested spectator.

The Thinking Machine ran over the bills and finally selected fifteen of them—bills that were new and crisp. They were of an issue by the Blank National Bank of Butte, Montana. The Thinking Machine stared at the money closely, then handed it to Hatch.

"Does that look like counterfeit to you?" he asked.

"Counterfeit?" gasped Hatch. "Counterfeit?" he repeated. He took the bills and examined them. "So far as I can see they seem to be good," he went on, "though I have never had enough experience with one-hundred-dollar bills to qualify as an expert."

"Do you know an expert?"

"Yes."

"See him immediately. Take fifteen bills and ask him to pass on them, each and every one. Tell him you have reason

—excellent reason—to believe that they are counterfeit. When he give his opinion come back to me."

Hatch went away with the money in his pocket. Then The Thinking Machine wrote another telegram, addressed to President Bell, cashier of the Butte Bank. It was as follows:

"Please send me full details of the manner in which money previously described was lost, with names of all persons who might have had any knowledge of the matter. Highly important to your bank and to justice. Will communicate in detail on receipt of your answer."

Then, while his visitor slept, The Thinking Machine quietly removed his shoes and examined them. He found, almost worn away, the name of the maker. This was subjected to close scrutiny under the magnifying glass, after which The Thinking Machine arose with a perceptible expression of relief on his face.

"Why didn't I think of that before?" he demanded of himself.

Then other telegrams went into the West. One was to a customs shoemaker in Denver, Colorado:

"To what financier or banker have you sold within three months a pair of shoes, Senate brand, calfskin blucher. number eight, D last? Do you know John Doane?"

A second telegram went to the Chief of Police of Denver. It was:

"Please wire if any financier, banker or business man has been out of your city for five weeks or more, presumably on business trip. Do you know John Doane?"

Then The Thinking Machine sat down to wait. At last the door bell rang and Hatch entered.

"Well?" demanded the scientist, impatiently.

"The expert declares those are not counterfeit," said Hatch.

Now The Thinking Machine was surprised. It was shown clearly by the quick lifting of the eyebrows, by the sudden snap of his jaws, by a quick forward movement of the yellow head.

"Well, well, well!" he exclaimed at last. Then again: "Well, well!"

"What is it?"

"See here," and The Thinking Machine took the hundred-dollar bills in his own hands. "These bills, perfectly new and crisp, were issued by the Blank National Bank of Butte, and the fact that they are in proper sequence would indicate that they were issued to one individual at the same time, probably recently. There can be no doubt of that. The numbers run from 846380 to 846395, all series B.

"I see," said Hatch.

"Now read that," and the scientist extended to the reporter the telegram Martha had brought in just before Hatch had gone away. Hatch read this:

"Series B, hundred-dollar bills 846380 to 846395 issued by this bank are not in existence. Were destroyed by fire, together with twenty-seven others of the same series. Government has been asked to grant permission to reissue these numbers.

"PRESTON BELL, *Cashier*."

The reporter looked up with a question in his eyes.

"It means," said The Thinking Machine, "that this man is either a thief or the victim of some sort of financial jugglery."

"In that case is he what he pretends to be—a man who doesn't know himself?" asked the reporter.

"That remains to be seen."

IV

Event followed event with startling rapidity during the next few hours. First came a message from the Chief of Police of Denver. No capitalist or financier of consequence was out of Denver at the moment, so far as his men could ascertain. Longer search might be fruitful. He did not know John Doane. One John Doane in the directory was a teamster.

Then from the Blank National Bank came another telegram signed "Preston Bell, Cashier," reciting the circumstances of the disappearance of the hundred-dollar bills. The Blank National Bank had moved into a new structure; within a week there had been a fire which destroyed it. Several packages of money, including one package of hundred-dollar bills, among them those specified by The Thinking Machine, had been burned. President Harrison of the bank immediately made affidavit to the Government that these bills were left in his office.

The Thinking Machine studied this telegram carefully and from time to time glanced at it while Hatch made his report. This was as to the work of the correspondents who had been seeking John Doane. They found many men of the name and reported at length on each. One by one The Thinking Machine heard the reports, then shook his head.

Finally he reverted again to the telegram, and after consideration sent another—this time to the Chief of Police of Butte. In it he asked these questions:

"Has there ever been any financial trouble in Blank National Bank? Was there an embezzlement or shortage at any time? What is reputation of President Harrison? What is reputation of Cashier Bell? Do you know John Doane?"

In due course of events the answer came. It was brief and to the point. It said:

"Harrison recently embezzled $175,000 and disappeared. Bell's reputation excellent; now out of city. Don't know John Doane. If you have any trace of Harrison, wire quick."

This answer came just after Doane awoke, apparently greatly refreshed, but himself again—that is, himself in so far as he was still lost. For an hour The Thinking Machine pounded him with questions—questions of all sorts, serious, religious and at times seemingly silly. They apparently aroused no trace of memory, save when the name Preston Bell was mentioned; then there was the strange, puzzled expression on Doane's face.

"Harrison—do you know him?" asked the scientist. "President of the Blank National Bank of Butte?"

There was only an uncomprehending stare for an answer. After a long time of this The Thinking Machine instructed

Hatch and Doane to go for a walk. He had still a faint hope that some one might recognize Doane and speak to him. As they wandered aimlessly on two persons spoke to him. One was a man who nodded and passed on.

"Who was that?" asked Hatch quickly. "Do you remember ever having seen him before?"

"Oh, yes," was the reply. "He stops at my hotel. He knows me as Doane."

It was just a few minutes before six o'clock when, walking slowly, they passed a great office building. Coming toward them was a well-dressed, active man of thirty-five years or so. As he approached he removed a cigar from his lips.

"Hello, Harry!" he exclaimed, and reached for Doane's hand.

"Hello," said Doane, but there was no trace of recognition in his voice.

"How's Pittsburg?" asked the stranger.

"Oh, all right, I guess," said Doane, and there came new wrinkles of perplexity in his brow. "Allow me, Mr.—Mr.—really I have forgotten your name—"

"Manning," laughed the other.

"Mr. Hatch, Mr. Manning."

The reporter shook hands with Manning eagerly; he saw now a new line of possibilities suddenly revealed. Here was a man who knew Doane as Harry—and then Pittsburg, too.

"Last time I saw you was in Pittsburg, wasn't it?" Manning rattled on, as he led the way into a nearby café. "By George, that was a stiff game that night! Remember that jack full I held? It cost me nineteen hundred dollars," he added, ruefully.

"Yes, I remember," said Doane, but Hatch knew that he did not. And meanwhile a thousand questions were surging through the reporter's brain.

"Poker hands as expensive as that are liable to be long remembered," remarked Hatch, casually. "How long ago was that?"

"Three years, wasn't it, Harry?" asked Manning.

"All of that, I should say," was the reply.

"Twenty hours at the table," said Manning, and again he laughed cheerfully. "I was woozy when we finished."

Inside the café they sought out a table in a corner. No one else was near. When the waiter had gone, Hatch leaned over and looked Doane straight in the eyes.

"Shall I ask some questions?" he inquired.

"Yes, yes," said the other eagerly.

"What—what is it?" asked Manning.

"It's a remarkably strange chain of circumstances," said Hatch, in explanation. "This man whom you call Harry, we know as John Doane. What is his real name? Harry what?"

Manning stared at the reporter for a moment in amazement, then gradually a smile came to his lips.

"What are you trying to do?" he asked. "Is this a joke?"

"No, my God, man, can't you see?" exclaimed Doane, fiercely. "I'm ill, sick, something. I've lost my memory, all of my past. I don't remember anything about myself. What is my name?"

"Well, by George!" exclaimed Manning. "By George! I don't believe I know your full name. Harry—Harry—what?"

He drew from his pocket several letters and half a dozen scraps of paper and ran over them. Then he looked carefully through a worn notebook.

"I don't know," he confessed. "I had your name and address in an old notebook, but I suppose I burned it. I remember, though, I met you in the Lincoln Club in Pittsburg three years ago. I called you Harry because everyone was calling everyone else by his first name. Your last name made no impression on me at all. By George!" he concluded, in a new burst of amazement.

"What were the circumstances, exactly?" asked Hatch.

"I'm a traveling man," Manning explained. "I go everywhere. A friend gave me a card to the Lincoln Club in Pittsburg and I went there. There were five or six of us playing poker, among them Mr.—Mr. Doane here. I sat at the same table with him for twenty hours or so, but I can't recall his last name to save me. It isn't Doane, I'm positive. I have an excellent memory for faces, and I know you're the man. Don't you remember me?"

"I haven't the slightest recollection of ever having seen you before in my life," was Doane's slow reply. "I have no recollection of ever having been in Pittsburg—no recollection of anything."

"Do you know if Mr. Doane is a resident of Pittsburg?" Hatch inquired. "Or was he there as a visitor, as you were?"

"Couldn't tell you to save my life," replied Manning. "Lord, it's amazing, isn't it? You don't remember me? You called me Bill all evening."

The other man shook his head.

"Well, say, is there anything I can do for you?"

"Nothing, thanks," said Doane. "Only tell me my name, and who I am."

"Lord, I don't know."

"What sort of a club is the Lincoln?" asked Hatch.

"It's a sort of a millionaire's club," Manning explained. "Lots of iron men belong to it. I had considerable business with them—that's what took me to Pittsburg."

"And you are absolutely positive this is the man you met there?"

"Why, I *know* it. I never forget faces; it's my business to remember them."

"Did he say anything about a family?"

"Not that I recall. A man doesn't usually speak of his family at a poker table."

"Do you remember the exact date or the month?"

"I think it was in January or February possibly," was the reply. "It was bitterly cold and the snow was all smoked up. Yes, I'm positive it was in January, three years ago."

After awhile the men separated. Manning was stopping at the Hotel Teutonic and willingly gave his name and permanent address to Hatch, explaining at the same time that he would be in the city for several days and was perfectly willing to help in any way he could. He took also the address of The Thinking Machine.

From the café Hatch and Doane returned to the scientist. They found him with two telegrams spread out on a table before him. Briefly Hatch told the story of the meeting with Manning, while Doane sank down with his head in his hands. The Thinking Machine listened without comment.

"Here," he said, at the conclusion of the recital, and he offered one of the telegrams to Hatch. "I got the name of a shoemaker from Mr. Doane's shoe and wired to him in Denver, asking if he had a record of the sale. This is the answer. Read it aloud."

Hatch did so.

"Shoes such as described made nine weeks ago for Preston Bell, cashier Blank National Bank of Butte. Don't know John Doane."

"Well—what—" Doane began, bewildered.

"It means that you are Preston Bell, said Hatch, emphatically.

"No," said The Thinking Machine, quickly. "It means that there is only a strong probability of it."

. . . .

The door bell rang. After a moment Martha appeared.

"A lady to see you, sir," she said.

"Her name?"

"Mrs. John Doane."

"Gentlemen, kindly step into the next room," requested The Thinking Machine.

Together Hatch and Doane passed through the door. There was an expression of—of—no man may say what—on Doane's face as he went.

"Show her in here, Martha," instructed the scientist.

There was a rustle of silk in the hall, the curtains on the door were pulled apart quickly and a richly gowned woman rushed into the room.

"My husband? Is he here?" she demanded, breathlessly. "I went to the hotel; they said he came here for treatment. Please, please, is he here?"

"A moment, madam," said The Thinking Machine. He stepped to the door through which Hatch and Doane had gone, and said something. One of them appeared in the door. It was Hutchinson Hatch.

"John, John, my darling husband," and the woman flung her arms about Hatch's neck. "Don't you know me?"

With blushing face Hatch looked over her shoulder into the eyes of The Thinking Machine, who stood briskly rubbing his hands. Never before in his long acquaintance with the scientist had Hatch seen him smile.

THE MAN WHO WAS LOST

V

For a time there was silence, broken only by sobs, as the woman clung frantically to Hatch, with her face buried on his shoulder. Then:

"Don't you remember me?" she asked again and again "Your wife? Don't you remember me?"

Hatch could still see the trace of a smile on the scientist's face, and said nothing.

"You are positive this gentleman is your husband?" inquired The Thinking Machine, finally.

"Oh, I know," the woman sobbed. "Oh, John, don't you remember me?" She drew away a little and looked deeply into the reporter's eyes. "Don't you remember me, John?"

"Can't say that I ever saw you before," said Hatch, truthfully enough. "I—I—fact is—"

"Mr. Doane's memory is wholly gone now," explained The Thinking Machine. "Meanwhile, perhaps you would tell me something about him. He is my patient. I am particularly interested."

The voice was soothing; it had lost for the moment its perpetual irritation. The woman sat down beside Hatch. Her face, pretty enough in a bold sort of way, was turned to The Thinking Machine inquiringly. With one hand she stroked that of the reporter.

"Where are you from?" began the scientist. "I mean where is the home of John Doane?"

"In Buffalo," she replied, glibly. "Didn't he even remember that?"

"And what's his business?"

"His health has been bad for some time and recently he gave up active business," said the woman. "Previously he was connected with a bank."

"When did you see him last?"

"Six weeks ago. He left the house one day and I have never heard from him since. I had Pinkerton men searching and at last they reported he was at the Yarmouth Hotel. I came on immediately. And now we shall go back to Buffalo." She turned to Hatch with a languishing glance. "Shall we not, dear?"

"Whatever Professor Van Dusen thinks best," was the equivocal reply.

Slowly the glimmer of amusement was passing out of the squint eyes of The Thinking Machine; as Hatch looked he saw a hardening of the lines of the mouth. There was an explosion coming. He knew it. Yet when the scientist spoke his voice was more velvety than ever.

"Mrs. Doane, do you happen to be acquainted with a drug which produces temporary loss of memory?"

She stared at him, but did not lose her self-possession.

"No," she said finally. "Why?"

"You know, of course, that this man is *not* your husband?"

This time the question had its effect. The woman arose suddenly, stared at the two men, and her face went white.

"Not?—not?—what do you mean?"

"I mean," and the voice reassured its tone of irritation, "I mean that I shall send for the police and give you in their charge unless you tell me the truth about this affair. Is that perfectly clear to you?"

The woman's lips were pressed tightly together. She saw that she had fallen into some sort of a trap; her gloved hands were clenched fiercely; the pallor faded and a flush of anger came.

"Further, for fear you don't quite follow me even now," explained The Thinking Machine, "I will say that I know all about this copper deal of which this so-called John Doane was the victim. *I know his condition now.* If you tell the truth you may escape prison—if you don't, there is a long term, not only for you, but for your fellow-conspirators. Now will you talk?"

"No," said the woman. She arose as if to go out.

"Never mind that," said The Thinking Machine. "You had better stay where you are. You will be locked up at the proper moment. Mr. Hatch, please 'phone for Detective Mallory."

Hatch arose and passed into the adjoining room.

"You tricked me," the woman screamed suddenly, fiercely.

"Yes," the other agreed, complacently. "Next time be sure you know your own husband. Meanwhile where is Harrison?"

"Not another word," was the quick reply.

"Very well," said the scientist, calmly. "Detective Mallory will be here in a few minutes. Meanwhile I'll lock this door."

"You have no right—" the woman began.

Without heeding the remark, The Thinking Machine passed into the adjoining room. There for half an hour he talked earnestly to Hatch and Doane. At the end of that time he sent a telegram to the manager of the Lincoln Club in Pittsburg, as follows:

"Does your visitors' book show any man, registered there in the month of January three years ago, whose first name is Harry or Henry? If so, please wire name and description, also name of man whose guest he was."

This telegram was dispatched. A few minutes later the door bell rang and Detective Mallory entered.

"What is it?" he inquired.

"A prisoner for you in the next room," was the reply. "A woman. I charge her with conspiracy to defraud a man who for the present we will call John Doane. That may or may not be his name."

"What do you know about it?" asked the detective.

"A great deal now—more after awhile. I shall tell you then. Meanwhile take this woman. You gentlemen, I should suggest, might go out somewhere this evening. If you drop by afterward there may be an answer to a few telegrams which will make this matter clear."

Protestingly the mysterious woman was led away by Detective Mallory; and Doane and Hatch followed shortly after. The next act of The Thinking Machine was to write a telegram addressed to Mrs. Preston Bell, Butte, Montana. Here it is:

"Your husband suffering temporary mental trouble here. Can you come on immediately? Answer."

When the messenger boy came for the telegram he found a man on the stoop. The Thinking Machine received the telegram, and the man, who gave to Martha the name of Manning, was announced.

"Manning, too," mused the scientist. "Show him in."

"I don't know if you know why I am here," explained Manning.

"Oh, yes," said the scientist. "You have remembered Doane's name. What is it, please?"

Manning was too frankly surprised to answer and only stared at the scientist.

"Yes, that's right," he said finally, and he smiled. "His name is Pillsbury. I recall it now."

"And what made you recall it?"

"I noticed an advertisement in a magazine with the name in large letters. It instantly came to me that that was Doane's real name."

"Thanks," remarked the scientist. "And the woman—who is she?"

"What woman?" asked Manning.

"Never mind, then. I am deeply obliged for your information. I don't suppose you know anything else about it?"

"No," said Manning. He was a little bewildered, and after a while went away.

For an hour or more The Thinking Machine sat with finger tips pressed together staring at the ceiling. His meditations were interrupted by Martha.

"Another telegram, sir."

The Thinking Machine took it eagerly. It was from the manager of the Lincoln Club in Pittsburg:

"Henry C. Carney, Harry Meltz, Henry Blake, Henry W. Tolman, Harry Pillsbury, Henry Calvert and Henry Louis Smith all visitors to club in month you name. Which do you want to learn more about?"

It took more than an hour for The Thinking Machine to establish long distance connection by 'phone with Pittsburg. When he had finished talking he seemed satisfied.

"Now," he mused. "The answer from Mrs. Preston."

It was nearly midnight when that came. Hatch and Doane had returned from a theater and were talking to the scientist when the telegram was brought in.

"Anything important?" asked Doane, anxiously.

"Yes," said the scientist, and he slipped a finger beneath the flap of the envelope. "It's clear now. It was an engaging problem from first to last, and now—"

He opened the telegram and glanced at it; then with bewilderment on his face and mouth slightly open he sank down at the table and leaned forward with his head on his arms. The message fluttered to the table and Hatch read this:

"Man in Boston can't be my husband. He is now in Honolulu. I received cablegram from him to-day.

"MRS. PRESTON BELL."

VI

It was thirty-six hours later that the three men met again. The Thinking Machine had abruptly dismissed Hatch and Doane the last time. The reporter knew that something wholly unexpected had happened. He could only conjecture that this had to do with Preston Bell. When the three met again it was in Detective Mallory's office at police headquarters. The mysterious woman who had claimed Doane for her husband was present, as were Mallory, Hatch, Doane and The Thinking Machine.

"Has this woman given any name?" was the scientist's first question.

"Mary Jones," replied the detective, with a grin.

"And address?"

"No."

"Is her picture in the Rogues' Gallery?"

"No. I looked carefully."

"Anybody called to ask about her?"

"A man—yes. That is, he didn't ask about her—he merely asked some general questions, which now we believe were to find out about her."

The Thinking Machine arose and walked over to the woman. She looked up at him defiantly.

"There has been a mistake made, Mr. Mallory," said the scientist. "It's my fault entirely. Let this woman go. I am sorry to have done her so grave an injustice."

Instantly the woman was on her feet, her face radiant. A look of disgust crept into Mallory's face.

"I can't let her go now without arraignment," the detective growled. "It ain't regular."

"You must let her go, Mr. Mallory," commanded The Thinking Machine, and over the woman's shoulder the detective saw an astonishing thing. The Thinking Machine winked. It was a decided, long, pronounced wink.

"Oh, all right," he said, "but it ain't regular at that."

The woman passed out of the room hurriedly, her silken skirts rustling loudly. She was free again. Immediately she disappeared The Thinking Machine's entire manner changed.

"Put your best man to follow her," he directed rapidly. "Let him go to her home and arrest the man who is with her as her husband. Then bring them both back here, after searching their rooms for money."

"Why—what—what is all this?" demanded Mallory, amazed.

"The man who inquired for her, who is with her, is wanted for a $175,000 embezzlement in Butte, Montana. Don't let your man lose sight of her."

The detective left the room hurriedly. Ten minutes later he returned to find The Thinking Machine leaning back in his chair with eyes upturned. Hatch and Doane were waiting, both impatiently.

"Now, Mr. Mallory," said the scientist, "I shall try to make this matter as clear to you as it is to me. By the time I finish I expect your man will be back here with this woman and the embezzler. His name is Harrison; I don't know hers. I can't believe she is Mrs. Harrison, yet he has, I suppose, a wife. But here's the story. It is the chaining together of fact after fact; a necessary logical sequence to a series of incidents, which are, separately, deeply puzzling."

The detective lighted a cigar and the others disposed themselves comfortably to listen.

"This gentleman came to me," began The Thinking Machine, "with a story of loss of memory. He told me that he knew neither his name, home, occupation, nor anything whatever about himself. At the moment it struck me as a case for a mental expert; still I was interested. It seemed to be a remarkable case of aphasia, and I so regarded it until he told me that he had $10,000 in bills, that he had no watch, that everything which might possibly be of value in establishing his identity had been removed from his clothing. This included even the names of the makers of his linen. That showed intent, deliberation.

"Then I knew it could *not* be aphasia. That disease strikes a man suddenly as he walks the street, as he sleeps, as he works, but never gives any desire to remove traces of one's identity. On the contrary, a man is still apparently sound mentally—he has merely forgotten something—and usually his first desire is to find out who he is. This gentleman had that desire, and in trying to find some clew he showed a mind capable of grasping at every possible opportunity. Nearly every question I asked had been anticipated. Thus I recognized that he must be a more than usually astute man.

"But if not aphasia, what was it? What caused his condition? A drug? I remembered that there was such a drug in India, not unlike hasheesh. Therefore for the moment I assumed a drug. It gave me a working basis. Then what did I have? A man of striking mentality who was the victim of some sort of plot, who had been drugged until he lost himself, and in that way disposed of. The handwriting might be the same, for handwriting is rarely affected by a mental disorder; it is a physical function.

"So far, so good. I examined his head for a possible accident. Nothing. His hands were white and in no way calloused. Seeking to reconcile the fact that he had been a man of strong mentality, with all other things a financier or banker, occurred to me. The same things might have indicated a lawyer, but the poise of this man, his elaborate care in dress, all these things made me think him the financier rather than the lawyer.

"Then I examined some money he had when he awoke. Fifteen or sixteen of the hundred-dollar bills were new and in sequence. They were issued by a national bank. To whom? The possibilities were that the bank would have a record. I wired, asking about this, and also asked Mr.

Hatch to have his correspondents make inquiries in various cities for a John Doane. It was not impossible that John Doane was his name. Now I believe it will be safe for me to say that when he registered at the hotel he was drugged, his own name slipped his mind, and he signed John Doane—the first name that came to him. That is *not* his name.

"While waiting an answer from the bank I tried to arouse his memory by referring to things in the West. It appeared possible that he might have brought the money from the West with him. Then, still with the idea that he was a financier, I sent him to the financial district. There was a result. The word 'copper' aroused him so that he fainted after shouting, 'Sell copper, sell, sell, sell.'

"In a way my estimate of the man was confirmed. He was or had been in a copper deal, selling copper in the market, or planning to do so. I know nothing of the intricacies of the stock market. But there came instantly to me the thought that a man who would faint away in such a case must be vitally interested as well as ill. Thus I had a financier, in a copper deal, drugged as result of a conspiracy. Do you follow me, Mr. Mallory?"

"Sure," was the reply.

"At this point I received a telegram from the Butte bank telling me that the hundred-dollar bills I asked about had been burned. This telegram was signed 'Preston Bell, Cashier.' If that were true, the bills this man had were counterfeit. There were no ifs about that. I asked him if he knew Preston Bell. It was the only name of a person to arouse him in any way. A man knows his own name better than anything in the world. Therefore was it his? For a moment I presumed it was.

"Thus the case stood: Preston Bell, cashier of the Butte bank, had been drugged, was the victim of a conspiracy, which was probably a part of some great move in copper. But if this man were *Preston Bell,* how came the signature there? Part of the office regulation? It happens hundreds of times that a name is so used, particularly on telegrams.

"Well, this man who was lost—Doane, or Preston Bell—went to sleep in my apartments. At that time I believed it fully possible that he was a counterfeiter, as the bills were supposedly burned, and sent Mr. Hatch to consult an expert. I also wired for details of the fire loss in Butte and names of persons who had any knowledge of the matter. This done, I removed and examined this gentleman's shoes for the name of the maker. I found it. The shoes were of fine quality, probably made to order for him.

"Remember, at this time I believed this gentleman to be Preston Bell, for reasons I have stated. I wired to the maker or retailer to know if he had a record of a sale of the shoes, describing them in detail, to any financier or banker. I also wired to the Denver police to know if any financier or banker had been away from there for four or five weeks. Then came the somewhat startling information, through Mr. Hatch, that the hundred-dollar bills were genuine. That answer meant that Preston Bell—as I had begun to think of him—was either a thief or the victim of some sort of financial conspiracy."

During the silence which followed every eye was turned on the man who was lost—Doane or Preston Bell. He sat staring straight ahead of him with hands nervously clenched. On his face was written the sign of a desperate mental struggle. He was still trying to recall the past.

"Then," The Thinking Machine resumed, "I heard from the Denver police. There was no leading financier or banker out of the city so far as they could learn hurriedly. It was not conclusive, but it aided me. Also I received another telegram from Butte, signed Preston Bell, telling me the circumstances of the supposed burning of the hundred-dollar bills. It did not show that they were burned at all; it was merely an assumption that they had been. They were last seen in President Harrison's office."

"Harrison, Harrison, Harrison," repeated Doane.

"Vaguely I could see the possibility of something financially wrong in the bank. Possibly Harrison, even Mr. Bell here, knew of it. Banks do not apply for permission to reissue bills unless they are positive of the original loss. Yet here were the bills. Obviously some sort of jugglery. I wired to the police of Butte, asking some questions. The answer was that Harrison had embezzled $175,000 and had disappeared. Now I knew he had part of the missing, supposedly burned, bills with him. It was obvious. Was Bell also a thief?

"The same telegram said that Mr. Bell's reputation was of the best, and he was out of the city. That confirmed my belief that it was an office rule to sign telegrams with the cashier's name, and further made me positive that this man was Preston Bell. The chain of circumstances was complete. It was two and two—inevitable result, four.

"Now, what was the plot? Something to do with copper, and there was an embezzlement. Then, still seeking a man who knew Bell personally, I sent him out walking with Hatch. I had done so before. Suddenly another figure came into the mystery—a confusing one at the moment. This was a Mr. Manning, who knew Doane, or Bell, as Harry—something; met him in Pittsburg three years ago, in the Lincoln Club.

"It was just after Mr. Hatch told me of this man that I received a telegram from the shoemaker in Denver. It said that he had made a shoe such as I described within a few months for Preston Bell. I had asked if a sale had been made to a financier or banker; I got the name back by wire.

"At this point a woman appeared to claim John Doane as her husband. With no definite purpose, save general precaution, I asked Mr. Hatch to see her first. She imagined he was Doane and embraced him, calling him John. Therefore she was a fraud. She did not know John Doane, or Preston Bell, by sight. Was she acting under the direction of some one else? If so, whose?"

There was a pause as The Thinking Machine readjusted himself in the chair. After a time he went on:

"There are shades of emotion, intuition, call it what you will, so subtle that it is difficult to express them in words. As I had instinctively associated Harrison with Bell's present condition I instinctively associated this woman with Harrison. For not a word of the affair had appeared in a newspaper; only a very few persons knew of it. Was it possible that the stranger Manning was backing the woman in an effort to get the $10,000? That remained to be seen. I questioned the woman; she would say nothing. She is clever, but she blundered badly in claiming Mr. Hatch for a husband."

The reporter blushed modestly.

"I asked her flatly about a drug. She was quite calm and her manner indicated that she knew nothing of it. Yet I presume she did. Then I sprung the bombshell, and she saw she had made a mistake. I gave her over to Detective Mallory and she was locked up. This done, I wired to the Lincoln Club in Pittsburg to find out about this mysterious 'Harry' who had come into the case. I was so confident then that I also wired to Mrs. Bell in Butte, presuming that there was a Mrs. Bell, asking about her husband.

"Then Manning came to see me. I knew he came because he had remembered the name he knew you by," and The Thinking Machine turned to the central figure in this strange entanglement of identity, "although he seemed surprised when I told him as much. He knew you as Harry Pillsbury. I asked him who the woman was. His manner told me that he knew nothing whatever of her. Then it came back to her as an associate of Harrison, your enemy for some reason, and I could see it in no other light. It was her purpose to get hold of you and possibly keep you a prisoner, at least until some gigantic deal in which copper figured was disposed of. That was what I surmised.

"Then another telegram came from the Lincoln Club in Pittsburg. The name of Harry Pillsbury appeared as a visitor in the book in January, three years ago. It was you—Manning is not the sort of man to be mistaken—and then there remained only one point to be solved as I then saw the case. That was an answer from Mrs. Preston Bell, if there was a Mrs. Bell. She would know where her husband was."

Again there was silence. A thousand things were running through Bell's mind. The story had been told so pointedly, and was so vitally a part of him, that semi-recollection was again on his face.

"That telegram said that Preston Bell was in Honolulu; that the wife had received a cable dispatch that day. Then, frankly, I was puzzled; so puzzled, in fact, that the entire fabric I had constructed seemed to melt away before my eyes. It took me hours to readjust it. I tried it all over in detail, and then the theory which would reconcile every fact in the case was evolved. That theory is right—as right as that two and two make four. It's logic."

It was half an hour later when a detective entered and spoke to Detective Mallory aside.

"Fine!" said Mallory. "Bring 'em in."

Then there reappeared the woman who had been a prisoner and a man of fifty years.

"Harrison!" exclaimed Bell, suddenly. He staggered to his feet with outstretched hands. "Harrison! I know! I know!"

"Good, good, very good," said The Thinking Machine.

Bell's nervously twitching hands were reaching for Harrison's throat when he was pushed aside by Detective Mallory. He stood pallid for a moment, then sank down on the floor in a heap. He was senseless. The Thinking Machine made a hurried examination.

"Good!" he remarked again. "When he recovers he will remember everything except what has happened since he has been in Boston. Meanwhile, Mr. Harrison, we know all about the little affair of the drug, the battle for new copper workings in Honolulu, and your partner there has been arrested. Your drug didn't do its work well enough. Have you anything to add?"

The prisoner was silent.

"Did you search his rooms?" asked The Thinking Machine of the detective who had made the double arrest.

"Yes, and found this."

It was a large roll of money. The Thinking Machine ran over it lightly—$70,000—scanning the numbers of the bills. At last he held forth half a dozen. They were among the twenty-seven reported to have been burned in the bank fire in Butte.

Harrison and the woman were led away. Subsequently it developed that he had been systematically robbing the bank of which he was president for years; was responsible for the fire, at which time he had evidently expected to make a great haul; and that the woman was not his wife. Following his arrest this entire story came out; also the facts of the gigantic copper deal, in which he had rid himself of Bell, who was his partner, and had sent another man to Honolulu in Bell's name to buy up options on some valuable copper property there. This confederate in Honolulu had sent the cable dispatches to the wife in Butte. She accepted them without question.

It was a day or so later that Hatch dropped in to see The Thinking Machine and asked a few questions.

"How did Bell happen to have that $10,000?"

"It was given to him, probably, because it was safer to have him rambling about the country, not knowing who he was, than to kill him."

"And how did he happen to be here?"

"That question may be answered at the trial."

"And how did it come that Bell was once known as Harry Pillsbury?"

"Bell is a director in United States Steel, I have since learned. There was a secret meeting of this board in Pittsburg three years ago. He went incog. to attend that meeting and was introduced at the Lincoln Club as Harry Pillsbury."

"Oh!" exclaimed Hatch.

The Great Auto Mystery

BY JACQUES FUTRELLE

The Great Auto Mystery

BY JACQUES FUTRELLE

I

WITH a little laugh of sheer light-heartedness on her lips and a twinkle in her blue eyes, Marguerite Melrose bound on a grotesque automobile mask, and stuffed the last strand of her recalcitrant hair beneath her veil. The pretty face was hidden from mouth to brow; and her curls were ruthlessly imprisoned under a cap held in place by the tightly tied veil.

"It's perfectly hideous, isn't it?" she demanded of her companions.

Jack Curtis laughed.

"Well," he remarked, quizzically, "it's just as well that we *know* you are pretty."

"We could never discover it as you are now," added Charles Reid. "Can't see enough of your face to tell whether you are white or black."

The girl's red lips were pursed into a pout, which ungraciously hid her white teeth, as she considered the matter seriously.

"I think I'll take it off," she said at last.

"Don't," Curtis warned her. "On a good road The Green Dragon only hits the tall places."

"Tear your hair off," supplemented Reid. "When Jack lets her loose it's just a pszzzzt!—and wherever you're going you're there."

"Not on a night as dark as this?" protested the girl, quickly.

"I've got lights like twin locomotives," Curtis assured her, smilingly. "It's perfectly safe. Don't get nervous."

He tied on his own mask with its bleary goggles, while Reid did the same. The Green Dragon, a low, gasoline car of racing build, stood panting impatiently, awaiting them at a side door of the hotel. Curtis assisted Miss Melrose into the front seat and climbed in beside her, while Reid sat behind in the tonneau. There was a preparatory quiver, the car jerked a little and then began to move.

The three persons in it were Marguerite Melrose, an actress who had attracted attention in the West five years before by her great beauty and had afterward, by her art, achieved a distinct place; Jack Curtis, a friend since childhood, when both lived in San Francisco and attended the same school, and Charles Reid, his chum, son of a mine owner at Denver.

The unexpected meeting of the three in Boston had been a source of mutual pleasure. It had been two years since they had seen one another in Denver, where Miss Melrose was playing. Now she was in Boston, pursuing certain vocal studies before returning West for her next season.

Reid was in Boston to lay siege to the heart of a young woman of society, Miss Elizabeth Dow, whom he first met in San Francisco. She was only nineteen years old, but despite this he had begun a siege and his ardor had never cooled, even after Miss Dow returned East. In Boston, he had heard, she looked with favor upon another man, Morgan Mason, poor but of excellent family, and frantically Reid had rushed, like Lochinvar out of the West, to find the rumor true.

Curtis was one who never had anything to do save seek excitement in a new and novel way. He had come East with Reid. They had been together constantly since their arrival in Boston. He was of a different type from Reid in that his wealth was distinctly a burden, a thing which left him with nothing to do, and opened illimitable possibilities of dissipation. The pace he led was one which caused other young men to pause and think.

Warm-hearted and perfectly at home with both Curtis and Reid, Miss Melrose, the actress, frequently took occasion to scold them. It was charming to be scolded by Miss Melrose, so much so in fact that it was worth while sinning again. Since she had appeared on the horizon Curtis had devoted a great deal of time to her; Reid had his own difficulties trying to make Miss Dow change her mind.

THE GREAT AUTO MYSTERY

The Green Dragon with its three passengers ran slowly down from the Hotel Yarmouth, where Miss Melrose was stopping, toward the Common, twisting and winding tortuously through the crowd of vehicles. It was half-past six o'clock in the evening.

"Cut across here to Commonwealth Avenue," Miss Melrose suggested. She remembered something and her bright blue eyes sparkled beneath the disfiguring mask. "I know a delightful old-fashioned inn out this way. It would be an ideal place to stop for supper. I was there once five years ago when I was in Boston."

"How far?" asked Reid.

"Fifteen or twenty miles," was the reply.

"Right," said Curtis. "Here we go."

Soon after they were skimming along Commonwealth Avenue, which at that time of day is practically given over to automobilists, past the Vendome, the Somerset and on over the flat, smooth road. It was perfectly light now, because the electric lights were about them; but there was no moon above, and once in the country it would be dark going.

Curtis was intent on his machine; Reid was thoughtful for a time, but after awhile leaned over and talked to Miss Melrose.

"I heard something to-day that might interest you," he remarked.

"What is it?" she asked.

"Don MacLean is in Boston."

"I heard that," she replied, casually.

"Who is he?" asked Curtis.

"A man who is frantically in love with Marguerite," said Reid, with a smile.

"Charlie!" the girl reproved, and a flush crept into her face. "It was never anything very serious."

Curtis looked at her curiously for a moment, then his eyes turned again to the road ahead.

"I don't suppose it's very serious if a man proposes to a girl seven times, is it?" Reid asked, banteringly.

"Did he do that?" asked Curtis, quickly.

"He merely made a fool of himself and me," replied the actress, with spirit, speaking to Curtis. "He was--in love with me, I suppose, but his family objected because I was on the stage and threatened to disinherit him, and all that sort of thing. So—it ended it. Not that I ever considered the matter seriously anyway," she added.

There was silence again as The Green Dragon plunged into the darkness of the country, the two brilliant lights ahead showing every dip and rise in the road. After a while Curtis spoke again.

"He's now in Boston?"

"Yes," said the girl. "At least, I've heard so," she added, quickly.

Then the conversation ran into other channels, and Curtis, busy with the great machine and the innumerable levers which made it do this or do that or do the other, dropped out of it. Reid and Miss Melrose talked on, but the whirr of the car as it gained speed made talking unsatisfactory and finally the girl gave herself up to the pure delight of high speed; a dangerous pleasure which sets the nerves atingle and makes one greedy for more.

"Do you smell gasoline?" Curtis asked suddenly, turning to the others.

"Believe I do," said Reid.

"Confound it! If I've sprung a leak in my tank it will be the deuce," Curtis growled amiably.

"Do you think you've got enough to get to the inn?" asked Miss Melrose. "It can't be more than five or six miles now."

"I'll run on until we stop," said Curtis. "We might be able to stir up some along here somewhere. I suppose they are prepared for autos."

At last lights showed ahead, many lights glimmering through the trees.

"I suppose that's the inn now," said Curtis. "Is it?" he asked of the girl.

"Really, I don't know, but I have an impression that it isn't. The one I mean seems farther out than this and it seems to me we passed one on the way. However, I don't remember very well."

"We'll stop and get some gasoline, anyhow," said Curtis.

Puffing and snorting odorously The Green Dragon came to

a standstill in front of an old house which stood back twenty feet or more from the road. It was lighted up, and from inside they could hear the cheery rattle of dishes and see white-aproned waiters moving about. Above the door was a sign, "Monarch Inn."

"Is this the place?" asked Reid.

"Oh, no," replied Miss Melrose. "The inn I spoke of was back from the road three or four hundred feet through a grove."

Curtis leaped out, and evidently dropped something from his pocket as he did so, for he stopped and felt around for a moment. Then he examined his tank.

It's a leak," he said, in irritation. "I haven't more than half a gallon left. These people must have some gasoline. Wait a few minutes."

Miss Melrose and Reid still sat in the car as he started away toward the house. Almost at the veranda he turned and called back:

"Charlie, I dropped something there when I jumped out. Get down and strike a match and see if you can find it. Don't go near that gasoline tank with the match."

He disappeared inside the house. Reid climbed out and struck several matches. Finally he found what was lost and thrust it into an outside pocket. Miss Melrose was gazing away down the road at two brilliant lights coming toward them rapidly.

"Rather chilly," Reid said, as he straightened up. "Want a cup of coffee or something?"

"Thanks, no," the girl replied.

"I think I'll run in and scare up some sort of a hot drink, if you'll excuse me?"

"Now, Charlie, don't," the girl asked, suddenly. "I don't like it."

"Oh, one won't hurt," he replied, lightly.

"I shan't speak to you when you come out," she insisted, half banteringly.

"Oh, yes, you will." He laughed, and passed into the house.

Miss Melrose tossed her pretty head impatiently and turned to watch the approaching lights. They were blinding as they drew nearer, clearly revealing her figure, in its tan auto coat, to the occupant of the other car. The newcomer stopped and then she heard whoever was in it—she couldn't see—speaking to her."

"Would you mind turning your car a little so I can run in off the road?"

"I don't know how," she replied, helplessly.

There was a little pause. The occupant of the other car was leaning forward, looking at her closely.

"Is that you, Marguerito?" he asked finally.

"Yes," she replied. "Who is that? Don?"

"Yes."

A man's figure leaped out of the other machine and came toward her.

. . . .

Curtis appeared beside The Green Dragon with a huge can of gasoline twenty minutes later. The two occupants of the car were clearly silhouetted against the sky, and Reid, leaning back in the tonneau, was smoking.

"Find it?" he asked.

"Yes," growled Curtis. And he began the work of repairing the leak and refilling his tank. It took only five minutes or so, and then he climbed up into the car.

"Cold, Marguerite?" he asked.

"She won't speak," said Reid, leaning forward a little. "She's angry because I went inside to get a hot Scotch."

"Wish I had one myself," said Curtis.

"Let's wait till we get to the next place," Reid interposed. "A little supper and trimmings will put all of us in a better humor."

Without answering, Curtis threw a lever, and the car pulled out. Two automobiles which had been standing when they arrived were still waiting for their owners. Annoyed at the delay, Curtis put on full speed. Finally Reid leaned forward and spoke to the girl.

"In a good humor?" he asked.

She gave no sign of having heard, and Reid placed his hand on her shoulder as he repeated the question. Still there was no answer.

"Make her talk to you, Jack," he suggested to Curtis.

"What's the matter, Marguerite?" asked Curtis, as he glanced around.

Still there was no answer, and he slowed up the car a little. Then he took her arm and shook it gently. There was no response.

"What *is* the matter with her?" he demanded. "Has she fainted?"

Again he shook her, this time more vigorously than before.

"Marguerite," he called.

Then his hand sought her face; it was deathly cold, clammy even about the chin. The upper part was still covered by the mask. For the third time he shook her, then, really frightened, apparently, he caught at her gloved wrist and brought the car to a standstill. There was no trace of a pulse; the wrist was cold as death.

"She must be ill—very ill," he said in some agitation. "Is there a doctor near here?"

Reid was leaning over the senseless body now, having raised up in the tonneau, and when he spoke there seemed to be fear in his tone.

"Better run on as fast as you can to the inn ahead," he instructed Curtis. "It's nearer than the one we just left. There may be a doctor there."

Curtis grabbed frantically at the lever and the car shot ahead suddenly through the dark. In three minutes the lights of the second inn were in sight. The two men leaped from the car simultaneously and raced for the house.

"A doctor, quick," Curtis breathlessly demanded of a waiter.

"Next door."

Without waiting for further instructions, Curtis and Reid ran to the auto, lifted the girl in their arms and took her to a house which stood just a few feet away. There, after much clamoring, they aroused some one. Was the doctor in? Yes. Would he hurry? Yes.

The door opened and the men laid the girl's body on a couch in the hall. Dr. Leonard appeared. He was an old fellow, grizzled, with keen, kindly eyes and rigid mouth.

"What's the matter?" he asked.

"Think she's dead," replied Curtis.

The doctor adjusted his glasses rather hurriedly.

"Who is she?" he asked, as he bent over the still figure and fumbled about the throat and breast.

"Miss Marguerite Melrose, an actress," explained Curtis, hurriedly.

"What's the matter with her?" demanded Reid, fiercely.

The doctor still bent over the figure. In the dim lamplight Curtis and Reid stood waiting anxiously, impatiently, with white faces. At last the doctor straightened up.

"What is it?" demanded Curtis.

"She's dead," was the reply.

"Great God!" exclaimed Reid. "How?" Curtis seemed speechless.

"This," said the doctor, and he exhibited a long knife, damp with blood. "Stabbed through the heart."

Curtis stared at him, at the knife, then at the inert figure, and lastly at the dead white of her face where it showed beneath the mask.

"Look, Jack!" exclaimed Reid, suddenly. "The knife!"

Curtis looked again, then sank down on the couch beside the body.

"Oh, my God! It's horrible!" he said.

II

To Hutchinson Hatch and half a dozen other reporters, Dr. Leonard, at his home late that night, told the story of the arrival of Jack Curtis and Charles Reid with the body of the girl, and the succeeding events so far as he knew them. The police and Medical Examiner Francis had preceded the newspaper men, and the body had been removed to a nearby village.

"They came here in great excitement," Dr. Leonard explained. They brought the body in with them, the man Curtis lifting her by the shoulders and the man Reid at the feet. They placed the body on this couch. I asked them who she was, and they told me she was Marguerite Melrose, an actress. That's all that was said of her identity.

"Then I made an examination of the body, seeking a trace of life. There was none, although the body was not then entirely cold. In examining her heart my hand struck the knife which had killed her—a heavy weapon, evidently used for rough work, with a blade of six or seven inches. I drew the knife out. Of course, knowing that it had pierced her heart, any idea of doing anything to save her was beyond question.

"One of the men, Curtis, seemed greatly excited about this knife after Reid called his attention to it. Curtis took the knife out of my hand and examined it closely, then asked if he might keep it. I told him it would have to be turned over to the medical examiner. He argued about it, and finally, to settle the argument, I took it out of his hand. Reid explained to Curtis that it was necessary for me to keep the knife, and finally Curtis seemed to agree to it.

"Then I suggested that the police be notified. I did this myself by telephone, the men remaining with me all the time. I asked if they could throw any light on the tragedy, but neither could. Curtis said he had been out searching for a man who had the keys to a shed where some gasoline was locked up, and it took fifteen or twenty minutes to find him. As soon as he got the gasoline he returned to the auto.

"Reid and Miss Melrose were at this time in the auto, he said. What had happened while he had been away Curtis didn't know. Reid said he, too, had stepped out of the automobile, and after exchanging a few words with Miss Melrose went into the inn. There he remained fifteen minutes or so, because inside he saw a woman he knew and spoke to her. He declared that any one of three waiters could verify his statement that he was in the Monarch Inn.

"After I had notified the police Curtis grew very uneasy in his actions—it didn't occur to me at the moment, but now I recall that it was so—and suggested to Reid that they go on to Boston and send out detectives—special Pinkerton men. I tried to dissuade them, but they went away. I couldn't stop them. They gave me their cards, however. They are at the Hotel Teutonic, and told me they could be seen there at any time. The medical examiner and the police came afterward. I told them, and one of the detectives started immediately for Boston. They have probably told their story to him by this time."

"What did the young woman look like?" asked Hatch.

"Really, I couldn't say," said the doctor. "She wore an automobile mask which covered all her face except the chin, and there was a veil tied over her cap, concealing her hair. I didn't remove these; I left the body just as it was for the medical examiner."

"How was she dressed?" Hatch went on.

"She wore a long tan automobile dust coat of what seemed to be rich material, and beneath this a handsome—not a fancy—gown. I believe it was tailor-made. She was a woman of superb figure."

That was all that could be learned from Dr. Leonard, and Hatch and the other men raced back to Boston. The next day the newspapers flamed with the mystery of the murder of Miss Melrose, a beautiful Western actress who was visiting Boston. Each newspaper watched the other greedily to see if there was a picture of Miss Melrose; neither had one.

The newspapers also carried the stories of Jack Curtis and Charles Reid in connection with the murder. The stories were in substance just what Dr. Leonard had said, but were given in more detail. It was the general presumption, almost a foregone conclusion, that some one had killed Miss Melrose while the two men were away from the auto.

Who was this some one? Man or woman? No one could answer. Reid's story of being inside the Monarch Inn, where he spoke to a lady he knew—but whose name he refused to give—was verified by Hatch's paper. Three waiters had seen him.

The medical examiner had made only a brief statement, in which he had said, in answer to a question, that the person who killed Miss Melrose might have been either at her right, in the position Curtis would have occupied while driving the car, or might have leaned forward from behind and stabbed her. Thus it was not impossible that one of the men in the car with her had killed her, yet against this possibility was the fact that each of the men was one whom one could not readily associate with such a crime.

The fact that the fatal blow was delivered from the right

was proven, said the astute medical examiner, by the fact that the knife slanted as a knife could not have been slanted conveniently by a person on her other side—her left. There were many dark, underlying intimations behind what the medical man said; but he refused to say any more. Meanwhile the body remained in the village where it had been taken. Efforts to get a photograph were unavailing; pleas of newspaper artists for permission to sketch her fell upon deaf ears.

Curtis and Reid, after their first statements, remained in seclusion at the Teutonic. They were not arrested because this did not seem necessary. Both had offered to do anything in their power to solve the riddle, had even employed Pinkerton men who were now on the case; but they would say nothing nor see anyone except the police. The police encouraged them in this attitude, and hinted darkly and mysteriously at clews which "would lead to an arrest within twenty-four hours."

Hatch read these intimations and smiled grimly. Then he went out to try what a little patience and perseverance and human intelligence would do. He learned something of Reid's little romance in Boston. Yet not all of it. It was a fact, however, that Reid had called at the home of Miss Elizabeth Dow on Beacon Hill just after noon and inquired for her.

"She is not in," the maid had replied.

"I'll leave my card for her," said Reid.

"I don't think she'll be back," the girl answered.

"Not be back?" Reid repeated. "Why?"

"Haven't you seen the afternoon papers?" asked the girl. "They will explain. Mrs. Dow, her mother, told me not to talk to anyone."

Reid left the house with a wrinkle in his brow and walked on toward the Common. There he halted a newsboy and bought an afternoon paper—many afternoon papers. The first pages were loaded with details of the murder of Miss Melrose, theories, conjectures, a thousand little things, with long dispatches of her history and her stage career from San Francisco.

Reid passed these over impatiently with a slight shiver

and looked inside the paper. There he found the thing to which the maid had referred.

"By George!" he exclaimed.

It was a story of the elopement of Elizabeth Dow with Morgan Mason, Reid's rival. It seemed that Miss Dow and Mason met by appointment at the Monarch Inn and went from there in an automobile. The bride had written to her parents before she started, saying she preferred Mason despite his poverty. The family refused to talk of the matter. But there in facsimile was the marriage license.

Reid's face was a study as he walked back to the hotel. In a private room off the café he found Curtis, who had been drinking heavily, yet who, with the strange mood of some men, was not visibly intoxicated. Reid threw the paper down, open at the elopement announcement.

"See that," he said shortly.

Curtis read it—or glanced at it—but did not make a remark until he came to the name, the Monarch Inn. Then he looked up.

"That's where the other thing happened, isn't it?" he asked, rather thickly.

"Yes."

Curtis rambled off into something else; studiously he avoided any reference to the tragedy, yet that was the one thing which was in his mind. It was in a futile effort to forget it that he was drinking now. He talked on as a drunken man will for a time, then turned suddenly to Reid.

"I loved her," he declared suddenly, passionately. "My God!"

"Try not to think of it," Reid advised.

"You'll never say anything about that other thing—the knife—will you?" pleaded Curtis.

"Of course not," said Reid, impatiently. "They couldn't drag it out of me. But you're drinking too much—you want to quit it. First thing you know you'll be saying more than —get up and go out and take a walk."

Curtis stared at Reid vacantly for a moment, as if not understanding, then arose. He had regained possession of himself to a certain extent, but his face was pale.

"I think I will go out," he said.

After a time he passed through the café door into a side street and, refreshed a little by the cool air, started to walk along Tremont Street toward the shopping district. It was two o'clock in the afternoon and the streets were thronged.

Half a dozen reporters were idling in the lobby of the hotel, waiting vainly for either Reid or Curtis. The newspapers were shouting for another story from the only two men who could know a great deal of the circumstances attending the tragedy. Reid, on his return, had marched boldly through the crowd of reporters, paying no attention to their questions. They had not seen Curtis.

As Curtis, now free of the reporters, crossed a side street off Tremont on his way toward the shopping district he met Hutchinson Hatch, who was bound for the hotel to see his man there. Hatch instantly recognized him and fell in behind, curious to see where he would go. At a favorable opportunity, safe beyond reach of the other men, he intended to ask a few questions.

Curtis turned into Winter Street and strolled along through the crowd of women. Half way down Winter Street Hatch followed, and then for a moment he lost sight of him. He had gone into a store, he imagined. As he stood at a door waiting, Curtis came out, rushed through the crowd of women, slinging his arms like a madman, with frenzy in his face. He ran twenty steps, then stumbled and fell.

Hatch immediately ran to his assistance, lifted him up and gazed into the staring, terror-stricken eyes and an ashen face.

"What is it?" asked Hatch, quickly.

"I—I'm very ill. I—I think I need a doctor," gasped Curtis. "Take me somewhere, please."

He fell back limply, half fainting, into Hatch's arms. A cab came worming through the crowd; Hatch climbed into it, assisting Curtis, and gave some directions to the cabby.

"And hurry," he added. "This gentleman is ill."

The cabby applied the whip and drove out into Tremont, then over toward Park Street. Curtis aroused a little.

"Where're we going?" he demanded.

"To a doctor," replied Hatch.

Curtis sank back with eyes closed and his face white—so

white that Hatch felt of the pulse to assure himself that the heart was still beating. After a few minutes the cab stopped and, still assisting Curtis, Hatch went to the door. An aged woman answered the bell.

"Professor Van Dusen here?" asked the reporter.

"Yes."

"Please tell him that Mr. Hatch is here with a gentleman who needs immediate attention," Hatch directed, hurriedly.

He knew his way here and, still supporting Curtis, walked in. The woman disappeared. Curtis sank down on a couch in the little reception room, looked at Hatch glassily for a moment, then without a sound dropped back on the couch unconscious.

After a moment the door opened and there came in Professor Augustus S. F. X. Van Dusen, The Thinking Machine. He squinted inquiringly at Hatch, and Hatch waved his head toward Curtis.

"Dear me, dear me," exclaimed The Thinking Machine.

He leaned over the prostrate figure a moment, then disappeared into another room, returning with a hypodermic. After a few anxious minutes Curtis sat up straight. He stared at the two men with unseeing eyes, and in them was unutterable terror.

"I saw her! I saw her!" he screamed. *"There was a dagger in her heart. Marguerite!"*

Again he fell back unconscious. The Thinking Machine squinted at Hatch.

"The man's got delirium tremens," he snapped impatiently.

III

For fifteen minutes Hatch silently looked on as The Thinking Machine worked over the unconscious man. Once or twice Curtis moved uneasily and moaned slightly. Hatch had started to explain the situation to The Thinking Machine, but the irascible scientist glared at him and the reporter became silent. After ten or fifteen minutes The Thinking Machine turned to Hatch more genially.

"He'll be all right in a little while now," he said. "What is it?"

"Well, it's a murder," Hatch began. "Marguerite Melrose, an actress, was stabbed through the heart last night, and—"

"Murder?" interrupted The Thinking Machine. "Might it not have been suicide?"

"Might have been; yes," said the reporter, after a moment's pause. "But it appears to be murder."

"When you say it *is* murder," said The Thinking Machine, "you immediately give the impression that you were there and saw it. Go on."

From the beginning, then, Hatch told the story as he knew it; of the stopping of The Green Dragon at the Monarch Inn, of the events there, of the whereabouts of Curtis and Reid at the time the girl received the knife thrust and of the confirmation of Reid's story. Then he detailed those incidents of the arrival of the men with the girl at Dr Leonard's house, of what had transpired there, of the effort Curtis had made to get possession of the knife.

With finger tips pressed together and squinting steadily upward, The Thinking Machine listened. At its end, which bore on the actions of Curtis just preceding his appearance in the room with them, The Thinking Machine arose and walked over to the couch where Curtis lay. He ran his slender fingers idly through the unconscious man's thick hair several times.

"Doesn't it strike you as perfectly possible, Mr. Hatch," he asked finally, "that Miss Melrose *did* kill herself?"

"It may be perfectly possible, but it doesn't appear so," said Hatch. "There was no motive."

"And certainly you've shown no motive for anything else," said the other, crustily. "Still," he mused, "I really can't say anything until I talk to him."

He again turned to his patient, and as he looked saw the red blood surge back into the face.

"Ah, now we're all right," he announced.

Thus it happened, for after another ten minutes the patient sat up suddenly on the couch and looked at the two men before him, bewildered.

"What's the matter?" he asked. The thickness was gone

from his speech; he was himself again, although a little shaky.

Briefly, Hatch explained to him what had happened, and he listened silently. Finally he turned to The Thinking Machine.

"And this gentleman?" he asked. He noted the queer appearance of the scientist, and stared into the squint eyes frankly.

"Professor Van Dusen, a distinguished scientist and physician," Hatch introduced. "I brought you here. He has been working with you for an hour."

"And now, Mr. Curtis," said The Thinking Machine, "if you will tell us *all* you know about the murder of Miss Melrose—"

Curtis paled suddenly.

"Why do you ask me?" he demanded.

"You said a great deal while you were unconscious," remarked The Thinking Machine, as he dreamily stared at the ceiling. "I know that worry over that and too much alcohol have put you in a condition bordering on nervous collapse. I think it would be better if you told it *all.*"

Hatch instantly saw the trend of the scientist's remarks, and remained discreetly silent. Curtis stared at both for a moment, then paced nervously across the room. He did not know what he might have said, what chance word might have been dropped. Then, apparently, he made up his mind, for he stopped suddenly in front of The Thinking Machine.

"Do I look like a man who would commit murder?" he asked.

"No, you do not," was the prompt response.

His recital of the story was similar to that of Hatch, but the scientist listened carefully.

"Details! details!" he interrupted once.

The story was complete from the moment Curtis jumped out of the car until the return to the hotel of Curtis and Reid. There the narrator stopped.

"Mr. Curtis, why did you try to induce Dr. Leonard to give up the knife to you?" asked The Thinking Machine, finally.

"Because—well, because—" He faltered, flushed and stopped.

"Because you were afraid it would bring the crime home to you?" asked the scientist.

"I didn't know *what* might happen," was the response.

"Is it your knife?"

Again the tell-tale flush overspread Curtis's face.

"No," he said, flatly.

"Is it Reid's knife?"

"Oh, no," he said, quickly.

"You were in love with Miss Melrose?"

"Yes," was the steady reply.

"Had she ever refused to marry you?"

"I had never asked her."

"Why?"

"Is this a third degree?" demanded Curtis, angrily, and he arose. "Am I a prisoner?"

"Not at all," said The Thinking Machine, quietly. "You may be made a prisoner, though, on what you said awhile unconscious. I am merely trying to help you."

Curtis sank down in a chair with his head in his hands and remained motionless for several minutes. At last he looked up.

"I'll answer your questions," he said.

"Why did you never ask Miss Melrose to marry you?"

"Because—well, because I understood another man, Donald MacLean, was in love with her, and she might have loved him. I understood she would have married him had it not been that by doing so she would have caused his disinheritance. MacLean is now in Boston."

"Ah!" exclaimed The Thinking Machine. "Your friend Reid didn't happen to be in love with her, too, did he?"

"Oh, no," was the reply. "Reid came here hoping to win the love of Miss Dow, a society girl. I came with him."

"Miss Dow?" asked Hatch, quickly. "The girl who eloped last night with Morgan Mason?"

"Yes," replied Curtis. "That elopement and this—crime have put Reid almost in as bad a condition as I am."

"What elopement?" asked The Thinking Machine.

Hatch explained how Mason had procured a marriage license, how Miss Dow and Mason had met at the Monarch Inn—where Miss Melrose must have been killed according to all stories—how Miss Dow had written to her parents from there of the elopement and then of their disappearance. The Thinking Machine listened, but without apparent interest.

"Have you such a knife as was used to kill Miss Melrose?" he asked at the end.

"No."

"Did you ever have such a knife?"

"Well, once."

"Where did you carry it when it was not in your auto kit?"

"In my lower coat pocket."

"By the way, what kind of looking woman was Miss Melrose?"

"One of the most beautiful women I ever met," said Curtis, with a certain enthusiasm. "Of ordinary height, superb figure—a woman who would attract attention anywhere."

"I believe she wore a veil and an automobile mask at the time she was killed?"

"Yes. They covered all her face except her chin."

"Could she, wearing an automobile mask, see either side of herself without turning?" asked The Thinking Machine, pointedly. "Had you intended to stab her, say while the car was in motion and had the knife in your hand, even in daylight, could she have seen it without turning her head? Or, if she had had the knife, could you have seen it?"

Curtis shuddered a little.

"No, I don't believe so."

"Was she blonde or brunette?"

"Blonde, with great clouds of golden hair," said Curtis, and again there was admiration in his tone.

"Golden hair?" Hatch repeated. "I understood Medical Examiner Francis to say she had dark hair?"

"No, golden hair," was the positive reply.

"Did you see the body, Mr. Hatch?" asked the scientist.

"No. None of us saw it. Dr. Francis makes that a rule."

The Thinking Machine arose, excused himself and passed into another room. They heard the telephone bell ring and then some one closed the door connecting the two rooms.

When the scientist returned he went straight to a point which Hatch had impatiently awaited.

"What happened to you this afternoon in Winter Street?"

Curtis had retained his composure well up to this point; now he became uneasy again. Quick pallor on his face was succeeded by a flush which crept up to the roots of his hair.

"I've been drinking too much," he said at last. "That and this thing have completely unnerved me. I am afraid I was not myself."

"What did you *think* you saw?" insisted The Thinking Machine.

"I went into a store for something. I've forgotten what now. I know there was a great crowd of women—they were all about me. There I saw—" He stopped and was silent for a moment. "There I saw," he went on with an effort, "a woman—just a glimpse of her, over the heads of the others in the store—and—"

"And what?" insisted The Thinking Machine.

"At the moment I would have sworn it was Marguerite Melrose," was the reply.

"Of course you know you were mistaken?"

"I know it now," said Curtis. "It was a chance resemblance, but the effect on me was awful. I ran out of there shrieking—it seemed to me. Then I found myself here."

"And you don't know what you said or did from that time until the present?" asked the scientist, curiously.

"No, except in a hazy sort of way."

After a while Martha, the scientist's aged servant, appeared in the doorway.

"Mr. Mallory and a gentleman, sir."

"Let them come in," said The Thinking Machine. "Mr. Curtis," and he turned to him gravely, "Mr. Reid is here. I sent for him as if at your request to ask him two questions, If he answers those questions, as I believe he will, I can demonstrate that you are not guilty of and have no connection with the murder of Miss Melrose. Let me ask these questions, without any hint or remark from you as to what the answer must be. Are you willing?"

"I am," replied Curtis. His face was white, but his voice was firm.

Detective Mallory, whom Curtis didn't know, and Charles Reid entered the room. Both looked about curiously. Mallory nodded brusquely at Hatch. Reid looked at Curtis and Curtis looked away.

"Mr. Reid," said The Thinking Machine, without any preliminary, "Mr. Curtis tells me that the knife used to kill Miss Melrose was your property. Is that so?" he demanded quickly, as Curtis faced about wonderingly.

"No," thundered Reid, fiercely.

"Is it Mr. Curtis's knife?" asked The Thinking Machine.

"Yes," flashed Reid. "It's a part of his auto kit."

Curtis started to speak; The Thinking Machine waved his hand toward him. Detective Mallory caught the gesture and understood that Jack Curtis was his prisoner for murder.

IV

Curtis was led away and locked up. He raved and bitterly denounced Reid for the information he had given, but he did not deny it. Indeed, after the first burst of fury he said nothing.

Once he was under lock and key the police, led by Detective Mallory, searched his rooms at the Hotel Teutonic and there they found a handkerchief stained with blood. It was slight, still it was a stain. This was immediately placed in the hands of an expert, who pronounced it human blood. Then the case against Curtis seemed complete; it was his knife, he had been in love with Miss Melrose, therefore probably jealous of her, and here was the tell-tale bloodstain.

Meanwhile Reid was permitted to go his way. He seemed crushed by the rapid sequence of events, and read eagerly every line he could find in the public prints concerning both the murder and the elopement of Miss Dow. This latter affair, indeed, seemed to have greater sway over his mind than the murder, or that a lifetime friend was now held as the murderer.

Meanwhile The Thinking Machine had signified to Hatch his desire to visit the scene of the crime and see what might be done there. Late in the aftrnoon, therefore, they started, taking a train for a village nearest the Monarch Inn.

"It's a most extraordinary case," The Thinking Machine said, "much more extraordinary than you can imagine."

"In what respect?" asked the reporter.

"In motive, in the actual manner of the girl meeting her death and in a dozen other details which I can't state now because I haven't all the facts."

"You don't doubt but what it was murder?"

"It doesn't necessarily follow," said The Thinking Machine, evasively. "Suppose we were seeking a motive for Miss Melrose's suicide, what would we have? We would have her love affair with this man MacLean whom she refused to marry because she knew he would be disinherited. Suppose she had not seen him for a couple of years—suppose she had made up her mind to give him up—that he had suddenly appeared when she sat alone in the automobile in front of the Monarch Inn—suppose, then, finding all her love reawakened, she had decided to end it all?"

"But Curtis's knife and the blood on his handkerchief?"

"Suppose, having made up her mind to kill herself, she had sought a weapon?" went on The Thinking Machine, as if there had been no interruption. "What is more natural than she should have sought something—the knife, say—in the tool bag or kit, which must have been near her? Suppose she stabbed herself while the men were away from the automobile, or even after they had started on again in the darkness?"

Hatch looked a little crestfallen.

"You believe, then, that she did kill herself?" he asked.

"Certainly not," was the prompt response. "I *don't* believe Miss Melrose killed herself—but as yet I know nothing to the contrary. As for the blood on Curtis's handkerchief, remember he helped carry the body to Dr. Leonard; it might have come from that—it might have come from a slight spattering of blood."

"But circumstances certainly implicate Curtis."

"I wouldn't convict any man of any crime on any circumstantial evidence," was the response. "It's worthless unless a man is forced to confess."

The reporter was puzzled, bewildered, and his face showed it. There were many things he did not understand, but the principal question in his mind took form:

"Why did you turn Curtis over to the police, then?"

"Because he is the man who owned the knife," was the reply. "I knew he was lying to me from the first about the knife. Men have been executed on less evidence than that."

The train stopped and they proceeded to the office of the medical examiner, where the body of the woman lay. Professor Van Dusen was readily permitted to see the body, even to offer his expert assistance in an autopsy which was then being performed; but the reporter was stopped at the door. After an hour The Thinking Machine came out.

"She was stabbed from the right," he said in answer to Hatch's inquiring look, "either by some one sitting at her right, by some one leaning over her right shoulder, or she might have done it herself."

Then they went on to Monarch Inn, five miles away. Here, after a comprehensive squint at the landscape, The Thinking Machine entered and for half an hour questioned three waiters there.

Did these waiters see Mr. Reid? Yes. They identified his published picture as a gentleman who had come in and taken a hot Scotch at the bar. Anyone with him? No. Speak to anyone in the inn? Yes, a lady.

"What did she look like?" asked The Thinking Machine.

"Couldn't say, sir," the waiter replied. "She came in an automobile and wore a mask, with a veil tied about her head and a long tan automobile coat."

"With the mask on you couldn't see her face?"

"Only her chin, sir."

"No glimpse of her hair?"

"No, sir. It was covered by the veil."

Then The Thinking Machine turned loose a flood of questions. He learned that the woman had been waiting at the inn for nearly an hour when Reid entered; that she had come there alone and at her request had been shown into a private parlor—"to wait for a gentleman," she had told the waiter.

She had opened the door when she heard Reid enter and had glanced out, but he had disappeared into the bar before she saw him. When he started away she looked out again. Then she saw him and he saw her. She seemed surprised and started to close the door, when he spoke to her. No one heard what was said, but he went in and the door was closed.

No one knew just when either Reid or the woman left the inn. Some half an hour or so after Reid entered the room a waiter rapped on the door. There was no answer. He opened the door and went in, but there was no one there. It was presumed then that the gentleman she had been waiting for had appeared and they had gone out together. It was a fact that an automobile had come up meanwhile—in addition to that in which Curtis, Miss Melrose and Reid had come—and had gone away again.

When all this questioning had come to an end and these facts were in possession of The Thinking Machine, the reporter advanced a theory.

"That woman was unquestionably Miss Dow, who knew Reid and who eloped that night with Morgan Mason."

The Thinking Machine looked at him a moment without speaking, then led the way into the private room where the lady had been waiting. Hatch followed. They remained there five or ten minutes, then The Thinking Machine came out and started toward the front door, only eight or ten feet from this room. The road was twenty feet away.

"Let's go," he said, finally.

"Where?" asked Hatch.

"Don't you see?" asked The Thinking Machine, irrelevantly, "that it would have been perfectly possible for Miss Melrose herself to have left the automobile and gone inside the inn for a few minutes?"

Following previously received directions The Thinking Machine now set out to find the man who had charge of the gasoline tank. They went away together and remained half an hour.

On the scientist's return to where Hatch had been waiting impatiently they climbed into the car which had brought them to the inn.

"Two miles down this road, then the first road to your right until I tell you to stop," was the order to the chauffeur.

"Where are you going?" asked Hatch, curiously.

"Don't know yet," was the enigmatic reply.

The car ran on through the night, with great, unblinking lights staring straight out ahead on a road as smooth as asphalt. The turn was made, then more slowly the car proceeded along the cross road. At the second house, dimly discernible through the night, The Thinking Machine gave the signal to stop.

Hatch leaped out, and The Thinking Machine followed. Together they approached the house, a small cottage some distance back from the road. As they went up the path they came upon another automobile, but it had no lights and the engine was still. Even in the darkness they could see that one of the forward wheels was gone, and the front of the car was demolished.

"That fellow had a bad accident," Hatch remarked.

An old woman and a boy appeared at the door in answer to their rap.

"I am looking for a gentleman who was injured last night in an automobile accident," said The Thinking Machine. "Is he still here?"

"Yes. Come in."

They stepped inside as a man's voice called from another room:

"Who is it?"

"Two gentlemen to see the man who was hurt," the woman called.

"Do you know his name?" asked The Thinking Machine.

"No, sir," the woman replied. Then the man who had spoken appeared.

"Would it be possible for us to see the gentleman who was hurt?" asked The Thinking Machine.

"Well, the doctor said we would have to keep folks away from him," was the reply. "Is there anything I could tell you?"

"We would like to know who he is," said The Thinking Machine. "It may be that we can take him off your hands."

"I don't know his name," the man explained; "but here are the things we took off him. He was hurt on the head, and hasn't been able to speak since he was brought here."

The Thinking Machine took a gold watch, a small note-book, two or three cards of various business concerns, two railroad tickets to New York and one thousand dollars in large bills. He merely glanced at the papers. No name appeared anywhere on them; the same with the railroad tickets. The business cards meant nothing at the moment. It was the gold watch on which the scientist concentrated his attention. He looked on both sides, then inside, carefully. Finally he handed it back.

"What time did this gentleman come here?" he asked.

"We brought him in from the road about nine o'clock," was the reply. "We heard his automobile smash into something and found him there beside it a moment later. He was unconscious. His car had struck a stone on the curve and he was thrown out head first."

"And where is his wife?"

"His wife?" The man looked from The Thinking Machine to the woman. "His wife? We didn't see anybody else."

"Nobody ran away from the machine as you went out?" insisted the scientist.

"No, sir," was the positive reply.

"And no woman has been here to inquire for him?"

"No, sir."

"Has anybody?"

"No, sir."

"What direction was the car going when it struck?"

"I couldn't tell you, sir. It had turned entirely over and was in the middle of the road when we found it."

"What's the number of the car?"

"It didn't have any."

"This gentleman has good medical attention, I suppose?"

"Yes, sir. Dr. Leonard is attending him. He says his condition isn't dangerous, and meanwhile we're letting him stay here, because we suppose he'll make it all right with us when he gets well."

"Thank you—that's all," said The Thinking Machine. "Good-night."

With Hatch he turned and left the house.

"What is all this?" asked Hatch, bewildered.

"That man is Morgan Mason," said The Thinking Machine.

"The man who eloped with Miss Dow?" asked Hatch, breathlessly.

"Now, where is Miss Dow?" asked The Thinking Machine, in turn.

"You mean—"

The Thinking Machine waved his hand off into the vague night; it was a gesture which Hatch understood perfectly.

V

Hutchinson Hatch was deeply thoughtful on the swift run back to the village. There he and The Thinking Machine took train to Boston. Hatch was turning over possibilities. Had Miss Dow eloped with some one besides Mason? There had been no other name mentioned. Was it possible that she killed Miss Melrose? Vaguely his mind clutched for a motive for this, yet none appeared, and he dismissed the idea with a laugh at its absurdity. Then, What? Where? How? Why?

"I suppose the story of an actress having been murdered in an automobile under mysterious circumstances would have been telegraphed all over the country, Mr. Hatch?" asked The Thinking Machine.

"Yes," said Hatch. "If you mean this story, there's not a city in the country that doesn't know of it by this time."

"It's perfectly wonderful, the resources of the press," the scientist mused.

Hatch nodded his acquiescence. He had hoped for a moment that The Thinking Machine had asked the question as a preliminary to something else, but that was apparently all. After a while the train jerked a little and The Thinking Machine spoke again.

"I think, Mr. Hatch, I wouldn't yet print anything about the disappearance of Miss Dow," he said. "It might be unwise at present. No one else will find it out, so—"

"I understand," said Hatch. It was a command.

"By the way," the other went on, "do you happen to re

member the name of that Winter Street store that Curtis went in?"

"Yes," and he named it.

It was nearly midnight when The Thinking Machine and Hatch reached Boston. The reporter was dismissed with a curt:

"Come up at noon to-morrow."

Hatch went his way. Next day at noon promptly he was waiting in the reception room of The Thinking Machine's home. The scientist was out—down in Winter Street, Martha explained—and Hatch waited impatiently for his return. He came in finally.

"Well?" inquired the reporter.

"Impossible to say anything until day after to-morrow," said The Thinking Machine.

"And then?" asked Hatch.

"The solution," replied the scientist positively. "Now I'm waiting for some one."

"Miss Dow?"

"Meanwhile you might see Reid and find out in some way if he ever happened to make a gift of any little thing, a thing that a woman would wear on the outside of her coat, for instance, to Miss Dow."

"Lord, I don't think *he'll* say anything."

"Find out, too, when he intends to go back West."

It took Hatch three hours, and required a vast deal of patience and skill, to find out that on a recent birthday Miss Dow had received a present of a monogram belt buckle from Reid. That was all; and that was not what The Thinking Machine meant. Hatch had the word of Miss Dow's maid for it that while Miss Dow wore this belt at the time of her elopement, it was underneath the automobile coat.

"Have you heard anything more from Miss Dow?" asked Hatch.

"Yes," responded the maid. "Her father received a letter from her this morning. It was from Chicago, and said that she and her husband were on their way to San Francisco and that the family might not hear from them again until after the honeymoon."

"How? What?" gasped Hatch. His brain was in a muddle. "She in Chicago, *with—her husband?*"

"Yes, sir."

"Is there any question about the letter being in her handwriting?"

"Not at all," replied the maid, positively. "It's perfectly natural," she concluded.

"But—" Hatch began, then he stopped.

For one fleeting instant he was tempted to tell the maid that the man whom the family had supposed was Miss Dow's husband was lying unconscious at a farmhouse not a great way from the Monarch Inn, and that there was no trace of Miss Dow. Now this letter! His head whirled when he thought of it.

"Is there any question but that Miss Dow did elope with Mr. Mason and not some other man?" he asked.

"It was Mr. Mason, all right," the girl responded. "I knew there was to be an elopement and helped arrange for Miss Dow to go," she added, confidentially. "It was Mr. Mason, I know."

Then Hatch rushed away and telephoned to The Thinking Machine. He simply couldn't hold this latest development until he saw him again.

"We've made a mistake," he bellowed through the 'phone.

"What's that?" demanded The Thinking Machine, aggressively.

"Miss Dow is in Chicago with her husband—family has received a letter from her—that man out there with the smashed head can't be Mason," the reporter explained hurriedly.

"Dear me, dear me!" said The Thinking Machine over the wire. And again: "Dear me!"

"Her maid told me all about it," Hatch rushed on, "that is, all about her aiding Miss Dow to elope, and all that. Must be some mistake."

"Dear me!" again came in the voice of The Thinking Machine. Then: "Is Miss Dow a blonde or brunette?"

The irrelevancy of the question caused Hatch to smile in spite of himself.

"A brunette," he answered. "A pronounced brunette."

"Then," said The Thinking Machine, as if this were merely dependent upon or a part of the blonde or brunette proposition, "get immediately a picture of Mason somewhere—I suppose you can—go out and see that man with the smashed head and see if it is Mason. Let me know by 'phone."

"All right," said Hatch, rather hopelessly. "But it is impossible—"

"Don't say that," snapped The Thinking Machine. "Don't say that," he repeated, angrily. "It annoys me exceedingly."

It was nearly ten o'clock that night when Hatch again 'phoned to The Thinking Machine. He had found a photograph, he had seen the man with the smashed head. They were the same. He so informed The Thinking Machine.

"Ah," said that individual, quietly. "Did you find out about any gift that Reid might have made to Miss Dow?" he asked.

"Yes, a monogram belt buckle of gold," was the reply.

Hatch was over his head and knew it. He was finding out things and answering questions, which by the wildest stretch of his imagination, he could not bring to bear on the matter in hand—the mystery surrounding the murder of Marguerite Melrose, an actress.

"Meet me at my place here at one o'clock day after tomorrow," instructed The Thinking Machine. "Publish as little as you can of this matter until you see me. It's extraordinary—perfectly extraordinary. Good-by."

That was all. Hatch groped hopelessly through the tangle, seeking one fact that he could grasp. Then it occurred to him that he had never ascertained when Reid intended to return West, and he went to the Hotel Teutonic for this purpose. The clerk informed him that Reid was to start in a couple of days. Reid had hardly left his room since Curtis was locked up.

Precisely at one o'clock on the second day following, as directed by The Thinking Machine, Hatch appeared and was ushered in. The Thinking Machine was bowed over a retort in his laboratory, and he looked up at the reporter with a question in his eyes.

"Oh, yes," he said, as if recollecting for the first time the purpose of the visit. "Oh, yes."

He led the way to the reception room and gave instructions to Martha to admit whoever inquired for him; then he sat down and leaned back in his chair. After a while the bell rang and two men were shown in. One was Charles Reid; the other a detective whom Hatch knew.

"Ah, Mr. Reid," said The Thinking Machine. "I'm sorry to have troubled you, but there were some questions I wanted to ask before you went away. If you'll wait just a moment."

Reid bowed and took a seat.

"Is he under arrest?" Hatch inquired of the detective, aside.

"Oh, no," was the reply. "Oh, no. Detective Mallory told me to ask him to come up. I don't know what for."

After a while the bell rang again. Then Hatch heard Detective Mallory's voice in the hall and the rustle of skirts; then the voice of another man. Mallory appeared at the door after a moment; behind him came two veiled women and a man who was a stranger to Hatch.

"I'm going to make a request, Mr. Mallory," said The Thinking Machine. "I know it will be a cause of pleasure to Mr. Reid. It is that you release Mr. Curtis, who is charged with the murder of Miss Melrose."

"Why?" demanded Mallory, quickly. Hatch and Reid stared at the scientist curiously.

"This," said The Thinking Machine.

The two women simultaneously removed their veils.

One was Miss Marguerite Melrose.

VI

"Miss Melrose that was," explained The Thinking Machine, "now Mrs. Donald MacLean. This, gentlemen, is her husband. This other young woman is Miss Dow's maid. Together I believe we will be able to throw some light on the death of the young woman who was found in Mr. Curtis's automobile."

Stupefied with amazement, Hatch stared at the woman whose reported murder had startled and puzzled the entire country. Reid had shown only slight emotion—an emotion of a kind hard to read. Finally he advanced to Miss Melrose, or Mrs. MacLean, with outstretched hand.

"Marguerite," he said.

The girl looked deeply into his eyes, then took the proffered hand.

"And Jack Curtis?" she asked.

"If Detective Mallory will have him brought here we can immediately end his connection with this case so far as your murder is concerned," said The Thinking Machine.

"Who—who was murdered, then?" asked Hatch.

"A little circumstantial development is necessary to show," replied The Thinking Machine.

Detective Mallory retired into another room and 'phoned to have Curtis brought up. On his assurance that there had been a mistake which he would explain later, Curtis set out from his cell with a detective and within a few minutes appeared in the room, wonderingly.

One look at Marguerite and he was beside her, gripping her hand. For a time he didn't speak; it was not necessary. Then the actress, with flushed face, indicated MacLean, who had stood quietly by, an interested but silent spectator.

"My husband, Jack," she said.

Quick comprehension swept over Curtis and he looked from one to another. Then he approached MacLean with outstretched hand.

"I congratulate you," he said, with deep feeling. "Make her happy."

Reid had stood unobserved meanwhile. Hatch's glance traveled from one to another of the persons in the room. He was seeking to explain that expression on Reid's face, vainly thus far. There was a little pause as Reid and Curtis came face to face, but neither spoke.

"Now, please, what does it all mean?" asked MacLean, who up to this time had been silent.

"It's a strange study of the human brain," said The Thinking Machine, "and incidentally a little proof that circumstantial evidence is absolutely worthless. For instance, here it was proven that Miss Melrose was dead, that Mr. Curtis was jealous of her, that while drinking he had threatened her—this I learned at the Hotel Yarmouth, but now it is unimportant—that his knife killed her, and finally that there was blood on one of his handkerchiefs. This is the complete circumstantial chain; and Miss Melrose appears, alive.

"Suppose we take the case from the point where I entered it. It will be interesting as showing the methods of a brain which reduces all things to tangible strands which may be woven into a whole, then fitting them together. My knowledge of the affair began when Mr. Curtis was brought to these apartments by Mr. Hatch. Mr. Curtis was ill. I gave him a stimulant; he aroused suddenly and shrieked: "I saw her. There was a dagger in her heart. Marguerite!"

"My first impression was that he was insane; my next that he had delirium tremens, because I saw he had been drinking heavily. Later I saw it was temporary mental collapse due to excessive drinking and a tremendous strain. Instantly I associated Marguerite with this—'a dagger in her heart.' Therefore, Marguerite dead or wounded. 'I saw her.' Dead or alive? These, then, were my first impressions.

"I asked Mr. Hatch what had happened. He told me Miss Melrose, an actress, had been murdered the night before. I suggested suicide, because suicide is always the first possibility in considering a case of violent death which is not obviously accidental. He insisted that he believed it was murder, and told me why. It was all he knew of the story.

"There was the stopping of The Green Dragon at the Monarch Inn for gasoline; the disappearance of Mr. Curtis, as he told the police, to hunt for gasoline—partly proven by the fact that he brought it back; the statement of Mr. Reid to the police that he had gone into the inn for a hot Scotch, and confirmation of this. Above all, here was the opportunity for the crime—if it were committed by any person other than Curtis or Reid.

"Then Mr. Hatch repeated to me the statement made to him by Dr. Leonard. The first thing that impressed me here was the fact that Curtis had, in taking the girl into the house, carried her by the shoulders. Instantly I saw, knowing that the girl had been stabbed through the heart, how it would be possible for blood to get on Mr. Curtis's hands, thence on his handkerchief or clothing. This was before I knew or considered his connection with the death at all.

"Curtis told Dr. Leonard that the girl was Miss Melrose. The body wasn't yet cold, therefore death must have come just before it reached the doctor. Then the knife was discovered. Here was the first tangible working clew—a rough knife, with a blade six or seven inches long. Obviously not the sort of knife a woman would carry about with her. Therefore, where did it come from?

"Curtis tried to induce the doctor to let him have the knife; probably Curtis's knife, possibly Reid's. Why Curtis's? The nature of the knife, a blade six or seven inches long, indicated a knife used for heavy work, not for a penknife. Under ordinary circumstances such a knife would not have been carried by Reid; therefore it may have belonged to Curtis's auto kit. He might have carried it in his pocket.

"Thus, considering *that it was Miss Melrose who was dead,* we had these facts: Dead only a few minutes, possibly stabbed while the two men were away from the car; Curtis's knife used—not a knife from any other auto kit, mind you, *because Curtis recognized this knife.* Two and two make four, not sometimes, but all the time."

Every person in the room was leaning forward, eagerly listening; Reid's face was perfectly white. The Thinking Machine finally arose, walked over and ran his fingers through Reid's hair, then sat again squinting at the ceiling. He spoke as if to himself.

"Then Mr. Hatch told me another important thing," he went on. "At the moment it appeared a coincidence, later it assumed its complete importance. This was that Dr. Leonard did not actually *see* the face of the girl—only the chin; that the hair was covered by a veil and the mask covered the remainder of the face. Here for the first time I saw that it was wholly possible that the woman *was not Miss Melrose at all.* I saw it as a possibility; not that I believed it. I had no reason to, then.

"The dress of the young woman meant nothing; it was

that of thousands of other young women who go automobiling—handsome tailor-made gown, tan dust coat. Then I tricked Mr. Curtis—I suppose it is only fair to use the proper word—into telling me his story by making him believe he made compromising admissions while unconscious. I had, I may say, too, examined his head minutely. I have always maintained that the head of a murderer will show a certain indentation. Mr. Curtis's head did not show this indentation, neither does Mr. Reid's.

"Mr. Curtis told me the first thing to show that the knife which killed the girl—I still believed her Miss Melrose then—could have pased out of his hands. He said when he leaped from the automobile he thought he dropped something, searched for it a moment, failed to find it, then, being in a hurry, went on. He called back to Mr. Reid to search for what he had lost. That is when Mr. Curtis lost the knife; that is when it passed into the possession of Mr. Reid. He found it."

Every eye was turned on Reid. He sat as if fascinated, staring into the upward turned face of the scientist.

"There we had a girl—presumably Miss Melrose—dead, by a knife owned by Mr. Curtis, last in the possession of Mr. Reid. Mr. Hatch had previously told me that the medical examiner said the wound which killed the girl came from her right, in a general direction. Therefore here was a possibility that Mr. Reid did it in the automobile—a possibility, I say.

"I asked Mr. Curtis why he tried to recover the knife from Dr. Leonard. He stammered and faltered, but really it was because, having recognized the knife, he was afraid the crime would come home to him. Mr. Curtis denied flatly that the knife was his, and in denying told me that it was. It was not Mr. Reid's I was assured. Mr. Curtis also told me of his love for Miss Melrose, but there was nothing there, as it appeared, strong enough to suggest a motive for murder. He mentioned you, Mr. MacLean, then.

"Then Mr. Curtis named Miss Dow as one whose hand had been sought by Mr. Reid. Mr. Hatch told me this girl—Miss Dow—had eloped the night before with Morgan Mason from Monarch Inn—or, to be exact, that her family had received a letter from her stating that she was eloping; that Mason had taken out a marriage license. Remember this was the girl that Reid was in love with; it was singular that there should have been a Monarch Inn end to that elopement as well as to this tragedy.

"This meant nothing as bearing on the abstract problem before me until Mr. Curtis described Miss Melrose as having golden hair. With another minor scrap of information Mr. Hatch again opened up vast possibilities by stating that the medical examiner, a careful man, had said Miss Melrose had *dark* hair. I asked him if he had seen the body; he had not. But the medical examiner told him that. Instantly in my mind the question was aroused: Was it *Miss Melrose* who was killed? This was merely a possibility; it still had no great weight with me.

"I asked Mr. Curtis as to the circumstances which caused his collapse in Winter Street. He explained it was because he had seen a woman whom he would have sworn was Miss Melrose if he had not known that she was dead. This, following the dark hair and blonde hair puzzle, instantly caused this point to stand forth sharply in my mind. Was Miss Melrose dead at all? I had good reason then to believe that she was *not.*

"Previously, with the idea of fixing for all time the ownership of the knife—yet knowing in my own mind it was Mr. Curtis's—I had sent for Mr. Reid. I told him Mr. Curtis had said it was his knife. Mr. Reid fell into the trap and did the very thing I expected. He declared angrily the knife was Mr. Curtis's, thinking Curtis had tried to saddle the crime on him. Then I turned Mr. Curtis over to the police. When he was locked up I was reasonably certain that he did not commit any crime, because I had traced the knife from him to Mr. Reid."

There was a glitter in Reid's eyes now. It was not fear, only a nervous battle to restrain himself. The Thinking Machine went on:

"I saw the body of the dead woman—indeed, assisted at her autopsy. She was a pronounced brunette—Miss Melrose was a blonde. The mistake in identity was not an impossible one in view of the fact that each wore a mask and had her hair tied up under a veil. That woman was stabbed from the right—still a possibility of suicide."

"Who was the woman?" demanded Curtis. He seemed utterly unable to control himself longer.

"Miss Elizabeth Dow, who was supposed to have eloped with Morgan Mason," was the quiet reply.

Instant amazement was reflected on every face save Reid's, and again every eye was turned to him. Miss Dow's maid burst into tears.

"Mr. Reid knew who the woman was all the time," said The Thinking Machine. "Knowing then that Miss Dow was the dead woman—this belief being confirmed by a monogram gold belt buckle, 'E. D.,' on the body—I proceeded to find out all I could in this direction. The waiters had seen Mr. Reid in the inn; had seen him talking to a masked and veiled lady who had been waiting for nearly an hour; had seen him go into a room with her, but had not seen them leave the inn. Mr. Reid had recognized the lady—not she him. How? By a glimpse of the monogram belt buckle which he knew because he probably gave it to her."

"He did," interposed Hatch.

"I did," said Reid, calmly. It was the first time he had spoken.

"Now, Mr. Reid went into the room and closed the door, carrying with him Mr. Curtis's knife," went on The Thinking Machine. "I can't tell you from *personal observation* what happened in that room, but I know. Mr. Reid learned in some way that Miss Dow was going to elope; he learned that she had been waiting long past the time when Mason was due there; that she believed he had humiliated her by giving up the idea at the last minute. Being in a highly nervous condition, she lost faith in Mason and in herself, and perhaps mentioned suicide?"

"She did," said Reid, calmly.

"Go on, Mr. Reid," suggested The Thinking Machine.

"I believed, too, that Mason had changed his mind," the young man continued, with steady voice. "I pleaded with Miss Dow to give up the idea of eloping, because, remember, I loved her, too. She finally consented to go on with our party, as her automobile had gone. We came out of the inn together. When we reached the automobile—The Green Dragon, I mean—I saw Miss Melrose getting into Mr. MacLean's automobile, which had come up meanwhile. Instantly I saw, or imagined, the circumstances, and said nothing to Miss Dow about it, particularly as Mr. MacLean's car dashed away at full speed.

"Now, in taking Miss Dow to The Green Dragon it had been my purpose to introduce her to Miss Melrose. She knew Mr. Curtis. When I saw Miss Melrose was gone I knew Curtis would wonder why. I couldn't explain, because every moment I was afraid Mason would appear to claim Miss Dow and I was anxious to get her as far away as possible. Therefore I requested her not to speak until we reached the next inn, and there I would explain to Curtis.

"Somewhere between the Monarch Inn and the inn we had started for Miss Dow changed her mind; probably was overcome by the humiliation of her position, and she used the knife. She had seen me take the knife from my pocket and throw it into the tool kit on the floor beside her. It was comparatively a trifling matter for her to stoop and pick it up, almost from under her feet, and—"

"Under all these circumstances, as stated by Mr. Reid," interrupted The Thinking Machine, "we understand why, after he found the girl dead, he didn't tell all the truth, even to Curtis. Any jury on earth would have convicted him of murder on circumstantial evidence. Then, when he saw Miss Dow dead, mistaken for Miss Melrose, he *could* not correct the impression without giving himself away. He was forced to silence.

"I realized these things—not in exact detail as Mr. Reid has told them, but in a general way—after my talk with the waiters. Then I set out to find out *why* Mason had not appeared. It was possibly due to accident. On a chance entirely I asked the man in charge of the gasoline tank at the Monarch if he had heard of an accident nearby on the night of the tragedy. He had.

"With Mr. Hatch I found the injured man. A monogram, 'M.M.,' on his watch, told me it was Morgan Mason. Mr. Mason had a serious accident and still lies unconscious. He was going to meet Miss Dow when this happened. He had two railroad tickets to New York—for himself and bride—in his pocket."

Reid still sat staring at The Thinking Machine, waiting. The others were awed into silence by the story of the tragedy.

"Having located both Mason and Miss Dow to my satisfaction, I then sought to find what had become of Miss Melrose. Mr. Reid could have told me this, but he wouldn't have, because it would have turned the light on the very thing which he was trying to keep hidden. With Miss Melrose alive, it was perfectly possible that Curtis *had* seen her in the Winter Street store.

"I asked Mr. Hatch if he remembered what store it was. He did. I also asked Mr. Hatch if such a story as the murder of Miss Melrose would be telegraphed all over the country. He said it would. It did not stand to reason that if Miss Melrose were in any city, or even on a train, she could have failed to hear of her own murder, which would instantly have called forth a denial.

"Therefore, where was she? On the water, out of reach of newspapers? I went to the store in Winter Street and asked if any purchases had been sent from there to any steamer about to sail on the day following the tragedy. There had been several purchases made by a woman who answered Miss Melrose's description as I had it, and these had been sent to a steamer which sailed for Halifax.

"Miss Melrose and Mr. MacLean, married then, were on that steamer. I wired to Halifax to ascertain if they were coming back immediately. They were. I waited for them. Otherwise, Mr. Hatch, I should have given you the solution of the mystery two days ago. As it was, I waited until Miss Melrose, or Mrs. MacLean, returned. I think that's all."

"The letter from Miss Dow in Chicago?" Hatch reminded him.

"Oh, yes," said The Thinking Machine. "That was sent to a friend in her confidence, and mailed on a specified date. As a matter of fact, she and Mason were going to New York and thence to Europe. Of course, as matters happened, the two letters—the other being the one mailed from the Monarch Inn—were sent and could not be recalled."

. . . .

THE GREAT AUTO MYSTERY

This strange story was one of the most astonishing news features the American newspapers ever handled. Charles Reid was arrested, established his story beyond question, and was released. His principal witnesses were Professor Augustus S. F. X. Van Dusen, Jack Curtis and Mrs. Donald MacLean.

The Flaming Phantom

BY JACQUES FUTRELLE

The Flaming Phantom

BY JACQUES FUTRELLE

I

HUTCHINSON HATCH, reporter, stood beside the City Editor's desk, smoking and waiting patiently for that energetic gentleman to dispose of several matters in hand. City Editors always have several matters in hand, for the profession of keeping count of the pulse-beat of the world is a busy one. Finally this City Editor emerged from a mass of other things and picked up a sheet of paper on which he had scribbled some strange hieroglyphics, these representing his interpretation of the art of writing.

"Afraid of ghosts?" he asked.

"Don't know," Hatch replied, smiling a little. "I never happened to meet one."

"Well, this looks like a good story," the City Editor explained. "It's a haunted house. Nobody can live in it; all sorts of strange happenings, demoniacal laughter, groans and things. House is owned by Ernest Weston, a broker. Better jump down and take a look at it. If it is promising, you might spend a night in it for a Sunday story. Not afraid, are you?"

"I never heard of a ghost hurting anyone," Hatch replied, still smiling a little. "If this one hurts me it will make the story better."

Thus attention was attracted to the latest creepy mystery of a small town by the sea which in the past had not been wholly lacking in creeping mysteries.

Within two hours Hatch was there. He readily found the old Weston house, as it was known, a two-story, solidly built frame structure, which had stood for sixty or seventy years high upon a cliff overlooking the sea, in the center of a land plot of ten or twelve acres. From a distance it was imposing, but close inspection showed that, outwardly, at least, it was a ramshackle affair.

Without having questioned anyone in the village, Hatch climbed the steep cliff road to the old house, expecting to find some one who might grant him permission to inspect it. But no one appeared; a settled melancholy and gloom seemed to overspread it; all the shutters were closed forbiddingly.

There was no answer to his vigorous knock on the front door, and he shook the shutters on a window without result. Then he passed around the house to the back. Here he found a door and dutifully hammered on it. Still no answer. He tried it, and passed in. He stood in the kitchen, damp, chilly and darkened by the closed shutters.

One glance about this room and he went on through a back hall to the dining-room, now deserted, but at one time a comfortable and handsomely furnished place. Its hardwood floor was covered with dust; the chill of disuse was all-pervading. There was no furniture, only the litter which accumulates of its own accord.

From this point, just inside the dining-room door, Hatch began a sort of study of the inside architecture of the place. To his left was a door, the butler's pantry. There was a passage through, down three steps into the kitchen he had just left.

Straight before him, set in the wall, between two windows, was a large mirror, seven, possibly eight, feet tall and proportionately wide. A mirror of the same size was set in the wall at the end of the room to his left. From the dining-room he passed through a wide archway into the next room. This archway made the two rooms almost as one. This second, he presumed, had been a sort of living-room, but here, too, was nothing save accumulated litter, an old-fashioned fireplace and two long mirrors. As he entered, the fireplace was to his immediate left, one of the large mirrors was straight ahead of him and the other was to his right.

Next to the mirror in the end was a passageway of a little more than usual size which had once been closed with a sliding door. Hatch went through this into the reception-hall of the old house. Here, to his right, was the main hall, connected with the reception-hall by an archway, and through this archway he could see a wide, old-fashioned stairway leading up. To his left was a door, of ordinary size, closed. He tried it and it opened. He peered into a big room beyond. This room had been the library. It smelled of books and damp wood. There was nothing here —not even mirrors.

Beyond the main hall lay only two rooms, one a drawing-room of the generous proportions our old folks loved, with its gilt all tarnished and its fancy decorations covered with dust. Behind this, toward the back of the house, was a small parlor. There was nothing here to attract his attention, and he went upstairs. As he went he could see through the archway into the reception-hall as far as the library door, which he had left closed.

Upstairs were four or five roomy suites. Here, too, in small rooms designed for dressing, he saw the owner's passion for mirrors again. As he passed through room after room he fixed the general arrangement of it in his mind, and later on paper, to study it, so that, if necessary, he could leave any part of the house in the dark. He didn't know but what this might be necessary, hence his care—the same care he had evidenced downstairs.

After another casual examination of the lower floor, Hatch went out the back way to the barn. This stood a couple of hundred feet back of the house and was of more recent construction. Above, reached by outside stairs, were apartments intended for the servants. Hatch looked over these rooms, but they, too, had the appearance of not having been occupied for several years. The lower part of the barn, he found, was arranged to house half a dozen horses and three or four traps.

"Nothing here to frighten anybody," was his mental comment as he left the old place and started back toward the village. It was three o'clock in the afternoon. His purpose was to learn then all he could of the "ghost," and return that night for developments.

He sought out the usual village bureau of information, the town constable, a grizzled old chap of sixty years, who realized his importance as the whole police department, and who had the gossip and information, more or less distorted, of several generations at his tongue's end.

The old man talked for two hours—he was glad to talk—seemed to have been longing for just such a glorious opportunity as the reporter offered. Hatch sifted out what he wanted, those things which might be valuable in his story.

It seemed, according to the constable, that the Weston house had not been occupied for five years, since the death of the father of Ernest Weston, present owner. Two weeks before the reporter's appearance there Ernest Weston had come down with a contractor and looked over the old place.

"We understand here," said the constable, judicially, "that Mr. Weston is going to be married soon, and we kind of thought he was having the house made ready for his Summer home again."

"Whom do you understand he is to marry?" asked Hatch, for this was news.

"Miss Katherine Everard, daughter of Curtis Everard, a banker up in Boston," was the reply. "I know he used to go around with her before the old man died, and they say since she came out in Newport he has spent a lot of time with her."

"Oh, I see," said Hatch. "They were to marry and come here?"

"That's right," said the constable. "But I don't know when, since this ghost story has come up."

"Oh, yes, the ghost," remarked Hatch. "Well, hasn't the work of repairing begun?"

"No, not inside," was the reply. "There's been some work done on the grounds—in the daytime—but not much of that, and I kind of think it will be a long time before it's all done."

"What is the story, anyway?"

"Well," and the old constable rubbed his chin thoughtfully. "It seems sort of funny. A few days after Mr. Weston was down here a gang of laborers, mostly Italians, came down to work and decided to sleep in the house—sort of camp out—until they could repair a leak in the barn and move in there. They got here late in the afternoon and didn't do much that day but move into the house, all upstairs, and sort of settle down for the night. About one o'clock they heard some sort of noise downstairs, and finally all sorts of a racket and groans and yells, and they just naturally came down to see what it was.

"Then they saw the ghost. It was in the reception-hall, some of 'em said, others said it was in the library, but anyhow it was there, and the whole gang left just as fast as they knew how. They slept on the ground that night. Next day they took out their things and went back to Boston. Since then nobody here has heard from 'em."

"What sort of a ghost was it?"

"Oh, it was a man ghost, about nine feet high, and he was blazing from head to foot as if he was burning up," said the constable. "He had a long knife in his hand and waved it at 'em. They didn't stop to argue. They ran, and as they ran they heard the ghost a-laughing at them."

"I should think he would have been amused," was Hatch's somewhat sarcastic comment. "Has anybody who lives in the village seen the ghost?"

"No; we're willing to take their word for it, I suppose," was the grinning reply, "because there never was a ghost there before. I go up and look over the place every afternoon, but everything seems to be all right, and I haven't gone there at night. It's quite a way off my beat," he hastened to explain.

"A man ghost with a long knife," mused Hatch. "Blazing, seems to be burning up, eh? That sounds exciting. Now, a ghost who knows his business never appears except where there has been a murder. Was there ever a murder in that house?"

"When I was a little chap I heard there was a murder or something there, but I suppose if I don't remember it nobody else here does," was the old man's reply. "It happened one Winter when the Westons weren't there. There was something, too, about jewelry and diamonds, but I don't remember just what it was."

"Indeed?" asked the reporter.

"Yes, something about somebody trying to steal a lot of jewelry—a hundred thousand dollars' worth. I know nobody ever paid much attention to it. I just heard about it when I was a boy, and that was at least fifty years ago."

"I see," said the reporter.

. . . .

That night at nine o'clock, under cover of perfect blackness, Hatch climbed the cliff toward the Weston house. At one o'clock he came racing down the hill, with frequent glances over his shoulder. His face was pallid with a fear which he had never known before and his lips were ashen. Once in his room in the village hotel Hutchinson Hatch, the nerveless young man, lighted a lamp with trembling hands and sat with wide, staring eyes until the dawn broke through the east.

He had seen the flaming phantom.

II

It was ten o'clock that morning when Hutchinson Hatch called on Professor Augustus S. F. X. Van Dusen—The Thinking Machine. The reporter's face was still white, showing that he had slept little, if at all. The Thinking Machine squinted at him a moment through his thick glasses, then dropped into a chair.

"Well?" he queried.

"I'm almost ashamed to come to you, Professor," Hatch confessed, after a minute, and there was a little embarrassed hesitation in his speech. "It's another mystery."

"Sit down and tell me about it."

Hatch took a seat opposite the scientist.

"I've been frightened," he said at last, with a sheepish grin; "horribly, awfully frightened. I came to you to know what frightened me."

"Dear me! Dear me!" exclaimed The Thinking Machine. "What is it?"

Then Hatch told him from the beginning the story of the haunted house as he knew it; how he had examined the house by daylight, just what he had found, the story of the old murder and the jewels, the fact that Ernest Weston was to be married. The scientist listened attentively.

THE FLAMING PHANTOM

"It was nine o'clock that night when I went to the house the second time," said Hatch. "I went prepared for something, but not for what I saw."

"Well, go on," said the other, irritably.

"I went in while it was perfectly dark. I took a position on the stairs because I had been told the—the THING—had been seen from the stairs, and I thought that where it had been seen once it would be seen again. I had presumed it was some trick of a shadow, or moonlight, or something of the kind. So I sat waiting calmly I am not a nervous man—that is, I never have been until now.

"I took no light of any kind with me. It seemed an interminable time that I waited, staring into the reception-room in the general direction of the library. At last, as I gazed into the darkness, I heard a noise. It startled me a bit, but it didn't frighten me, for I put it down to a rat running across the floor.

"But after a while I heard the most awful cry a human being ever listened to. It was neither a moan nor a shriek —merely a—a cry. Then, as I steadied my nerves a little, a figure—a blazing, burning white figure—grew out of nothingness before my very eyes, in the reception-room. It actually grew and assembled as I looked at it."

He paused, and The Thinking Machine changed his position slightly.

"The figure was that of a man, apparently, I should say, eight feet high. Don't think I'm a fool—I'm not exaggerating. It was all in white and seemed to radiate a light, a ghostly, unearthly light, which, as I looked, grew brighter. I saw no face to the THING, but it had a head Then I saw an arm raised and in the hand was a dagger, blazing as was the figure.

"By this time I was a coward, a cringing, frightened coward—frightened not at what I saw, but at the weirdness of it. And then, still as I looked, the—the THING—raised the other hand, and there, in the air before my eyes, wrote with his own finger—*on the very face of the air,* mind you —one word: 'Beware!'"

"Was it a man's or woman's writing?" asked The Thinking Machine.

The matter-of-fact tone recalled Hatch, who was again being carried away by fear, and he laughed vacantly.

"I don't know," he said. "I don't know."

"Go on."

"I have never considered myself a coward, and certainly I am not a child to be frightened at a thing which my reason tells me is not possible, and, despite my fright, I compelled myself to action. If the THING were a man I was not afraid of it, dagger and all; if it were not, it could do me no injury.

"I leaped down the three steps to the bottom of the stairs, and while the THING stood there with upraised dagger, with one hand pointing at me, I rushed for it. I think I must have shouted, because I have a dim idea that I heard my own voice. But whether or not I did I—"

Again he paused. It was a distinct effort to pull himself together. He felt like a child the cold, squint eyes of The Thinking Machine were turned on him disapprovingly.

"Then—the THING disappeared just as it seemed I had my hands on it. I was expecting a dagger thrust. Before my eyes, while I was staring at it, I suddenly saw *only half of it.* Again I heard the cry, and the other half disappeared—my hands grasped empty air.

"Where the THING had been there was nothing. The impetus of my rush was such that I went right on past the spot where the THING had been, and found myself groping in the dark in a room which I didn't place for an instant. Now I know it was the library.

"By this time I was mad with terror. I smashed one of the windows and went through it. Then from there, until I reached my room, I didn't stop running. I couldn't. I woudn't have gone back to the reception-room for all the millions in the world."

The Thinking Machine twiddled his fingers idly; Hatch sat gazing at him with anxious, eager inquiry in his eyes.

"So when you ran and the—the THING moved away or disappeared you found yourself in the library?" The Thinking Machine asked at last.

"Yes."

"Therefore you must have run from the reception-room through the door into the library?"

"Yes."

"You left that door closed that day?"

"Yes."

Again there was a pause.

"Smell anything?" asked The Thinking Machine.

"No."

"You figure that the THING, as you call it, must have been just about in the door?"

"Yes."

"Too bad you didn't notice the handwriting—that is, whether it seemed to be a man's or a woman's."

"I think, under the circumstances, I would be excused for omitting that," was the reply.

"You said you heard something that you thought must be a rat," went on The Thinking Machine. "What was this?"

"I don't know."

"Any squeak about it?"

"No, not that I noticed."

"Five years since the house was occupied," mused the scientist. "How far away is the water?"

"The place overlooks the water, but it's a steep climb of three hundred yards from the water to the house."

That seemed to satisfy The Thinking Machine as to what actually happened.

"When you went over the house in daylight, did you notice if any of the mirrors were dusty?" he asked.

"I should presume that all were," was the reply. "There's no reason why they should have been otherwise."

"But you didn't notice particularly that some were not dusty?" the scientist insisted.

"No. I merely noticed that they were there."

The Thinking Machine sat for a long time squinting at the ceiling, then asked, abruptly:

"Have you seen Mr. Weston, the owner?"

"No."

"See him and find out what he has to say about the place, the murder, the jewels, and all that. It would be rather a queer state of affairs if, say, a fortune in jewels should be concealed somewhere about the place, wouldn't it?"

"It would, said Hatch. "It would."

"Who is Miss Katherine Everard?"

"Daughter of a banker here, Curtis Everard. Was a reigning belle at Newport for two seasons. She is now in Europe, I think, buying a trousseau, possibly."

"Find out all about her, and what Weston has to say, then come back here," said The Thinking Machine, as if in conclusion. "Oh, by the way," he added, "look up something of the family history of the Westons. How many heirs were there? Who are they? How much did each one get? All those things. That's all."

Hatch went out, far more composed and quiet than when he entered, and began the work of finding out those things The Thinking Machine had asked for, confident now that there would be a solution of the mystery.

That night the flaming phantom played new pranks. The town constable, backed by half a dozen villagers, descended upon the place at midnight, to be met in the yard by the apparition in person. Again the dagger was seen; again the ghostly laughter and the awful cry were heard.

"Surrender or I'll shoot," shouted the constable, nervously.

A laugh was the answer, and the constable felt something warm spatter in his face. Others in the party felt it, too, and wiped their faces and hands. By the light of the feeble lanterns they carried they examined their handkerchiefs and hands. Then the party fled in awful disorder.

The warmth they had felt was the warmth of blood—red blood, freshly drawn.

III

Hatch found Ernest Weston at luncheon with another gentleman at one o'clock that day. This other gentleman was introduced to Hatch as George Weston, a cousin. Hatch instantly remembered George Weston for certain eccentric exploits at Newport a season or so before; and also as one of the heirs of the original Weston estate.

Hatch thought he remembered, too, that at the time Miss

Everard had been so prominent socially at Newport, George Weston had been her most ardent suitor. It was rumored that there would have been an engagement between them, but her father objected. Hatch looked at him curiously; his face was clearly a dissipated one, yet there was about him the unmistakable polish and gentility of the well-bred man of society.

Hatch knew Ernest Weston as Weston knew Hatch; they had met frequently in the ten years Hatch had been a newspaper reporter, and Weston had been courteous to him always. The reporter was in doubt as to whether to bring up the subject on which he had sought out Ernest Weston, but the broker brought it up himself, smilingly.

"Well, what is it this time?" he asked, genially. "The ghost down on the South Shore, or my forthcoming marriage?"

"Both," replied Hatch.

Weston talked freely of his engagement to Miss Everard, which he said was to have been announced in another week, at which time she was due to return to America from Europe. The marriage was to be three or four months later, the exact date had not been set.

"And I suppose the country place was being put in order as a Summer residence?" the reporter asked.

"Yes. I had intended to make some repairs and changes there, and furnish it, but now I understand that a ghost has taken a hand in the matter and has delayed it. Have you heard much about this ghost story?" he asked, and there was a slight smile on his face.

"I have seen the ghost," Hatch answered.

"You have?" demanded the broker.

George Weston echoed the words and leaned forward, with a new interest in his eyes, to listen. Hatch told them what had happened in the haunted house—all of it. They listened with the keenest interest, one as eager as the other.

"By George!" exclaimed the broker, when Hatch had finished. "How do you account for it?"

"I don't," said Hatch, flatly. "I can offer no possible solution. I am not a child to be tricked by the ordinary illusion, nor am I of the temperament which imagines things, but I can offer no explanation of this."

"It must be a trick of some sort," said George Weston.

"I was positive of that," said Hatch, "but if it is a trick, it is the cleverest I ever saw."

The conversation drifted on to the old story of missing jewels and a tragedy in the house fifty years before. Now Hatch was asking questions by direction of The Thinking Machine; he himself hardly saw their purport, but he asked them.

"Well, the full story of that affair, the tragedy there, would open up an old chapter in our family which is nothing to be ashamed of, of course," said the broker, frankly; "still it is something we have not paid much attention to for many years. Perhaps George here knows it better than I do. His mother, then a bride, heard the recital of the story from my grandmother."

Ernest Weston and Hatch looked inquiringly at George Weston, who lighted a fresh cigarette and leaned over the table toward them. He was an excellent talker.

"I've heard my mother tell of it, but it was a long time ago," he began. "It seems, though, as I remember it, that my great-grandfather, who built the house, was a wealthy man, as fortunes went in those days, worth probably a million dollars.

"A part of this fortune, say about one hundred thousand dollars, was in jewels, which had come with the family from England. Many of those pieces would be of far greater value now than they were then, because of their antiquity. It was only on state occasions, I might say, when these were worn, say, once a year.

"Between times the problem of keeping them safely was a difficult one, it appeared. This was before the time of safety deposit vaults. My grandfather conceived the idea of hiding the jewels in the old place down on the South Shore, instead of keeping them in the house he had in Boston. He took them there accordingly.

"At this time one was compelled to travel down the South Shore, below Cohasset anyway, by stagecoach. My grandfather's family was then in the city, as it was Winter, so he made the trip alone. He planned to reach there at night, so as not to attract attention to himself, to hide the jewels about the house, and leave that same night for Boston again by a relay of horses he had arranged for. Just what happened after he left the stagecoach, below Cohasset, no one ever knew except by surmise."

The speaker paused a moment and relighted his cigarette.

"Next morning my great-grandfather was found unconscious and badly injured on the veranda of the house. His skull had been fractured. In the house a man was found dead. No one knew who he was; no one within a radius of many miles of the place had ever seen him.

"This led to all sorts of surmises, the most reasonable of which, and the one which the family has always accepted, being that my grandfather had gone to the house in the dark, had there met some one who was stopping there that night as a shelter from the intense cold, that this man learned of the jewels, that he had tried robbery and there was a fight.

"In this fight the stranger was killed inside the house, and my great-grandfather, injured, had tried to leave the house for aid. He collapsed on the veranda where he was found and died without having regained consciousness. That's all we know or can surmise reasonably about the matter."

"Were the jewels ever found?" asked the reporter.

"No. They were not on the dead man, nor were they in the possession of my grandfather."

"It is reasonable to suppose, then, that there was a third man and that he got away with the jewels?" asked Ernest Weston.

"It seemed so, and for a long time this theory was accepted. I suppose it is now, but some doubt was cast on it by the fact that only two trails of footsteps led to the house and none out. There was a heavy snow on the ground. If none led out it was obviously impossible that anyone came out."

Again there was silence. Ernest Weston sipped his coffee slowly.

"It would seem from that," said Ernest Weston, at last, "that the jewels were hidden before the tragedy, and have never been found."

George Weston smiled.

"Off and on for twenty years the place was searched, according to my mother's story," he said. "Every inch of the cellar was dug up; every possible nook and corner was searched. Finally the entire matter passed out of the minds of those who knew of it, and I doubt if it has ever been referred to again until now."

"A search even now would be almost worth while, wouldn't it?" asked the broker.

George Weston laughed aloud.

"It might be," he said, "but I have some doubt. A thing that was searched for for twenty years would not be easily found."

So it seemed to strike the others after a while and the matter was dropped.

"But this ghost thing," said the broker, at last. "I'm interested in that. Suppose we make up a ghost party and go down to-night. My contractor declares he can't get men to work there."

"I would be glad to go," said George Weston, "but I'm running over to the Vandergrift ball in Providence to-night."

"How about you, Hatch?" asked the broker.

"I'll go, yes," said Hatch, "as one of several," he added with a smile.

"Well, then, suppose we say the constable and you and I?" asked the broker; "to-night?"

"All right."

After making arrangements to meet the broker later that afternoon he rushed away—away to The Thinking Machine. The scientist listened, then resumed some chemical test he was making.

"Can't you go down with us to-night?" Hatch asked.

"No," said the other. "I'm going to read a paper before a scientific society and prove that a chemist in Chicago is a fool. That will take me all evening."

"To-morrow night?" Hatch insisted.

"No—the next night."

This would be on Friday night—just in time for the feature which had been planned for Sunday. Hatch was compelled to rest content with this, but he foresaw that he would have it all, with a solution. It never occurred to him that this problem, or, indeed, that any problem, was beyond the mental capacity of Professor Van Dusen.

Hatch and Ernest Weston took a night train that evening, and on their arrival in the village stirred up the town constable.

"Will you go with us?" was the question.

"Both of you going?" was the counter-question.

"Yes."

"I'll go," said the constable promptly. "Ghost!" and he laughed scornfully. "I'll have him in the lockup by morning."

"No shooting, now," warned Weston. "There must be somebody back of this somewhere; we understand that, but there is no crime that we know of. The worst is possibly trespassing."

"I'll get him all right," responded the constable, who still remembered the experience where blood—warm blood—had been thrown in his face. "And I'm not so sure there isn't a crime."

That night about ten the three men went into the dark, forbidding house and took a station on the stairs where Hatch had sat when he saw the THING—whatever it was. There they waited. The constable moved nervously from time to time, but neither of the others paid any attention to him.

At last the—the THING appeared. There had been a preliminary sound as of something running across the floor, then suddenly a flaming figure of white seemed to grow into being in the reception-room. It was exactly as Hatch had described it to The Thinking Machine.

Dazed, stupefied, the three men looked, looked as the figure raised a hand, pointing toward them, and wrote a word in the air—positively in the air. The finger merely waved, and there, floating before them, were letters, flaming letters, in the utter darkness. This time the word was: "Death."

Faintly, Hatch, fighting with a fear which again seized him, remembered that The Thinking Machine had asked him if the handwriting was that of a man or woman; now he tried to see. It was as if drawn on a blackboard, and there was a queer twist to the loop at the bottom. He sniffed to see if there was an odor of any sort. There was not.

Suddenly he felt some quick, vigorous action from the constable behind him. There was a roar and a flash in his ear, he knew the constable had fired at the THING. Then came the cry and laugh—almost a laugh of derision—he had heard them before. For one instant the figure lingered and then, before their eyes, faded again into utter blackness. Where it had been was nothing—nothing.

The constable's shot had had no effect.

IV

Three deeply mystified men passed down the hill to the village from the old house. Ernest Weston, the owner, had not spoken since before the—the THING appeared there in the reception-room, or was it in the library? He was not certain—he couldn't have told. Suddenly he turned to the constable.

"I told you not to shoot."

"That's all right," said the constable. "I was there in my official capacity, and I shoot when I want to."

"But the shot did no harm," Hatch put in.

"I would swear it went right through it, too," said the constable, boastfully. "I can shoot."

Weston was arguing with himself. He was a cold-blooded man of business; his mind was not one to play him tricks. Yet now he felt benumbed; he could conceive no explanation of what he had seen. Again in his room in the little hotel, where they spent the remainder of the night, he stared blankly at the reporter.

"Can you imagine any way it could be done?"

Hatch shook his head.

"It isn't a spook, of course," the broker went on, with a nervous smile; "but—but I'm sorry I went. I don't think probably I shall have the work done there as I thought."

They slept only fitfully and took an early train back to Boston. As they were about to separate at the South Station, the broker had a last word.

"I'm going to solve that thing," he declared, determinedly. "I know one man at least who isn't afraid of it—or of anything else. I'm going to send him down to keep a lookout and take care of the place. His name is O'Heagan, and he's a fighting Irishman. If he and that—that—THING ever get mixed up together—"

Like a schoolboy with a hopeless problem, Hatch went straight to The Thinking Machine with the latest developments. The scientist paused just long enough in his work to hear it.

"Did you notice the handwriting?" he demanded.

"Yes," was the reply; "so far as I *could* notice the style of a handwriting that floated in air."

"Man's or woman's?"

Hatch was puzzled.

"I couldn't judge," he said. "It seemed to be a bold style, whatever it was. I remember the capital D clearly."

"Was it anything like the handwriting of the broker—what's-his-name?—Ernest Weston?"

"I never saw his handwriting."

"Look at some of it, then, particularly the capital D's," instructed The Thinking Machine. Then, after a pause: "You say the figure is white and seems to be flaming?"

"Yes."

"Does it give out any light? That is, does it light up a room, for instance?"

"I don't quite know what you mean."

"When you go into a room with a lamp," explained The Thinking Machine, "it lights the room. Does this thing do it? Can you see the floor or walls or anything by the light of the figure itself?"

"No," replied Hatch, positively.

"I'll go down with you to-morrow night," said the scientist, as if that were all.

"Thanks," replied Hatch, and he went away.

Next day about noon he called at Ernest Weston's office. The broker was in.

"Did you send down your man O'Heagan?" he asked.

"Yes," said the broker, and he was almost smiling.

"What happened?"

"He's outside. I'll let him tell you."

The broker went to the door and spoke to some one and O'Heagan entered. He was a big, blue-eyed Irishman, frankly freckled and red-headed—one of those men who look trouble in the face and are glad of it if the trouble can be reduced to a fighting basis. An everlasting smile was about his lips, only now it was a bit faded.

"Tell Mr. Hatch what happened last night," requested the broker.

O'Heagan told it. He, too, had sought to get hold of the flaming figure. As he ran for it, it disappeared, was obliterated, wiped out, gone, and he found himself groping in the darkness of the room beyond, the library. Like Hatch, he took the nearest way out, which happened to be through a window already smashed.

"Outside," he went on, "I began to think about it, and I saw there was nothing to be afraid of, but you couldn't have convinced me of that when I was inside. I took a lantern in one hand and a revolver in the other and went all over that house. There was nothing; if there had been we would have had it out right there. But there was nothing. So I started out to the barn, where I had put a cot in a room.

"I went upstairs to this room—it was then about two o'clock—and went to sleep. It seemed to be an hour or so later when I awoke suddenly—I knew something was happening. And the Lord forgive me if I'm a liar, but there was a cat—a ghost cat in my room, racing around like mad. I just naturally got up to see what was the matter and rushed for the door. The cat beat me to it, and cut a flaming streak through the night.

"The cat looked just like the thing inside the house—that is, it was a sort of shadowy, waving white light like it might be afire. I went back to bed in disgust, to sleep it off. You see, sir," he apologized to Weston, "that there hadn't been anything yet I could put my hands on."

"Was that all?" asked Hatch, smilingly.

"Just the beginning. Next morning when I awoke I was bound to my cot, hard and fast. My hands were tied and my feet were tied, and all I could do was lie there and yell. After awhile, it seemed years, I heard some one outside and shouted louder than ever. Then the constable came up and let me loose. I told him all about it—and then I came to Boston. And with your permission, Mr. Weston, I resign right now. I'm not afraid of anything I can fight, but when I can't get hold of it—well—"

Later Hatch joined The Thinking Machine. They caught a train for the little village by the sea. On the way The Thinking Machine asked a few questions, but most of the time he was silent, squinting out the window. Hatch respected his silence, and only answered questions.

"Did you see Ernest Weston's handwriting?" was the first of these.

"Yes."

"The capital D's?"

"They are not unlike the one the—the THING wrote, but they are not wholly like it," was the reply.

"Do you know anyone in Providence who can get some information for you?" was the next query.

"Yes."

"Get him by long-distance 'phone when we get to this place and let me talk to him a moment."

Half an hour later The Thinking Machine was talking over the long-distance 'phone to the Providence correspondent of Hatch's paper. What he said or what he learned there was not revealed to the wondering reporter, but he came out after several minutes, only to re-enter the booth and remain for another half an hour.

"Now," he said.

Together they went to the haunted house. At the entrance to the grounds something else occurred to The Thinking Machine.

"Run over to the 'phone and call Weston," he directed. "Ask him if he has a motor-boat or if his cousin has one. We might need one. Also find out what kind of a boat it is—electric or gasoline."

Hatch returned to the village and left the scientist alone, sitting on the veranda gazing out over the sea. When Hatch returned he was still in the same position.

"Well?" he asked.

"Ernest Weston has no motor-boat," the reporter informed

him. "George Weston has an electric, but we can't get it because it is away. Maybe I can get one somewhere else if you particularly want it."

"Never mind," said The Thinking Machine. He spoke as if he had entirely lost interest in the matter.

Together they started around the house to the kitchen door.

"What's the next move?" asked Hatch.

"I'm going to find the jewels," was the startling reply.

"Find them?" Hatch repeated.

"Certainly."

They entered the house through the kitchen and the scientist squinted this way and that, through the reception-room, the library, and finally the back hallway. Here a closed door in the flooring led to a cellar.

In the cellar they found heaps of litter. It was damp and chilly and dark. The Thinking Machine stood in the center, or as near the center as he could stand, because the base of the chimney occupied this precise spot, and apparently did some mental calculation.

From that point he started around the walls, solidly built of stone, stooping and running his fingers along the stones as he walked. He made the entire circuit as Hatch looked on. Then he made it again, but this time with his hands raised above his head, feeling the walls carefully as he went. He repeated this at the chimney, going carefully around the masonry, high and low.

"Dear me, dear me!" he exclaimed, petulantly. "You are taller than I am, Mr. Hatch. Please feel carefully around the top of this chimney base and see if the rocks are all solidly set."

Hatch then began a tour. At last one of the great stones which made this base trembled under his hand.

"It's loose," he said.

"Take it out."

It came out after a deal of tugging.

"Put your hand in there and pull out what you find," was the next order. Hatch obeyed. He found a wooden box, about eight inches square, and handed it to The Thinking Machine.

"Ah!" exclaimed that gentleman.

A quick wrench caused the decaying wood to crumble. Tumbling out of the box were the jewels which had been lost for fifty years.

V

Excitement, long restrained, burst from Hatch in a laugh —almost hysterical. He stooped and gathered up the fallen jewelry and handed it to The Thinking Machine, who stared at him in mild surprise.

"What's the matter?" inquired the scientist.

"Nothing," Hatch assured him, but again he laughed.

The heavy stone which had been rolled out of place was lifted up and forced back into position, and together they returned to the village, with the long-lost jewelry loose in their pockets.

"How did you do it?" asked Hatch.

"Two and two always make four," was the enigmatic reply. "It was merely a sum in addition." There was a pause as they walked on, then: "Don't say anything about finding this, or even hint at it in any way, until you have my permission to do so."

Hatch had no intention of doing so. In his mind's eye he saw a story, a great, vivid, startling story spread all over his newspaper about flaming phantoms and treasure trove—$100,000 in jewels. It staggered him. Of course he would say nothing about it—even hint at it, yet. But when he did say something about it—!

In the village The Thinking Machine found the constable.

"I understand some blood was thrown on you at the Weston place the other night?"

"Yes. Blood—warm blood."

"You wiped it off with your handkerchief?"

"Yes."

"Have you the handkerchief?"

"I suppose I might get it," was the doubtful reply. "It might have gone into the wash."

"Astute person," remarked The Thinking Machine.

"There might have been a crime and you throw away the one thing which would indicate it—the blood stains."

The constable suddenly took notice.

"By ginger!" he said. "Wait here and I'll go see if I can find it."

He disappeared and returned shortly with the handkerchief. There were half a dozen blood stains on it, now dark brown.

The Thinking Machine dropped into the village drug store and had a short conversation with the owner, after which he disappeared into the compounding room at the back and remained for an hour or more—until darkness set in. Then he came out and joined Hatch, who, with the constable, had been waiting.

The reporter did not ask any questions, and The Thinking Machine volunteered no information.

"Is it too late for anyone to get down from Boston tonight?" he asked the constable.

"No. He could take the eight o'clock train and be here about half-past nine."

"Mr. Hatch, will you wire to Mr. Weston—Ernest Weston—and ask him to come to-night, sure. Impress on him the fact that it is a matter of the greatest importance."

Instead of telegraphing, Hatch went to the telephone and spoke to Weston at his club. The trip would interfere with some other plans, the broker explained, but he would come. The Thinking Machine had meanwhile been conversing with the constable and had given some sort of instructions which evidently amazed that official exceedingly, for he kept repeating "By ginger!" with considerable fervor.

"And not one word or hint of it to anyone," said The Thinking Machine. "Least of all to the members of your family."

"By ginger!" was the response, and the constable went to supper.

The Thinking Machine and Hatch had their supper thoughtfully that evening in the little village "hotel." Only once did Hatch break this silence.

"You told me to see Weston's handwriting," he said. "Of course you knew he was with the constable and myself when we saw the THING, therefore it would have been impossible—"

"Nothing is impossible," broke in The Thinking Machine. "Don't say that, please."

"I mean that, as he was with us—"

"We'll end the ghost story to-night," interrupted the scientist.

Ernest Weston arrived on the nine-thirty train and had a long, earnest conversation with The Thinking Machine, while Hatch was permitted to cool his toes in solitude. At last they joined the reporter.

"Take a revolver by all means," instructed The Thinking Machine.

"Do you think that necessary?" asked Weston.

"It is—absolutely," was the emphatic response.

Weston left them after awhile. Hatch wondered where he had gone, but no information was forthcoming. In a general sort of way he knew that The Thinking Machine was to go to the haunted house, but he didn't know when; he didn't even know if he was to accompany him.

At last they started, The Thinking Machine swinging a hammer he had borrowed from his landlord. The night was perfectly black, even the road at their feet was invisible. They stumbled frequently as they walked on up the cliff toward the house, dimly standing out against the sky. They entered by way of the kitchen, passed through to the stairs in the main hall, and there Hatch indicated in the darkness the spot from which he had twice seen the flaming phantom.

"You go in the drawing-room behind here," The Thinking Machine instructed. "Don't make any noise whatever."

For hours they waited, neither seeing the other. Hatch heard his heart thumping heavily; if only he could see the other man; with an effort he recovered from a rapidly growing nervousness and waited, waited. The Thinking Machine sat perfectly rigid on the stair, the hammer in his right hand, squinting steadily through the darkness.

At last he heard a noise, a slight nothing; it might almost have been his imagination. It was as if something had glided across the floor, and he was more alert than ever. Then came the dread misty light in the reception-hall, or was it in the library? He could not say. But he looked, looked, with every sense alert.

Gradually the light grew and spread, a misty whiteness which was unmistakably light, but which did not illuminate anything around it. The Thinking Machine saw it without the tremor of a nerve; saw the mistiness grow more marked in certain places, saw these lines gradually grow into the figure of a person, a person who was the center of a white light.

Then the mistiness fell away and The Thinking Machine saw the outline in bold relief. It was that of a tall figure, clothed in a robe, with head covered by a sort of hood, also luminous. As The Thinking Machine looked he saw an arm raised, and in the hand he saw a dagger. The attitude of the figure was distinctly a threat. And yet The Thinking Machine had not begun to grow nervous; he was only interested.

As he looked, the other hand of the apparition was raised and seemed to point directly at him. It moved through the air in bold sweeps, and The Thinking Machine saw the word "Death," written in air luminously, swimming before his eyes. Then he blinked incredulously. There came a wild, demoniacal shriek of laughter from somewhere. Slowly, slowly the scientist crept down the steps in his stocking feet, silent as the apparition itself, with the hammer still in his hand. He crept on, on toward the figure. Hatch, not knowing the movements of The Thinking Machine, stood waiting for something, he didn't know what. Then the thing he had been waiting for happened. There was a sudden loud clatter as of broken glass, the phantom and writing faded, crumbled up, disappeared, and somewhere in the old house there was the hurried sound of steps. At last the reporter heard his name called quietly. It was The Thinking Machine.

"Mr. Hatch, come here."

The reporter started, blundering through the darkness toward the point whence the voice had come. Some irresistible thing swept down upon him; a crashing blow descended on his head, vivid lights flashed before his eyes; he fell. After a while, from a great distance, it seemed, he heard faintly a pistol shot.

THE FLAMING PHANTOM

VI

When Hatch fully recovered consciousness it was with the flickering light of a match in his eyes—a match in the hand of The Thinking Machine, who squinted anxiously at him as he grasped his left wrist. Hatch, instantly himself again, sat up suddenly.

"What's the matter?" he demanded.

"How's your head?" came the answering question.

"Oh," and Hatch suddenly recalled those incidents which had immediately preceded the crash on his head. "Oh, it's all right, my head, I mean. What happened?"

"Get up and come along," requested The Thinking Machine, tartly. "There's a man shot down here."

Hatch arose and followed the slight figure of the scientist through the front door, and toward the water. A light glimmered down near the water and was dimly reflected; above, the clouds had cleared somewhat and the moon was struggling through.

"What hit me, anyhow?" Hatch demanded, as they went. He rubbed his head ruefully.

"The ghost," said the scientist. "I think probably he has a bullet in him now—the ghost."

Then the figure of the town constable separated itself from the night and approached.

"Who's that?"

"Professor Van Dusen and Mr. Hatch."

"Mr. Weston got him all right," said the constable, and there was satisfaction in his tone. "He tried to come out the back way, but I had that fastened, as you told me, and he came through the front way. Mr. Weston tried to stop him, and he raised the knife to stick him; then Mr. Weston shot. It broke his arm, I think. Mr. Weston is down there with him now."

The Thinking Machine turned to the reporter.

"Wait here for me, with the constable," he directed. "If the man is hurt he needs attention. I happen to be a doctor; I can aid him. Don't come unless I call."

For a long while the constable and the reporter waited. The constable talked, talked with all the bottled-up vigor of days. Hatch listened impatiently; he was eager to go down there where The Thinking Machine and Weston and the phantom were.

After half an hour the light disappeared, then he heard the swift, quick churning of waters, a sound as of a powerful motor-boat maneuvering, and a long body shot out on the waters.

"All right down there?" Hatch called.

"All right," came the response.

There was again silence, then Ernest Weston and The Thinking Machine came up.

"Where is the other man?" asked Hatch.

"The ghost—where is he?" echoed the constable.

"He escaped in the motor-boat," replied Mr. Weston, easily.

"Escaped?" exclaimed Hatch and the constable together.

"Yes, escaped," repeated The Thinking Machine, irritably. "Mr. Hatch, let's go to the hotel."

Struggling with a sense of keen disappointment, Hatch followed the other two men silently. The constable walked beside him, also silent. At last they reached the hotel and bade the constable, a sadly puzzled, bewildered and crestfallen man, good-night.

"By ginger!" he remarked, as he walked away into the dark.

Upstairs the three men sat, Hatch impatiently waiting to hear the story. Weston lighted a cigarette and lounged back; The Thinking Machine sat with finger tips pressed together, studying the ceiling.

"Mr. Weston, you understand, of course, that I came into this thing to aid Mr. Hatch?" he asked.

"Certainly," was the response. "I will only ask a favor of him when you conclude."

The Thinking Machine changed his position slightly, readjusted his thick glasses for a long, comfortable squint, and told the story, from the beginning, as he always told a story. Here it is:

"Mr. Hatch came to me in a state of abject, cringing fear and told me of the mystery. It would be needless to go over his examination of the house, and all that. It is enough to say that he noted and told me of four large mirrors in the dining-room and living-room of the house; that he heard and brought to me the stories in detail of a tragedy in the old house and missing jewels, valued at a hundred thousand dollars, or more.

"He told me of his trip to the house that night, and of actually seeing the phantom. I have found in the past that Mr. Hatch is a cool, level-headed young man, not given to imagining things which are not there, and controls himself well. Therefore I knew that anything of charlatanism must be clever, exceedingly clever, to bring about such a condition of mind in him.

"Mr. Hatch saw, as others had seen, the figure of a phantom in the reception-room near the door of the library, or in the library near the door of the reception-room, he couldn't tell exactly. He knew it was near the door. Preceding the appearance of the figure he heard a slight noise which he attributed to a rat running across the floor. Yet the house had not been occupied for five years. Rodents rarely remain in a house—I may say never—for that long if it is uninhabited. Therefore what was this noise? A noise made by the apparition itself? How?

"Now, there is only one white light of the kind Mr. Hatch described known to science. It seems almost superfluous to name it. It is phosphorus, compounded with Fuller's earth and glycerine and one or two other chemicals, so it will not instantly flame as it does in the pure state when exposed to air. Phosphorus has a very pronounced odor if one is within, say, twenty feet of it. Did Mr. Hatch smell anything? No.

"Now, here we have several facts, these being that the apparition in appearing made a slight noise; that phosphorus was the luminous quality; that Mr. Hatch did not smell phosphorus even when he ran though the spot where the phantom had appeared. Two and two make four; Mr. Hatch saw phosphorus, passed through the spot where he had seen it, but did not smell it, therefore it was not there. It was a reflection he saw—a reflection of phosphorus. So far, so good.

"Mr. Hatch saw a finger lifted and write a luminous word

in the air. Again he did not actutlly see this; he saw a reflection of it. This first impression of mine was substantiated by the fact that when he rushed for the phantom *a part of it* disappeared, first half of it, he said—then the other half. So his extended hands grasped only air.

"Obviously those reflections had been made on something, probably a mirror as the most perfect ordinary reflecting surface. Yet he actually passed through the spot where he had seen the apparition and had not struck a mirror. He found himself in another room, the library, having gone through a door which, that afternoon, he had himself closed. He did not open it then.

"Instantly a sliding mirror suggested itself to me to fit all these conditions. He saw the apparition in the door, then saw only half of it, then all of it disappeared. He passed through the spot where it had been. All of this would have happened easily if a large mirror, working as a sliding door, and hidden in the wall, were there. Is it clear?"

"Perfectly," said Mr. Weston.

"Yes," said Hatch, eagerly. "Go on."

"This sliding mirror, too, might have made the noise which Mr. Hatch imagined was a rat. Mr. Hatch had previously told me of four large mirrors in the living and dining-rooms. With these, from the position in which he said they were, I readily saw how the reflection could have been made.

"In a general sort of way, in my own mind, I had accounted for the phantom. Why was it there? This seemed a more difficult problem. It was possible that it had been put there for amusement, but I did not wholly accept this. Why? Partly because no one had ever heard of it until the Italian workmen went there. Why did it appear just at the moment they went to begin the work Mr. Weston had ordered? Was it the purpose to keep the workmen away?

"These questions arose in my mind in order. Then, as Mr. Hatch had told me of a tragedy in the house and hidden jewels, I asked him to learn more of these. I called his attention to the fact that it would be a queer circumstance if these jewels were still somewhere in the old house. Suppose some one who knew of their existence were searching for them, believed he could find them, and wanted something which would effectually drive away any inquiring persons, tramps or villagers, who might appear there at night. A ghost? Perhaps.

"Suppose some one wanted to give the old house such a reputation that Mr. Weston would not care to undertake the work of repair and refurnishing. A ghost? Again perhaps. In a shallow mind this ghost might have been interpreted even as an effort to prevent the marriage of Miss Everard and Mr. Weston. Therefore Mr. Hatch was instructed to get all the facts possible about you, Mr. Weston, and members of your family. I reasoned that members of your own family would be more likely to know of the lost jewels than anyone else after a lapse of fifty years.

"Well, what Mr. Hatch learned from you and your cousin, George Weston, instantly, in my mind, established a motive for the ghost. It was, as I had supposed, an effort to drive workmen away, perhaps only for a time, while a search was made for the jewels. The old tragedy in the house was a good pretext to hang a ghost on. A clever mind conceived it and a clever mind put it into operation.

"Now, what one person knew most about the jewels? Your cousin George, Mr. Weston. Had he recently acquired any new information as to these jewels? I didn't know. I thought it possible. Why? On his own statement that his mother, then a bride, got the story of the entire affair direct from his grandmother, who remembered more of it than anybody else—who might even have heard his grandfather say where he intended hiding the jewels."

The Thinking Machine paused for a little while, shifted his position, then went on:

"George Weston refused to go with you, Mr. Weston, and Mr. Hatch, to the ghost party, as you called it, because he said he was going to a ball in Providence that night. He did not go to Providence; I learned that from your correspondent there, Mr. Hatch; so George Weston might, possibly, have gone to the ghost party after all.

"After I looked over the situation down there it occurred to me that the most feasible way for a person, who wished to avoid being seen in the village, as the perpetrator of the ghost did, was to go to and from the place at night in a motor-boat. He could easily run in the dark and land at the foot of the cliff, and no soul in the village would be any the wiser. Did George Weston have a motor-boat? Yes, an electric, which runs almost silently.

"From this point the entire matter was comparatively simple. I *knew*—the pure logic of it told me—how the ghost was made to appear and disappear; one look at the house inside convinced me beyond all doubt. I knew the motive for the ghost—a search for the jewels. I knew, or thought I knew, the name of the man who was seeking the jewels; the man who had fullest knowledge and fullest opportunity, the man whose brain was clever enough to devise the scheme. Then, the next step to prove what I knew. The first thing to do was to find the jewels."

"Find the jewels?" Weston repeated, with a slight smile.

"Here they are," said The Thinking Machine, quietly.

And there, before the astonished eyes of the broker, he drew out the gems which had been lost for fifty years. Mr. Weston was not amazed; he was petrified with astonishment and sat staring at the glittering heap in silence. Finally he recovered his voice.

"How did you do it?" he demanded. "Where?"

"I used my brain, that's all," was the reply. "I went into the old house seeking them where the owner, under all conditions, would have been most likely to hide them, and there I found them."

"But—but—" stammered the broker.

"The man who hid these jewels hid them only temporarily, or at least that was his purpose," said The Thinking Machine, irritably. "Naturally he would not hide them in the woodwork of the house, because that might burn; he did not bury them in the cellar, because that has been carefully searched. Now, in that house there is nothing except woodwork and chimneys above the cellar. Yet he hid them in the house, proven by the fact that the man he killed was killed in the house, and that the outside ground, covered with snow, showed two sets of tracks into the house and none out. Therefore he did hide them in the cellar. Where? In the stonework. There was no other place.

"Naturally he would not hide them on a level with the eye, because the spot where he took out and replaced a stone would be apparent if a close search were made. He would, therefore, place them either above or below the eye level. He placed them above. A large loose stone in the chimney was taken out and there was the box with these things."

Mr. Weston stared at The Thinking Machine with a new wonder and admiration in his eyes.

"With the jewels found and disposed of, there remained only to prove the ghost theory by an actual test. I sent for you, Mr. Weston, because I thought possibly, as no actual crime had been committed, it would be better to leave the guilty man to you. When you came I went into the haunted house with a hammer—an ordinary hammer—and waited on the steps.

"At last the ghost laughed and appeared. I crept down the steps where I was sitting in my stocking feet. I knew what it was. Just when I reached the luminous phantom I disposed of it for all time by smashing it with a hammer. It shattered a large sliding mirror which ran in the door inside the frame, as I had thought. The crash startled the man who operated the ghost from the top of a box, giving it the appearance of extreme height, and he started out through the kitchen, as he had entered. The constable had barred that door after the man entered; therefore the ghost turned and came toward the front door of the house. There he ran into and struck down Mr. Hatch, and ran out through the front door, which I afterward found was not securely fastened. You know the rest of it; how you found the motorboat and waited there for him; how he came there, and—"

"Tried to stab me," Weston supplied. "I had to shoot to save myself."

"Well, the wound is trivial," said The Thinking Machine. "His arm will heal up in a little while. I think then, perhaps, a little trip of four or five years in Europe, at your expense, in return for the jewels, might restore him to health."

"I was thinking of that myself," said the broker, quietly. "Of course, I couldn't prosecute."

"The ghost, then, was—?" Hatch began.

"George Weston, my cousin," said the broker. "There are some things in this story which I hope you may see fit to leave unsaid, if you can do so with justice to yourself."

Hatch considered it.

"I think there are," he said, finally, and he turned to The Thinking Machine. "Just where was the man who operated the phantom?"

"In the dining-room, beside the butler's pantry," was the reply. "With that pantry door closed he put on the robe already covered with phosphorus, and merely stepped out. The figure was reflected in the tall mirror directly in front, as you enter the dining-room from the back, from there reflected to the mirror on the opposite wall in the living-room, and thence reflected to the sliding mirror in the door which led from the reception-hall to the library. This is the one I smashed."

"And how was the writing done?"

"Oh, that? Of course that was done by reversed writing on a piece of clear glass held before the apparition as he posed. This made it read straight to anyone who might see the last reflection in the reception-hall."

"And the blood thrown on the constable and the others when the ghost was in the yard?" Hatch went on.

"Was from a dog. A test I made in the drug store showed that. It was a desperate effort to drive the villagers away and keep them away. The ghost cat and the tying of the watchman to his bed were easily done."

All sat silent for a time. At length Mr. Weston arose, thanked the scientist for the recovery of the jewels, bade them all good-night and was about to go out. Mechanically Hatch was following. At the door he turned back for the last question.

"How was it that the shot the constable fired didn't break the mirror?"

"Because he was nervous and the bullet struck the door beside the mirror," was the reply. "I dug it out with a knife. Good-night."

The Mystery of a Studio

BY JACQUES FUTRELLE

The Mystery of a Studio

BY JACQUES FUTRELLE

I

WHERE the light slants down softly into one corner of a noted art museum in Boston there hangs a large picture. Its title is "Fulfillment." Discriminating art critics have alternately raved at it and praised it; from the day it appeared there it has been a fruitful source of acrimonious discussion. As for the public, it accepts the picture as a startling, amazing thing of beauty, and there is always a crowd around it.

"Fulfillment" is typified by a woman. She stands boldly forth against a languorous background of deep tones. Flesh tints are daringly laid on the semi-nude figure, diaphanous draperies hide, yet, reveal, the exquisite lines of the body. Her arms are outstretched straight toward the spectator, the black hair ripples down over her shoulders, the red lips are slightly parted. The mysteries of complete achievement and perfect life lie in her eyes.

Into this picture the artist wove the spiritual and the worldly; here he placed on canvas an elusive portrayal of success in its fullest and widest meaning. One's first impression of the picture is that it is sensual; another glance shows the underlying typification of success, and love and life are there. One by one the qualities stand forth.

The artist was Constans St. George. After the first flurry of excitement which the picture caused there came a whirlwind of criticism. Then the artist, who had labored for months on the work which he had intended and which proved to be his masterpiece, collapsed. Some said it was overwork—they were partly right; others that it was grief at the attacks of critics who did not see beyond the surface of the painting. Perhaps they, too, were partly right.

However that may be, it is a fact that for several months after the picture was exhibited St. George was in a sanitarium. The physicians said it was nervous collapse—a total breaking-down, and there were fears for his sanity. At length there came an improvement in his condition, and he returned to the world. Since then he had lived quietly in his studio, one of many in a large office building. From time to time he had been approached with offers for the picture, but always he refused to sell. A New York millionaire made a flat proposition of fifty thousand dollars, which was as flatly refused.

The artist loved the picture as a child of his own brain; every day he visited the museum where it was exhibited and stood looking at it with something almost like adoration in his eyes. Then he went away quietly, tugging at his straggling beard and with the dim blindness of tears in his eyes. He never spoke to anyone; and always avoided that moment when a crowd was about.

Whatever the verdict of the critics or of the public on "Fulfillment," it was an admitted fact that the artist had placed on canvas a representation of a wonderfully beautiful woman. Therefore, after a while the question of who had been the model for "Fulfillment" was aroused. No one knew, apparently. Artists who knew St. George could give no idea—they only knew that the woman who had posed was not a professional model.

This led to speculation, in which the names of some of the most beautiful women in the United States were mentioned. Then a romance was woven. This was that the artist was in love with the original and that his collapse was partly due to her refusal to wed him. This story, as it went, was elaborated until the artist was said to be pining away for love of one whom he had immortalized in oils.

As the story grew it gained credence, and a search was still made occasionally for the model. Half a dozen times Hutchinson Hatch, a newspaper reporter of more than usual astuteness, had been on the story without success; he had seen and studied the picture until every line of it was firmly in his mind. He had seen and talked to St. George twice. The artist would answer no questions as to the identity of the model.

THE MYSTERY OF A STUDIO

This, then, was the situation on the morning of Friday, November 27, when Hatch entered the reportorial rooms of his newspaper. At sight of him the City Editor removed his cigar, placed it carefully on the "official block" which adorned his flat-topped desk, and called to the reporter.

"Girl reported missing," he said, brusquely. "Name is Grace Field, and she lived at No. 195 —— Street, Dorchester. Employed in the photographic department of the Star, a big department store. Report of her disappearance made to the police early to-day by Ellen Stanford, her room-mate, also employed at the Star. Jump out on it and get all you can. Here is the official police description."

Hatch took a slip of paper and read:

"Grace Field, twenty-one years, five feet seven inches tall, weight 151 pounds, profuse black hair, dark-brown eyes, superb figure, oval face, said to be beautiful."

Then the description went into details of her dress and other things which the police note in their minute records for a search. Hatch absorbed all these things and left his office. He went first to the department store, where he was told Miss Stanford had not appeared that day, sending a note that she was ill.

From the store Hatch went at once to the address given in Dorchester. Miss Stanford was in. Would she see a reporter? Yes. So Hatch was ushered into the modest little parlor of a boarding-house, and after a while Miss Stanford entered. She was a petite blonde, with pink cheeks and blue eyes, now reddened by weeping.

Briefly Hatch explained the purpose of his visit—an effort to find Grace Field, and Miss Stanford eagerly and tearfully expressed herself as willing to tell him all she knew.

"I have known Grace for five months," she explained; "that is, from the time she came to work at the Star. Her counter is next to mine. A friendship grew up between us, and we began rooming together. Each of us is alone in the East. She comes from the West, somewhere in Nevada, and I come from Quebec.

"Grace has never said much about herself, but I know that she had been in Boston a year or so before I met her. She lived somewhere in Brookline, I believe, but it seems that she had some funds and did not go to work until she came to the Star. This is as I understand it.

"Three days ago, on Tuesday it was, there was a letter for Grace when we came in from work. It seemed to agitate her, although she said nothing to me about what was in it, and I did not ask. She did not sleep well that night, but next morning, when we started to work, she seemed all right. That is, she was all right until we got to the subway station, and then she told me to go on to the store, saying she would be there after a while.

"I left her, and at her request explained to the manager of our floor that she would be late. From that time to this no one has seen her or heard of her. I don't know where she could have gone." and the girl burst into tears. "I'm sure something dreadful has happened to her."

"Possibly an elopement?" Hatch suggested.

"No," said the girl, quickly. "No. She was in love, but the man she was in love with has not heard of her either. I saw him the night after she disappeared. He called here and asked for her, and seemed surprised that she had not returned home, or had not been at work."

"What's his name?" asked Hatch.

"He's a clerk in a bank," said Miss Stanford. "His name is Willis—Victor Willis. If she had eloped with him I would not have been surprised, but I am positive she did not, and if she did not, where is she?"

"Were there any other admirers you know of?" Hatch asked.

"No," said the girl, stoutly. "There may have been others who admired her, but none she cared for. She has told me too much—I—I know," she faltered.

"How long have you known Mr. Willis?" asked Hatch.

The girl's face flamed scarlet instantly.

"Only since I've known Grace," she replied. "She introduced us."

"Has Mr. Willis ever shown you any attention?"

"Certainly not," Miss Stanford flashed, angrily. "All his attention was for Grace."

There was the least trace of bitterness in the tone, and

Hatch imagined he read it aright. Willis was a man whom both perhaps loved; it might be in that event that Miss Stanford knew more than she had said of the whereabouts of Grace Field. The next step was to see Willis.

"I suppose you'll do everything possible to find Miss Field?" he asked.

"Certainly," said the girl.

"Have you her photograph?"

"I have one, yes, but I don't think—I don't believe Grace—"

"Would like to have it published?" asked Hatch. "Possibly not, under ordinary circumstances—but now that she is missing it is the surest way of getting a trace of her. Will you give it to me?"

Miss Stanford was silent for a time. Then apparently she made up her mind, for she arose.

"It might be well, too," Hatch suggested, "to see if you can find the letter you mentioned."

The girl nodded and went out. When she returned she had a photograph in her hand; a glimpse of it told Hatch it was a bust picture of a woman in evening dress. The girl was studying a scrap of paper.

"What is it?" asked Hatch, quickly.

"I don't know," she responded. "I was searching for the letter when I remembered she frequently tore them up and dropped them into the waste-basket. It had been emptied every day, but I looked and found this clinging to the bottom, caught between the cane."

"May I see it?" asked the reporter.

The girl handed it to him. It was evidently a piece of a letter torn from the outer edge just where the paper was folded to put it into the envelope. On it were these words and detached letters, written in a bold hand:

sday
ill you
to the
ho

Hatch's eyes opened wide.

"Do you know the handwriting?" he asked.

The girl faltered an instant.

"No," she answered, finally.

Hatch studied her face a moment with cold eyes, then turned the scrap of paper over. The other side was blank. Staring down at it he veiled a glitter of anxious interest.

"And the picture?" he asked, quietly.

The girl handed him the photograph. Hatch took it and as he looked it was with difficulty he restrained an exclamation of astonishment—triumphant astonishment. Finally, with his brain teeming with possibilities, he left the house, taking the photograph and the scrap of paper. Ten minutes later he was talking to his City Editor over the 'phone.

"It's a great story," he explained, briefly. "The missing girl is the mysterious model of St. George's picture, 'Fulfillment.' "

"Great," came the voice of the City Editor.

II

Having laid his story before his City Editor, Hatch sat down to consider the fragmentary writing. Obviously "sday" represented a day of the week—either Tuesday, Wednesday, or Thursday, these being the only days where the letter "s" preceded the "day." This seemed to be a definite fact, but still it meant nothing. True, Miss Field had last been seen on Wednesday, but then?—nothing.

To the next part of the fragment Hatch attached the greatest importance. It was the possibility of a threat, —— "ill you." Did it mean "kill you" or "will you" or "till you" or—or what? There might be dozens of other words ending in "ill" which he did not recall at the moment. His imagination hammered the phrase into his brain as "kill you." The "to the"—the next words—were clear, but meant nothing at all. The last letters were distinctly "ho," possibly "hope."

Then Hatch began real work on the story. First he saw the bank clerk, Victor Willis, who Miss Stanford had said loved Grace Field, and whom Hatch suspected Miss Stanford loved. He found Willis a grim, sullen-faced young man of twenty-eight years, who would say nothing.

From that point Hatch worked vigorously for several hours. At the end of that time he had found out that on Wednesday, the day of Miss Field's disappearance, a veiled woman—probably Grace Field—had called at the bank and inquired for Willis. Later, Willis, urging necessity, had asked to be allowed the day off and left the bank. He did not appear again until next morning. His actions did not impress any of his associates with the idea that he was a bridegroom; in fact, Hatch himself had given up the idea that Miss Field had eloped. There seemed no reason for an elopement.

When Hatch called at the studio, and home, of Constans St. George, to inform him of the disappearance of the model whose identity had been so long guarded, he was told that Mr. St. George was not in; that is, St. George refused to answer knocks at the door, and had not been seen for a day or so. He frequently disappeared this way, his informant said.

With these facts—and lack of facts—in his possession on Friday evening, Hatch called on Professor S. F. X. Van Dusen. The Thinking Machine received him as cordially as he ever received anybody.

"Well, what is it?" he asked.

"I don't believe this is really worth your while, Professor," Hatch said, finally. "It's just a case of a girl who disappeared. There are some things about it which are puzzling, but I'm afraid it's only an elopement."

The Thinking Machine dragged up a footstool, planted his small feet on it comfortably and leaned back in his chair.

"Go on," he directed.

Then Hatch told the story, beginning at the time when the picture was placed in the art museum, and continuing up to the point where he had seen Willis after finding the photograph and the scrap of paper. He had always found that it saved time to begin at the beginning with The Thinking Machine; he did it now as a matter of course.

"And the scrap of paper?" asked The Thinking Machine.

"I have it here," replied the reporter.

For several minutes the scientist examined the fragment and then handed it back to the reporter.

"If one could establish some clear connection between that and the disappearance of the girl it might be valuable," he said. "As it is now, it means nothing. Any number of letters might be thrown into the waste-basket in the room the two girls occupied, therefore dismiss this for the moment."

"But isn't it possible—" Hatch began.

"Anything is possible, Mr. Hatch," retorted the other, belligerently. "You might take occasion to see the handwriting of St. George, the artist, and see if that is his—also look at Willis's. Even if it were Willis's, however, it may mean nothing in connection with this."

"But what could have happened to Miss Field?"

"Any one of fifty things," responded the other. "She might have fallen dead in the street and been removed to a hospital or undertaking establishment; she might have been arrested for shoplifting and given a wrong name; she might have gone mad and gone away; she might have eloped with another man; she might have committed suicide; she might have been murdered. The question is not what *could* have happened, but what *did* happen."

"Yes, I thoroughly understand that," Hatch replied, with a slight smile. "But still I don't see—"

"Probably you don't," snapped the other. "We'll take it for granted that she did none of these things, with the possible exception of eloping, killing herself, or was murdered. You are convinced that she did not elope. Yet you have only run down one possible end of this—that is, the possibility of her elopement with Willis. You don't believe she did elope with him. Well, why not with St. George?"

"St. George?" gasped Hatch. "A great artist elope with a shop-girl?"

"She was his ideal in a picture which you say is one of the greatest in the world," replied the other, testily. "That being true, it is perfectly possible that she was his ideal for a wife, isn't it?"

The matter had not occurred to Hatch in just that light. He nodded his head, with a feeling of having been weighed and found wanting.

"Now, you say, too, that St. George has not been seen around his studio for a couple of days," said the scientist. "What is more possible than that they are together somewhere?"

"I see," said the reporter.

"It was understood, too, as I understand it, that St. George was in love with her," went on The Thinking Machine. "So, I should imagine a solution of the mystery might be reached by taking St. George as the center of the affair. Suicide may be passed by for the moment, because she had no known motive for suicide—rather, if she loved Willis, she had every reason to live. Murder, too, may be passed for the moment—although there is a possibility that we might come back to that. Question St. George. He will listen if you make him, and then he must answer."

"But his place is all closed up," said Hatch. "It is supposed he is half crazy."

"Possibly he might be," said The Thinking Machine. "Or it is possible that he is keeping to his studio at work—or he might even be married to Miss Field and she might be there with him."

"Well, I see no way to ascertain definitely that he is there," said the reporter, and a puzzled wrinkle came into his face. "Of course I might remain on watch night and day to see if he comes out for food, or if anything to eat is sent in."

"That would take too long, and besides it might not happen at all," said The Thinking Machine. He arose and went into the adjoining room. He returned after a moment, and glanced at the clock on the mantel. "It is just nine o'clock now," he commented. "How long would it take you to get to the studio?"

"Half an hour."

"Well, go there now," directed the scientist. "If Mr. St. George is in his studio he will come out of it to-night at thirty-two minutes past nine. He will be running, and may not wear either a hat or coat."

"What?" and Hatch grinned, a weak, puzzled grin.

"You wait where he can't see you when he comes out," the scientist went on. "When he goes he may leave the door open. If he does go on see if you find any trace of Miss

Field, and then, on his return, meet him at the outer door, ask him what you please, and come to see me to-morrow morning. He will be out of his studio about twenty minutes."

Vaguely Hatch felt that the scientist was talking rot, but he had seen this strange mind bring so many odd things to pass that he could not doubt this, even if it were absurd on its face.

"At thirty-two minutes past nine to-night," said the reporter, and he glanced at his watch.

"Come to see me to-morrow after you see the handwriting of Willis and St. George," directed the scientist. "Then you may also tell me just what happens to-night."

. . . .

Hatch was feeling like a fool. He was waiting in a darkened corner, just a few feet from St. George's studio. It was precisely half-past nine o'clock. He had been there for seven minutes. What strange power was to bring St. George, who for two days had denied himself to everyone, out of that studio, if, indeed, he were there?

For the twentieth time Hatch glanced at his watch, which he had set with the little clock in The Thinking Machine's home. Slowly the minute hand crept around, to 9:31, 9:31½, and he heard the door of the studio rattle. Then suddenly it was thrown open and St. George appeared.

Without a glance to right or left, hatless and coatless, he rushed out of the building. Hatch got only a glimpse of his face; his lips were pressed tightly together; there was a glint of madness in his eyes. He jerked at the door once, then ran through the hall and disappeared down the stairs leading to the street. The studio door stood open behind him.

III

When the clatter of the running footsteps had died away and Hatch heard the outer door slam, he entered the studio, closing the door behind him. It was close here, and there was a breath of Chinese incense which was almost stifling. One quick glance by the light of an incandescent told Hatch that he stood in the reception-room. Typically, from floor to ceiling, the place was the abode of an artist; there was a rich gradation of color and everywhere were scraps af art and half-finished studies.

The reporter had given up the idea of solving the mystery of why St. George had so suddenly left his apartments; now he devoted himself to a quick, minute search of the place. He found nothing to interest him in the reception-room, and went on into the studio where the artist did his work.

Hatch glanced around quickly, his eyes taking in all the details, then went to a little table which stood, half-covered with newspapers. He turned these over, then bent forward suddenly and picked up—a woman's glove. Beside it lay its mate. He stuffed them into his pocket.

Eagerly he sought now for anything that might come to hand. At last he reached another door, leading into the bedroom. Here on a large table was a chafing dish, many dishes which had not been washed, and all the other evidences of a careless man who did a great deal of his own cooking. There was a dresser here, too, a gorgeous, mahogany affair. Hatch didn't stop to admire this because his eye was attracted by a woman's veil which lay on it. He thrust it into his pocket.

"Quite a haul I'm making," he mused, grimly.

From this room a door, half open, led into a bathroom. Hatch merely glanced in, then looked at his watch. Fifteen minutes had elapsed. He must get out, and he started for the outer door. As he opened it quietly and stepped into the hall he heard the street door open one flight below, and started down the steps. There, half way, he met St. George.

"Mr. St. George?" he asked.

"No," was the reply.

Hatch knew his man perfectly, because he had seen him half a dozen times and had talked to him twice. The denial of identity therefore was futile.

"I came to tell you that Grace Field, the model for your 'Fulfillment,' has disappeared," Hatch went on, as the other glared at him.

"I don't care," snapped the other. He darted up the steps. Hatch listened until he heard the door of the studio close.

It was ten minutes to ten o'clock when Hatch left the building. Now he would see Miss Stanford and have her identify the gloves and the veil. He boarded a car and drew out and closely examined the gloves and veil. The gloves were tan, rather heavy, but small, and the veil was of some light, cobwebby material which he didn't know by name.

"If these are Grace Field's," the reporter argued, to himself, "it means something. If they are not, I'm simply a burglar."

There was a light in the Dorchester house where Miss Stanford lived, and the reporter rang the bell. A servant appeared.

"Would it be possible for me to see Miss Stanford for just a moment?" he asked.

"If she has not gone to bed."

He was ushered into the little parlor again. The servant disappeared, and after a moment Miss Stanford came in.

"I hated to trouble you so late," said the reporter, and she smiled at him frankly, "but I would like to ask if you have ever seen these?"

He laid in her hands the gloves and the veil. Miss Stanford studied them carefully and her hands trembled.

"The gloves, I know, are Grace's—the veil I am not so positive about," she replied.

Hatch felt a great wave of exultation sweep over him, and it stopped his tongue for an instant.

"Did you—did you find them in Mr. Willis's possession?" asked the girl.

"I am not at liberty to tell just where I found them," Hatch replied. "If they are Miss Field's—and you can swear to that, I suppose—it may mean that we have a clew."

"Oh, I was afraid it would be this way," gasped the girl, and she sank down weeping on a couch.

"Knew what would be which way?" asked Hatch, puzzled.

"I knew it! I knew it!" she sobbed. "Is there anything to connect Mr. Willis directly with the—*the murder?*"

The reporter started to say something, then paused. He wasn't quite sure of himself. He had uncovered something, he didn't know what yet.

"It would be better, Miss Stanford," he explained, gently, "if you would tell me all you know about this affair. The things which are now in my possession are fragmentary—if you could give me any new detail it would be only serving the ends of justice."

For a little while the girl was silent, then she arose and faced him.

"Is Mr. Willis yet under arrest?" she asked, calmly now.

"Not yet," said the reporter.

"Then I will say nothing else," she declared, and her lips closed in a straight line.

'What was the motive for murder?" Hatch insisted.

"I will say nothing else," she replied, firmly.

"And what makes you positive there was murder?"

"Good-night. You need not come again, for I will not see you."

Miss Stanford turned and left the room.

Hatch, sadly puzzled, bewildered, stood staring after her a moment, then went out, his brain alive with possibilities, with intangible ends which would not be connected. He was eager to lay the new facts before The Thinking Machine.

From Dorchester the reporter took a car for his home. In his room, with the tangible threads of the mystery spread out on a table, he thought and surmised far into the night, and when he finally replaced them all in his pocket and turned down the light it was with a hopeless shake of his head.

On the following morning when Hatch arose he picked up a paper and went to breakfast. He spread the paper before him and there—the first thing he saw—was a huge headline, stating that a burglar had entered the room of Constans St. George and had tried to kill Mr. St. George. A shot had been fired at him and had passed through his left arm.

Mr. St. George had been asleep when the door of his apartments was burst in by the thief. The artist arose at the noise, and as he stepped into the reception-room had been shot. The wound was trivial. The burglar escaped; there was no clew.

THE MYSTERY OF A STUDIO

IV

It was a long story of seemingly hopeless complications that Hatch told The Thinking Machine that morning. Nothing connected with anything, and yet here was a series of happenings, all apparently growing out of the disappearance of Miss Field, and which must have some relation one to the other. At the conclusion of the story, Hatch passed over the newspaper containing the account of the burglary in the studio. The artist had been removed to a hospital.

The Thinking Machine read the newspaper account and turned to the reporter with a question:

"Did you see Willis's handwriting?"

"Not yet," replied the reporter.

"See it at once," instructed the other. "If possible, bring me a sample of it. Did you see St. George's handwriting?"

"No," the reporter confessed.

"See that and bring me a sample if you can. Find out first if Willis has a revolver now or has ever had. If so, see it and see if it is loaded or empty—its exact condition. Find out also if St. George has a revolver—and if he has one, get possession of it if it is in your power."

The scientist twisted the two gloves and the veil which Hatch had given to him in his fingers idly, then passed them to the reporter again.

Hatch arose and stood waiting, hat in hand.

"Also find out," The Thinking Machine went on, "the exact condition of St. George—his mental condition particularly. Find out if Willis is at his office in the bank today, and, if possible, where and how he spent last night. That's all."

"And Miss Stanford?" asked Hatch.

"Never mind her," replied The Thinking Machine. "I may see her myself. These other things are of immediate consequence. The minute you satisfy yourself come back to me. Quickness on your part may prevent a tragedy."

The reporter went away hurriedly. At four o'clock that afternoon he returned. The Thinking Machine greeted him; he held a piece of letter-paper in his hand.

"Well?" he asked.

"The handwriting is Willis's," said Hatch, without hesitation. "I saw a sample—it is identical, and the paper on which he writes is identical."

The scientist grunted.

"I also saw some of St. George's writing," the reporter went on, as if he were reciting a lesson. "It is wholly dissimilar."

The Thinking Machine nodded.

"Willis has no revolver that anyone ever heard of," Hatch continued. "He was at dinner with several of his fellow employees last night, and left the restaurant at eight o'clock."

"Been drinking?"

"Might have had a few drinks," responded the reporter. "He is not a drinking man."

"Has St. George a revolver?"

"I was unable to find that out or do anything except get a sample of his writing from another artist," the reporter explained. "He is in a hospital, raving crazy. It seems to be a return of the trouble he had once before, except it is worse. The wound itself is not bad."

The scientist was studying the sheet of paper.

"Have you that scrap?" he asked.

Hatch produced it, and the scientist placed it on the sheet; Hatch could only conjecture that he was fitting it to something else already there. He was engaged in this work when Martha entered.

"The young lady who was here earlier to-day wants to see you again," she announced.

"Show her in," directed The Thinking Machine, without raising his eyes.

Martha disappeared, and after a moment Miss Stanford entered. Hatch, himself unnoticed, stared at her curiously, and arose, as did the scientist. The girl's face was flushed a little, and there was an eager expression in her eyes.

"I know he didn't do it," she began. "I've just gotten a letter from Springfield stating that he was there on the day Grace went away—and—"

"Know who didn't do what?" asked the scientist.

"That Mr. Willis didn't kill Grace," replied the girl, her enthusiasm suddenly checked. "See here."

The scientist read a letter which she offered, and the girl sank into a chair. Then for the first time she saw Hatch and her eyes expressed her surprise. She stared at him a moment, then nodded a greeting, after which she fell to watching The Thinking Machine.

"Miss Stanford," he said, at length, "you made several mistakes when you were here before in not telling me the truth—all of it. If you will tell me all you know of this case I may be able to see it more clearly."

The girl reddened and stammered a little, then her lips trembled.

"Do you *know*—not conjecture, but *know*—whether or not Miss Field, or Grace, as you call her, was engaged to Willis?" the irritated voice asked.

"I—I know it, yes," she stammered.

"And you were in love with Mr. Willis—you *are* in love with him?"

Again the tell-tale blush swept over her face. She glanced at Hatch; it was the nervousness of a girl who is driven to a confession of love.

"I regard Mr. Willis very highly," she said, finally, her voice low.

"Well," and the scientist arose and crossed to where the girl sat, "don't you see that a very grave charge might be brought home to you if you don't tell all of this? The girl has disappeared. There might be even a hint of murder in which your name would be mentioned. Don't you see?"

There was a long pause, and the girl stared steadily into the squint eyes above her. Finally her eyes fell.

"I think I understand. Just what is it you want me to answer?"

"Did or did you not ever hear Mr. Willis threaten Miss Field?"

"I did once, yes."

"Did or did you not know that Miss Field was the original of the painting?"

"I did not."

"It is a semi-nude picture, isn't it?"

Again there was a flush in the girl's face.

"I have heard it was," she said. "I have never seen it. I

suggested to Grace several times that we go to see it, but she never would. I understand why now."

"Did Willis know she was the original of that painting? That is, knowing it yourself now, do you have any reason to suppose that he previously knew?"

"I don't know," she said, frankly. "I know that there was something which was always causing friction between them—something they quarreled about. It might have been that. That was when I heard Mr. Willis threaten her—it was something about shooting her if she ever did something—I don't know what."

"Miss Field knew him before you did, I think you said?"

"She introduced me to him."

The Thinking Machine fingered the sheet of paper he held.

"Did you know what those scraps of paper you brought me contained?"

"Yes, in a way," said the girl.

"Why did you bring them, then?"

"Because you told me you knew I had them, and I was afraid it might make more trouble for me and for Mr. Willis if I did not."

The Thinking Machine passed the sheet to Hatch.

"This will interest you. Mr. Hatch," he explained. "Those words and letters in parentheses are what I have supplied to complete the full text of the note, of which you had a mere scrap. You will notice how the scrap you had fitted into it."

The reporter read this:

"If you go to th(at stud)io Wednesday to see that artist, (I will k)ill you bec(ause I w)on't have it known to the world tha(t you a)re a model. I hope you will heed this warning. "V. W."

The reporter stared at the patched-up letter, pasted together with infinite care, and then glanced at The Thinking Machine, who settled himself again comfortably in the chair.

"And now, Miss Stanford," asked the scientist, in a most matter-of-fact tone, "where is the body of Miss Field?"

THE MYSTERY OF A STUDIO

V

The blunt question aroused the girl, and she arose suddenly, staring at The Thinking Machine. He did not move. She stood as if transfixed, and Hatch saw her bosom rise and fall rapidly with the emotion she was seeking to repress.

"Well?" asked The Thinking Machine.

"I don't know," flamed Miss Stanford, suddenly, almost fiercely. "I don't even know she is dead. I know that Mr. Willis did not kill her, because, as that letter I gave you shows, he was in Springfield. I won't be tricked into saying anything further."

The outburst had no appreciable effect on The Thinking Machine beyond causing him to raise his eyebrows slightly as he looked at the defiant little figure.

"When did you last see Mr. Willis have a revolver?"

"I know nothing of any revolver. I know only that Victor Willis is innocent as you are, and that I love him. Whatever has become of Grace Field I don't know."

Tears leaped suddenly to her eyes, and, turning, she left the room. After a moment they heard the outer door slam as she passed out. Hatch turned to the scientist with a question in his eyes.

"Did you smell anything like chloroform or ether when you were in St. George's apartments?" asked The Thinking Machine as he arose.

"No," said Hatch. "I only noticed that the place seemed close, and there was an odor of Chinese incense—joss sticks—which was almost stifling."

The Thinking Machine looked at the reporter quickly, but said nothing. Instead, he passed out of the room, to return a few minutes later with his hat and coat on.

"Where are we going?" asked Hatch.

"To St. George's studio," was the answer.

Just then the telephone bell in the next room rang. The scientist answered it in person.

"Your City Editor," he called to Hatch.

Hatch went to the 'phone and remained there several minutes. When he came back there was a new excitement in his face.

"What is it?" asked the scientist.

"Another queer thing my City Editor told me," Hatch responded. "Constans St. George, raving mad, has escaped from the hospital and disappeared."

"Dear me, dear me!" exclaimed the scientist, quickly. It was as near surprise as he ever showed. "Then there is danger."

With quick steps he went to the telephone and called up Police Headquarters.

"Detective Mallory," Hatch heard him ask for. "Yes. This is Professor Van Dusen. Please meet me immediately here at my house. Be here in ten minutes? Good. I'll wait. It's a matter of great importance. Good-by."

Then impatiently The Thinking Machine moved about, waiting. The reporter, whose acquaintance with the logician was an extended one, had never seen him in just such a state. It started when he heard St. George had escaped.

At last they left the house and stood waiting on the steps until Detective Mallory appeared in a cab. Into that Hatch and The Thinking Machine climbed, after the latter had given some direction, and the cabby drove rapidly away. It was all a mystery to Hatch, and he was rather glad of it when Detective Mallory asked what it meant.

"Means that there is danger of a tragedy," said The Thinking Machine, crustily. "We may be in time to avert it. There is just a chance. If I'd only known this an hour ago—even half an hour ago—it might have been stopped."

The Thinking Machine was the first man out of the cab when it stopped, and Hatch and the detective followed quickly.

"Is Mr. St. George in his apartments?" asked the scientist of the elevator boy.

"No, sir," said the boy. "He's in hospital, shot."

"Is there a key to his place? Quick."

"I think so, sir, but I can't give it to you."

"Here, give it to me, then!" exclaimed the detective. He flashed a badge in the boy's eyes, and the youth immediately lost a deal of his coolness.

"Gee, a detective! Yes, sir."

"How many rooms has Mr. St. George?" asked the scientist.

"Three and a bath," the boy responded.

Two minutes later the three men stood in the reception-room of the apartments. There came to them from somewhere inside a deadly, stifling odor of chloroform. After one glance around The Thinking Machine rushed into the next room, the studio.

"Dear me, dear me!" he exclaimed.

There on the floor lay huddled the figure of a man. Blood had run from several wounds on his head. The Thinking Machine stooped a moment, and his slender fingers fumbled over the heart.

"Unconscious, that's all," he said, and he raised the man up.

"Victor Willis!" exclaimed Hatch.

"Victor Willis!" repeated The Thinking Machine, as if puzzled. "Are you sure?"

"Certain," said Hatch, positively. "It's the bank clerk."

"Then we are too late," declared the scientist.

He arose and looked about the room. A door to his right attracted his attention. He jerked it open and peered in. It was a clothes press. Another small door on the other side of the room was also thrown open. Here was a kitchenette, with a great quantity of canned stuffs.

The Thinking Machine went on into the little bedroom which Hatch had searched. He flung open the bathroom and peered in, only to shut it immediately. Then he tried the handle of another door, a closet. It was fastened.

"Ah!" he exclaimed.

Then on his hands and knees he sniffed at the crack between the door and the flooring. Suddenly, as if satisfied, he arose and stepped away from the door.

"Smash that door in," he directed.

Detective Mallory looked at him stupefied. There was a similar expression on Hatch's face.

"What's—what's in there?" the detective asked.

"Smash it," said the other, tartly. "Smash it, or God knows what you'll find in there."

The detective, a powerful man, and Hatch threw their

weight against the door; it stood rigid. They pulled at the handle; it refused to yield.

"Lend me your revolver?" asked The Thinking Machine.

The weapon was in his hand almost before the detective was aware of it, and, placing the barrel to the keyhole, The Thinking Machine pulled the trigger. There was a resonant report, the lock was smashed and the detective put out his hand to open the door.

"Look out for a shot," warned The Thinking Machine, sharply.

VI

The Thinking Machine drew Detective Mallory and Hatch to one side, out of immediate range of any person who might rush out, then pulled the closet door open. A cloud of suffocating fumes—the sweet, sickening odor of chloroform—gushed out, but there was no sound from inside. The detective looked at The Thinking Machine inquiringly.

Carefully, almost gingerly, the scientist peered around the edge of the door. What he saw did not startle him, because it was what he expected. It was Constans St. George lying prone on the floor as if dead, with a blood-spattered revolver clasped loosely in one hand; the other hand grasped the throat of a woman, a woman of superb physical beauty, who also lay with face upturned, staring glassily.

"Open the windows—all of them, then help me," commanded the scientist.

As Detective Mallory and Hatch turned to obey the instructions, The Thinking Machine took the revolver from the inert fingers of the artist. Then Hatch and Mallory returned and together they lifted the unconscious forms toward a window.

"It's Grace Field," said the reporter.

In silence for half an hour the scientist labored over the unconscious forms of his three patients. The detective and reporter stood by, doing only what they were told to do. The wind, cold and stinging, came pouring through the windows, and it was only a few minutes until the chloroform odor was dissipated. The first of the three unconscious ones to show any sign of returning comprehension was Victor Willis, whose presence at all in the apartments furnished one of the mysteries which Hatch could not fathom.

It was evident that his condition was primarily due to the wounds on his head—two of which bled profusely. The chloroform had merely served to further deaden his mentality. The wounds were made with the butt of the revolver, evidently in the hands of the artist. Willis's eyes opened finally and he stared at the faces bending over him with uncomprehending eyes.

"What happened?" he asked.

"You're all right now," was the scientist's assuring answer. "This man is your prisoner, Detective Mallory, for breaking and entering and for the attempted murder of Mr. St. George."

Detective Mallory was delighted. Here was something he could readily understand; a human being given over to his care; a tangible thing to put handcuffs on and hold. He immediately proceeded to put the handcuffs on.

"Any need of an ambulance?" he asked.

"No," replied The Thinking Machine. "He'll be all right in half an hour."

Gradually as reason came back Willis remembered. He turned his head at last and saw the inert bodies of St. George and Grace Field, the girl whom he had loved.

"She was here, then!" he exclaimed suddenly, violently. "I knew it. Is she dead?"

"Shut up that young fool's mouth, Mr. Mallory," commanded the scientist, sharply. "Take him in the other room or send him away."

Obediently Mallory did as directed; there was that in the voice of this cold, calm being, The Thinking Machine, which compelled obedience. Mallory never questioned motives or orders.

Willis was able to walk to the other room with help. Miss Field and St. George lay side by side in the cold wind from the open window. The Thinking Machine had forced a little whisky down their throats, and after a time St. George opened his eyes.

The artist was instantly alert and tried to rise. He was

weak, however, and even a strength given to him by the madness which blazed in his eyes did not avail. At last he lay raving, cursing, shrieking. The Thinking Machine regarded him closely.

"Hopeless," he said, at last.

Again for many minutes the scientist worked with the girl. Finally he asked that an ambulance be sent for. The detective called up the City Hospital on the telephone in the apartments and made the request. The Thinking Machine stared alternately at the girl and at the artist.

"Hopeless," he said again. "St. George, I mean."

"Will the girl recover?" asked Hatch.

"I don't know," was the frank reply. "She's been partly stupefied for days—ever since she disappeared, as a matter of fact. If her physical condition was as good as her appearance indicates she may recover. Now the hospital is the best place for her."

It was only a few minutes before two ambulances came and the three persons were taken away; Willis a prisoner, and a sullen, defiant prisoner, who refused to speak or answer questions; St. George raving hideously and cursing frightfully; the woman, beautiful as a marble statue, and colorless as death.

When they had all gone, The Thinking Machine went back into the bedroom and examined more carefully the little closet in which he had found the artist and Grace Field. It was practically a padded cell, relatively six feet each way. Heavy cushion of felt two or three inches thick covered the interior of the little room closely. In the top of it there was a small aperture, which had permitted some of the fumes of the chloroform to escape. The place was saturated with the poison.

"Let's go," he said, finally.

Detective Mallory and Hatch followed him out and a few minutes later sat opposite him in his little laboratory. Hatch had told a story over the telephone that made his City Editor rejoice madly; it was news, great, big, vital news.

"Now, Mr. Hatch, I suppose you want some details," said The Thinking Machine, as he relapsed into his accustomed attitude. "And you, too, Mr. Mallory, since you are holding Willis a prisoner on my say-so. Would you like to know why?"

"Sure," said the detective.

"Let's go back a little—begin at the beginning, where Mr. Hatch called on me," said The Thinking Machine. "I can make the matter clearer that way. And I believe the cause of justice, Mr. Mallory, requires absolute accuracy and clarity in all things, does it not?"

"Sure," said the detective again.

"Well, Mr. Hatch told me at some length of the preliminaries of this case," explained The Thinking Machine. "He told me the history of the picture; the mystery as to the identity of the model; her great beauty; how he found her to be Grace Field, a shop-girl. He also told me of the mental condition of the artist, St. George, and repeated the rumor as he knew it about the artist being heartbroken because the girl—his model—would not marry him.

"All this brought the artist into the matter of the girl's disappearance. She represented to him, physically, the highest ideal of which he could conceive—hope, success, life itself. Therefore it was not astonishing that he should fall in love with her; and it is not difficult to imagine that the girl did not fall in love with him. She is a beautiful woman, but not necessarily a woman of mentality; he is a great artist, eccentric, childish even in certain things. They were two natures totally opposed.

"These things I could see instantly. Mr. Hatch showed me the photograph and also the scrap of paper. At the time the scrap of paper meant nothing. As I pointed out, it might have no bearing at all, yet it made it necessary for me to know whose handwriting it was. If Willis's, it still might mean nothing; if St. George's, a great deal, because it showed a direct thread to him. There was reason to believe that any friendship between them had ended when the picture was exhibited.

"It was necessary, therefore, even that early in the work of reducing the mystery to logic to center it about St. George. This I explained to Mr. Hatch and pointed out the fact that the girl and the artist might have eloped—were possibly together somewhere. First it was necessary to get to the artist; Mr. Hatch had not been able to do so.

"A childishly simple trick, which seemed to amaze Mr. Hatch considerably, brought the artist out of his rooms after he had been there closely for two days. I told Mr. Hatch that the artist would leave his rooms, if he were there, one night at 9:32, and told him to wait in the hall, then if he left the door open to enter the apartments and search for some trace of the girl. Mr. St. George did leave his apartments at the time I mentioned, and—"

"But why, how?" asked Hatch.

"There was one thing in the world that St. George loved with all his heart," explained the scientist. "That was his picture. Every act of his life has demonstrated that. I looked at a telephone book; I found he had a 'phone. If he were in his rooms, locked in, it was a bit of common sense that his telephone was the best means of reaching him. He answered the 'phone; I told him, just at 9:30, that the Art Museum was on fire and his picture in danger.

"St. George left his apartments to go and see, just as I knew he would, hatless and coatless, and leaving the door open. Mr. Hatch went inside and found two gloves and a veil, all belonging to Miss Field. Miss Stanford identified them and asked if he had gotten them from Willis, and if Willis had been arrested. Why did she ask these questions? Obviously because she knew, or thought she knew, that Willis had some connection with the affair.

"Mr. Hatch detailed all his discoveries and the conversation with Miss Stanford to me on the day after I 'phoned to St. George, who, of course, had found no fire. It showed that Miss Stanford suspected Willis, whom she loved, of the murder of Miss Field. Why? Because she had heard him threaten. He's a hare-brained young fool, anyway. What motive? Jealousy. Jealousy of what? He knew in some way that she had posed for a semi-nude picture, and that the man who painted it loved her. There is your jealousy. It explains Willis's every act."

The Thinking Machine paused a moment, then went on:

"This conversation with Mr. Hatch made me believe Miss Stanford knew more than she was willing to tell. In what way? By a letter? Possibly. She had given Mr. Hatch a scrap of a letter; perhaps she had found another letter, or more of this. I sent her a note, telling her I knew she had these scraps of letters, and she promptly brought them to me. She had found them after Mr. Hatch saw her first somewhere in the house—in a bureau drawer she said, I think.

"Meanwhile, Mr. Hatch had called my attention to the burglary of St. George's apartments. One reading of that convinced me that it was Willis who did this. Why? Because burglars don't burst in doors when they think anyone is inside; they pick the lock. Knowing, too, Willis's insane jealousy, I figured that he would be the type of man who would go there to kill St. George if he could, particularly if he thought the girl was there.

"Thus it happened that I was not the only one to think that St. George knew where the girl was. Willis, the one most interested, thought she was there. I questioned Miss Stanford mercilessly, trying to get more facts about the young man from her which would bear on this, trying to trick her into some statement, but she was loyal to the last.

"All these things indicated several things. First, that Willis didn't actually know where the girl was, as he would have known had he killed her; second, that if she had disappeared with a man, it was St. George, as there was no other apparent possibility; third, that St. George would be with her or near her, even if he had killed her; fourth, the pistol shot through the arm had brought on again a mental condition which threatened his entire future, and now as it happens has blighted it.

"Thus, Miss Field and St. George were together. She loved Willis devotedly, therefore she was with St. George against her will, or she was dead. Where? In his rooms? Possibly. I determined to search there. I had just reached this determination when I heard St. George, violently insane, had escaped from the hospital. He had only one purpose then—to get to the woman. Then she was in danger.

"I reasoned along these lines, rushed to the artist's apartments, found Willis there wounded. He had evidently been there searching when St. George returned, and St. George had attacked him, as a madman will, and with the greater strength of a madman. Then I knew the madman's first step. It would be the end of everything for him; therefore the death of the girl and his own. How? By poison preferably, because he would not shoot her—he loved beauty too much. Where? Possibly in the place where she had been all along, the closet, carefully padded and prepared to withstand noises. It is really a padded cell. I have an idea that the artist, sometimes overcome by his insane fits, and knowing when they would come, prepared this closet and used it himself occasionally. Here the girl could have been kept and her shrieks would never have been heard. You know the rest."

The Thinking Machine stopped and arose, as if to end the matter. The others arose, too.

"I took you, Mr. Mallory, because you were a detective, and I knew I could force a way into the apartments which I imagined would be locked. I think that's all."

"But how did the girl get there?" asked Hatch.

"St. George evidently asked her to come, possibly to pose again. It was a gratification to the girl to do this—a little touch of vanity that Willis was fighting so hard, and which led to his threats and his efforts to kill St. George. Of course the artist was insane when she came; his frantic love for her led him to make her a prisoner and hold her against her will. You saw how well he did it."

There was an awed pause. Hatch was rubbing the nap of his hat against his sleeve, thoughtfully. Detective Mallory had nothing to say; it was all said. Both turned as if to go, but the reporter had two more questions.

"I suppose St. George's case is hopeless?"

"Absolutely. It will end in a few months with his death."

"And Miss Field?"

"If she is not dead by this time she will recover. Wait a minute." He went into the next room and they heard the telephone bell jingle. After a time he came out. "She will recover," he said. "Good-afternoon."

Wonderingly, Hutchinson Hatch, reporter, and Detective Mallory passed down the street together.

Gentleman Coggins: Alias Towers

BY OSWALD CRAWFURD, C.M.G.

Gentleman Coggins: Alias Towers

BY OSWALD CRAWFURD, C. M. G.

CHAPTER I

CAPTAIN TOWERS

"I HAVE always considered," said my friend, Inspector Morgan, when he paid me a late after-dinner visit, "I have always considered that the greatest help a detective can have in following up and finding out about a crime is to know something beforehand of the criminal's own private and particular way of looking at things.

"To prove that I should like to tell you the real story of the great jewel robbery at Balin Abbey, and how the place was broken into by Ikey Coggins, commonly called Gentleman Coggins, *alias* Towers. You read about it, I dare say, at the time, in the newspapers?"

"I did," I said; "I remember the case vaguely."

"You only read part of the real story; for the general public never got to know more than a little bit of what actually happened. The real story is a very curious one."

"I should like to hear it from you."

"You shall," said the Inspector, "only you must let me tell you about it from the beginning, and in my own way."

Inspector Morgan then told me the following story:

"My first years of services in the army were passed in India and in the Colonies, and when I got my company and came home, I exchanged into a smart cavalry regiment. From that time, things went wrong with me. I had meant, being a comparatively poor man, and very ambitious, to work hard and make a serious career of my profession, and, so far, I had done so; but when I got into the —— I confess I led a fool's life. Few men can fight against their environment. The regiment was a sporting regiment, and it was quartered in Ireland. Unfortunately for me, I had a fair seat in the saddle, a light hand on the reins, and I could ride under ten stone. My fellow-officers were good fellows and sportsmen. The talk at mess was of nothing but polo, drag-hunts, and steeplechases. I fell into their way. Anything like serious study was impossible. I bought two polo ponies. I had part ownership in a famous steeplechaser which I had ridden more than once to a win. I lost a good deal more than I could afford at cards. My polo stud was expensive. I was running fast into debt, but I looked to pull myself free at a great race meeting in our near neighborhood. The two chief events of that meeting were the Hunt Steeplechase, in which I was to ride a friend's hunter, and the Great West of Ireland Handicap, in which my mount was the horse in which I held a part ownership, a very famous steeplechaser, named The Leprochaun. On both events I had laid to win heavily.

"Now, I have every reason to believe I should have won both races, paid my debts, pulled myself together, seen what an idiot I had been making of myself, changed into a quieter regiment, and made the army a career and perhaps a successful one. I say I might have done all this but for one man, my evil genius, Captain Towers, who, about this time, came into our regiment. He had done service in the Colonies. No one knew much about him, but he brought with him a reputation as a sportsman and a rider. Towers was never liked at mess. He was a cold, quiet, cynical fellow, with a pale, sinister face, and a horseman's build, broad-shouldered, clean-limbed, strong, spare, and wiry. I saw at once that I had a rival in the saddle, and I was not sorry, for, in point of fact, I had had it too much my own way for the last year or two, being the only man in the regiment who fulfilled all the requirements of a race rider, seat, hand, experience, nerve, and low weight.

"The regiment was at that time mad upon bridge, and Towers played a good, quiet game. He had certain rare advantages as a bridge player; he never abused his partner or made cynical remarks; he won without triumphing, and he lost gaily. Not that he lost often, and it was soon observed that no man ever enjoyed so consistent a run of good luck as Captain Towers.

"He and I having so much in common were thrown together—but we were never friends. Indeed, I disliked him and distrusted him from the first. He was not a genial fellow. He was a man who never lost a chance of sneering at the four or five things on which men at large do not care to listen to cynical speech—religion, politics, women, social honor, and social honesty. He and I sometimes quarreled, as two men will when one is quick-tempered and the other coldly cynical. I was fool enough to lend him a hundred pounds when he first came to the regiment, and he had the impudence to look upon my loan to him as the act of a fool. 'Why,' he said, 'you never expected to get it back, did you?'

"'You are chaffing, Captain Towers,' I said stiffly.

"'Oh,' he said, 'you may call it chaffing if you like; you won't get the money out of me! You haven't my I.O.U.'

"'Then,' I said, losing my temper, 'you'll allow me to have my opinion of your conduct, and to let my friends know what I think.'

"'Do, and be hanged to you!' he said.

"We parted uncomfortably. What an infernal blackguard! I thought. The great race was still in the far future, when one day Towers came to me and said, overlooking the bad terms we were on, 'Captain Morgan, I want your opinion on a matter in which you know more than I do.'

"'What can that be?' I asked, rather amused, for Towers was not, as a rule, overmodest.

"'The points of a horse.'

"I said nothing, but I thought, What is he driving at now?

"If I had been able to give the right answer to that question, my life would perhaps have been a different life to what it has been.

"'The fact is,' he said, 'I am in rather a hole. I got a letter from a friend in Dublin, last week, offering me a chaser for sale—the price was reasonable, the mare young and untried, but she could jump and she could gallop, and I was tempted. "Send her down," I wired. Well, she has come; she is standing at Simpson's, and, to look at her, she is the greatest brute I ever saw. Come and see her.'

"A lover of horses does not lose a chance of seeing something out of the way in the horse line. Certainly I never saw a less promising animal than the mare in Simpson's stable; ewe-necked, a huge, ugly head, vicious eyes, looking round at us with the whites showing, as we came near the stall.

"'Do you see any points about that mare?" asked Towers.

"'She has big quarters,' I said, 'she ought to gallop, but her shoulder is straight.'

"'She's the devil's own of a temper, your honor,' said the groom, 'when a man's on her back; and she cries out if she's vexed, like a woman. We call her The Squealer.'

"'The Squealer!' said Towers. 'I'll christen her that—she's unnamed as yet—that is, if I keep her. But shall I? Shall I pay her journey back to Dublin and send a fiver and try to be off the bargain?'

"Irish grooms are free with their opinions.

"'Begorra, sir, I'd send a tenner wid her and make sure!'

" 'Better see what she can do first,' I said, hadn't you? Take her out with the drag-hounds to-morrow.'

"'Put a saddle and bridle on her now, Pat, and we'll try her in Simpson's field.'

"Irishmen resent the general use of that common patronymic which Englishmen think it knowing and friendly to apply to every Irishman they meet.

"'Me name's Terence, with yer honor's leave,' said the groom.

"'Is that so? Then, Terence, my man, if you can manage to sit astride of a horse, perhaps you won't mind putting the mare round the field.'

"The groom was offended. Every Irishman in or near a stable can ride, and it was clear that Terence had the seat and the hand of a good workman when he was on the mare's back, shoulders well set back, knees forward, hands held low on either side of the mare's withers. Perhaps the ill-humor of the man communicated itself to the mare—for there is no sympathy so close as that between horse and rider—or perhaps, as Terence had said, she had a bad temper of her own. Certainly a more cantankerous mount no man ever had. While she walked, the whites of her wicked eyes and the wrinkling of her nostrils were the only sign, but when Terence put her to a canter, she went short, she bucked, she threw her head up, then put it down to nearly between her knees, and she stopped in her stride to kick.

"'By Jove,' I said, 'that fellow can keep his seat!'

"'Now we'll try her over the fences,' said Towers.

"The outer circle at Simpson's field was a lane of green turf. An inner circle was set with fences to represent the obstacles in a steeplechase or the hunting-field, and was used to test Mr. Simpson's hunters.

"The groom put the mare at the first fence. She went at it at ninety miles an hour, stopped suddenly as she came close up, gave a squeal of ill-temper such as I never heard from a horse before, and reared badly.

"Towers laughed heartily, while the man was, I could see, in imminent danger of a broken neck.

"'Drop the curb, Terence!' I shouted, but the advice came too late. The mare was standing nearly bolt upright, her head straight up in the air. 'Slip off her, man!' I called out, and he did so, just in time to save himself from being crushed. Relieved of his weight, the mare fell to her fore feet again.

"'I knew she'd rear if he touched the curb, that's her way,' Towers said, with a broad grin.

"'What! You knew that, and you let him ride her on the curb?'

"'Pooh! What does a fellow like that signify?'

"The groom had seized the reins and led her back to us.

"'Sure the mare's got an imp of Satan inside her to make her want to kill the two of us that way!' said Terence.

"'Put on a plain running snaffle,' said Towers, 'and I'll try her.'

"'You're risking your neck, Towers, for no good. She's a brute, and you'll make nothing of her for hunting or racing. Send her back, even if you lose money by it.'

"He did not listen to me, and presently he was on the mare's back.

"'I want to let her extend herself and see if she can gallop.'

"She went freer in the snaffle as Towers galloped her round the outer circle. She seemed to go a little short for a racer, showing no indications whatever of any remarkable turn of speed. I have had good reason since to suspect that Towers, a clever rider, took particularly good care not to put the mare, as the saying is, 'on the stretch.'

"When Towers rode at the fences, the mare's behavior was quite changed. She went round the ring at a slow canter, taking every fence, large and small, in her stride, and taking them well and easily.

"'What do you think of that?' said Captain Towers, as he brought the mare back to us.

"'Bedad, sir,' said Terence, putting in his say, 'when she's in that humor she'd be the very mount for a nervous old gentleman who loves a quiet day with hounds.'

"'What do you think of her, Captain Morgan?'

"'I agree with Terence, and I don't think she has the making of a racer in her. Did you try to extend her just now?'

"'All she'd let me,' said Towers.

"'I'd send her back to Dublin, if you'd care to have my advice,' said I.

"'Wid fifteen golden sovereigns tied to her tail!' suggested Terence.

"'I'll take your advice, Morgan.'

"When I next spoke to Towers about the mare it was three days afterward, and he looked vexed.

"'Would you believe it? They've stuck me with that infernal mare! The man refused to be off his bargain at any price, and now I've got her on my hands.'

"'A white elephant! Shall you put her in training?'

"'Is she worth it?'

"Towers never did put the mare into regular training—he never even let her be properly clipped or singed, and as the winter came on her coat grew ragged and her fetlocks were left untrimmed. He took her out once or twice with the hounds, and he entered her regularly at the drag meets, but though she jumped cleverly she was never forward with hounds, and she never came near winning the drag.

"Needless to say he and his unfortunate purchase came in for a good deal of chaff at mess. He took it in fairly good part, and defended the mare. 'The more I know her,' he said, 'the more I like her. She has a temper and is too lazy to gallop, but I believe she can.'

"'Not with that shape, my dear fellow,' said Major O'Gorman, a keen sportsman, but too stout to ride his own horses on the turf. 'A horse wants shoulders to land him as well as hind legs to send him forward, and your mare has shoulders like a sheep's.'

"'You know more of horses than I do,' said Towers almost humbly.

"'Not difficult,' said O'Gorman behind his moustache. But Towers did not hear, or pretended not to hear.

"'I'd back her even now,' said Towers, 'over a stiff course against some horses I could name.'

"The weakness we all have for our own property blinds the wisest of us! and we were a little sorry even for Towers when we saw O'Gorman's eagerness to take him at his word. It was a little over-sharp of O'Gorman, we thought, upon the newcomer.

"'Do you mean any of my lot, Captain Towers? because if you mean that, I'll do business with you.'

"'I suppose it's cheek of me, but I did mean The Clipper.'

"There was a peal of laughter at the mess table.

"'Owners up?' suggested Towers, and the laugh turned against the red-faced, burly major.

"'Certainly not,' said O'Gorman; 'you know I never ride my own horses. I'll put Morgan up.'

"Then I must choose the course!' said Towers sharply and decisively.

"O'Gorman suspected a trap and hesitated. 'Four miles of fair hunting country?' he suggested.

"'Quite so,' answered Towers, 'and I to choose it.'

"So the matter was agreed upon for £100 a side. The Clipper was a clever chaser who had won many a hurdle race and many a local steeplechase. He was thought even to have a good chance against The Leprochaun for the Great West of Ireland Race, having to receive no less than 11 lbs. from that famous crack. The Clipper could gallop and could jump, and if his jumping was not always very free, that would not matter in a match when he could follow a lead over every fence, for his great turn of speed would enable him to beat nearly any horse in the last run in.

"There was little betting till the last, so hollow a thing did the race seem, and so foregone a conclusion its result. At the last, among the few hundred of sporting men from the neighborhood and officers from the garrison, almost any odds could have been obtained against Towers' mare. He himself, already in the saddle, in his jockey cap and jacket, went among the crowd and was received with chaff and laughter. 'What odds do you want?' they asked him.

"'What offer?' Towers called out.

"One man in derision offered ten to one. Towers shook his head and laughed. The other raised his offer to 25 to 1, and the Captain, saying 'Done with you!' booked the bet in tenners.

"Others followed half in fun, half in the wish to make a sovereign or two out of the match, and before Towers and I stood at the starting-point he must have booked over a thousand pounds in bets. He asked me, as we stood waiting for the start, if I would give him the current odds, but I wouldn't take advantage of him.

"A match between a fast horse who is not a safe and ready fencer and a slower horse who can jump is generally a very dull affair. My riding orders were simple. 'Follow Towers' lead over every fence and race in from the last,' O'Gorman had said. I did as I was bid, and the race was conducted mostly at a walk. The fences were big and various; doubles, bullfinches, a stiff post and rail. A big flying leap at a brook, the last jump before the finish was also a brook, but quite a narrow one, not more than 12 feet of water with a good take off and landing. The brook lay at the bottom of a slope, so that, coming at it, we had a good view of the water, and it looked bigger than it was. I could see why Towers had insisted upon choosing the course. The Clipper, like most horses, preferred any kind of jump to water. If he refused anything, he would refuse a water jump, but O'Gorman's riding orders had provided for this, and with a lead over the fences there was no danger of his refusing anything. The most refusing of jumpers will always follow another horse over a fence.

"Towers and I went over the course at our ease, chaffing each other. He gave me a good lead over the big brook, and then pulled up in the middle of the field to let me follow and rejoin him.

" 'There's no use my trying to get away from you,' he said, 'is there? By Jove, The Clipper is a clipper, and no mistake; and my last chance is gone, I suppose, if he can do water like that. Come along!'

"I really thought the race was over and was admiring Towers' pluck. He was always a good loser.

"We were coming back in a great four-mile circle to the starting-field where the crowd stood and where also was the winning-post not more than 300 yards from the last fence, the brook before mentioned.

"We rode pretty fast at it, nearly side by side, The Clipper only half a length behind Towers' mare. I could see the green winning flags, beyond the two red ones which marked the spot where we were to take the brook, and I was already pulling myself together for the effort to race in.

"We were within five yards of the water when Towers' mare showed her temper—or perhaps was made to. She stopped dead short at the edge of the water, gave the strange squeal I had heard before, and began to rear.

"I jammed The Clipper at the little brook, but the sight of the water, or more probably the unexpected refusal of the mare whom he had been following, scared him. He stuck his fore feet obstinately together at the take off, and then swerved suddenly some twenty yards to the left.

"As I made a half circle to put my horse again at the jump, I could not well see what Towers was about, but they told me afterward that what happened was this: The mare almost immediately came down from her rear, and Towers, who, by-the-bye, carried no whip and wore no spurs, without turning back, urged his mare to take the brook standing. She did so at once, with so big a bound as surprised the lookers on, and then she began to canter very slowly up the slope toward the winning-post.

"I put The Clipper fast at the brook; he took it splendidly, and, seeing the slow pace of The Squealer, I made no doubt of overtaking her, but Towers, looking round, saw me coming up and mended his own pace. We raced in, I was overtaking him fast, I had reached his mare's quarters, then the saddle, then her neck, amid shouts of 'The Clipper wins! The Clipper wins!' but Towers squeezed past the post, a winner by half a head! There was a moment's silence among the onlookers, so unexpected was the issue of the race. Then in a moment came a great huzzaing for Captain Towers. He became at once the hero of the crowd and his win the cleverest bit of jockeyship ever seen on an Irish racecourse.

"Was it accident, or was it design? Had the mare's temper prevailed for a moment, or had Towers induced it at the critical moment? The crowd never doubted but that Towers had managed the whole thing, nor, to be sure, did I or any one who saw the race run and knew Towers, have the slightest doubt on the subject. The ethics of horse-racing are not very strict, and a trick of this sort is held to be fair by the majority of racing men. Even O'Gorman laughed over his loss, like the good sportsman and gentleman he was, and was seen to shake hands openly on the course with the winner of the match—whereat the Irish crowd cheered both gentlemen heartily.

"This affair, however, did not increase Captain Towers' reputation in the regiment. The race might be all right, but that long-continued belittling of an animal that if she could only gallop fairly well could at least jump superbly. Many of us, too, had lost considerably to him at cards. Good as his play was, it was not enough to justify his almost constant winning at bridge, and some of the more suspicious among us began to make unpleasant remarks, and one or two of the heaviest losers were so convinced of the unfairness of his play that they set themselves to watch him. They found, of course, nothing. Towers was a most scrupulous player, he always called attention to a player who held his hand carelessly. His own eyes never traveled beyond his own hand and the cards on the table. It was noticed that he was clumsy in handling the pack, that he shuffled and cut awkwardly, dealing slowly, and carrying his hand, as some old-fashioned players do, with every card dealt, and dealing them into four regular little heaps on the table. The watchers noted all this, and then gave up watching him as a bad job.

"'It's all luck,' said some of us. 'He'll make up for his run of luck some day, somehow'—a prediction which came true in the end, but not quite in the way the prophets had meant.

"Rather to our surprise, after the exhibition of lack of speed which The Squealer had made in the match with The Clipper, Towers had entered his mare for the two chief events in the Great West of Ireland Race meeting—namely, for the Hunters' Sweepstakes, for which The Squealer had qualified, and for the Great West of Ireland Race. We could not quite make this out, for the mare could not have a chance in the Hunt Steeplechase even though no better horse than The Clipper ran in it, and I had every reason to believe The Clipper would win the race. I had backed him heavily. That Towers should put his mare into the Great West of Ireland Handicap, that he should enter such an animal as The Squealer against all the best chasers in Ireland, and among them against the famous Leprochaun, seemed nothing short of madness. Yet there were some of us who, after Towers' exploit against The Clipper, were quite willing to take long odds against The Squealer for both races. Towers was one of them. He said he thought he might win. He laid freely against any horse in the race, and took all the long odds that he could get against his own mount. By the day of the race he had a book which must have totaled over ten thousand pounds.

"I will not tell you the story of that day's racing," said Inspector Morgan. "Even now the memory of it is too unpleasant and the feeling I have against that swindling scoundrel too bitter. Enough to say that Towers won both races.

"When he appeared on the course in his preliminary canter, on his ragged-coated mare, with her ewe neck, her ugly head, and her shambling, lurching gallop, a shout of derision went up among the racecourse crowd, and the usual cheap wit was indulged in.

"'How much the pound, Captain?' 'What price cat's meat to-day?' 'Take her home and cut her hair, sir, do!'

"When the race began and they saw her take every fence as if it was playtime with her, keep her place in the first rank, and that although the race was being run at the usual break-neck pace of modern steeplechases, an unaccustomed silence fell upon the crowd. Towers and I were again alone, every other horse in the race having either fallen or been outpaced. This time we rode abreast, and I took no lead. The Clipper was full of go to-day, and full of courage, facing every jump and clearing everything safely and well. We raced hard over the last sweep three fields off the finish, and took the last three jumps simultaneously and abreast. I could not shake off the mare: we were neck and neck. I plied whip and spurs, and the brave beast responded, but I could not get past Towers, and, almost at the post, The Squealer forged ahead, and won the race by a narrow half length.

"Amid the shouting of the crowd and the congratulations of brother sportsmen, Towers kept his usual cool cynicism as he was being led back to the weighing yard. He caught sight of O'Gorman's red face in the lane of sportsmen through which he was being led.

"'I told you, O'Gorman,' he said quietly, 'that I thought the mare might have a turn of speed in her.'

"The history of the great race of the day was the history of the Hunt race over again. The mare never made a mistake at her fences, never seemed to exert herself, and Captain Towers drew alongside of me on The Leprochaun, and raced that famous chaser over the last few hundred yards, beating him as he had beaten The Clipper by the narrowest of distances at the post.

"That race was the end of my army career. I was in debt far beyond my solvency. I had lost some hundreds at cards, and my chances of recouping myself at the race meeting had been hindered by Captain Towers and his mysterious mare.

"It was not quite the end of Towers' career, but it was the beginning of the end. It was not till all racing debts had been paid to him and done with, that something happened which was to solve the problem of The Squealer and how she had come to beat the best horses in Ireland, but another rather startling event was to happen first, and this also led to unexpected developments.

"Captain Towers' exploits on the turf had made him famous, and in sporting circles outside our mess he was even popular, for he had other claims to society success. He was musical and had a capital voice, and he was beyond compare the best amateur actor I have ever known. His specialty was what on the stage is known as character parts, old men, particularly foreign old men, when he would make up and talk in a way to make one entirely forget his own individuality. The complicated Jew nature he seemed to have studied as few men have—when and where I could never guess. He impersonated Shylock once in the trial scene from the 'Merchant of Venice.' Portia, the Duke, Bassanio, and Antonio were all forgotten. We had eyes and ears for him alone.

"In a silly melodrama which the Amateur Dramatists of the garrison town played in for a charity, Towers had been asked to choose his part. He chose, to the surprise of every one, the character of 'Ikey Moses,' a young Cockney Jew, dealer in old clothes, who, in some way, comes into collision with the noble Christian hero of the piece and gets the worse of the encounter. His part consisted only of a dozen or two of words, but they were delivered at rehearsals with such an unctuous roll of the lips, such a broad and humorous accent, half Cockney, half Yiddish, that our stage-manager—a professional—suggested a little writing up of the part. At the next rehearsal Towers had put in a few lines and delivered them with marvelous effect. The whole company applauded and entreated him to work on, upon the same lines. At every rehearsal the part grew. Ikey Moses was from the first a ridiculous, somewhat hateful character—mean, subservient to his superiors, a bully to his inferiors—spurned by the low-born heroine, to whom he presumes to offer his obnoxious addresses. Towers with great skill preserved all the mean and ridiculous elements in the character, but he converted the Jew's presumptuous courting of the heroine into a genuine love. The better elements in the man were seen to be fighting against his baser side. There was the true dramatic struggle and contention of passion with passion.

Pathos and even tragedy were latent in the struggle. The part extended day by day till at last it literally filled the play. It *was* the play—the parts of the leading gentleman and lady were ruthlessly cut down, and when the piece came to be acted, Ikey Moses, with his comic lisp, his mixture of knowingness, knavery, and simplicity, was on the stage during nearly the whole of the four acts, and there was a scene between him and his sweetheart while he pleads, and she half pities, half despises him, and finally rejects him, which stirred the house to unwonted tragic depths. Towers was cheered when he came on and when he went off, and when the curtain fell it was amid a tumult of applause.

"I mention this to show what a versatile and accomplished fellow Towers was, and also because his mimetic powers have a distinct relation to something I shall have to tell you presently. With all these talents, enough to raise any man to a pinnacle of success in almost any line of life, there was in Towers an instinct toward evil, that demoniac tendency which drives men to their doom, that mysterious, little understood impulse which lies deep at the heart of every great criminal, the tendency to set evil above good which finally destroys the man's soul.

"Now," Morgan went on, "I must tell you of the incident which led to the first of a series of catastrophes in Towers' military career. I have told you how he systematically won at cards, and how, though we all began to suspect him of foul play, we never could find anything to justify any suspicions. The cards he played with belonged to the mess, and were procured in the usual way by the mess committee for the time being. Towers went on winning, and we had no excuse but to go on playing with him.

"There was one young fellow among us who did not take it so calmly—Terence O'Grady, a hot-headed young Tipperary giant—a good fellow, popular among us all, a distant relative of my own, and a man whom I loved as a brother. He had lost night after night when he played against Towers, and won only when he found himself Towers' partner.

"'I know the beggar cheats!' he cried out.

"'Hush!' said an older officer. 'You can't prove it, whatever you think, and you'd best hold your tongue till you're sure.'

"'Then I'll make sure!' said O'Grady. 'I'll pin him, sir, never fear but I'll pin him!'

"We laughed at this vague threat—not for a moment guessing what he meant by his vague threat of pinning Captain Towers.

"That night O'Grady and I played against Towers and O'Gorman. It happened that every one of the three of us had already, in previous play, lost heavily to Towers—O'Gorman in particular, and O'Grady far more than he could afford. Towers dealt. We watched with an ill-defined suspicion the slow and deliberate movements of the dealer. We always expected something fantastic in the way of a declaration when Towers dealt, but this time it surprised me to find that he declared no trumps, for, sitting third hand, I held seven hearts to the Quart Major in my own hand. I immediately redoubled, and, to my surprise, Towers redoubled again. Knowing that my partner would follow the 'heart convention' and play me a heart, I doubled again, and on a seeming certainty, and so it went on to the extreme limit. Eventually we stood to win or lose 100 points on each trick.

"What was my surprise when O'Grady failed to lead a heart. He had none. Towers easily discarded the few hearts in his own hand, kept the lead, my hearts never came in, and we lost the whole thirteen tricks, Grand Slam!

"'Now,' thought I, 'how could Towers possibly have dared to redouble and to continue to redouble, unless he had felt sure that O'Grady, with the blind lead, had not a single heart in his hand? How could he have known this by any fair means? He could not even have caught a chance glance at O'Grady's hand, for that young Irishman is short-sighted, and never holds his cards more than three inches from his nose.

"I looked at O'Gorman, who is a fine player. He wore a very grave look. I saw he had arrived at the same conclusion as I had. Indeed, it was too obvious to miss. O'Grady's face worked. I thought he meant mischief.

"The score was marked down, Towers cut for O'Grady and

the game went on with varied success till the turn came again for Towers to deal.

"'Hearts!' said Towers, after a glance at his hand.

"He laid his cards in a neat heap on the table, sat back and waited for developments; as he did so, he rested both hands for a moment on his knees. It is an ordinary action which I have seen many an innocent bridge-player adopt, but it suggested foul doings to O'Grady.

"'May I play?' he asked me, but his voice was choked with some strong emotion.

"'Yes,' I answered, and Towers raised his hands from the table and proceeded to take up his cards. In the moment of his doing so, and before he could touch the cards, O'Grady shot out his right hand and grasped Towers by the wrist so strongly that he could not move it. O'Grady was a fellow of prodigious strength.

"Poor O'Grady's feat was a poor parody of the old story of the man who pierces the sharper's hand to the table with a dagger and offers to apologize if there is not a card beneath it.

"'I'll make you my apologies, Captain Towers,' says O'Grady, 'if you don't hold a false card in your hand.'

"As is usual in such catastrophes, there was a moment's silence. Towers, though he could not disengage his hand, could turn it, and he did so, and showed that it was empty.

"'You young idiot!' O'Gorman called out. 'Let go! No one cheats at bridge that way.'

"O'Grady, out of countenance, withdrew his hand, but, before he had quite done so, Towers had clenched his left hand, and, half raising himself from his seat, brought his fist with prodigious force full on O'Grady's temple. As the young Irishman's right arm and shoulder were extended, his head inclined somewhat away from the shoulder, and the temple lying flat to the blow, received it full and without a glance. O'Grady groaned, his head dropped forward—he had been felled, as an ox is felled, by the terrible force of the blow delivered by an angry man.

"'You brute!' I said, but I felt, as I said it, that the provocation almost justified the assault.

"'I presume the rubber is over for the present,' said O'Gorman, cold-bloodedly. 'I'll gather up the cards,' he added, and he proceeded to put them together in the order they lay on the table and placed them in his pocket.

"Towers had left the room.

"'Do you feel any better yet, O'Grady, my boy?' asked O'Gorman, but the young Irishman lay still. 'Give him time,' said O'Gorman, 'and a spoonful of whisky, but I say, what a biceps that fellow must have to deliver such a smasher, eh!'

"I was dragging O'Grady's lifeless form to a sofa, helped by O'Gorman, and presently we forced a drop or two of raw whisky between his lips.

"He opened his eyes.

"'I pinned him, didn't I?' he asked, 'and then I seem to forget. What happened then?'

"'What naturally would,' said O'Gorman. 'You lay hold of a man's hand and suggest that he cheats, and he hits you hard over the ear.'

"'I'll have him out for it!' says O'Grady.

"'No, you won't, my boy. It's tit for tat, and that's good law all the world over.'

"'My head aches infernally,' muttered the young man, 'but I'll have him out on the field and shoot him.'

"'We'll have the blackguard into court first, and get him time and hard labor for cheating at cards—'

"'Then we've found him out.'

"O'Gorman went to the door and locked it. 'Look here, you two,' he said, and he took the pack of cards out of his pocket and spread them, face up, on the card-table. He counted out the first thirteen. 'There, that was Towers' hand. This is O'Grady's,' and he counted a second thirteen. 'This is mine, his dummy, and this is Morgan's. Now you heard him call hearts, didn't you? Let us see what he did it on. See here, Captain Morgan, he had just three hearts in his hand, knave, ten, and four, with some strength in the three other suits. Does any sane man declare hearts with only three of the suit in his hand? Never. But he might if he happened to know that his dummy holds five hearts.'

"'How could he guess that?'

"'By some devil's cantrip, sir! That's his secret, Captain Morgan, and Satan's, his master!'

"The thing had gone beyond a mess scandal. It was made a matter of regimental inquiry. Just about this time, too, ugly rumors began to circulate as to Towers' doings on the turf. The Colonel had received anonymous letters, of which he took at first no notice, alleging that Towers' mare, entered under the name of The Squealer as a six-year-old, was in fact a well-known steeplechaser named The Scapegoat, who had run in the Grand National at Liverpool two years before, and had come very near to winning that important event. A letter from a friend of the Colonel's, a well-known Irish sportsman, testified to the same effect. He had had his suspicions aroused, he said, on the day of the race, but not being sure, for the mare's coat was ragged and her appearance changed, he had held his tongue. It was not till some time had passed that he and a companion had examined the mare in Simpson's stables and he had found his suspicions confirmed. It was The Scapegoat sure enough. The mare's teeth had been tampered with, she bore 'mark of mouth' at variance with the length of her teeth, and that mark had evidently been 'faked.' Moreover, there was a conspicuous scar on the coronet of the off hind leg of The Scapegoat which was hidden by the unusual growth of hair on the fetlocks of Captain Towers' mare. This mark was looked for and found on the animal in Simpson's stable.

"On this evidence Towers was summoned before a Regimental Court of Inquiry and required to give an explanation. He was also called upon to explain the incidents during the bridge rubber, interrupted by the action of Lieutenant O'Grady. He had no excuse to offer for his redoubling 'No Trumps' and declaring 'hearts' with only three of that suit in his hand, except that he always played a forward, dashing game, and found it a winning one. As to his mare, he denied that she was anything but a young mare 'rising six,' and declared that a friend had picked her up for him in a Dublin livery stable.

"The inquiry was adjourned for further expert testimony. A Dublin vet. deposed that the mare's mouth had been 'faked,' that the length of her teeth indicated her age to be not less than eight. At that age the depression in the corner teeth of a horse, known as 'mark of mouth,' has disappeared for more than a twelvemonth. The mare indeed possessed 'mark of mouth,' but it was easy to see that it was a mark which had been produced by artificial means.

"Captain Towers being asked to explain why he had failed to singe or clip the mare and thus let her run at disadvantage to herself with half her winter coat on, replied that he was opposed to excessive removal of a horse's natural covering.

"Asked if the growth of hair allowed to grow on her fetlocks was not designed by him to conceal a scar or blemish on the mare's coronet, Captain Towers said the same answer would apply as he had made to the court's former question.

"An eminent detective officer had been brought from Scotland Yard, an expert in the ways of card-sharping. On being told of the circumstances of the last rubber played by Captain Towers, the detective asked for the packs that had been used. He examined the cards carefully, picked out sixteen cards from each pack, looking only at the backs, and dealt them into two heaps, face downward on the table, at which the officers on the inquiry were sitting.

"We looked at Captain Towers. For the first time his assumed smile left him and he showed some emotion. He had turned pale. 'You will probably find, gentlemen,' said Inspector Medlicott, 'that these two heaps consist of the whole suit of hearts and the three remaining aces. He turned up the cards and it proved to be as he said. There lay exposed all four aces and all the hearts in each pack.

"He handed the bundle of sixteen cards to the President.

"'You will see nothing, sir, in these cards unless you look with a powerful magnifying glass, and you will feel nothing, but the man who takes the precaution of slightly rubbing down the skin of the ball of the thumb and of his second finger with pumice stone, and so increasing the sensibility of the skin, can perceive in handling the cards that each ace has received the prick of a fine needle point, moving from face to back, and all the hearts similar pricks, from back to front—the pricks in the case of the hearts varying in number according to the value of the card. Now that supplies information enough to a good player to enable him to win heavily on every rubber.'

"Inspector Medlicott gathered up the cards of one pack into his hand, shuffled them and turned to the President.

"'If you will allow me, sir, to deal this pack, as if I were the dealer at a game of bridge, I will show you the *modus operandi* of the swindler at the game of bridge.'

"'Certainly, Mr. Inspector,' said the Colonel from the head of the board table, 'do as you say.'

"Every one in the room was a bridge player, and we watched the movements of the detective with deep interest. I glanced at the accused.

"He had turned to a death-like pallor.

"'This,' said Inspector Medlicott, 'is how a card-sharper, using these needle-marked cards, would probably deal.'

"He dealt the cards and, to my astonishment, he exactly repeated the slow method of dealing practiced by Captain Towers—the hand in each case following the card and laying each card, in its turn, on its respective heap.

"'By so doing,' said the inspector, "the ball of the thumb and of the second finger have time to come into contact with the prick marks on each card.'

"The cards now lay in four heaps on the table.

"'I am able now to tell you, sir,' said Inspector Medlicott, looking to the President, 'that I have dealt two aces to my dummy and one to each of my adversaries. I have, as it happens, given myself four good hearts; there are five small hearts in my dummy's hand, and my adversaries have each two. I should accordingly declare hearts on this deal though I have only four in the suit, and am quite sure to win heavily.'

"He turned up the cards and showed that he had correctly described them.

"The evidence was conclusive.

"We looked at Captain Towers. He had covered his face with his hands. A report of the inquiry was forwarded to headquarters, and Captain Towers was ordered to submit himself to a court martial or quit the service. But Towers did not wait for any instructions from headquarters. He disappeared suddenly from our midst. The day following the inquiry he was gone. He had left numerous creditors behind, which we thought the more iniquitous, as his short career among us had left him a winner at cards and on the turf of over £15,000. He had never repaid advances made by O'Gorman, O'Grady, and myself. Simpson had an unpaid bill of £50 against him with the mare as set-off, but a steeple-chaser whose teeth have been tampered with is not a very realizable asset, and he was glad to take £100 from Major O'Gorman for the animal, with the understanding that the balance was to be paid to any legal claimant who might turn up.

"I will observe that the mare's bad temper was a fiction of Towers'. She had nothing wrong with her but a delicate mouth, and the touch of the curb was an agony to her that caused her to rear. She became O'Gorman's favorite hunter, and won him many a race, but she had to carry weight in consideration of her previous performances as The Scapegoat, her old name, which was honestly restored to her.

"A terrible catastrophe followed Towers' disappearance. If he had not entirely ruined me, he was the actual sole cause of the ruin of my poor young kinsman, Lieutenant O'Grady. He had borrowed money from O'Grady when he had any to lend, won from him at cards and, we now knew, cheated him, besides inducing him to make absurd books on horse-races with him. O'Grady was irretrievably insolvent. He came of a family of good and honorable soldiers. He felt that honor soiled and sullied, and on the day following Towers' departure, O'Grady blew his brains out.

"I shall never forget our meeting after the funeral. We swore among us that if ever the chance presented itself we would be even with the cold-blooded villain Towers. It has happened that I alone among us was able to redeem that oath.

"I cannot lay all the blame of my own misfortunes upon Captain Towers. Some of it at least was due to my own stupidity and my own extravagance.

"I could only just pay my debts and I was nearly a pauper, with no chances left. My purpose was to enlist in some regiment going to India or the Colonies. I mentioned my intention to Inspector Medlicott, as a man of wide experience, to whose society I had taken a fancy.

"'Don't do anything so rash with your life, sir,' he said. 'Don't waste it—you've had your lesson. You've learnt a lot without knowing that you've learnt anything. Go where you can use what you have learnt.'

"'And where's that, Mr. Inspector? I am too old and ignorant of business for an office, and I don't know any situation where they have any use for the sort of thing I know.'

"'Come to us,' said the Inspector, 'work your way up from the ranks. It's more interesting than soldiering, and quite as dangerous.'

"This is how I came to enter the detective force, and I never have regretted taking Inspector Medlicott's advice. Nevertheless, I did not take it quite at once. It is a big jump from being an officer in a smart cavalry regiment to the rank and file of the Force at Scotland Yard. I hesitated for a time and tried other ways, but I need dwell no longer at present upon that interval in my career."

CHAPTER II

THE GREAT JEWEL ROBBERY AT BALIN ABBEY

"You began, Mr. Morgan," I said, "by telling me that you would give me some account of the great jewel robbery at Balin Abbey, and the burglar you call Gentleman Coggins."

"I have been telling you about Gentleman Coggins," said Inspector Morgan, "all along. Captain Towers and Gentleman Coggins are one and the same person."

"What!" I said, "an officer in the army turned London burglar! Towers sank so low as that, did he?"

"Don't say 'sank,'" said Morgan, laughing, "say rather he rose. There is rank in crime as in every other profession. No man stands so high as Coggins—Ikey Coggins. Captain Towers, who cheated us all at cards and won those thousands of pounds on the turf and then let himself be found out, is not to be named in rank and social position with Ikey Coggins—*alias* Conkey Coggins—*alias* Gentleman Coggins. He stands at the head of his profession in Great Britain. He has been suspected and watched by the police for years, and never once been nabbed, never once been sent to jail, never once even been brought before a court of justice. It is a proud position!"—The Inspector smiled.

"Did he go at once from soldiering to burglary?" I asked.

"No," said Morgan. "Captain Towers went first to America. After a short and successful career in that country, finding it got too hot to hold him, he got killed in an accident."

I laughed—"A sham accident, I presume."

"No, the accident was serious enough. One of the biggest things of the kind in America of that season. Sixty drowned, forty burned to death, and over a hundred injured for life, but I don't suppose Towers was anywhere near the place where it happened. I have kept the announcement of his death in the *Morning Post*. It is a curiosity."

The Inspector drew from his pocket a newspaper cutting and read aloud: "'*Obituary Notice.* We regret to announce the death, in the recent accident on the Wabash & Susquehanna Railway, America, of Captain Towers, late of H.M. . . . The great success of Captain Towers as a gentleman rider on the Irish Turf, his fine horsemanship and his phenomenal winnings will be in the recollection of our readers. Captain Towers was not only a gentleman rider of remarkable skill, but a sportsman of rare integrity. His winning of a fortune on the Irish Turf was the immediate cause of his honorable retirement from the British Army. The sudden melancholy demise of Captain Towers has cut short what promised to become a very brilliant sporting career in the United States, where he leaves many admiring friends.'

"The fact is," said Inspector Morgan, "that Pinkerton's police were hot upon his scent, and he bolted over here, under a false name, just in time to save himself. He had won quite a lot of American money."

"He must have been a rich man with his winnings on both sides of the water."

"Yes, but not too rich for the position he aspired to take up in the profession."

"What!" I said. "It takes capital to set up as a London burglar?"

"A very large capital. That is, if you have ambition to take rank. Recollect, too, it is one of the most lucrative professions in the world. Great lawyers, great surgeons, great jockeys, are not in it with great burglars. When you may look to net from £50 to £200,000 a year, you must not stint in preliminary expenses."

"I don't really see, Mr. Morgan, what a burglar can require beyond a set of burglary tools, a pair of list slippers, a mask, a dark lantern, a revolver, and perhaps a few skeleton keys and center-bits."

Morgan smiled. "That is not enough for the modern professional. It was all very well for the old-fashioned cracksman. The modern burglar leads a double life. He passes half his time in society—of a kind—the other half among his pals. He has to keep in his pay an army of retainers as large as a mediæval baron. Some of them are his agents, some his spies, half the criminal classes in town are his pensioners, and good pay, too, they get, for if he give less than the police offer, the rascals would betray him at once. Then he has to pay for the defense in court of his agents when they get caught. I calculate that a man in the position of Ikey Coggins, lately Captain Towers, does not pay away less than twelve or fifteen thousand a year."

"And it pays him to do that?"

"Handsomely. Why, a single haul like the one at Balin Abbey must have brought in not far short of £100,000. Even the papers said £60,000, but ladies, we find, invariably lessen their losses in these cases."

"Was Towers' name mentioned in the case? I don't remember his name in the papers."

"He was only known among us as Coggins. His identity with Captain Towers did not come out at the trial. No one but four or five persons can know the truth about it. Of course, my chiefs at the office know, for I told them."

"Is it to be a secret still?"

"I don't see that it's any use making a secret of it any longer. It's ancient history now. Certainly not to you, who are, if you will allow me to call you so, a brother official and something of a colleague.

"You honor me, Morgan, by calling me so. But tell me this story of the jewel robbery if it's fresh in your memory. It's anything but fresh in mine."

"It is in mine. It was my first big job, and it won my inspectorship for me."

"Then, please, Mr. Morgan, tell me the story, and tell it in your own way. I don't know a better. You give the length and breadth and look of things and let me see their working out, so that I could do it all myself if I wanted to. I never get that sort of thing in books. I suppose it's a detective's way of telling a story to his brother detective."

"I suppose it may be that," said Inspector Morgan. "We know the importance of detail. One nail-hole in a footprint on a dusty road may make all the difference between finding our man or losing him."

I interrupted him as he was beginning his story.

"One thing I want to know first. You said the swindler Towers, who had given himself out as dead in that name, was leading a double life in London. Surely he has not come to life again and resumed his own name?"

Morgan paused. "Well, he *is* undoubtedly living a double life. That is certain, for 'Coggins' disappears from time to time, but, so to say, his life activity goes on.

"And what's his new name? What is his other life?"

"The answer to that question," said Inspector Morgan, "is the answer to the problem I set myself to discover. You will see that I did discover it. More by a strange sort of accident than by any cleverness of mine it came out. That he kept his secret so long was due to his wonderful talent."

"You mean that the police knew Coggins and could lay their hands on him when they would, but the other life of the man was a mystery to them?"

"Just so, and what was the good of arresting Coggins? He managed that there should never be a scrap of evidence against him, though we know he was behind every big thing in London and 100 miles round London.

"Why, when Balin Abbey was broken into, Coggins was at Pangford, eight miles away, and our fellows had been there watching him for a week. He was staying at the Balin Arms at Pangford as Monsieur Dubois, traveling for a Lyons silk firm and booking a good many orders for silk skirtings and dress pieces. The man was the life and soul of the Commercial Room, speaking fluent English with a French accent and singing French songs to the piano in the travelers' room! What can you do with such a fellow!"

"What made your people watch him?"

"We had got notice from trustworthy sources that he had gone to crack a crib, as they call it, on the outskirts of Pangford. We had three good men on the watch, Sergeant Smith and two others under him, and they reported that he was seen at odd hours to be watching and studying this particular house—a retired manufacturer's villa."

"A blind, I suppose?"

"Not exactly; the house was broken into the very night following the affair at Balin Abbey, when every one was full of that, and the fellow got off with £5,000 in plate and jewelry. The burglary, however, could not be traced to Coggins, though of course we suspected him.

"It was the day after the great affair at the Abbey that my chief sent for me. 'There is something going on down in Somersetshire,' he said, 'which beats us all. Coggins is in it. I can tell you that much, but I can tell you no more. We are going to give you a chance of unraveling matters.'"

"Stop, Morgan," I said. "Pray, did your chief know or did you guess that Coggins and Towers were the same person?"

"He did not and I did not—at that time. All we knew of Coggins was that he was a burglaring luminary of the first order, who had come from nowhere about four years before and had beaten all our best men."

"Please go on. Forgive me for interrupting. I won't again."

Morgan continued: "'The case,' said my chief, when I went before him, 'is peculiar, and we are taking unusual measures to come at the truth. The facts, as we know them, are these—(Forget what you have read in the newspapers, the reporters have got hold of some things by the wrong end). The plain facts are these:

ALIAS TOWERS

"'Lord and Lady Balin were entertaining a house party at the Abbey some days ago. On the 23d of this month of January there was a big shoot on. The day was fine, dry and frosty; the wind got up at night and some rain had fallen.

"'The ladies joined the guns at lunch time at a point in the Balin woods some two miles from the Abbey. Every one of the ladies had elected to walk, except two: the hostess, Lady Balin, and Lady Drusilla Lancaster, an elderly lady, a first cousin of Lord Balin. These two ladies were driven to the luncheon place in her Ladyship's pony phaeton.

"'The fact is important; because that night the Abbey was broken into, and the room of every one of the ladies was entered by the burglar, or burglars, except Lady Drusilla's.'

"'Lady Balin's room was not entered?'

"'Yes, it was,' said my chief, 'and the famous Balin emeralds were abstracted. They are historical jewels, and cannot be worth less than £20,000.'

"'Then the inference which you wish me to draw, that the four-mile walk and the day in the open air would have made all the ladies drowsy except the hostess and Lady Drusilla, partly breaks down.'

"My chief smiled. 'Only partly. Lady Balin is a stout lady, and presumably a heavy sleeper. That fact would be known to the dwellers at the Abbey—servants and others.'

"'Ah,' I said, 'you suspect connivance of some one in the house?'

"'We are sure of it. The burglar had learnt when to break in, where to break in, and, being in, where to go. The house is ancient and very large, and the corridors and passages and bedrooms are a perfect rabbit warren; no one but an inmate could make his way about. He made no mistake. He went into every room where there were jewels to be got, and he took everything except the pearls and diamonds of Lady Drusilla. The old lady is more careless even than most ladies with her jewels, and insists upon her maid leaving the string of pearls—about the biggest in the country—hanging by the side of her mirror, and her diamond necklace and pendant fastened to her pincushion, where she can see both from her bed in the light of her night-light. Coggins, or his agent, never troubled her, however, and her diamonds and pearls were safe in the morning.'

"The chief had turned over the pages of a little MS. pocket-book, and he referred to an entry in it as he read these particulars in the habits and behavior of Lady Drusilla Lancaster.

"'Lord Balin,' my chief went on, 'was here this morning. He asks, with the sanction of the local police, for the help of Scotland Yard. He wished to offer a great reward. I dissuaded him. He was himself of opinion that the burglar must have a confederate in the house. I told him I had no doubt of it. I told him I would send a couple of my men down to make inquiries. These inquiries, as you know, Sergeant, made openly and to the knowledge of every one, are worth next to nothing. I told Lord Balin so; but told him that, with his leave, I would also send down a competent officer with two assistants, who, while the other officers would fill the eyes of the people at Balin, would carry on a real inquiry. Would Lord Balin agree to receive such an officer as a guest?'

"'Lord Balin hesitated. He said, 'Would the detective be enough used to the ways of the world not to be discovered at once by the rest of my guests?'

"'The person I shall choose,' said my chief, 'will run no such risk.'

"Lord Balin bowed. 'I have an idea,' he said. 'I have a distant cousin in Australia of whom I often talk, I have never seen him since he was a child. Let your officer impersonate him.'

"'What is his age?"

"'About thirty or thirty-five,' said Lord Balin.

"'Rich or poor?' asked the chief.

"'Fabulously rich. A squatter who has speculated successfully in gold mines in Western Australia.'

"'The very thing. My officer shall go down in a motor, with a chauffeur, and an Irish valet, both trustworthy officers in the force. Pray, Lord Balin, may I ask if you have lunched?'

"'Not yet. I propose to do so at my club.'

"'Please do, and when you come back I will introduce you to your relative from Australia!'

"'Before Lord Balin went off to lunch,' said my chief, 'I took down from his lips certain intimate particulars relative to every guest staying in the Abbey. Here are my memoranda. Put them in your pocket and study them at your leisure.'

"My chief, having given me these details of his conversation with Lord Balin with his accustomed succinctness and lucidity, turned to me and said:

"'You will guess, Sergeant Morgan, that the cousin from Australia, whose name is Stanley, is yourself. Macgregor is your chauffeur, and O'Brien your valet and servant, both in your division; they will, of course, take their orders directly from you. Go with O'Brien to the stores now and make yourself ready to go down to Somersetshire. You know what a smart man's outfit should be on a country visit. As you are a millionaire, you may safely outdo good taste. You will take my own 24 h.p. Napier. Macgregor is accustomed to drive it, and he will carry you down in less than five hours. Try to get there before ten, so as to see the guests and make a good impression before you turn in for the night. The rest I leave entirely to you. Go now and make your preparations and purchases, and in two hours' time come back here and make Lord Balin's acquaintance.'

"When I returned Lord Balin was with my chief.

"He received me very pleasantly. Lord Balin is known for a charm of manner not common among Englishmen of his class. In his case it is explainable by the fact that he was in diplomacy before he succeeded to the peerage. I think my chief had said more in my favor than he had told me, for Lord Balin smoothed over a difficult position cleverly and kindly. He seemed particularly struck by the humor of the situation, and acted the part of a long-separated relation to perfection.

"'Well, Mr. Stanley, you have changed less than I expected. It is true you were a chubby infant of four when your father carried you off to the Antipodes; you've grown, my boy, but not out of remembrance. I could swear to those eyes of yours. You don't remember me, Mr. Stanley—

Stanley, I mean, for I must drop the Mr. with Dick Stanley's son.

"'Now tell me, my dear Stanley, one thing. Can you shoot? Have you taken after your poor father in that?'

"'I used to shoot pretty straight,' I said, 'years ago. I hope I haven't forgotten how.'

"'I'm very glad to hear it. We have a big shoot on to-morrow, and we want an extra gun. Moreton is half blind, Pulteney nervous, and there is only myself left to account for the pheasants, and you, if you will help me. You didn't bring your guns from Australia?' asked Lord Balin slily.

"'No,' I said, 'I'm afraid I left them behind.'

"'Never mind, we can find you all that at the Abbey. I thought, Sir Henry,' said Lord Balin, addressing my chief, 'that I would not put off this shoot. It is one planned on pretty much the same scale as the one we had on the 23d, the day of the robbery, and I thought it would help our friend'—he turned to me—'that everything should take place to-morrow as it took place on the day the Abbey was broken into.'

"'Excellent idea! Pray, Lord Balin, combine your plans with Sergeant—with Mr. Stanley.' He laughed, shook hands with Lord Balin, nodded to me, and went off. 'You have your last orders, Sergeant,' he said to me as he left the room.

"Lord Balin and I talked over things in the chief's room, and the more we talked the more did Lord Balin smooth over the awkwardness of the situation in which I found myself about to plunge, into the midst of a kind of society in which I had practically taken no part for over six years, and in which I was to appear—with the best of motives, of course—under false pretences, and in a name which did not belong to me.

"It was a pleasant drive down to Balin Abbey in Somersetshire: cold but pleasant. We three professionals talked naturally of nothing but the great jewel robbery. Certainly our chief could not have given me a better staff. Macgregor is a young Scotsman of great intelligence and promise. He would take advantage of his superior position in the house as chauffeur to deal with the upper servants. Phelim O'Brien, a clever, good-looking, lively Irishman, who had himself served in the Irish Constabulary, had found the county work in that service too dull, enlisted into a line regiment, had been an officer's servant, but gave that up for harder work of a higher kind, and found his way at last to Scotland Yard. We trusted to him to find out what was going on among the valets and ladies' maids in the servants' hall. We naturally talked of 'Coggins,' the mysterious factor in the criminal world. Coggins, who went about evading us—the king of burglars, a master of disguise and make-up, admired and feared by every thief, bully, and hooligan in the streets—and though always suspected, never arrested. The very boys chaffed the policeman on his beat with '*Yah! Pinch Coggins—caunt yer? garn!*'—and here was this impudent scoundrel settled down at Pangford, within a few miles of the scene of his last successful exploit—and not a single ounce of evidence against him!"

CHAPTER III

THE CIRCLE AT BALIN ABBEY

"Balin Abbey, in Somersetshire, is a huge, stately building of Shakespeare's time, untouched by the hand of the restorer—a gray pile that stands up amid a wide, flat area of grounds and gardens contemporary with itself, with stone paved courts and pathways and tall rectilineal yew hedges. As we drew up, the moonlight of a wind-still winter night shone full upon its walls and the few ancient cedars that grew thereby, and displayed the armorial carvings on wall surfaces and gable ends.

"The ground is a plain, far and near, and the park studded with oak trees of great size. No high road runs within a mile of the Abbey, and I asked myself how the burglar could approach the house for purposes even of inspection without arousing observation, but Macgregor reminded me that the Abbey was one of the famous show houses of England, containing many valuable works of the great foreign masters and also priceless family portraits by Reynolds, Romney, and Raeburn.

" 'Be jabers,' said Phelim O'Brien, 'I hope the knowledge of that same won't reach 'Gentleman Coggins' at Pangford. If it does, the devil a picture will be left on the walls of Balin Abbey.'

"I never was so cordially, even so exuberantly, welcomed. Lord Balin could not better have played the part of a host welcoming a long-parted relative. His guests, many of whom had known and heard of my supposed father, came forward as cordially as their host. It was fortunate for me that I had done garrison duty in Australia, or I should have been puzzled by some of the questions I was expected to answer.

"For a moment I was confounded at the responsibility of my new part and even ashamed of my imposture. I was like an actor thrust forward upon the stage to act some important part that he feels to be beyond his powers, and is astounded at his own undeserved success and the applause of his audience.

"I could see that there was not a shadow of suspicion in any of the company that I was anybody but the person I was impersonating. Presently I began to reflect that to do any good to my superior and to Lord Balin and his despoiled guests I must do my utmost to second Lord Balin's endeavors to put me in the shoes of Dick Stanley's son. So I let myself go forward, and presently I was, as the saying is, in the very skin of my part, and I began to be almost persuaded that I was no other than young Robert Stanley, Australian squatter and millionaire. I had studied my chief's note-book in coming down. Most of the guests seemed to me thoroughly commonplace and uninteresting people. Lord and Lady Moreton and their two plain, good-humored daughters, Lord Pulteney, a young man with every appearance of health and strength, but, according to his own account, a nerve-shattered neurasthenic, who got one into corners to complain of his health and the last new theories on serums, microbes, and what not. Two persons in the company struck me as standing apart, both were women.

"One was the elderly lady whom I have mentioned before,

Lady Drusilla Lancaster; the other a remarkably smart and handsome woman who was introduced to me as Mrs. Townley. I should call her an unusually well-dressed woman from the milliner's point of view, for I have eye enough to know what women and milliners mean by well dressed. It generally leaves men who are worth anything cold, but this woman had evidently thought less of the fashion plates, in dressing herself, than of her remarkable beauty of face, hair, eyes and figure, and dressed to enhance these attributes. Her gown and its garniture seemed to me to be simple in defiance of the present mode which is not simple.

"When I put this point of view, admiringly, to Lady Drusilla Lancaster, that wise lady placed her double eyeglass upon her austere and aquiline nose and contemplated Mrs. Townley's half-reclining form with a severe expression.

"'Pretty creature!' she said, with more contempt than admiration in her tone. 'That soft cloudy mauve goes wonderfully with that bright complexion of hers and her golden brown hair. And that great diamond-clasped pearl dog-collar on her neck and the pearl embroidery on her dress and the dog-collar bracelets of diamond and pearls suit her white skin perfectly. But I think you said, simple?'

"'The effect is simple.'

"'My dear man!'—it was a favorite old-fashioned form of speech with Lady Drusilla—'my dear man, if simple means easy and if simple means cheap, that confection is nothing of the sort. Trust a woman's eyes! Paquin or Raudnitz has had sleepless nights over that dress, and you may be sure those *nuits blanches* will be represented in Paquin's or Raudnitz's bills!'

"Mrs. Townley is rich, I believe?"

"'She is a widow, or rather a grass widow, without children, whose husband came into, or made, a great fortune the other day—so I hear. Her wealth is one of her many charms.'

"'I never thought wealth was a charm.'

"'It never was one in my best time. It is now. Hideous people with horrid manners come among us, and if they are rich, we overlook their looks, and their ways, and adore them. Then, just imagine what we do with rich people with sweet faces and figures, who know how to dress and talk, like Mrs. Townley!'

"'You say *her* charm. Is her husband, then, a person of no importance?'

"'On the contrary, a man of great importance and intelligence; for does he not manufacture the money that pays for all that luxury?'

"'A dull, money-grubbing sort of man, I suppose?'

"'My cousin Balin says not—says he is charming. His only fault is that he is never, so to say, anywhere. He is always traveling—always in pursuit of fortune, and always overtaking it. He even traveled here one day to see his wife and make Lord Balin's acquaintance. Balin says he is a delightful man and clever and learned beyond words. He was interested in everything—the architecture, the abbey ruins, and, above all, the pictures. It seems he found out all sorts of masterpieces in the gallery that no one had ever suspected. The next morning before breakfast he had disappeared, had rushed down to Southampton to catch the next steamer for Tokio or the River Plate, I forget which.'

"'I am glad you approve of Mrs. Townley,' I said. 'She is certainly charming.'

"'She is; but pray do not go and fall in love with her, Mr. Stanley. Believe me, she is horrid in some ways, and I owe it to the son of my old friend Dick Stanley to tell him so.'

"'Horrid?'

"'Horrid! A baddish, indiscriminate flirt, a heartless woman, and a very selfish one, insincere and—all the rest of it. Mind, I don't say not virtuous. I am sure she is as good as gold. It makes it all the worse, for it deprives her of the excuse of temptation.'

"I was so taken aback by this outspokenness that I said nothing for a minute. 'Now,' said the lady, 'that I have given myself away, and made you think me a spiteful old cat, I'll tell you why I said it all.'

"I smiled. 'You spoke out, and I am rather afraid your voice reached to Mrs. Townley's ears.'

"'My dear man! I talked loud just that I might not be heard. That woman has the ears of a lynx. If I had dropped my voice she would have overheard every word I said. She is not like one of us, who never condescend to listen when people abuse us. But no, I change my mind, I won't say why I abuse her. Let's leave her alone. You see I hate her! Tell me about yourself and your father. I knew him well and liked him immensely. Shall I confess the truth? I admired him—we most of us did. You have just his eyes, Mr. Stanley, and you would be like him but for that horrid beard of yours. Forgive me for saying that! He was in the Guards when I knew him first. Then he got into debt—all the nice ones do—and exchanged into a crack cavalry regiment—which? the Scots Greys, I think—ruined himself entirely, and we had to let him go to the land of kangaroos and gold. Dear Mr. Stanley, if you wore your moustache only, you would be the image of him. You have just his height, his square shoulders and his light figure.'

"I may remark here that I had let my beard grow when I had left the army, short and trimmed back, to be sure—but it was a most complete disguise. I passed my oldest friends in the street and they never knew me. There is no such disguise as a beard.

"Lord Balin followed the hospitable custom of showing his latest guest his bedroom. I noticed that the guests left the drawing-room in a body, and we found ourselves in the great hall from which broad flights of polished oaken stairs lead in three directions to the bedrooms on the floor above. On the hall table were two great silver trays, on one of which had been ranged decanters of white wines and spirits, with mineral waters. On the other were great crystal decanters of what looked like barley water. Most of the men and all the women drank copiously of this soothing and harmless beverage. All except Lady Drusilla. I filled a glass and brought it to her. She took it and touched the rim with her lips, barely tasting the liquid.

"'It is bad luck, isn't it?' she said, smiling (there are few things more taking than the rare smile of an austere old woman), 'to refuse the first thing one is offered by a new friend, and I want nothing bad to come between us two.'

"'Thank you,' I said. 'You don't like barley water?'

"'Well,' she said, 'if I drank as much dry champagne and

sweet Benedictine as some of the women, perhaps I should be thirsty too. Besides which,' said Lady Drusilla with a curious bluntness, 'I don't like my drink meddled with by other people.'

"'How meddled with?'

"'Well, the other night I came out just before the others. I was sleepy, and I saw a woman stirring up the barley water with a long spoon. "What are you doing?" I asked, staring at her. "Only putting in a little more sugar. It is never quite sweet enough for me," she said.'

"'I wonder who it was?' I remarked. 'The housekeeper, perhaps.'

"Lady Drusilla did not appear to hear my question. 'Good-night,' she said, 'and don't dream of burglars.'

"'I shall lock my door,' I said, laughing.

"'I shall not lock mine,' she said, 'for all the burglars in England, besides—'

"I laughed. 'You are not afraid of seeing a masked figure with a dark lantern in one hand and a revolver in the other—'

"'Not at all,' she said, laughing in her turn. 'That is not the sort of figure I should see. I don't think I should see a man at all. Oh! I shouldn't be afraid.'

"We both laughed. I don't quite know why.

"Mrs. Townley had interrupted her talk with young Lord Pulteney and was watching us. Was she, like the man in the old play, sure we were talking of her because we laughed so heartily?

"I followed Lord Balin after the others had all said their last good-nights and had gone to the bedrooms. He showed me into mine. No sooner had he shut the door behind him than he sat down and laughed heartily.

"'Now, did I do it well?' he asked. 'I used to be rather good at private theatricals, but, by Jove, I don't think I ever played so well as to-night. And you? Do you know the whole lot of them have been congratulating me on my new-found kinsman. Lady Drusilla raves about you, and the beautiful Mrs. Townley is sulking with her for monopolizing you all the evening. I say, though, my boy, there's one thing I'm sorry for—damned sorry for!'

"'What is that, Lord Balin?'

"'Why, that it isn't true—that you are not Bob Stanley and come to settle in the Old Country.'

"I had come to discharge a rather difficult and disagreeable duty, and, behold, I found myself in a Capua!

"'It's my great wealth that does it, I suppose. Lady Drusilla tells me wealth is the modern *open sesame* into society and into men's and women's hearts.'

"'Not into mine, Stanley—and, by Jove, if you knew her, not into my cousin Drusilla's either.'

"I thought it about time to get Lord Balin to give me some particulars. He was prepared. He had brought a plan of the first floor of the house.

Morgan took out his note-book, and on a blank sheet of it drew a rough sketch.

"The cross marks the place where the burglar had forced an entry, by entering the conservatory, climbing up a ladder inside, pushing up a skylight, and entering the corridor which leads to all the bedrooms of the guests. Observe that the bedroom marked A is mine, opposite to me is the bedrom B, occupied on the night of the robbery by Mrs. Townley. While her bedroom was entered and valuable jewels taken, Lady Drusilla's, marked C, was left unentered, although the burglar must have passed her door on his way to the other wing of the house, where every room occupied by a lady was entered and the jewels abstracted. The passing by of Lady Drusilla's door, though it was known to every one what a prize lay there unguarded for the taking, was unaccountable, and perhaps should furnish some clue to the thief and the motives of the thief.

"I asked Lord Balin if the forcing of the window leading from the end of the corridor on the flat roof of the conservatory might not be a sham entry, while all the time the real thief was some one, perhaps a servant, in the house.

"Lord Balin had considered that, but he did not think it possible. In the first place, the entry had been effected, according to the testimony of the two officers from Scotland Yard, with such skill that it could be the work of no one but a skilled professional. They would no doubt report all the circumstances to me, when I should deem it prudent to see them. I told Lord Balin that the officer Macgregor had been instructed by me to act as intermediary between myself and the two detectives, so as not to arouse suspicion by my speaking to them myself.

"Then," said Lord Balin, 'I can't do better than let you ring for your valet and chauffeur, interview them and leave you together. If you want to see me in private, you will always find me alone in the library.'

"Macgregor and O'Brien came and brought with them the report of the two detectives on the spot. They exactly confirmed what Lord Balin had told me. The window of the corridor was strongly barred with iron, and a bar had been removed from its soldered inlet in the stonework of the window. A circular hole had been cut through the thick plate-glass window, exactly over the bolt in the heavy oaken shutter, the shutter likewise had been neatly perforated with a burglar's center-bit, the bolt pushed back, and window and shutter opened. No one but a very clever professional burglar could do such work so neatly, and even so it was a job that would take some time to execute. There was the mark of a hand on the glass and on the shutter, but the hand had been gloved. No betraying finger-marks had been left. There were plentiful footprints on the turf near where the entrance had been effected, the night having been rainy and the wind high. There were even muddy marks where a man had trodden in the corridor, but, after four or five steps, the muddy impressions got fainter, as they naturally would, and presently disappeared altogether. The prints were untraceable for this reason, that rough socks had been drawn over the wearer's boots. So much for the burglar's entry. The wonder was that any one could break into Balin Abbey, for a night fireman was on duty all night in the hall. It is true he was a very old man, and that he remained on the ground floor and only patrolled the hall and the rooms on that floor, but the hall runs up nearly to the roof of the house, and any movement in the corridors would presumably be visible or audible from below. It seemed, moreover, impossible to come near the house without being observed, for, at nightfall, two under-keepers patrol the grounds, with two fierce bloodhounds in leash. After this patrolling, the dogs, which are kept shut up in the dark all day, are let loose, and only taken in again and fed at daylight. This practice, a precaution against poachers and tramps, had been followed for years, and was known all over the neighborhood. Under these difficult circumstances a burglarious entry of the premises had always seemed to the owners and inmates of Balin Abbey an impossible circumstance.

"I had suggested to Lord Balin almost at once upon my introduction to him that the robbery might have been done by a servant, male or female, either in the service of a guest or of the family. Lord Balin had told me that this was in the last degree improbable, from the fact of a curious domestic usage in existence at the Abbey from the days when the building had been a conventual house. All the men servants sleep in the east wing of the third story, and the women in the west wing—neither inmates of the separate sleeping apartments being able to reach the lower part of the house without, in the case of the men, their passing through a door of which the key is kept by the house steward; in the case of the women, without their passing through the bedroom of the housekeeper.

"'This circumstance by itself, therefore, almost precludes the possibility of collusion between an outside burglar and a servant.'

"It left this, then, as the inevitable conclusion. The crime which, from its nature and all the circumstances of difficulty surrounding it, could not have been committed by any single unaided burglar, must have been the joint action of a skilful professional criminal, acting in confederacy either with an inmate of the house, not a servant, or else with the connivance and help of one of the gamekeepers, of whom there was a small army at Balin Abbey. I put this latter possibility aside almost as soon as it occurred to me, for it is well known to members of our profession that criminality, of anything more than a petty larceny character, is nearly unknown among the gamekeeper class in this country. Taking them as a whole, a more respectable and honest community of men does not exist. Apart from which, the keepers have no access to the dwelling part of the house, and it was proved that the burglar's confederate had a very complete and intimate knowledge not only of where the possessors of the jewels slept, but of exactly where, in what drawers, cabinets or receptacles, the jewels were kept by their owners.

"I went to sleep that night with the problem summed up in its shortest terms: A great and successful jewel robbery, clear traces of burglarious entry by a most skilful operator, the fact that the most notorious burglar in Great Britain had taken up his residence in a town in the neighborhood, the still more unaccountable circumstance that he still remained there after the jewels were stolen. What could be the only deduction from these facts but that, though the robbery had been successful, the jewels had not yet been carried off by the principal in the affair. They must therefore still be in the Abbey. Since the robbery, I had been told that two additional bloodhounds had been let loose every night. The ways of these animals are well known, they are the fiercest among the race of dogs, their natural prey is man, and they never give tongue but when they scent their quarry. Unlike almost every other description of dog, they never bark or bay without cause. Therefore, if a single hound gives tongue in the night, it would be a signal to the other hounds that their quarry was afoot, the night would be filled by their baying, and the whole house instantly on the alert. With four such animals at large it was certain that no stranger would dare to approach the windows of Balin Abbey. This, then, was probably the explanation of the mystery of the continued stay at Pangford of the burglar Coggins, if indeed he was the author of the crime. He was waiting to receive the proceeds of the robbery from his confederate, an inmate of the Abbey. Why could not the jewels be made up into a parcel and sent away by post? The answer is that such a proceeding, since the advent of the police officers in the house, would be an extremely risky operation. Every postal packet would be scrutinized.

"So far my conclusions had now led me. I had ordered Macgregor to be ready for me with the motor by daylight. O'Brien was to be on the watch round the house as soon as the hounds were called in, which was always done as soon as the eye could travel a hundred yards across the lawns.

"The next day was to bring with it several remarkable surprises and discoveries.

CHAPTER IV

THE FIRST DISCOVERY

"I was up and was dressing before dawn, and from my window watched the great walls of yew turn from black to green, and their shadows, across the frost-covered lawns, slowly shorten, as the sun's globe rose from the eastern woods. I heard the keepers whistle, and saw the four fawn-coated hounds gallop slowly and lurchingly toward the sound. As they went they left their footprints on the white rime which lay on turf, paths, and flower beds. It was going to be a glorious day, and presently the sun, in a cloudless sky, would draw up the slight hoar frost. I went down and went out. I could hear the snorting of the motor in the stable-yard where I had told Macgregor to wait for me, but I would go round, first, by the conservatory under Mrs. Townley's and my windows, and take a survey of the ground. I could see for myself how, through the flat roof of the conservatory, half glass, half lead, the burglar had made his way, and how, from the roof, he had climbed by the thick stem of a wistaria to the window of the corridor—a bold and difficult feat, and one that only a master of his craft could attempt. How had a man, doing all this at night, escaped the bloodhounds which were at large every night? It puzzled me. And the explanation only came later.

"I walked along a broad stone-paved path that leads from the conservatory, and looked back at the house. Every blind was down and every shutter closed. The path leads to the lawn tennis ground. I reached a grassy plot of turf beyond where the few ruins of the ancient Abbey are visible, ruined bits of walls and archways rising sheer from level well-shorn turf. The ground all round was at present one level sheet of hoar frost, dazzlingly white in the red rays of the rising sun.

"My eye was caught suddenly by a curious break in the whiteness, a little circular patch of green, no larger across than the palm of a man's hand, close to a ruined archway that rose out of the ground and broke the level monotony of white. Clearly a piece of wood, probably the top of some half-rotted post, just under the surface, had raised the temperature and prevented the deposition of frost crystals in that particular spot.

"Though quite satisfied with my explanation, the fancy took me to examine into the thing more closely. I went down on my knees, and perceived at once that the circle was artificially made, probably by a gardener's trowel. I perceived that the tool had cut deep all round the little circle. I took hold of the grass and pulled at it, but the slight frost had frozen all together. I took a pen-knife from my pocket and passed the longest blade deep round the circle and pulled again at the blades of grass. The bit of turf lifted as the top of a box lifts up and revealed the hole in the ground, entirely filled by a brown paper parcel a little larger than a man's fist.

"The jewels? No! Only their gold settings.

"I put the parcel half opened in my pocket, filled in the hole with a clod of earth, replaced the turfy covering, stamped all down smooth, and knew that, in half an hour, when the sun should have melted the hoar frost, not a trace would be left of my morning's work.

"Who had done this? Who had detached the gems from their setting and deposited them in this hiding-place? And why had it been done? To answer the last question first: The settings were clearly removed to lessen the chance of detection, and to make the jewels more easy to pass or send away. Who had taken the stones from the setting? Clearly not the burglar. It was a two hours' job for an expert, working with pliers and pincers. He would not have had the time. Clearly it was the work of his confederate, the inmate of the house, and he, or she, had hidden the gold settings in a place where they might reasonably be expected to lie, lost to man's cognizance, forever. The place of concealment was admirably chosen—it was a secluded, unfrequented part of the grounds, where the Abbey ruins lay—and a person engaged in making the *cache* in such a spot could safely count on not being observed by guests or gardeners.

"I communicated my discovery to Macgregor as we motored to Pangford, where I desired to see the chief of our agents who were there to watch the suspected Coggins.

" 'It's growing warm, sir,' said Macgregor, when I showed him the jewel settings. 'It's growing warm!'

"I thought so too, yet we were as far as ever from bringing the thing home to the man we were morally sure was the real author of the crime—'Gentleman Coggins.' "

CHAPTER V

SERGEANT SMITH: HIS OPINIONS AND ADVENTURES

"Sergeant Smith is in charge of the party deputed to watch the redoubtable Coggins at Pangford. The Sergeant is a North country man, senior to me in the force, but of more recent promotion, a very hard-working, conscientious man, but, to tell truth, I felt that Smith was not quite a match for the wily Coggins. I did not let Macgregor take the motor into the town, but waited outside the houses while Macgregor went on foot and brought Sergeant Smith to report and confer with me.

"Sergeant Smith had a strange tale to relate. It appears to him that Coggins has his heart in his new business. The Sergeant prudently keeps out of Coggins' way himself for fear of recognition, but neither of his men have ever seen him or been seen by him, and they drop from time to time into the bar parlor of the Balin Arms. From that 'coign of vantage' they can hear Coggins in the commercial room, talking loud in broken English, laughing, singing snatches of French songs, vociferating in his foreign way, joking with his fellow-travelers, boasting of his commercial successes, and then again talking over his many customers. For he has introduced some wonderful 'cheap lines,' as commercial people call them, in silk ties, smart handkerchiefs, all sold at remarkably low prices. He is out day after day, and at all times of the day, with the inn dog-cart and the hostler's boy,

He visits all the neighboring village shops, and talk of him has gone round the country. 'I suppose,' said Sergeant Smith, 'he will get a dozen calls in a day from the small shopkeepers in the towns and villages round about to get more of his cheap stuff.'

"'And no one, I suppose, has any suspicion about him?' I asked.

"'No danger! They just think him a smart business man opening up a new line, and willing to let his stuff go cheap at first. Naturally, they want to make hay while the sun shines—and sometimes, Sergeant Morgan, I ask myself if this Mr. Dubois, as he calls himself—' Sergeant Smith pondered.

"'You ask yourself,' I suggested, 'if Mr. Dubois is really Gentleman Coggins after all?'

"'Just so,' said Smith, laughing. 'We are beginning here to ask ourselves that.'

"'I cannot help you, Sergeant Smith, I've never seen Coggins—but you have.'

"'That's just it,' said Smith. 'I've taken many a squint at this fellow Dubois through windows and the like, and for the life of me I can't spot him. The real Coggins is a sallow, clean-shaven fellow, just like one of those actor chaps you can see any day by the dozen in the Strand, and the real Coggins pulls a long face. Now this man is a rosy-gilled fellow—that's smiling and laughing all the time, no moustache, but a stiff black beard, shaved a bit on the cheeks, and going under his chin like a Newcastle ruff—French fashion.'

"'I don't think the office have made any mistake. Stick to him, Sergeant. It's Coggins, you bet!'

"'I will stick to him, and I have stuck to him, Coggins or not Coggins,' said Sergeant Smith, 'and I'll give you an example of how I've done it. Yesterday he ordered the inn dog-cart and drove out. It was close upon three o'clock in the afternoon. I thought I would follow him on my bicycle, as I had often done before in the last three weeks that we have been watching him. I had not noticed that he had taken his own bicycle with him in the cart, covered with a rug. He drove to a village beyond Balin, got out and did business at the general shop. I held back out of sight, and when I came up to the trap again the hostler's lad was driving alone.'

"'Why,' said I to the boy, 'where's Mr. Dubois?'

"'He had his bicycle with him,' said the lad, 'and he goes to Pincote village and gets me to leave samples at places on the way back to Pangford.'

"'Gone to Pincote, is he?'

"'So I pedaled on fast, and presently got him in sight again, and he led me a pretty chase long past Pincote, up and down very bad roads, and I thought I'd just go up to him for once, and ask him what the devil he was up to. Just at this moment Dubois dashed into a narrow lane and I followed him. I felt I had the speed of him, and was overhauling him fast, when—whuff!—I ran over something and punctured my tyre badly, very badly, and presently I had to pull up. I got down, it was a clean cut, and in another part of the tyre were two tin tacks stuck fast. Had Coggins, or Dubois, whichever it is, sprinkled the road with glass and tacks, or was it the work of some cantankerous fellow who lived near the lane? I saw my man pedaling steadily ahead, and presently he was out of sight.

"'My bicycle was useless, and I stood over it, thinking what I should do next. As I stood there cursing my luck I heard a rustic come singing and whistling down the lane from the direction toward which I had been traveling.

"'He was a simple-looking young fellow in a tucked-up smock frock and leather gaiters, with a little battered wide-awake hat on the back of his head. He carried a bill-hook on his shoulder, and tied to the bill by a bit of string was a pair of thick, rough hedger's gauntlets.

"'He stopped whistling *The Girl I Left Behind Me,* as he saw me—stood and stared with his mouth open for a good minute, then began to grin from ear to ear like an idiot.

"'Practicing to grin through a horse collar, are you, my lad?' I said. 'Did you never see a punctured tyre before?'

"'Forgie I,' said the fellow, in a strong Somersetshire brogue. 'Forgie I, zur, fer a venturing to laugh, but I niver zee two punctured uns in Farmer Joyce's lane, a one day afoor!' and he laughed out loud.

"'What?' I said. 'Is the other fellow caught too?'

"'Ay, zur, at t'other end of the lane, and a swearing a

terrible bad I had to move away from he. Ha! ha! It do tickle I!'

"Then he looked suddenly serious. 'Yer moightend want a bit o' hedging and ditching done, zur? I foinds my own gloves and my own bill 'uk.'

"'He leant his bill-hook on the ground and dangled his great leathern gloves at me.

"'I'm reckoned a foine worker!' he added.

"'Tell me where's the nearest blacksmith's forge,' I said, 'and I'll give you sixpence.'

"'Will ee now, zur?' he said with a greedy look in his eyes, and he came near and held his hand out. 'T'other gentleman gave I a shilling for tellin' he, but I'll take sixpence from you, zur.'

"'I put a shilling into his open hand and he began to direct me. 'You be to go up droo the lane and keep a trending and a turning to your left and then to your right, and then to your left and then to your right again, droo the moorland till you come plump on to a horse pond that's just over against Jem Bevan's forge, only yer can't see the forge rightly till you'm turned the next carner. Do ee understand I, zur? and thanking yer for your shilling, I'll be going on whoam, zur.'

"'The young rustic was whistling again, and presently he broke into his song again of *The Girl I left Behind Me*. I suppose it was a sort of rustic chaff on his part.

"'I dragged my bicycle up through the lane and out upon the common, but I never saw a trace of the man I was after, nor did I find Jem Bevan's forge.'

"'But I suspect, Sergeant Smith, that you had found Gentleman Coggins himself.'

"'What, the grinning idiot with the bill-hook! Never! Remember, I know Coggins by sight. This fellow was just a silly Somersetshire lad with an accent you could cut with a knife.'

"I said no more, but I had my doubts. 'Tell me one thing, Sergeant Smith. Is the man Dubois often away in the night-time? Did you miss him, for instance, on the night of the 23d when the burglary at the Abbey was done?'

"'No, Sergeant Morgan, we did not.' The detective took

out his note-book, and turning back to the date in question, read out the following

"'January 23d.—Dubois, supposed Coggins, went out on bicycle in early morning and never returned till dark. Saw several visitors before leaving, said to be from neighboring villages—some of them took samples away with them. He received these customers mostly in little private office off his bedroom—my man had looked into this office in his absence one day, found it spread with samples, mostly cheap silks and neckties. Same day, brisk business. Inn servants and people in commercial room complain of Dubois's noisiness. At 9.30 in the evening, a man, said to be from Pincote, came to see him. Dubois angry, sent him away, reproved him loudly for coming to see him late and just as he was going to bed.

"'Allowed man to take parcel of samples, but refused to do other business with him, told him he must come again at nine next morning. Dubois called out in the hearing of inn servants that he was going to turn in. Man left muttering. Dubois was heard overhead in his bedroom for some time. Officer remained on watch all night in neighborhood of inn. Dubois did not go out. Nothing further happened.'

"'Thank you, Sergeant Smith. Tell your men to keep their eyes skinned. They have to deal with a sharp fellow in Coggins—very clever at disguises. Let them be sure he doesn't go out disguised and leave one of his fellows to stamp about on the floor overhead, making them think Coggins himself is at home.'

"Sergeant Smith did not relish my advice.

"'I thank you, Sergeant,' he said stiffly, 'for your counsel. I will do my duty to the best of my ability.'

CHAPTER VI

THE NEW BEATER

"We drove back to the Abbey, and I was in good time to sit down with the party at breakfast and hear all the preparations for the coming shoot.

"After breakfast Lord Balin took me into the gun-room

and let me choose a couple of guns. As my host is of about my own height and arm-length, I found no difficulty in finding two that he had discarded with advancing age, a rather heavy Lancaster and a lighter Westley Richards.

"We drove to the woods about a mile away where the shooting was to begin. Great traditions of sport are followed at Balin—a company of keepers marshals and directs an army of beaters, and the procession of shooters, beaters and guns through the great beech wood is most interesting. Pheasants and ground game abound, but the shooting is varied. An occasional roe-deer starts before the beaters in the copses. Now and again, a glade in the woods opens and discloses a mere surrounded with willows, rushes and sedges, where mallard, teal, widgeon and snipe rise before the guns.

"The day was clear and the air ringing. It is the good old fashion at Balin Abbey not to repress the homely humor of the rustic beaters. They seemed to enjoy the sport quite as much as the gentlemen, and one heard jests and laughter and mutual chaff among them. Now and again, when the covert was more than usually thick, I heard singing along the line. Some one with a clear, resonant voice had started the well-known Somersetshire song, 'Cham a Zummerzetshire man,' and keepers and beaters and even 'the guns' themselves joined in the chorus to this air, known to every soul in Somerset.

" 'Who is it with that good voice?' I asked of one of my loaders.

" 'It is a queer half-cracked fellow that one of the keepers picked up on the road, looking for a job of hedging and ditching. He doesn't shirk his work in the woods, doesn't Joe, and he keeps the line in heart with his songs and catches.'

"I remembered the misadventures of poor Sergeant Smith. 'What,' I thought, 'has Coggins the impudence to venture into the lion's den?'

" 'Is the fellow,' I asked, 'a Somersetshire man?'

" 'By his talk,' said the loader, I should say he comes more Devonshire way, but he knows all our West Country ditties. Hark to him now, sir!'

"The singer began the first verse of that queer old Somersetshire ballad—

> A shepherd kept sheep on a hill so high,
> And there came a fair lady riding by.

The long line of beaters and keepers burst out with the odd uncouth words that form the chorus of the old ballad, and beat the measure out vigorously with their sticks against the tree trunks—then the ballad went on with the singer's ready memory, and the verses were broken into now and again with the rustle of a pheasant's wings through the tree branches, the cries of a keeper, 'Hare back,' or 'Cock forward,' or the banging of the guns. At the end of the song the gentleman cried 'Bravo!'

"'Where have I heard that voice?' I asked myself, 'that fine, rolling baritone?'

"We stopped to lunch at an enchanting spot in the great beech woods. The ladies had already arrived and were sitting or standing under the trees where the great bulging roots of the beech trees, covered with moss, emerald green, formed convenient seats. On the dry bare earth, still spangled with the fallen leaves, russet gold, the servants from the Abbey were laying the cloth for luncheon and handing out dishes from the hampers they had brought.

"The keepers and beaters sat down round a good midday meal, fifty yards away from us. Much laughter, chaff and talk was going on among them. We men went forward to look at the game, laid out in rows on a grassy bank. Lord Balin congratulated me heartily on my shooting. He and I between us had accounted for more than three-fourths of the whole bag.

"We lunched, and the meal was gay.

"'Did you have that delightful Joe again among the beaters?' asked Lady Drusilla—'the rustic with the lovely voice?'

"The men told her of his singing of the Somersetshire ballad and how they had enjoyed it.

"'When one thinks,' said Lady Drusilla, 'that a man with a voice and memory like that could earn a fortune at those hateful London music-halls!—and lose his country complexion, his country figure, and his country health in a season! How lucky it is no one tells him!'

"The point was debated. Mrs. Townley said he ought to be told the truth and have his choice offered. She said, 'Surely ignorance is never bliss in this world, and poverty, I am quite sure, was never a blessing to any one.'

"The discussion went on and only ended by our begging our host to let the man come and sing to the ladies.

"He came. It was just the man Sergeant Smith had told me of in the lane, the same leather gaiters, the same tucked-up smock frock, the same little battered wide-awake hat set back on his head, that gave him, with his upraised eyebrows and perpetual smile, an air of rustic simplicity and innocence. Could this possibly be the redoubtable Coggins? I had reproved Sergeant Smith for not suspecting him in this very guise, and now I could hardly bring myself to consider him anything but what he seemed to be, a simple West Country lout who was accepted for such in a company of his own West Countrymen.

"He stood leaning on his beating stick, with his hat in his hand, seeming half shy, half proud that he had attracted the attention of 'the quality.'

"He began to sing the old ballad. At first his voice was a little shaky as if with a natural diffidence before the strange company. Then he gained confidence and sang, and his voice rang out clear and ringing. At the end of every verse came the queer chorus, joined in by the rustics' voices from the distance, and presently the ladies and gentlemen caught up the air too, and the woods re-echoed with a melody perhaps as old as themselves. Something quaint and old world, something of rustic wit, rustic humor, and rustic romance that our modern hurry has quite let slip from our lives was in the old song. Lord Balin's guests were delighted. They cheered the singer heartily and asked for another song.

"I watched every look and turn of the man's face, every inflection of his voice. Where, when, and in what different circumstances had it all been present to me?—not the song indeed, that was new to me, but the ring of the singer's voice, and all his inflections, all his tricks of manner. Memory sometimes shuts the gates of consciousness very close, but a whisper comes at times through the locked portals.

"Mrs. Townley rose and approached the singer—she said a word or two of praise to him. He took off his hat, bowed with a bashful, rustic grace, and held it out toward her, asking unmistakably for a tip. The men laughed at the broad hint and felt for their purses, and Mrs. Townley searched in the knotted corner of her lace handkerchief—a lady's purse—for a coin.

"I stepped quickly forward between Mrs. Townley and the singer and looked hard at her hands. The man, seeing himself watched, stepped quickly back. Mrs. Townley laughed nervously. 'You must sing us another song, Mr. Joe,' she said, 'and then I'll make a collection for you.'

"I said to myself, 'You will drop nothing into Joe's hat with my leave, madam,' and I kept a sharper watch than ever upon the two. I knew not much as yet, but something told me that I was in the presence of the two chief actors of the drama at Balin Abbey. Why was Coggins here? for that the singer was Coggins I had no doubt at all now. Had I had any before, Mrs. Townley's action and manner would have sufficed to banish these doubts.

"To what criminal end was Coggins still here? For no possible reason, I was sure, except that his confederate had had no opportunity as yet of passing into his hands the stolen gems whose setting she had hidden among the Abbey ruins.

"How was it I had come to fix the guilt of confederacy so confidently on Mrs. Townley? The actual evidence was almost *nil.* I answer that I arrived partly intuitively at this conclusion, partly by the elimination of every other possible personage in the house. That there was a confederate was certain. The cleverest burglar could not have acted alone. Who, then, was it? I saw at once that only two persons were intellectually capable of the difficult *rôle* played by the confederate—Lady Drusilla and Mrs. Townley. Lady Drusilla's character, her age, her antecedents and a certain air of uprightness about her, put her beyond all possibility of suspicion. There was nothing of all this in Mrs. Townley. I had been at once impressed by a tone of insincerity in her voice, a false gaiety in her manner, a feigned seriousness, and a constant pretense of sham enthusiasm and sham earnestness She was never quite at home among the people of more assured social position than herself at the Abbey. She had not their ease and naturalness. All this had set me against her in spite of her great beauty and her obvious desire to please and attract. I must confess too that Lady Drusilla's strong disparagement almost at starting had been for something in my distrust. With pretty women it is often the first stroke that wins the game, or loses it for them. If they make that first happy stroke to their advantage, their charm and beauty tell on us and they score; if it is we who get in the first winning point, it is they who lose. Mrs. Townley never made the first winning stroke; I was in opposition to her from the first.

"When I saw her rise to go toward the man I knew now to be the disguised burglar—when I saw her fumble with her knotted handkerchief, I knew that in another minute the jewels would have passed from her to him. I had stopped her, and the moment afterward I almost regretted that I had done so. What if I had let her pass the stolen gems and then immediately arrested the culprit with the property on him? What a coup! What a bold and dramatic situation! Yes! and what an extremely unpleasant one to every guest present, and what if a single link in my long line of suppositions and intuitions and conclusions had broken? What if the new beater was, after all, a harmless rustic, the jewels not in his possession at all? What if Mrs. Townley was an innocent lady? My blood ran cold at the thought of such a catastrophe of misadventures happening in this delightful woodland scene.

"Mrs. Townley returned to her seat under the beech tree. I stood watching them both in seeming eager talk with the other guests.

"'Won't he sing us another song?' asked Lady Drusilla.

"Lord Balin asked him. The fellow took off his hat and grinned from ear to ear.

"'Do, Mr. Joe,' said Mrs. Townley, 'some good old country ditty, and after that we will make a collection for you.'

"Joe played at being the diffident, over-honored minstrel. At last he set his hat again upon the back of his head, and slanting his long stick upon his shoulder, he began the first bars of an air that is known to every English soldier. It is called 'Turmut Hoeing,' and is the regimental march of the Wiltshire that was once the 36th Regiment. The words are simple, rustic and homely, like the air. Here they are, for I know them by heart:

"Some love to plow and some to sow,
  And some delight in mowing.
Some, 'mid the hay, will stand all day,
  And loves to be a throwing
The new mown hay wi' pitchfork up—
  Gie I the turmut hoeing!
Gie I my hoe and let me go
  To do the turmut hoeing.
Oh! the hoe! 'tis the hoe, the hoe I loves to handle!
And 'tis just so! ay! 'tis just so, that the hoe I loves to handle.

"The disguised burglar suited his action to the words, using his beater's staff as a hoe.

"For 'tis the pay, five bob a day,
  The farmer is a owing!
Five bob a day will jolly well pay
  To set the ale-pot flowing!
So that's the reason that in the season,
  When turmut flies be blowing,
I takes my hoe and off I go
  To do the turmut hoeing!
    Oh! the hoe, &c.

"Some loves to sing of early spring
  And days of barley sowing,
Some love to rhyme of sweet May time
  When daffodils be blowing.
Gie I the moon that shines in June
  When turmut fields want hoeing.
Ah! he's no fool who loves the tool
  That does the turmut hoeing!
    Oh! the hoe, &c.

"The pretended rustic had not sung the first line before the scales seemed to fall from my eyes—air, voice, and manner all came back to me in a moment, and, now that I could remember so much, the face itself began to reveal itself through all its disguises. I had heard the song sung a score of times at our mess by Captain Towers, Towers the turf swindler, Towers the card-sharper, Towers the author of my ruin, Towers the cause of my kinsman's death, Towers whose own death I had read in the papers and believed in, three years before, Towers himself was before me! Here was a revelation indeed. In a flash and by a sort of accident I had learnt more than the whole police force of London knew. If this indeed were Coggins, then Coggins the burglar and Towers the swindler were one and the same man, and my triumph was that here stood I face to face with him and he knew me not! I knew his secret and he never suspected mine. In truth he had not heard my voice, except in those tones that a man does not often use in the society of men, either his equals or inferiors. I had spoken but a word to Mrs. Townley in his hearing. My face he would not know, it was sufficiently disguised by my beard.

"I listened to his song, as he sang with excellent comic effect and in the broadest of Wiltshire accents. The song is well known in the West, and I want you to read into it all the character and cleverness which the disguised criminal was employing, in the presence of his former victim. There is a humor in naked facts even greater sometimes than the humor in words, tone and manner, and that form of humor I was enjoying to the utmost and all to myself, while the scoundrel was priding himself upon taking us all in.

"The ladies liked the turn the song took in the third stanza. They thought it poetical. I thought the whole thing, song included, was more than poetical. It was an ethical drama charged with human interest, working itself out toward what critics, I believe, call poetical justice, and I was being the instrument of all this, and, as I have said, the sole member of the audience who really understood the plot of the play!

"When the song and the applause that followed had ended, Mrs. Townley said, addressing us all, 'Now, please, the collection.' The singer took off his hat and held it to one after another of the party of ladies and gentlemen, receiving from each a coin or two. He came toward Mrs. Townley, who had taken her seat some way back from the others, as I guessed with the subject that if anything passed between her and the singer the action should not be visible to the others. He had stepped forward and was reaching out his hat toward her. Just as he was approaching her, I held out my arm and barred his passage. 'Stop,' I said, 'here is my contribution,' and I dropped half a crown into the hat. Then suddenly I took the hat from his hand and handed it myself to Mrs. Townley. I glanced quickly at both their countenances. They kept them admirably. There was a smile on hers, a continued grin on his.

"'Thank you, my lord,' he said to me with a mock gratitude.

"Mrs. Townley fumbled awkwardly for a moment with her handkerchief, and after a little delay, produced a silver coin.

"I had baffled them once again.

"Presently Mrs. Townley changed her seat and sat down on the outlying root of a great beech tree. She seemed, for a moment, to be lost in reverie; she began to trace fantastic figures on the bare earth with the point of her parasol.

"I went up to Lord Balin and began to talk to him, but my eyes were fixed upon Mrs. Townley's movements. 'Lord Balin,' I said, 'will you manage to let me walk with you alone for a hundred yards, when we go from here? I have something important to ask you.' I spoke below my voice.

"'Certainly,' said Lord Balin. 'I will manage that,' and again he began loudly to praise my shooting.

"I smiled, and seemed all ears, but my eyes were following the point of Mrs. Townley's parasol.

"She had drawn what looked to me like the rude representation of a tennis racket. Mrs. Townley was, I had heard an enthusiastic tennis player—was her drawing done in mere distraction? We are all given to trace meaningless lines and figures if we happen to hold a stick in our hands, while our thoughts are otherwise engaged. Yet it looked to be the representation of a very palpable racquet. The parasol point had drawn a circle and filled it with cross lines.

Then it drew the shape of a handle. It could surely be nothing on earth but a racquet. Then came a strange figure, an arch with a straight line under it. Finally the figure 7. Could these symbols have any possible meaning for any one? To Coggins? He was still making his rounds of the guests with his hat and grinning out his effusive thanks. He repassed the spot where Mrs. Townley's parasol had been busy. She had hardly raised her eyes for a second as he went by, but, when he had passed, she began at once to obliterate the figures. Presently nothing remained, but the drawn lines were fast in my memory. The figure of the arch, the numeral 7, and a racquet.

"That it was a signal I had not the slightest doubt—a signal to Coggins, and I knew that if I could not interpret it, the jewels would pass to him and be lost for ever.

"An archway, the figure 7, and a racquet.

"Seven might mean seven o'clock—a racquet might indicate the lawn-tennis court—but the archway? I had it—it meant the secluded place beyond the tennis court where the ruins of the Abbey lay, half buried in the turf. One of the remains was an archway. Yes, it clearly indicated the very spot where the jewel settings had been buried. Evidently something was to happen at seven o'clock that evening, or at seven next morning, in this unfrequented spot. I would anticipate the event, whatever it might be, by going there myself at both hours.

"We had another large covert to shoot, and the keepers and beaters went off to take up their line. The ladies started to go home, and Lord Balin and I found ourselves walking across the fields.

" 'You have had no time to do much yet, I suppose?' he said.

" 'I have learnt a good deal,' I said, 'in the last half hour.'

" 'You don't say so, my dear Stanley! What a wonderful fellow you are! Why, I have hardly had my eye off you all day. You have been busy eating your lunch and laughing and talking with the women. Come, now! What can you have found out?'

" 'First, I have made sure that the burglar is in league with an inmate in your house.'

" 'Not a servant?'

" 'No, not a servant.'

" 'Mrs. ——?' He did not utter the name.

"I nodded.

" 'Are you quite sure?'

" 'I am quite sure now. I have seen signals passing between her and the burglar who broke into the Abbey.'

" 'The burglar who broke into— Are you dreaming? My keepers—why I could go bail for the whole of them.'

" 'So could I, I believe.'

" 'Then who is the man, and are you sure?'

" 'The man I mean is Coggins—Gentleman Coggins, the smartest operator in his line, who has been living at Pangford for three weeks past.'

" 'Yes, I know that; and how can that lady make signals to him there from our beech woods?'

" 'I could see that Lord Balin was beginning to find my statements difficult of belief—perhaps he half doubted my sanity.

" 'Mrs. Townley,' I said, 'twice tried to pass something to the person I know to be the burglar. Twice I was able to stop her. Then she traced a signal to him with the point of her parasol on the ground.'

" 'And what did she try to pass?'

" 'The stolen jewels.'

" 'What! they are in her possession?'

" 'Yes.'

" 'But they would be bulky—all the stolen jewelry together would make too big a parcel to pass.'

" 'Yes, in their settings—but they have been taken out of the settings. In their present form they would hardly fill a tea cup.'

" 'How do you know that?'

" 'Because the settings are here in my pocket.'

"I showed them. They were squeezed and pressed together.

" 'Good heavens!' said Lord Balin. 'Where did they come from?'

"I explained how I found them.

"Lord Balin could hardly understand it. 'You were at work early,' he said. 'By-the-bye, you have not mentioned one thing. Who is the criminal, the man who has broken into my house, and to whom you say Mrs. Townley twice tried to pass the jewels, and to whom she made signals? Who is this man? Where is he?'

"'Joe the beater, the man who sang "Turmut hoeing" to us.'

"'Joe the beater!' said Lord Balin, stopping to look me in the face. 'Why, surely not that weak-brained fellow!'

"'He is the most dangerous criminal in all London.'

"'Is it possible? And I have myself encouraged my keepers to engage him! He seemed such a merry, harmless sort of fellow, just a rustic innocent. I even suggested that he might be taken on as an under-beater and watcher.'

"I told the story of how Sergeant Smith had pursued him, how he had spoilt Smith's bicycle, and then, hiding his own, had turned back disguised (the very disguise he had employed to-day), had sent the Sergeant on a wild goose chase in search of a forge which never existed, and how this self-same innocent rustic had been beating the woods all day, and singing country ditties to us.

"'And what can he be doing here?'

"'Waiting,' I said, 'to get hold of the jewels.'

"'Look here!' said Lord Balin, taking out a whistle and giving three loud blasts on it. That will bring the head keeper here—anyhow, we'll get Joe the beater turned off the place at once.'

"I begged Lord Balin to do nothing of the sort. I undertook to watch that he did no harm. If he were sent off, I said, his confederate might devise some new way of hiding, or getting off with, the jewels.

"When the keeper came up I pretended to be interested in Joe and his singing.

"'He's a good companionable fellow,' said the keeper. 'We all like him, and as his lordship desires me to engage him as under keeper, we take him with us on the rounds at night.'

"'Ah,' thought I, 'that accounts for a good deal.'

"Lord Balin sent the keeper back to his duties, and the shooting began.

"I am afraid my loaders were less pleased with me during

the afternoon shooting than in the morning. The first condition of good shooting is to have one's attention entirely concentrated on the matter in hand. A second lost in recalling one's wandering thoughts is generally the chance of a shot missed, a head of game thrown away. My thoughts wandered all the afternoon. What mischief was my old enemy Towers, now Ikey Coggins, meditating? What did Mrs. Townley's signal mean? What was the signification of the mysterious figure of the racquet? Surely the archway was enough to indicate the spot. The racquet must be a further special signal agreed upon between the confederates to which I had no clue. Mrs. Townley would be at home three hours before me, and would have time to plot many things.

"I thought of sending a message by one of my loaders to Macgregor to bid him and O'Brien keep watch on her movements. Then I heard the cheery voice of Joe the beater hallooing in the woods, and I thought that, at least while he was with us, no great misfortune could happen.

"While my thoughts were thus engaged I missed three rocketers in succession. My head loader, pulling out his whisky flask, remarked that I was a bit off my shooting as compared with the morning. 'This morning, sir,' he was pleased to say, 'you hardly let a thing pass. Perhaps I may make so bold as to recommend a drop of this.'

"I took a sip at the proffered flask, and made an effort to pull myself together, with the good result that I knocked down a couple of pheasants right and left almost immediately, and recovered my shooting for the rest of the afternoon.

"It was nearly dark when we reached home, and I asked Lord Balin to let me slip off quietly to my room. From my window I saw Mrs. Townley coming back from the lawn tennis courts. She was an enthusiastic player, and sometimes went out with a boy to field the balls while she practiced services by the hour. It was by now so dark that I could not see whether she carried her racquet with her. As soon as she had come in I sent for O'Brien.

" 'Get me,' I said, 'a stable lantern and carry it unlighted, with matches, on to the lawn tennis ground there to wait for me, letting no one see you if you can help it. At what time are the bloodhounds let loose?'

"'Not till ten, or half-past if no carriage-folk are coming to the Abbey or going away. They are that fierce they'd be after the horses in a carriage and pulling the coachman off his box.'

"'Whistle twice in answer to me, softly, when you hear me coming.'

"'I will, sir.'

"It was half-past six. I stole out a few minutes afterward, wrapped in an ulster. I stumbled up the walk in the pitch darkness, giving a low whistle when I thought I was near the tennis ground. Then I made toward O'Brien's double whistle.

"'Here I am, sir,' came O'Brien's whisper close to me.

"'Light the lantern,' I whispered, 'and keep your body between it and the house.'

"He struck three or four matches before he succeeded in getting it alight.

"'Don't throw the matches down,' I whispered. 'Put them in your pocket.'

"'I'm doing that, sir,' said O'Brien.

"I took the lantern in my hand and lighted our way to the Abbey ruins. I held it high up and could make out no one and nothing. We walked slowly all round the space occupied by the ruined remains .

"'Is that what you're looking for, sir?' said O'Brien, pointing to the ruined archway.

"'I see nothing.'

"'It's a spade, or something like it, leaning against that bit of ruined arch,' said O'Brien, walking toward it.

"'Is it a tennis racquet, O'Brien?'

"'I'm thinking it may be, sir. Yes, 'tis just that very identical thing.'

"He handed me a large, heavy, substantial racquet.

"'One of the ladies has been playing in the court,' I said, 'and forgot to bring in her racquet.'

"'Sure, 'tis a mighty heavy tool for a lady to handle, sir.'

"'Yes,' I said, 'and I'd choose a lighter one myself for convenience. O'Brien, my man,' I said, weighing the racquet in my hand, 'I'm thinking we may have found what we came down to Balin Abbey to look for. Go in now and open the side door, which is bolted inside. See here, I button this racquet under my ulster. I don't want to go through the hall where the ladies and gentlemen are and let any of them guess at what I'm carrying. Then you'll bring Macgregor up to my bedroom, and perhaps I'll show you both something queer.'

"When the two officers were in my room I bade them lock the door.

"'If I'm not mistaken,' I said, taking up the racquet, 'here is the end of all our trouble.'

"The two detectives looked upon me as one who has taken leave of his senses. The handle of the racquet had, what many racquets have, a roughened covering of red-dish india-rubber. I pulled it off, and the handle at first sight seemed to be fashioned just like the handle of any other racquet, but a close inspection showed an unusually large protuberance at the end. It seemed to be jointed to the handle, but our united strength could not pull it off, or unscrew it. Macgregor happened to have a little steel wrench, belonging to his motor car, in his pocket. He closed down the holder on the protuberance and held it fast while I turned the racquet in his hands. The screw worked loose, and presently the top was off, showing that a hole about three-quarters of an inch in diameter had been bored down into the whole length of the handle.

"I looked in and saw that the cavity was packed tight with pink cotton wool.

"'Which of you has a corkscrew?' I asked.

"The Scotsman and the Irishman each produced, in great haste, a neat extracting tool.

"I spread a sheet of newspaper on the table, entangled the point of the corkscrew with the cotton wool in the handle of the racquet and gave the screw a turn. I drew forth a great hank of cotton wool. As the cotton fell upon the table, gems of extraordinary size came tumbling out with it—some remained embedded in the cotton, some leapt out upon the paper—emeralds, green as grass, flat, and as large as a man's forefinger nail, great blood-red rubies, some faceted, some cabochon-shaped, sapphires, blue as southern skies, and diamonds of uncommon size and brilliancy, and this profusion of precious things lay on the table between us three men, under the three-fold light of the electric lamps above our heads, shining and glistening as if they were living, moving things.

"There is, I think, something almost awe-inspiring about precious stones of such lustre and size to persons unaccustomed to see and handle them. The two men retired a step or two from the great treasure before them.

"'There's enough to fill the windows of a dozen jewelers' shops in Broad Street,' said the practical Scotsman.

"'Bedad! It's nothing short of a king's ransom,' said the more poetical Irishman.

"I carefully turned up the corners of the newspaper and made a small parcel of the gems.

"'See, Macgregor, if there's any more inside the racquet.'

"Macgregor banged the handle of the racquet down on the table—nothing came out. Then Macgregor held up the racquet to the electric light and squinted into the hole. 'It's all out, sir.'

"'We must leave it as it was. I will spare you some of the cotton wool to repack it with.'

"It amused the men to drop bits of coal from the grate into the cavity that had contained the gems, to fill up the interstices with cotton wool, pack all tightly, replace the top, screw it on tightly, and roll on the indiarubber handle cover.

"'Now,' I said to Macgregor, 'carry it down—don't let any one see you, and hang it up in the passage near the conservatory with the other lawn tennis things.'

"Macgregor presently returned. It was now a quarter to eight, and I was dressing as fast as I could for dinner. He returned to report to me that as soon as he had finished hanging up the racquet with the others, he had gone toward the conservatory, just, as he said, from curiosity to find out if the door leading out was locked at that early hour of the night. As he went toward it he encountered Mrs. Townley coming in from outside through the conservatory. She was wrapped round in a long sealskin cloak, but, for all that, he could see that she was carrying some sort of a bundle underneath it.

"'Very odd!' I said. 'What do you make of that, Macgregor?'

"'I make nothing of it, sir, but it seems queer that a young lady should be out at this hour of the night and come in carrying a big bundle.'

"'Did she pass through the passage where you had hung the racquet?'

"'She did, sir, and I was close behind her.'

"'Did she seem to notice that you had put back the racquet in its place?'

"'She hurried through the passage and looked neither to right nor left.'

"'Is the night still very dark, Macgregor?'

"'Very dark and overcast, after the fine day, and a little drizzle of rain has set in.'

"'There's no moon, I think, Macgregor, to-night?'

"'Not till the small hours, sir, by the almanac, and but little then.'

"'A good night for cracking a crib, eh?' I remarked, dressing in haste.

"'Well, sir,' said Macgregor, smiling, 'not with those four savage bloodhounds roaming round the house.'

"'What would you say, Macgregor, if our friend Coggins had not only humbugged Sergeant Smith, but had got round the keepers here, and even Lord Balin himself? He has been going the rounds every night with the watchers. The hounds must know him by now, and he can come and go as he will by night or day. What do you say to that?'

"O'Brien stood with my white tie in his hand.

"He laughed. 'That beats all, sir! That's cleverness, if you like, but don't let him beat us, sir, for the dear Lord's sake! don't let him beat us!'

"'I'm thinking,' said Macgregor, 'that going the rounds won't help him far with the dogs. They've a kennel of a dozen of them here. The head keeper showed it me to-day. Bloodthirsty brutes, every one of them. I'd sooner face four hungry tigers from the Zoo. Ever since the burglary here these four fresh hounds have been let loose every night.'

"'That's good news, anyhow,' I said. 'Keep a sharp look out all the same, you two. See that the conservatory door is locked—keep my window open, and one of you stay in the room without a light burning. You may chance to hear or see something. I'll be back with you as soon as I can.'

"'I hurried down, but I was not the last. Mrs. Townley was still to appear, and she kept the party waiting. When she did at last come in, she abounded in pretty apologies—smiling, nervous, I thought, but full of life and movement. She wore a resplendent red dress with embroidery of seed pearl, and a great string of large oriental pearls coiled twice round her neck and the ends hanging down. Pearls, she had told me, were her favorite wear. We were told she had lost a necklace of great pearls and diamonds in the burglary, as well as two pendants of pearl and diamond of great price. She deplored these losses hourly, but the wealth of this beautiful woman even after her losses impressed us all immensely. I remarked to myself, as I admired the superb pearls on her neck, that we had not discovered one single pearl among the wealth of precious stones hidden in the racquet. The fact, of course, had nothing astonishing for me.

"I took an opportunity of telling Lord Balin that I had good news for him, but that I would beg him to allow me to say nothing till the morning. 'The night,' I said, 'may bring its further developments.'

CHAPTER VII

FURTHER DEVELOPMENTS

"We spoke at dinner of the wonderful voice and cleverness of the beater, Joe. Mrs. Townley was particularly loud in her praises, and I myself was quite as enthusiastic about him as she. Such a man, I said, was much more than a clever village singer, he had artistic and other talents too, and I was sure it would not be long before he was heard of in London.

"Lord Balin's eye met mine, but he did not smile.

"'We shall miss him when he leaves us!' he said, and he pinched his lips together as if a sudden emotion held him. Knowing Lord Balin's sense of humor, I feared an explosion, and hastened to change the subject. I spoke of the last woodcock that had got up out of shot and had never been seen again. A woodcock is a subject of conversation that will always take English sportsmen from any other talk.

"When I got upstairs it was nearly twelve o'clock. O'Brien and Macgregor were both in my room, the lights turned off and the windows open. The four hounds had been let loose an hour before, they told me, and the keepers gone home. Leaning out of the window, I could just hear the patter of the bloodhounds' feet, and their panting breath, as these fierce creatures ranged over the grass plots and through the shrubberies round the house.

"'The moon,' I said, 'rises at three o'clock. If nothing happens between this and then, we may all go to bed.'

"I had an intuition that something would happen, because I knew the burglar, being disappointed at not finding the jewels in the racquet, as he had been promised, would take some further steps to get hold of them.

"Assuming that he guessed nothing of the arrival of myself and my two subordinates, and there was indeed nothing to betray any of us to Mrs. Townley, or to himself, he would naturally conclude that his accomplice had been prevented by an accident from keeping her word. He would never dream that so clever a woman had been outwitted. The jewels were therefore, he would think, still in her possession, and he would, probably, present himself under his confederate's window at some appointed hour in the night and Mrs. Townley would throw out to him the packet of jewels. This simple and obvious way of getting hold of the jewels had, till now, been rendered impossible in my eyes by the fact that the grounds were closely patrolled by keepers every night up to a certain hour, and after that by fierce bloodhounds.

"But the keeper's revelation that day shook my confidence in the dogs, for, if Coggins went about at night with the watchers and their dogs, these latter would naturally get used to him. I had no doubt that it had been Coggins's original intention to get hold of the jewels in this simple manner. But then, after the night of the robbery, the head keeper, to make things safe, had, as I have said, let loose four instead of two hounds, and Coggins would of course be a stranger to two of these animals, if not to all four. So, to get the jewels, he had to resort to other methods. Hence the attempts of Mrs. Townley to pass the jewels in the wood and the later manœuvre of the tennis racquet. Now that he had been baffled in every attempt, what would he do next? He could not know, yet, that the stolen property had passed for good out of his confidante's possession. What did the heavy bundle brought in by Mrs. Townley portend? What could it contain except some means of getting into the house, possibly a rope ladder, or, more likely, one of those knotted ropes which have lately become a common implement in a modern housebreaker's trade? Did Coggins meditate breaking in, a second time, into Balin Abbey? I was pretty sure that he did—not for purposes of robbery, but to secure the booty he had obtained through his confederate.

"I had made a fair guess, but I had really no idea to what lengths the audacity and insolence of this Prince of Professional Burglars were prepared to carry him.

CHAPTER VIII

COGGINS'S CROWNING EFFORT

"There was an empty bedroom in one of the two towers which rise on either front of Balin Abbey. I had Lord Balin's permission to use it for purposes of observation, and I directed Macgregor to go thither and watch. He came to me in about half an hour to report that he could hear nothing of the hounds. Generally one or other of them were on the move all through the night, and their footsteps could be heard, or their panting as they galloped slowly across the turf, or the rustling of the evergreens as they pushed their way through the shrubberies; to-night he had not heard a sign of them.

"'The scoundrel has drugged them or poisoned them!' I said.

"It looked like it.

"'Then he means to be up to something to-night,' said O'Brien.

"'Go back to the tower, Macgregor, and watch for what

happens. Go, both of you, and keep a good look out, and let O'Brien come here and report when you notice anything.'

"The tower stands out from the corner of the main building, and the windows command full views of two sides of the house, of the front and of the western side where the conservatory is and to which Mrs. Townley and my rooms look. Only on this side can the house be broken into. Here, then, was the point of danger.

"I had waited in the dark for nearly two hours, and, tired out with my day's shooting and my many anxieties, was all but asleep, with my arms on the table and my head resting on them, when O'Brien opened the door hastily and said in a loud whisper:

" 'The rascal's at work, sir!'

" 'What's happened?' I asked, hardly daring to believe the good news.

" 'We heard Mrs. Townley open her window just now, and chuck something out.'

" 'The knotted rope!'

" 'We can't see a thing, the night's so thick, but we can hear him climbing up against the creepers on the wall, hand over hand.'

" 'Send Macgregor here, and you run to the two constables below and tell them to post themselves in the passage leading to the conservatory. There is no hurry. There let them stay till they hear me give three stamps on the floor overhead. Then they are to run out and nab any one coming down a rope from Mrs. Townley's window. Explain it all clearly to them, O'Brien. Let them stick closely to my instructions; and then you come back quietly into my room. Pull your boots off as you come upstairs.'

"Macgregor and I waited a good ten minutes. We removed our boots as a matter of precaution. Presently O'Brien entered the room barefoot. We had heard, or thought we heard, some one stirring in Mrs. Townley's room, but it was only after some minutes' waiting that we heard the door softly open. We waited a few minutes. Then I opened the door of my room and listened. I could hear the sound of stockinged feet some way up the corridor. I knew it must be Coggins.

"I followed the footsteps, after whispering to Macgregor to follow on some yards behind me.

"'What is he at?' I wondered, as I cautiously went forward through the darkness in the direction of the footfall. To what was he leading me? I wondered, for he did not go in the direction of the living part of the house.

"He seemed to know every inch of the way in the dark, and turned sharp to the right and left more than once.

"Finally he came to a sudden stop. I heard the opening of a door; he went forward, half closing it behind him. I waited for a moment to let Macgregor come up. I could see now that the burglar carried a dark lantern with him. He turned it on, flashing the light upon the walls. To my astonishment he had entered the famous picture gallery of Balin Abbey. I saw the light of his lantern flash upon great luminous canvases of Rubens, upon sweet portraits of girls by Romney and Reynolds, upon masterpieces of Velasquez and Titian. Was O'Brien's prediction come true? Was the rascal coveting some of the works of the great masters which Lady Drusilla told me the Mr. Townley, whom I made no doubt was Coggins, had once criticized so acutely? I almost laughed at the fellow's audacity.

"This certainly was his object, and he now set to work to carry it out. He began with a beautiful picture of three nymphs in a woodland landscape by Rubens. It was a picture full of a golden and rosy light, and the bright surface reflected the gleam of the bull's-eye lantern carried at his waist-belt. The reflected light clearly revealed all his movements in outline. He took from his pocket a knife and cut along the bottom line of the inner frame, then as high as he could reach on each side. Then, standing on a table which he had moved in front of the picture, he cut along the top and sides. In another moment he had put up his two hands and was steadily ripping the canvas down and off the backing of the frame, with a dull rasping noise as when a saw passes through soft wood; then he turned, and for a moment we could see his face and the knife with its gleaming blade between his teeth. I saw, too, the handle of a revolver protruding from his breast pocket.

"He leaped lightly from the table and rolled the canvas

up. His actions were almost monkey-like in their nimbleness. He moved the table to another picture and we saw the light stream upon it. It was the portrait of a lady in a gray dress slashed with black and embroidered with silver lace on the shoulders and sleeves—the portrait of a young queen, by Velasquez—a face with a proud disdainful smile. I saw him use his knife upon this lifelike presentment of a noble woman, with something of the horror with which I should see him prepare to attack a living human being. The painted face and figure formed a point of light in that great vault of blackness which is before me at this moment that I speak to you as vividly as I saw it that night.

"Macgregor pressed forward as Coggins passed the knife quickly round the edge of the picture. I laid my hand on his shoulder and whispered 'Wait!' in his ear. When the burglar put up his hand and began drawing off the canvas from the back, I took advantage of the sound of tearing to throw wide open the door and, together, we rushed in upon the burglar. Together, we leaped up at him on the table, but before we could reach him he had heard us, turned, taken the knife in one hand and drawn the revolver with the other. Macgregor had seized one wrist, I the other, in the uncertain light. The table fell, and all three of us lay struggling on the ground. One barrel of the revolver went off, and he stabbed at us both repeatedly with the knife. The burning powder singed my hair, but the ball struck neither of us, and after a minute Macgregor got the pistol from him. He had struck Macgregor once savagely with the knife on the shoulder, but I had hold of his wrist and the blow glanced, and though it cut through the cloth of Macgregor's coat, it only just grazed the skin. The struggle on the floor lasted but a minute or two. Then we overmastered him. O'Brien ran up as we held him and slipped the handcuffs over his wrists. The Irishman picked up the lantern, which had fallen to the ground and had cast only a flickering and uncertain light during our fight with the criminal. Not a word had been spoken by any of us.

" 'Take him to the room in the tower, Macgregor,' I whispered in Macgregor's ear, 'and answer no questions if the prisoner asks any. Make no noise as you go.'

"I had expected the gallery to fill at once with people from the house, roused by the crash of the falling table, and more still by the report of the pistol, but nothing of the sort happened. The picture gallery lies far away from the inhabited portion of the Abbey, being reached through long and tortuous corridors. The door had shut to as Macgregor and I rushed in, and though the noise of the pistol discharge seemed deafening to us, as it reverberated through the vaulted roof of the gallery, it turned out that not a soul but ourselves had heard anything.

"I went downstairs and brought up the two officers from their post near the conservatory. I told them we had captured our man, and that their duty would be to watch him during the night.

"It was now nearly three o'clock. By daylight I was up again and had gone out. I saw the keepers assembled on the lawn. They were greatly disturbed by the non-appearance of the bloodhounds. The dogs had not answered, as usual, to the keepers' call, and a search in the shrubberies presently resulted in finding the bodies of all four of them lying dead and stark.

"I spent two hours in writing a report to my chief. I felt that luck had greatly befriended me all through—I had succeeded in every point. I had recovered the lost jewels. I had brought the robbery home to the actual thieves—that is, morally brought it home, for even now it was doubtful if legal evidence could have been brought against Coggins for the jewel robbery, but I had established a clear case of burglary in the matter of the pictures against the man suspected so often and never yet in durance for an hour.

"It was nine o'clock. I dressed and sent in word to Lord Balin that I would like to see him before breakfast.

"I said, 'My business is done. I have found the stolen jewels—here they are,' and I laid the paper parcel before him. 'One of the thieves was Mrs. Townley, but the instigator and real criminal was Coggins, *alias* Towers, who is the husband of Mrs. Townley. The man Coggins broke into the Abbey last night for the second time, and we were able to arrest him in the very act of stealing your pictures. He is now a prisoner in the tower room. No one in the house knows anything of the matter, not even Mrs. Townley.'

"'Stop! stop!' said Lord Balin, raising his hands. 'You overwhelm me! What! found the jewels and arrested the thief? Why—why, you are the most extraordinary fellow in the whole world—you shoot my pheasants for me when I couldn't get any one else to, you entertain my guests as no one else does—and now, in a turn of the hand, you find the lost property and arrest the thief. You are a wonderful fellow, my dear Stanley!'

"'Morgan now, Lord Balin—Sergeant Morgan, at your service. The comedy is over.'

"'Nothing is over, Morgan—if you will let me call you that and,' he added, holding out his hand, 'and my friend; and do not forget that I owe you a debt of gratitude that I shall never be able to discharge.'

"Then he changed the subject suddenly. 'And that poor woman, Morgan? What are we to do with her—arrest her too, charge her with the theft, and get her put into prison?'

"'It seems hard upon her,' I said; 'she acted under the influence and compulsion of her husband.'

"'It is damned hard, Morgan. Though I confess I never liked the woman; but a pretty woman and my guest! No, no!'

"'The moral evidence,' I said, 'against Mrs. Townley is overwhelming—the legal evidence almost *nil*. I doubt if we could secure a conviction. I have told my chief so. Counsel for her defense would be sure to argue, If she was the thief, why did Coggins run the risk of breaking into the house?'

"'To be sure,' said Lord Balin, 'why did he?'

"'Because he would know that he couldn't trust her to do the trick herself. It takes pluck, nerve and experience which no ordinary woman possesses. Even if she had all the will in the world, Mrs. Townley could not have gone through the rooms single-handed and stolen the jewels herself.'

"'Then you think he did it alone?'

"'Alone or together, who can tell?'

"'I tell you what, Morgan. Let's think it over presently. Come in to breakfast now—the second gong has gone long ago—come in and be Robert Stanley once more. Let us ignore everything for the moment and see what this wretched woman will do and say.'

"'Remember,' I said, 'that she can know nothing as yet. My men are to be trusted, and they won't have spoken to any one in the house. The man passed through her bedroom toward the picture gallery. She certainly knew his errand, for he had brought a dark lantern and a sharp-cutting knife with him. He did not return. She would guess that he found it best to make his escape in some other way than back through her room, for she, having heard nothing of the struggle, would naturally conclude that her friend got safe off.'

"'Just so,' said Lord Balin. 'I will call her in here after breakfast and tell her what has happened. I shall tell her she must leave my house at once and for good, but I will tell her also that, so far as I am concerned, I will not prosecute her. If the authorities choose to press for a prosecution it shall not be my act or by my advice.'

"I thought that line was equitable, and I said so. I ventured to doubt if it were strictly legal.

"Lord Balin laughed. 'Law be hanged, Morgan! equity and poetical justice forever! But come to breakfast; you must be hungry after your night's work.'

"We had sat down and taken our places before Mrs. Townley entered the room. I cannot say that her face was pale, for it was more highly colored than ever, but her unquiet eyes and her trembling mouth told the tale of the night's anguish. Lord Balin greeted her with no change of his accustomed morning cordiality. She was more carefully, more exquisitely dressed than usual, and her hair seemed to have undergone the attentions of a professional hair-dresser. She talked and laughed freely, but I could see that she looked and listened for any stray revelation of the events of that terrible night.

"The butler came in and spoke in a low voice to Lord Balin.

"'His Lordship half rose from his seat in anger. Poisoned them! What! all four? Confound the sneaking villain!' Then he sat down, having mastered his wrath.

"'I beg your pardon,' he said, turning to his guests, 'but what do you think? The scoundrel who robbed this house three days ago, and who has been hanging about the neighborhood for weeks past, has poisoned four of my bloodhounds!'

"I looked at Mrs. Townley. She gave a nervous start, and a shudder shook her whole body for a moment. Lord Balin caught sight of her frightened face, and in a moment his chivalry to a guest and a woman came back to him.

"He smiled and changed the subject. So did the meal pass off, and I could not but marvel at the possibility of what may happen in a great house, in the night-time, in the way of moving human drama, and its inmates, guests and servants, have no inkling of what has passed.

"'Mrs. Townley,' said Lord Balin, but so much in his usual tone that I could see it did not alarm his guest, 'I have some news for you. Will you join me in the library presently?'

"Then he left his guests, giving me a look to follow him. Mrs. Townley rose to leave the room. I opened the door for her, and followed her into Lord Balin's private room.

"He motioned her to a seat and began at once.

"'It is very painful, Mrs. Townley, for me to have to say what I am going to. Don't please interrupt me till I have quite finished, and then say what you will.'

"Lord Balin's tone was not stern. It was rather sad, but he spoke without hesitation.

"'I want to speak to you about the robbery of jewels here three days ago. This gentleman'—he looked at me—'is an officer of the detective service, and he authorizes me to say that the settings of the lost gems were found hidden among the Abbey Ruins; the gems themselves, which you twice endeavored to pass to the disguised burglar—'

"'Lord Balin!' exclaimed the unhappy woman.

"Lord Balin went on: 'The stones themselves were finally found, as had been indicated by you in a signal to the man Coggins, in the handle of your racquet.'

"Mrs. Townley groaned and hid her face.

"'They are all there,' said Lord Balin, pointing to a cabinet, 'except the pearls and diamonds which you told us you had lost. We have reason to know that your husband broke into this house on the 23d, and went or induced you to go to the rooms of the persons who had drunk of the barley water that you had drugged.'

"Mrs. Townley groaned again.

"'Your husband broke in for the second time again last night, passing through your bedroom. He intended to rob me of the pictures which he had admired at his visit here, and of which no one knew better than himself the value.'

"When Lord Balin had got so far, Mrs. Townley probably made sure that her husband had baffled the police once more and got safely away. She looked up, smiled through her tears, and shook her head.

"'He was arrested in the very act,' Lord Balin went on, 'and will stand his trial for burglary.'

"The woman's face fell, she almost shrieked out the word 'Arrested!'

"Lord Balin bowed. 'You do not, I suppose, seek to deny any part of what I have said?'

"The unhappy woman muttered some incoherent words, and again hid her face in her hands.

"'I have no intention of prosecuting you, Mrs. Townley. I shall advise the authorities not to do so, on the ground that you acted under the compulsion of your husband.'

"Mrs. Townley raised her head, with something of a reprieved look in her face.

"'Lord Balin! you are very generous to me—very generous'—she wept—'to a most unhappy woman—guilty, yes, but, oh, if you could only know!'

"'Mrs. Townley,' said Lord Balin, almost kindly, 'I wish to force no confession from you, but one thing I must tell you. You must leave my house at once, pretexting some sudden call of business. You will do so without again seeing my other guests. I will not betray you to them. Now go,' he said more sternly, 'and make your preparations to leave. The carriage will take you to the station in two hours' time from now.'

"Mrs. Townley got up, and without any leave-taking quitted the room. Again, as before, I opened the door to let her go out.

"'Lord Balin,' said I, 'may I ask you a favor?'

"'*May* you ask me!' said my host, smiling.

"'It is that you will allow me to have a parting interview with a lady I have reason to respect very greatly.'

"'My cousin, Drusilla Lancaster?'

"'Yes.'

"Lord Balin rang the bell and told the butler to beg Lady Drusilla Lancaster to come to the library in order to hear some important news.

"'Tell her, please,' I said, 'when she comes, who I am and why I came here.'

"'I will, Morgan,' said Lord Balin; 'I will, my dear fellow; but, I say, we won't give that poor woman away even to Lady Drusilla?'

"'No! no! On no account.'

"'Drusilla,' said Lord Balin, 'I have a confession to make to you, and to you alone, mind, from my friend here. He is not Robert Stanley; he is Mr. Morgan, of the detective service.'

"'I thought he was too nice for a millionaire,' said Lady Drusilla, smiling, and otherwise unimpressed.

"'I owe him an enormous debt of gratitude,' Lord Balin went on. 'He has recovered all the jewels that were stolen here, and he has arrested the thief.'

"'The thief?' asked Lady Drusilla, with a curiously shrewd look.

"'Yes, the famous burglar, Coggins—Gentleman Coggins, who has baffled the whole London police for four years. Last night he made an attempt upon my picture gallery, and Mr. Morgan arrested him in the act.'

"'Well done!' said Lady Drusilla, turning to me.

"'I have begged Lord Balin,' I said, 'to give me the chance of apologizing to you for the miserable part I played with you—'

"'Miserable part!' exclaimed Lady Drusilla; 'why, this sort of thing is nearly the only real action possible in this tame age. In my eyes—Mr.—Mr.—what am I to call you?'

"'Morgan,' said Lord Balin.

"'In my eyes, Mr. Morgan, you are a knight errant—you think and you act in the interests of the rest of us, and that is to be the only sort of knight errant and hero possible in these days.'

"She came forward and took my hand in both hers.

"'Mr. Morgan, you and I are going to be great friends,

are we not?' she laughed. 'Do, if you please, come and have tea with me in Hill Street, next Friday.'

"I have nothing more to say about this case at Balin Abbey except this. My short twenty-four hours' work at Balin Abbey won me inspectorship, and, on my favorable report, Macgregor and O'Brien were promoted to be Sergeants.

"But I have gained what I esteem even more highly, the life-long friendship of my host at the Abbey and of Lady Drusilla Lancaster.

"The authorities took Lord Balin's advice and did not prosecute Mrs. Townley.

"Gentleman Coggins, *alias* Towers, *alias* Townley, got five years' penal servitude.

"Mrs. Townley resumed her luxurious life in Park Lane. Her jewels, her dress, her motor cars, her yacht, her chef, her charming dinners, her bridge evenings (when the play runs high) are more than ever the talk of the town. She is said to be the richest grass widow on this side of the Atlantic; for she admits herself that grass widow is now quite an applicable name for her. 'It is too bad of my husband,' she says; 'he never seems to have time to come home. One day I get a postcard from Pekin telling me of how he has a valuable concession from the Dowager Empress, two months later a wire comes from South America, then he is heard of in Japan! It is very hard upon his poor wife.'

"The supposed financial wanderer is, however, still doing time at Broadmoor, and we, in the force, are wondering whether, when he comes out, he will resume the very lucrative business of Ikey Coggins or the far less profitable but safer profession of city financier. We hope he will continue in the burglaring rather than the financing line. We know more now about Gentleman Coggins than we did, and believe we could catch him tripping; anyhow, we can always follow a criminal in that line with some hopes of running him in, whereas the person who practices the more speculative branches of the profession is mostly quite beyond the reach of the law."

The Murder at Jex Farm

BY OSWALD CRAWFURD, C.M.G.

The Murder at Jex Farm

BY OSWALD CRAWFURD, C.M.G.

CHAPTER I

CHARLES JEX

INSPECTOR MORGAN and I were sitting over the fire one particularly cheerless winter night at my lodgings in Duke Street. The Inspector had brought with him a thick bundle of documents. He threw them on the table between us as he came in. As usual, our talk had fallen upon the art, or science of crime detection.

"Do you remember," asked Morgan, "my once saying that the first thing a clever criminal does is to try his best to block the way of the man who has to follow up the track of his crime?"

"I shall do that myself," said I, "if I ever commit a serious crime."

"Of course you would, so should I, and so, I suppose, would any man with his senses about him. Well, that is just what a man coming green to detective work is apt to forget. I came near to forgetting it myself when they sent me down to Jex Farm to inquire about the murder there. You must remember the case, for it made a great stir at the time."

"I hope you are going to tell me all about it, Morgan. One does not carry these things in one's head. One big crime gets mixed up with another."

"I came here meaning to tell you the whole story," said the Inspector, taking hold of the bundle of papers and untying the knots of red tape which bound them together.

"Are these documents in the case?" I asked.

"Plans and reports, and cuttings from newspapers, but I am only going to ask you to look at some of them."

THE MURDER AT JEX FARM

"If I am not mistaken, Morgan, the papers spoke very handsomely of your conduct of the Jex Farm case."

"They did, but they had little reason to. If they had known all the facts as well as you will presently know them, they might have handled me differently. It is wonderful what the papers do get to know, but, naturally, they can't see things from the inside as we can."

"Well, Morgan, get to the story. I want to hear it."

"There is not much of a story to tell, so far as the outside facts were concerned. It is only the inside working of things that made it interesting. A young girl had been found lying at the orchard gate of the farm, 37½ yards from the house, dead, with three pistol bullets in her head. Suicide was out of the question, the three wounds and the three bullets precluded that, and there was no pistol about. Moreover, it was not in evidence that the girl had any cause for despondency. There was no reason for her taking her life. But then, again, she was not known to have an enemy."

The Inspector took out a newspaper from the bundle of documents, docketed *Jex Murder Case,* and handed it to me. I read as follows:

"Murder in Surrey.—Jex Farm, one mile from the village of Bexton, in Surrey, was the scene of a terrible and mysterious crime, on the evening of Wednesday last. A young unmarried lady of the name of Judson, a niece of Mrs. Jex, the widowed owner of Jex Farm, was found murdered, late on Wednesday night, just inside the orchard gate of the farm, and within a stone's throw of the house. There were no signs of a struggle, but Miss Judson's gold watch and chain were missing. The crime must have been committed at late dusk on Wednesday evening, 17th inst. (October). It is singular that no sound of firearms was heard by any inmate of the house; and the crime was not discovered till the family were about to meet at supper, when Miss Judson's absence was noticed.

"After waiting a while and calling the name of the young lady in vain, the night being very dark and gusty, young Mr. Jex and the farm-laborers started out with lanterns. They almost immediately came upon the dead body of the unfortunate young lady, which was lying on the walk just inside the orchard gate, and it is stated that the first discoverer of the tragedy was Mr. Jex himself. It adds one more element of gloom to the fearful event when we add that it is rumored in the neighborhood that Mr. Jex, the only son of the lady who owns the farm, was engaged to be married to the victim of this terrible tragedy.

"No clue has yet been obtained. It is clear that the motive of the crime was robbery—the young lady's valuable gold watch and chain were missing—and it is supposed in the neighborhood that, as the high road runs within twenty yards of the scene of the tragedy, the perpetrator may have been one of a very rough set of bicyclists who were drinking at the Red Lion at Bexton in the afternoon, and who were seen, at nightfall, to retrace their journey in the direction of Jex Farm. We understand that Inspector Morgan, the well-known London detective, has been despatched from Scotland Yard to the scene of the murder. Inspector Morgan is the officer whose name has recently attained considerable prominence in connection with the discovery and conviction of the perpetrator of the great jewel robbery at Balin Abbey."

"Rather penny-a-lining and wordy," observed Mr. Morgan as I finished reading the paragraph aloud, "but barring the too-flattering allusion to myself, on the whole, a fair enough account of the facts.

"I found that it was young Mr. Jex himself who supplied the information about the bicyclists. He had been shooting rabbits at an outlying farm of his own a couple of miles beyond Bexton, and, stopping to get a glass of beer at the chief inn there, found himself surrounded in the bar by a group of rowdy bicyclists. The Surrey countryman generally dislikes the cycling Londoners who travel along the roads of his county in extraordinary numbers. Mr. Jex had noticed that these men, instead of continuing their journey toward London, had turned again in the direction of Jex Farm. If they repassed the Lion at Bexton, they must have done so at night, for they were not seen again.

"Mr. Jex is a fine young man with good looks, a little over thirty years of age, six foot one in height, a sportsman, and popular in the neighborhood. But I will confess at once to you that the ways and manners of the man did not find much favor with me. However, he seemed very ready to give me every assistance in his power. He is resolved, he says, to bring the villains to justice.

"His mother is a kind and motherly old lady, rather infirm in health and slightly deaf. She herself gave me to understand that she fully approved of the approaching marriage of her son. I gather in the neighborhood that Mr. Jex, like so many of his class, has been very hard hit by the prevailing agricultural depression, and that his proposed marriage with his cousin, Miss Judson, an orphan, with a considerable fortune of her own, was something of a godsend to himself and his family.

"My written orders from headquarters had been to instal myself in the house, if I could obtain an invitation, in order the better to unravel the facts of the crime, and I was to take my full time in the investigation. I showed my instructions on this head to Mrs. Jex and her son, and was by them at once cordially invited to consider the farm my home for the time being. I thought it best to leave my two subordinate officers to do outside work and hear and report outside rumors. They put up at the Lion at Bexton.

"It was a somewhat delicate situation, and I put it plainly to each of the inmates of Jex Farm, to Mr. Jex, to his mother, and to a young lady on a visit to them, Miss Lewsome. I was a detective officer, I told them, on a mission to detect a great crime. Though I was a guest at the farm, I was bound, as a police officer, to make a minute inquiry into everybody's conduct since, and before, the murder. They must not take it amiss if I was particular in my questions, and vexatious in my way of putting them. The reasonableness of all this was apparent to them all, and I at once began my investigations at the farm and outside it.

"The first person I interviewed was young Mr. Jex himself. Now, I repeat that I did not quite like young Mr. Jex's manner. Some witnesses are too shy and too holding back, and others a good deal too forward, not to say impatient. Jex was of this class, and I was a little sharper with him in consequence than I should otherwise have been. On the 17th he told me he had returned from shooting at his farm on the other side of Bexton, and he stopped on his way home for a drink at the Red Lion.

"'At what time?' I asked.

"'It was growing dusk,' said Jex. 'I should say it was within a few minutes of half-past five or getting on for six; three men were drinking at the bar, bicyclists; I was thinking they would be overtaken by night; I did not like the looks of those men.'

"'Never mind the bicyclists, for the present, Mr. Jex You stayed some time in the bar?'

"'An hour or more.'

"'Did you meet any one you knew at the Lion? Any neighbors?'

"'Yes, I met James Barton and—'

"'Don't trouble yourself with their names just now! You met friends who can speak to your being at the inn?'

"'I did.'

"'That will do. I want to get to the dates. At about 6:30 you started for home?'

"'It was on the stroke of seven, by the clock of the Lion.'

"'You had no doubt taken a glass or two of ale?'

"'No, I took a glass of whisky and water.'

"'Or two?'

"'I took two glasses.'

"'You took two glasses of whisky and water, good; and then you set off for the farm? Was your man still with you?'

"'What man?'

"'The man who carried your game, or was it a boy?'

"'I had no man, or boy, with me. I had brought three rabbits in my pocket, and these I left as a present to Mrs. Jones of the Lion.'

"'You were carrying your gun, of course?'

"'Of course I was.'

"'Was it loaded?'

"'Yes, but I drew the charges as I neared home.'

"'You noticed nothing unusual as you came in?'

"'Nothing.'

"'Yet you passed within a yard of the orchard gate where the poor girl must have been lying dead?'

"'I did, of course, but it was pitch dark under the trees. I saw nothing but the lights in the parlor windows from the time I opened the gate out of the road.'

"'And coming along the road from Bexton you did not notice, or hear anything?'

"'Yes, I saw the lanterns of three cyclists coming toward me when I had got only a few hundred yards from the Lion. I never saw men traveling faster by night; they nearly got me down in the road between them.'

"'Were they the men who had been drinking at the Lion?'

"'I couldn't see, it was too dark. They never slackened speed; I just felt the swish and wind of their machines as they shaved past me.'

"'You noticed nothing else on the road home?"

"'Yes, I thought I heard some shots far away—poachers, I thought at the time—in Squire Watson's woods.'

"'How many shots?'

"'Three.'

"'Close together?'

"'As close as I speak now: one—two—three.'

"'Was this long after you met the cyclists?'

"He took a moment to think. 'Come, Mr. Jex, you can't want time to answer such a simple question?'

"'It was some time before I met them.'

"'How far might it have been from the Lion when you heard the three shots?'

"'A matter of half a mile or so.'

"'Then it was *after* you met the cyclists?'

"'No, it was before.'

"'It was after, for you told me just now you met them a few hundred yards on your way home, and now you say you heard the shots when you were half a mile on your way home. Half a mile is not a few hundred yards; it is 880 yards.'

"Mr. Jex seemed puzzled.

"'You are too sharp on a fellow!' he said.

"'I had need to be, perhaps, Mr. Jex,' I answered.

"'Now, Mr. Jex,' I said, 'there is another point on which I am afraid I must question you.'

"'I guess what it is,' said he; 'go ahead. You mean about me and Miss Judson?'

"'That is so, about Miss Judson and yourself. You were engaged to her?'

"'I was.'

"'Had the engagement lasted long?'

"'A month.'

"'And she had been two months your mother's guest at the farm?'

"'Going on for three.'

"'And there was nothing standing against your wishes?'

"'I don't understand what sort of thing you mean.'

"'Well, any misunderstanding between you—quarrels, you know?'

"'Oh, lovers' quarrels! They don't amount to much, do they? We had the usual number, I suppose.' (This is a queer, indifferent sort of a lover, I thought.)

"'Well, even a lover's quarrel has a cause, I suppose—and it's mostly jealousy; perhaps there was some neighbor you did not fancy the look of?'

"'God bless you, no! Miss Judson hardly knew the neighbors.'

"'Or some old London friend the young lady may have had a liking for once?'

"'Couldn't be,' said Jex positively. 'Because Mary only had one friend. She had been engaged to him, and she threw him over. She fancied me better, you see. She told me all about him. She told me everything, you know.'

"'Ah, I suppose women always do!"

"'They do when they care for a fellow,' said Jex warmly.

"The man's way of talking of the poor dead girl grated upon me most unpleasantly.

"'Well, perhaps they do, Mr. Jex, but you see, here's a mysterious crime, and I want to find a motive for it.'

"'Who could have a motive?' asked Mr. Jex.

"'Possibly a disappointed rival—from London.'

"'Why, man,' said Jex, 'I tell you it couldn't be; the man I spoke of is in New Zealand—thousands of miles away. I tell you the motive was robbery. Why! wasn't the girl's gold watch and chain taken?'

"'That might be a blind, Mr. Jex,' said I, looking him straight in the face; 'it's a common trick, that.'

"'Oh, nonsense; we all agreed at the inquest it was robbery, and we fastened it on to those three cyclists I saw at the Lion, coming back along the road, hot-foot, just in the nick of time to do the trick. Don't you go wasting your time, Mr. Morgan, over rivals, and rot of that kind!'

"I let this very positive gentleman run on, but I thought well presently to throw a little cold water over his cocksureness.

"'Mr. Jex,' I said, 'do you remember that at the inquest the county police put in plaster casts of all the footprints found next morning round about where the body had lain?'

"'Well, what if they did?'

"'Only that I've just compared those footprints with the bootprints of the inmates of this house, and the marks correspond with the boots worn by the three laborers at the farm, and—by yourself.'

"This seemed to stagger him a bit.

"'Of course,' he said, 'we made those marks when we brought the body in.'

"'I know that,' I said.

"'And one country boot,' said Jex, 'is just as like another as one pea is like another.'

"'Not quite so like as that, Mr. Jex, and did you ever know a cyclist to ride his machine in hobnailed boots? There was no single footprint in or near the place but what had heavy hobnails showing. So, you see, the murderer could not be one of your bicyclists.'

"Jex kept silence for a minute, and paled as I watched him.

"'The man who committed this murder, Mr. Jex,' I said, 'never wore a cyclist's shoe or boot.'

"'I'll tell you what,' said Jex, after a longish pause, 'we'd trampled down the ground a good bit all round; we must have trampled out the murderer's footprints.'

"'It's just possible,' I said, 'but not likely that he shouldn't have left a square inch of shoeprint anywhere. However, that is of no matter to me at present. I've another bit of evidence that I'll work out first.'

"'A clue?' asked Jex eagerly. 'What is it?'

"'Well, Mr. Jex, you'll excuse me for not mentioning it just at present. You'll know soon enough.' I gave him a moment to think over the matter, then I went on:

"'Now, sir, I should like to ask you one or two more questions, if you're quite agreeable.'

"'Fire away,' said Jex. 'I'm here to answer you.'

"'I'm told you used to meet Miss Judson on your return from shooting, or what not, at the orchard gate leading out of the flower garden?'

"'That's so.'

"'At nightfall?'

"'Yes, as it grew from dusk to dark.'

"'Might she be expecting you there on the 17th, just as night fell?'

"'Likely she might.'

"'But about that time you were drinking in the bar-parlor of the Lion?'

"'Well, if you call two small goes of whisky and water after a long walk, drinking, I was.'

"'The landlady is an old friend of your mother's, I'm told?'

"Jex laughed. Whoever told you that, told you wrong; my mother does not particularly cotton to Mrs. Jones.'

"'What! the two old ladies don't hit it off?'

"'Who told you that Mrs. Jones was an old lady?' said Jex. "She's a young widow, and a pretty one into the bargain.'

"'That accounts,' said I, 'for the present of rabbits, eh?'

"Jex winked. Decidedly I don't like this young man."

CHAPTER II

MAUD LEWSOME AND HER DIARY

I have mentioned a fourth inmate at Jex Farm at the time of the murder, in the person of Miss Maud Lewsome, a young lady friend of Miss Judson's, and a distant cousin of hers, but no blood relation of the Jex family. Miss Lewsome had come as a friend of Miss Judson, and had resided at the farm some five or six weeks. She is a tall, dark, handsome girl, gentle and reserved in manner, but, as I should judge, extremely intelligent. I hear that her profession in life is the literary one, but whether in the way of novel-writing, or journalism, I am not told. She had also been for a short time on the stage. I have, as yet, had hardly any conversation with Miss Lewsome, so overcome is she with the nervous shock of the tragedy of her dearest friend.

I need not reproduce here at any length the evidence of

the country surgeon who made the *post-mortem,* as given at the inquest. It was to the effect that death had resulted from three bullet wounds in the side of the head, one just behind the ear and two just above it. The shots must have been fired from the distance of some few yards, for there was no burning or discoloration of the skin. That they must have been fired in rapid succession was evident from the fact of the three wounds being within a circle whose diameter was not more than three inches in length. The charges of powder, in the doctor's opinion, must have been light, for, after passing through the walls of the skull, there was little penetration. The bullets, all three, had been extracted—very small round leaden bullets hardly bigger than large peas, and not of the conical shape used in revolvers of the more expensive kind. Death must have been instantaneous, for the bullets were all three found buried in the brain, one still spherical, the others flattened by contact with bone.

Now, it is obvious that this circumstance increases the difficulty connected with the fact that no one at the farm, neither Mrs. Jex nor Miss Lewsome, nor any of the laborers or female servants, who were indoors and at supper at the time, had heard the sound of firearms. It is true that on the evening of the 17th half a gale of wind was blowing from the northwest, and the orchard, where the fatal shots were fired, is nearly south of the house. All doors and windows were closed, the night having turned cold and rainy, but the sitting-room faces the southeast, and, though a tall yew hedge interposed, it was difficult to understand how three pistol shots, fired less than forty yards away, should not be audible by the inmates of the room. Was Mrs. Jex hard of hearing? I asked her. Only very slightly so, she declared. Had she heard positively nothing? Nothing but the roaring of the wind in the chimney and, every now and then, the rattling of the windows. Was she absorbed in reading, or talk? No, she was knitting by the fireside. Miss Lewsome had been writing at the table all the evening. From time to time, Mrs. Jex told me, she had talked with Miss Lewsome, who had remained with her in the sitting-room from before sundown till supper time.

I then examined Miss Lewsome by herself, as I had already

examined Mrs. Jex. She corroborated what that lady had said. The wind was loud that night, said Miss Lewsome. It rattled the windows and made a great noise in the chimney. She was writing all the evening, she said.

"Forgive my curiosity," I said, "was it something that took up your attention and would have prevented your hearing a noise outside?"

She hesitated. "I was writing up my diary," she answered.

"You keep a regular diary?"

"Yes."

"May I see it?"

"Oh, no!" she said. "That would be impossible. I could not show it to any one. You must really not ask to see it."

"I am sorry," I said, "I am afraid you must let me read it."

"Why?"

"Because I am a police officer, and am here to inquire into the death by violence of Miss Mary Judson, and because your diary may throw some light upon the circumstances of the crime."

"How can it help you? It is all—personal; all about myself."

"I am not in a position to say how the diary can help me till I have seen it; but see it I must."

She still hesitated; after a pause she asked:

"Do you really insist?"

"I am afraid I must."

She walked to her desk, opened it, and gave me a leather-covered book, locked, and put it, with the key, into my hands.

That night I read the diary. The entries were, as Miss Lewsome had told me, scanty, that is, at first, referring to such trivial events as her arrival at the farm, for the diary began with the beginning of her visit. As it went on, however, the entries became fuller, and the occurrences of the six or seven days previous to the murder were narrated with considerable fullness. Before I had ended my perusal of the book, certain vague suspicions that had already formed themselves in my mind began to gather in strength and to acquire full corroboration.

Inspector Morgan picked out, from the bundle of documents, one marked: *Extracts from Miss Lewsome's Diary* This is what he read out to me:

THE MURDER AT JEX FARM

October 3.—The more I see of what is going on between Charles and Mary the more I blame myself for my fatal weakness. Had I only known of their engagement! . . . why, oh, why, did they keep it a secret from me? He never should have learned my passion for him—never should have . . . oh, fool, fool that I have been! Poor Charles, I hardly blame him. In honor he is bound to poor Mary, and yet I see, day by day, that he is getting colder and colder to her and more and more devoted to me. In honor he can't break off his engagement. Poor fellow, too, he needs his cousin's money. Without it, I know, ruin stares him in the face. Were it not for that, as he says, he would break with Mary to-morrow. I believe him.

October 5.—What am I to do? The situation becomes more and more difficult every day. I see that I must leave Jex Farm, but it will break my heart, and I fear it will break Charles's too.

October 6.—Mary suspects nothing, though Charles grows daily colder to her.

October 11.—Charles and I have had an explanation. I have told him that I can bear it no longer. He said he could not break off the engagement; if he could, he would. He spoke almost brutally. "I must have Mary's money," he said. "Without it my mother, I, my sisters and brothers and the farm must all go to the devil. I hate the woman!" he cried out. "Don't—don't say that, Charles; it is so dreadfully cruel and wicked. What has poor Mary done to you?" "She has come between me and the only woman I ever loved. Is not that enough?" "But you have told me that your cousin's money must come to you some day or other?" "Yes, but only on her death." "Don't, Charles, it is too dreadful." "Yes, isn't it? Just awful!" "Well, but—" He laughed. "Oh, women never understand business, but I see what you are driving at, my dear, a *post obit,* or a sale of the reversion of Mary's estate, eh?" I nodded, just wishing to see what his meaning was, but, of course, never dreaming of anything so mercenary and hateful. He went on: "Then you think, I suppose, that with the cash in hand I could break off with Mary and make amends for the wrong I have done you? Is that your little game?" At that moment I almost hated

Charles. Tears of mortification came into my eyes. "Oh, Charles, don't think so meanly of me!" "Meanly! Why, hang it, it was in my own head, why should it not be in yours, too? You are the cleverest girl I know, for all you are so quiet; of course, you thought of it! So did I, only that cock won't fight, my girl. Oh, no; I consulted a lawyer, and he upset all my little plans. 'You could not raise a penny,' says he, 'for Miss Judson might marry, and if she does and dies, her estate goes to her children, if she has any. Anyhow, you can't touch the reversion till she dies single, or dies childless.'" "Then, Charles, there is nothing for me to do but to go out into the wide world, poor, abandoned and miserable, with all the weight of my sin on me!" He looked at me a long time with a curious expression in his eyes, frowning. Then he kissed me suddenly on the mouth. "Maud," he said, "you love me—really? really? really?" "I love you," I said, "with all my heart and soul and strength." "And what?" he asked, "what would you do to gain my—my company forever?" I made him no answer, for I did not understand him. I do not understand him now. Then he said suddenly, "If you look at me like that with those great brown eyes of yours and kiss me with those lips I would . . . by Jove! there is nothing, nothing I would not—" Then, without another reasonable word and with an oath, he broke from me and left the room.

The last entry in Miss Lewsome's diary was made and dated on the evening of the murder, and it was no doubt written at the very moment that the tragedy was being enacted within a few yards of the farmhouse windows. The handwriting of this last entry, I noticed, was as firm as it had been throughout—such a hand as I should have expected from what I knew and had heard of this young lady's character and temperament. She is a strikingly beautiful, dark-skinned girl, quiet and reticent in manner, impulsive and headstrong, perhaps, where her passions lead her—the diary proves this only too clearly—but gentle, repressed in all her ways and speech; a woman, in short, with such powers of fascination as few men can resist. It is just such a girl as this for whom men commit untold follies, and just such a girl as would hold such an obstinate, dull-witted, overbearing, young fellow as I see Charles Jex to be, in the hollow of her hand. These lines that follow are the last in the diary.

"I have had a long talk with Mary to-day. Charlie has at last spoken to her about his feelings toward her and his feelings toward me. He has told her plainly that he no longer cares for her, but that he will marry her if she insists upon holding him to his promise. The communication has come upon her as a shock, she said. She was overwhelmed. She could give him no answer. She could not believe that I had encouraged him. Did I love him? she asked me. Did he really love me? Was it not all a horrible dream? I told her the truth, or as much of it as I dared. I told her he had made me care for him long before I knew, or even guessed, there was anything between him and her. I would go at once. To-morrow I could take the train to town and never trouble him, or her, or any one connected with Jex Farm again. Poor Mary cried—she behaved beautifully. She said, 'Maud, you love him, he loves you. You can make him happy, I see now that I cannot. His happiness is more to me than my own. I will go away, and you shall be his wife. I will never marry any one.' We did not speak for several minutes. I could not at first believe in such a reversal of misery. Then all the difficulties of the situation flashed upon me. My poverty; the financial ruin he had to face; the wealth that would save him. 'No,' I said, 'Mary, it cannot be. You are generous, and I love you, but it cannot be! I cannot allow you to make this sacrifice.' We talked long together, and we both of us cried a great deal. I do not think the world holds so sweet and unselfish a woman as Mary Judson. Whatever our lots are in life, hers and mine, we shall always be as sisters one to the other. To-morrow I leave Jex Farm."

CHAPTER III

FRESH EVIDENCE

The immediate effect upon my mind of the reading of Miss Lewsome's diary was to supply me with what had been wanting: a motive for the crime. Everything had pointed in my estimation to treachery in the household; everything seemed to be against the possibility of the crime being committed by an outsider.

Assuming thieves and murderers not connected with the household, what possible reason could have brought them to run such a risk as to shoot down an innocent, unoffending girl within forty yards of a dwelling-house, where probably several men were within call, and certainly within earshot of the sound of firearms? Then again, if a stranger had done this thing for the sake of robbery, how could he be sure that the girl would have money or a watch about her? A third and stronger reason against any stranger criminal was the fact that no stranger had left the imprint of his steps in the garden plot near the gate on the further side of which the girl had fallen. Her head, as she lay, all but touched the lower bar of the orchard gate. She had been shot down at her accustomed trysting-place with her lover, in the dusk, and under deep shadow of the trees, in the darkness of late evening. What stranger could guess she would be there? What stranger could know so well where and how she would stand as to be able to fire three following shots, through the shadows of falling night, with such deadly aim as to take effect within an inch of each other on the poor girl's temple?

I abandoned the idea of a murder for the sake of robbery. It was untenable. I scouted the theory suggested by Charles Jex, and persevered in by him with curious insistence, that the murderers were the bicyclists whom he had seen in the bar at the Lion. The murderer was an inmate of Jex Farm; of that there could be no manner of doubt; the evidence of the footprints was proof enough for that.

Who, then, was the murderer?

Before I answer that question, I put in another document, a very important piece of evidence. It is the report—the very concise and careful report—of one of the most conscientious, painstaking and intelligent provincial officers I have ever had the pleasure of doing business with, Sergeant Edwardes, of the Surrey Constabulary.

The Inspector took up the bundle, selected one paper and gave me to read—*Sergeant Edwardes's Report on the foot-*

prints near the spot where the body of Miss Judson was found at 9:35 P.M. *of October* 17, 189—. It ran as follows:

"I have counted 43 distinct human footsteps and 54 partial imprints. Of the 43, 24 are made by the left foot and only 19 by the right. Of the 54 faint or partial impressions I found 17 of the left foot and only 12 of the right, the rest are not distinctive enough to pronounce upon.

"Of the total number of the fainter footprints 18 are deeply marked in the soft clay, and others are less strongly impressed. Of the 18 that are deeply marked, 11 are made by the left foot, 7 by the right.

"This accords with what I was told subsequently—that Mr. Jex's three laborers, and Mr. Jex himself, on finding Miss Judson's body, at once took it up in their arms and bore it to the house.

"Bearers of a heavy weight, such as a dead body, walking together, invariably bear heavily upon the left foot, both those who are supporting it on the left and those who are supporting it on the right side.

"Distinguishing the bootprints by their length, breadth, and the pattern of the nail-marks upon them, I find that they are the footprints of five separate persons, all of them men. I also found, clearly impressed, the footprints of a sixth person, a woman, namely, those of the victim herself.

"There had been heavy rain in the morning of the 17th, and the soil is a sticky clay. I examined the marks at daybreak on the morning of the 18th, and, as it had not rained during the night, the impressions were as fresh as if they had just been made. By my orders no one had been allowed to come near the spot where the body was found during the night. Just inside the gate of the orchard the grass has been long ago trodden away by passers-by, leaving the earth bare; and this patch of bare earth forms an area rather broader than the gate. On this area the body had fallen, and round about the spot where it had lain, I found all the footprints on which I am reporting.

"I have compared the boots worn by the laborers with the impressions near the gate. They correspond in every particular.

"In the case of the footprints of the three laborers a majority of the deeper impressions are made by the left boot.

"I therefore conclude that all three men came upon the spot only to carry away the body of the girl, and hold no hand in her death. I argue the same from the footprints made by Mr. Jex. He also had borne more heavily with the left than with the right foot. He also, therefore, must have come on the spot only to bear off the body, and could have taken no part in the girl's murder.

"There are almost an exactly equal number of impressions, plain or faint, of the footprints of these four persons.

"There remain the footprints of a fifth person. They are the impressions of a man's foot, but the hobnailed boots that made them, though full-sized, are of a rather lighter make than the others, and the nail-marks are smaller, the boots are newer, for the sides of the impressions have a cleaner cut, and, what is important, the impressions *of the left foot are in no case deeper than those of the right.*

"This person, therefore, clearly did not assist in carrying the body. The person who left these footprints is, in my opinion, the man who, on the night of the 17th of October last, murdered Miss Mary Judson."

CHAPTER IV

MORE FACTS IN THE CASE

The conclusion, so clearly and so logically arrived at by Inspector Edwardes, at once narrowed the field of investigation. My own inquiries bring out a still more startling discovery. The footprints alleged by Sergeant Edwardes to be those of the murderer—the almost self-convicted murderer—correspond in length and breadth, and in the number of nail-marks, twelve in the print of the left foot, ten (there being two gaps) in that of the right, with a pair of boots in the possession of Mr. Charles Jex.

I did not, however, allow this very damning fact to press too heavily against Charles Jex. It is absolutely necessary in inquiries of this very grave character to proceed with caution and deliberation. Another man might have worn the boots with intent to deception on the night of the murder. A murderer, using the devilish cunning of one who seeks to compass the death of a fellow-being without risk of detection, frequently employs such wily precautions as this.

I must first of all seek for a possible criminal among the inmates of the house. There was Miss Lewsome—but it could not have been Miss Lewsome, for, first, there was the direct evidence of old Mrs. Jex that the young lady had not left her side, in the sitting-room, from sundown till after the body was found. There is the almost stronger indirect, undesigned, and internal evidence of Miss Lewsome's diary, with the entry of this very date calmly and fully set out at the very time the murder must have been committed.

Then, again, there are the two maids, to all seeming well-behaved, innocent, rustic girls. It could be neither of them, for their presence in the kitchen the whole evening was vouched for by the evidence of the other servants. The same applied to the three farm laborers. Not one of the servants, male or female, had left the kitchen or scullery that night. From sundown to supper-time is the hour of rest and recreation at a farm, and the day generally ends in talk and laughter. The whole five of them had been enjoying themselves noisily round the kitchen fire. Their loud talk and the blustering wind that roared about the farm chimneys on this tempestuous evening had, doubtless, prevented any one of them from hearing the three revolver shots on the night of the murder.

There remains Mr. Jex. Let us impartially examine the acts that throw suspicion upon him. Here is a man who clearly no longer loves, probably never did love, the girl whom he is about to marry for her money; who certainly does care for another woman; who has entangled himself in an intrigue with this second woman, which he may reasonably expect to come to light at any moment and endanger his prospects of a rich marriage. Here is a man who, by the impartial evidence of that woman's diary, has indulged in vague threats against the murdered girl. He is the only person who could benefit by her death, and would enjoy a welcome and immediate relief, by this event, from impending bankruptcy.

On the other hand, Mr. Jex, at the moment of the crime's commission, represented himself to have been at Bexton, or on the homeward road; but we have, of course, no exact knowledge of the hour at which Mary Judson met with her death. It clearly took place a little time before or a little after half past six o'clock. It might be, for all we know, a good half hour later than Mr. Jex's return to the farm. We know nothing of Mr. Jex's movements from the time of his coming home till his entry, at nine o'clock, into the sitting-room where his mother and Miss Lewsome were awaiting him. No servant opened the door for him; he let himself in. No one saw or heard him enter. What was he doing during all the time that elapsed between his coming home and the discovery of the murder? By his own statement there was an hour and a half to be accounted for. He says he was taking off his wet things and putting on dry ones, lounging about in his bedroom, resting. It may be so, but the time so occupied seems unnecessarily long.

Charles Jex had shown himself, in his talk with me, not a little of a fool, as well as (assuming his guilt) a brutal and cruel murderer. It was the very extremity of his stupidity, indeed, that almost inclined me to hope him innocent. It was almost unthinkable that such a shrewd fellow as Jex had the character of being in the countryside—keen at a bargain, quick at a joke, a hearty, jovial companion at board and bar, knowing and clever in all the signs of coming change in weather and market—should have proved so clumsy and stupid in this deadly affair; leaving traces enough and supplying motives enough to hang a dozen men. Of all men, one would suppose that a man of the fields and a sportsman, used to the marks and tracking of game, would be careful how he left the imprint of his footsteps on the soft clay. Why, that evidence alone, with time fitting and motive thrown in, was enough to bring him to the gallows!

As if this was not enough, further most damning evidence was presently forthcoming.

I will trace out for you, step by step, the history of the murder, on the assumption that Jex was the actual murderer. As to motive I have said enough. No one but Jex had a pecuniary motive for the murder of the girl, whom he certainly did not love. The evidence of the footprints was very strong, but I have said enough of them. To touch upon the immediate cause of the girl's death, there were three small bullets found in the brain. I have already told you that these bullets were not of the conical kind usually found in revolver catridges. They were round, and of the size that is used in the dangerous toys known as drawing-room pistols. During one of Jex's absences on the farm, I had carefully overhauled the saddle-room, where the young farmer kept his guns and ammunition. I found all his guns, cartridge-fillers, wads, shots of different sizes, arranged with the neat order that a good sportsman uses. The guns, carefully cleaned and oiled, were slung on the wall. Two were of the ordinary kind—twelve-inch bore and double-barreled. A third was a heavy, single-barreled, percussion-action duck gun, no doubt meant for use in the neighboring marsh. Half a dozen old-fashioned shot pouches hung along the wall, full, or half full, of shot.

These receptacles, as every one knows, were formerly employed for muzzle-loaders, when men put in, first, the powder, then the wadding, then the shot, with a second wad over that, and finally a percussion cap on the lock nipple. One of these old-fashioned pouches caught my eye. It was of a larger size than the others. I took it from the wall, held it mouth downward over my left hand, and pressed the spring which releases a charge of shot. No shot fell into my hand, but three slugs of the size of small pistol bullets. I snapped the spring again, and three slugs again fell out. I repeated the experiment again and again, every time with the same result. The brass measure, meant to hold an ordinary charge of shot that would weigh about one ounce, held just three of the slugs, neither more nor less, every time it was opened and shut. It was a revelation, for the slugs were identical in size and weight with those found in the brain of the unfortunate girl! The obvious conclusion was that the murderer had loaded his gun from this leather pouch.

There was another corollary to be drawn. The theory of three shots from a revolver was no longer tenable; it seemed clear that the fatal shot had been fired at one discharge, and from a gun. It was also certain, from other evidence, that the person who fired the shot had been one well acquainted with firearms and their use. He would have been anxious that the discharge of his gun should make as little noise as possible. A man, knowing in gun-firing, knows that, to do that, he must use a minimum of powder, with a soft paper wadding in place of the usual tightly fitting circular wad. So fired, the report of a gun is little louder than the clap of a man's two hands when he holds them half-curved. It was in evidence that the bullets had made but little penetration, only just enough to kill, and that therefore the charge was light. It is true that no such paper wadding as I believed had been employed to muffle the sound of the discharge had been found near the scene of the murder. There were further conclusions still to be drawn. The gun was heavy and unhandy. It could hardly have been used but by a strongish man. A further conclusion still was this, that for the three bullets in the charge not to scatter in their trajectory, the gun must have been held close to the girl's head.

It was well, though not absolutely indispensable, in order to bring home the perpetration of the crime to Jex, and in order to show that it was the deed of an expert—in order to show that his story of his hearing the three shots was a lie, invented to find a reason for the gun report, fired so close to the house, having been unheard by its inmates—it was well, I say, to show that the noise had actually been deadened by the use of soft paper wadding.

I walked straight to the orchard gate. I placed myself where the murderer must have stood, within two or three yards of it; he must have fired point-blank at the girl, suddenly and quickly, in the half dark, before she would have had time to move. She had, probably, with her hands resting on the top rail, stood waiting for her lover. The paper wadding would have flown out from the gun barrel, at an angle, more or less acute, to the line of fire, right or left of it, some four or five yards from the muzzle of the gun, and would have fallen, and must now be lying hidden in the grass across the gate, on one side or the other of the orchard path.

I searched the long wisps of grass, and, in two or three minutes, had the satisfaction of finding, half hidden among them, first one, and then a second piece of crumpled paper charred and blackened with gunpowder. Inspector Edwardes had overlooked this important piece of evidence. By the time I had spread the papers out upon a board, there was little left of them but a damp film, but enough was left of their original appearance to show that they were pieces of the county paper, taken in regularity by Mr. Jex.

The man who fired that shot therefore was a proved expert. He was one who had strong reason for not wishing the shot to be heard; and, with half a charge of powder, a light load of shot, and loose paper wadding, he had taken the very best means to effect this purpose. Who in the household was thus expert in firearms? Who, alone, could have known of the existence of the bullet in the saddle-room? Clearly, no one but Charles Jex. He had loaded the gun, too, with paper obtainable in his own house.

I had now more than evidence enough to justify Jex's arrest for the murder of Mary Judson, but I was willing to accumulate still more. I therefore contented myself with obtaining a warrant for his arrest from the magistrates at Bilford, the nearest large town, and prepared to execute it the moment circumstances should make it expedient. Jex had, for some time, shown himself to be uneasy. He shunned me; it was clear he suspected me of having got upon the trail of the crime. I became anxious lest he should think the game was up, and try to escape from justice. I wired for two officers, and instructed them to watch the farm by night, and lay hands on the farmer if he should attempt to break away in the darkness. By day I could keep my own eye upon him. I did not let him get far out of my sight, but, careful as I was, he showed signs of knowing he was watched.

On the morning of the 22d of October—it was my third day on this job—he came down early, dressed rather more smartly than usual, and, before breakfast, he went round to the stables. I affected not to have observed this suspicious movement, and, in the course of the morning, I accepted Miss Lewsome's invitation to accompany her on a walk to Bexton. We both went to make ready. Jex left the room at the same moment. He went toward the stables; I was watching him from my bedroom window. I ran downstairs, prepared for what was coming, and, making my way quickly into the road, stood behind the tall, quickset hedge.

Presently I heard the hurried steps of the groom in the avenue; in a moment more he had opened the gate wide, and as he did so, the dog-cart appeared with Jex driving his gray mare very fast. He called to his servant to look sharp, and hardly stopped the trap for the man to climb up behind. I moved quickly in front of the mare.

"Hulloa, Mr. Jex, you're in a hurry this morning!"

"Yes, confound you, I am; get out of my way, please, or we shall do you a mischief," and he whipped up the mare and tried to drive past me.

"Easy! easy! if you please." I took hold of the reins and kept a firm hold.

"Well, what is it?" he asked.

"Going to catch a train, Mr. Jex?" He hesitated.

"You're in good time for the 12:10 up, you know. Going to town, perhaps?"

"N—no—I'm not. Going to meet a friend at Lingham Junction, that's all."

"Will you take me with you, Mr. Jex?"

"No room, Inspector. My friend and his things, and my fellow will take all there is to spare."

"Oh, leave Sam behind. I can hold your mare at the station, you know." He muttered an oath stupidly, but there was no way for him out of the scrape.

"Jump up, then," he said sulkily. "Sam," he called to his man, "you can go back to your horses."

I sat by his side in the cart, and we drove at a fair pace to the station without half a dozen words passing between us.

No doubt he was thinking the matter out; so was I. I knew just what was passing in his thick head. He was devising how he might slip into the train while I stood outside, holding the horse. He forgot the telegraph. Dealing with these rustic criminals and their simple ways, is bad practice for us London officers, who have to set our wits, in town, against some of the sharpest rogues in creation. I thought, as I sat by Charles Jex, of my old friend Towers, *alias* Ikey Coggins, and I laughed to myself as I compared the one criminal with the other. We got in good time to the station. The up-train signal only went up as we drove to the gate.

"Now, Mr. Jex, you'll be wanting to meet your friend; shall I walk the mare about?"

"Please to do so, Mr. Morgan," said Jex. "You might

take her two hundred yards, or so, up the road. Keep her behind that outhouse, where she can't see the train passing, will you? when it comes in. The mare is a bit nervous."

I laughed in my sleeve at the fellow's shallowness.

"All right, give me the ribbons. Hulloa, you've got a bag!"

"Only a parcel for the up-train."

"Oh, I see; only a parcel for the up-train. Look sharp, then, and get it booked while there's time."

I looked up and down the line; the train was not yet in sight; there was no need for hurry. I turned the mare round and drove her slowly toward the building Jex had pointed to. I saw him watch us from the station gateway before he went in. As he disappeared I beckoned to a boy standing by.

"Here's a shilling job, my lad! Just you walk the mare up to that outhouse, and keep her there out of sight of the train till I come back."

Then I slipped into the station, and, keeping out of sight, saw, as I fully expected I should, Jex taking his ticket.

I waited till the train was in, and as the young farmer, bag in hand, stepped on to the footboard of a second-class carriage, I walked up to him and laid my hand upon his shoulder.

"Charles Jex," I said, speaking loud and clear, for him and the others around to make no mistake about it, "I arrest you for the murder, on the 17th instant, of Miss Mary Judson!"

There was a crowd of ten to fifteen porters, guards, farmers, and others round us in a minute. Jex just swore once. Most criminals that I have taken this way lose their pluck and turn pale, but Jex behaved differently. It was clear that my move had not taken him by surprise.

"I expected as much," he said. He looked round at the people on the platform—his friends to a man, for the young farmer was popular in the neighborhood. "Half a minute more," said he, under his breath, "and I'd have done it."

I slipped one of a pair of handcuffs over his wrist—and clicked the catch, keeping fast hold of the other iron.

"Anyhow, the game's up now," I said.

"You're right, Inspector, the game's up now, sure enough."

The crowd of his friends became rather obstreperous. I called on the station-master and his guards to stand by me, telling him and the people about who I was.

There was a bit of a hustle, and rough talk and threats, and I tried to get the other handcuff on, but my prisoner and I were being pushed about in spite of what the station people did to help us, and I should not have managed it but for Jex himself. He held his free hand out alongside of the manacled one. "Oh, damn it, Morgan, if that's what you want, get done with it, and let's be off out of this."

I put the second handcuff on and clicked the lock.

The sight angered his friends, the farmers standing about, and one of them shouted:

"Now, then, boys, one more rush to goal and we score!"

"Hold on, gentlemen, if you please," I cried. "I warn you, in the King's name! This is my lawful prisoner; I'm an Inspector of Police and I hold a warrant for the arrest of the body of Charles Jex, for murder."

They held back at this for a moment, and I hurried my prisoner through the station entrance, and the porters, guards, and station-master closed round and shut the gate in the faces of the crowd. I never yet knew a man take it so coolly as Jex. When we got to the dog-cart, he said:

"I guess you'll have to drive yourself, Mr. Inspector. With these damned things on my wrists, I can't."

We got in, and I took the reins and drove off fast.

We had traveled some half a mile from the station, and Jex had not opened his lips. I said:

"So you were going to town, were you, Mr. Jex?"

"Mr. Inspector," he said quietly, "haven't you forgotten to caution your prisoner before you ask him any questions? Isn't that the law?" He had me there, sure enough.

"I warn you," I said, coming in with it rather late, I must admit, "that any statement you make may be used against you on trial."

"That's just what I had in my mind, Inspector," said Jex, and he never uttered another word till we neared the farm.

Just as we sighted the farm buildings, I made out on the road, in the distance, a woman's figure. It was Miss Lewsome. She stood in the middle of the road, and I should have driven over her if I had not pulled up.

"What is this, Mr. Morgan?" she cried as we drove up. "Why is it you who are driving? Tell me—tell me quick."

"You'll know soon enough, Miss Lewsome. Stand aside, if you please."

"Oh! what is it? Charles, speak, for God's sake, speak!"

Jex had kept his hands under the apron; he did not say a word, but presently he held out his two wrists, manacled together, for the girl to see. She gave a loud scream.

"O God! you have arrested him, Mr. Morgan! No, no, you can't—you—"

As she was speaking a faintness came over her; she turned from red to very pale, muttering incoherent words which we could not catch, and staggered back against a road gate. But for the bar of the gate to which she clung, she would have fallen. "Help her," said Jex. "Get down and help the girl. You know I can't."

"It's all right, she'll get over it. We'll let her be, and send the women to her presently," and I drove the cart the forty or fifty yards that took us into the stable-yard.

It had been my intention to lodge my prisoner, after dark, that evening, in the keeping of the county police, but events were to happen before nightfall that put a quite different face upon the whole case. As soon as I had given the young farmer into my men's charge, with orders that one or the other was to be with him till we should give him over to the police at Bilford, I called to two of the women of the farm, and went with them to the help of Miss Lewsome.

We found her lying by the roadside, in a dead faint. A farmer's wife—a passer-by—was kneeling by her side, and trying to recall her to her senses.

"Poor thing!" she was saying. "It's only a bit of a swound. She'll come to, if we wait a little."

In two or three minutes Miss Lewsome opened her eyes, and presently stood up, and, with our help, she walked to the house. She said nothing, in her seemingly bewildered condition, of what had happened, and presently afterward she was induced to lie down in her bedroom, and, for the time, I saw no more of her.

In little more than an hour, however, I had a message from her through one of the farm girls. She desired to see me at once, and alone.

I found her sitting up in an armchair, pale and excited in

looks, but, at first, she did not speak. I drew a chair near hers and sat down. She did not notice the few phrases of condolence I uttered. Suddenly she spoke, and I could judge what she must have felt by the strained tones of her voice.

"He is innocent, Mr. Morgan."

I said nothing. Poor girl! My heart bled for her.

"Innocent, I tell you! Innocent, and you must release him at once!"

"You must not excite yourself about this matter, Miss Lewsome. It is not a thing for a young lady to meddle with."

"Yes, but I must meddle with it! I must, I must!"

She raised her voice to a scream.

"Yes, yes, my poor girl, I know how shamefully you have been treated."

"I, shamefully treated? No, no! He has treated me so well. No one could be so good and loyal as he has been."

"Your diary, Miss Lewsome?"

"Lies, all lies, all wicked, cowardly lies, to save myself and hurt him. Yes, to hurt the only man I ever loved. Oh, I am a devil, a malignant, hateful devil! No woman, since the world began, ever schemed so hellish a thing as I schemed."

She covered her face with her hands and sobbed.

What should I do? I was wasting my time in listening to the raving of a love-sick, hysterical girl. I rose to leave her.

"You are doing your health no good, dear Miss Lewsome. You must see the doctor, not me; he shall give you a sleeping-draught, and you will be all right again in the morning."

"By the morning you will have gone away, and you will have taken Charles with you to disgrace, perhaps to death. No, they can't, they can't! The law can't convict him, can it?"

"It is not for me to say. The evidence is very strong."

"Very strong? But there is not a particle of evidence! There can be none!"

"If that man did not murder Mary Judson," said I, getting impatient with her hysterical nonsense, "who did?"

She did not answer for a space of time in which I could have counted twenty, slowly; but she kept her eyes on me with a look in them that almost frightened me.

"I did!" she cried out, at last.

"Ah no! young lady, I see what you're driving at, but it

won't do. No, Miss Lewsome, it's a forgivable thing, your saying this to save your friend, but I tell you it won't do."

"I murdered Mary Judson!" I shook my head and smiled.

"I tell you, I shot Mary Judson on Wednesday night. I did it because I was a jealous, malignant devil, and hated her, and hated him."

"Quite impossible. You never left Mrs. Jex's side all the evening, from before sundown till supper-time. It's in evidence."

"She says so—she believes I did not. She dozes for an hour every evening, and does not even know that she does. I went from the room. I slipped out the moment she dozed off, and came back before she woke. Oh, I had plenty of time."

"But your footprints were not there, and Jex's were."

"I put on his boots over my own. I had often done it, in fun. I did it that day in earnest."

"Did you want to hang him?"

"I did. I hated him so—then."

"Why, in your diary you say you loved him!"

"I did; oh, I do now! But then, when she was alive, I hated them both—her and him. But you can't understand. Men can't understand women. I was mad."

"You are mad now, Miss Lewsome, if you think to save your lover by telling me these falsehoods—for you know they are falsehoods. Mind, I don't blame you for saying what you are saying, but don't expect me, or any one, to believe you."

"I shot Mary Judson in the dusk, at the gate, with his gun! I put three little balls in it that I took from a shot-pouch in the saddle-room."

"You couldn't load the double-barrel with powder and balls, without a cartridge, and none was used."

I thought to catch her tripping in her invention here.

"I did not use the double-barrel. I used the single-barrel. I loaded it as I had seen Charles load it. I put a bit of paper over the powder, and another over the bullets, and rammed them down as I have seen Charles do, and I put a cap on as he had shown me how."

"Come now, that gun with a full charge would have knocked you down."

"I know it would, but I put in only half a charge."

"Stop a bit now, Miss Lewsome, and I will catch you out.

I have found the paper wadding in the grass. What sort of paper was it you put in—brown paper?"

"No, a bit of newspaper; the county paper. I tore off a bit of the *Surrey Times.*" The thing was beginning to puzzle me.

"Another question, Miss Lewsome. You say Mr. Jex is an innocent man. Then why does he attempt to run away? He tried this very day to throw dust in my eyes and go by the express to London."

"I guessed he would, and that is why I wished to get you out of his way this morning."

"Had you told Mr. Jex, then, what you tell me now?"

"No, but he suspects me—oh, I am sure he knows it is I who have done this dreadful thing!"

"If he knows that you are the real murderer and himself innocent, why did he try to escape? You see your story won't hang together, Miss Lewsome."

"Mr. Jex tried to escape, I tell you, to save me."

"But why should he put his own neck in the halter to save a guilty woman—if guilty you are?"

"Because he loves me. He would be suspected, not I."

She was certainly in one story about it all.

"Yes, he loves me so that he has run this great risk to save me from being found out and hanged."

"He told you this?"

"No, he has told me nothing, nor have I told him anything; but these last days I have guessed, by his face, that he knows. I have seen it in his eyes. Oh, he loathes and despises me now!" I said nothing for a few moments.

"Now, Miss Lewsome, I will ask you once more deliberately, and, mind you, your story will be sifted to the utmost, and what you say now may be used against yourself in court. You tell me you shot Miss Mary Judson after sundown on the night of the 17th of October?"

"I did."

"You used Mr. Jex's gun, and you charged it yourself?"

"Yes."

"You wore Mr. Jex's boots when you went out in the dark to kill your dearest friend, and you committed this black crime in order to throw suspicion upon Mr. Jex, who was your lover?"

"Yes. Oh, I was quite mad! I can't understand it. But there was only hatred and bitterness in my heart, and I saw nothing but blood—there was blood in my eyes."

"And what was your object? What did you think would come of it?"

"Nothing, only I hated her so. I was too miserable, because the time was coming near when he would marry her and I be left alone."

"But, according to your first story, you were writing your diary, if not at the time of the murder, at least immediately after it was done. Do you wish me to believe that a murderess, hot-handed, can sit down and write long entries in a diary?"

"It was a lie I told to take you in. I wrote that entry in the diary—all those lies, to throw dust in your eyes—in the forenoon."

"You expected nothing, then, from the murder?"

"I think I expected that perhaps Charles would inherit her money and be able to marry me, when it had all blown over."

"But why did you say, just now, that you hated him, and had committed this cruel crime to spite him? You must have guessed that you would bring him in peril of his life."

"Ah, you don't understand women. Women understand women; men never do. I tell you I felt a devil. Why did he want to make her his wife and leave me in the cold? Oh, I hated him for that; I should never have killed her if I had not so hated him."

"Surely you could not have expected him to marry a woman who had committed a murder?"

"I never thought he would guess. I never thought of all these discoveries. No one would have known, if you had not taken him up."

"But you brought that about by wearing his boots, and firing with his gun and his ammunition."

"Ah, yes, there is the pity. I did not reason; I wanted to punish him for his jilting of me. He would be in my power. Oh, I did not reason. I only felt a vindictive devil. Have no mercy on me; I deserve everything. I hate myself!"

I got up. "We will talk of this again to-morrow," I said, "when you are calmer."

"Yes," she said quietly, "when I am calmer."

"You will let me send for the doctor?"

"Why?"

"To give you a sleeping-draught."

"Yes, send for him; but you won't tell Mrs. Jex. She is old and feeble."

"No, I will tell her nothing to-night, at any rate—nothing of what has happened. She need not even know that her son has been arrested. He will not go from here to-night."

"Can you manage that?"

"Yes, I can manage that."

The farm servants, of course, knew that their master was in custody. I told them they were to keep it from the old lady. I sent one of them for the doctor, and when he came I bade him give a strong sleeping-draught to Miss Lewsome.

I went into Jex's bedroom. He was lying on the bed, with the handcuffs on his wrists. My two men were with him. I motioned them to leave me.

I took out my key, unfastened the irons and removed them.

"What's up?" he asked.

"I've some fresh evidence, that is all."

"Am I no longer under arrest, then?"

"Please to consider yourself in custody for the present. I have said nothing to your mother about all this. She knows nothing. Isn't that better so?"

"Much better. I'll come down to supper, to keep it up."

"I was going to ask you to."

"How is Miss Lewsome?"

"Very excited and disturbed. I've sent for the doctor to give her a sleeping-draught. Miss Lewsome has made a communication to me."

"Ay, ay." He showed no further curiosity in the matter.

The doctor came, gave Miss Lewsome a pretty strong dose of chloral, and departed, having learned nothing, by my express orders to the servants, of what had taken place that day at Jex Farm. One of my men remained that night in Mr. Jex's bedroom, and the other had orders to watch the house from the outside.

Miss Lewsome's absence was easily accounted for to Mrs. Jex, who was too old and feeble to be easily roused to curiosity, by a story of a chill and a headache that had obliged her guest to keep to her bedroom.

The hours after breakfast, next morning, passed slowly. No fresh developments of any kind occurred. Jex asked no questions, and I did not care to speak to him.

I waited for Miss Lewsome's awakening and deliberated as to my next step. Was her confession to be seriously acted upon? It had shaken me, but not quite convinced me, curiously supported though it was by a whole chain of circumstantial evidence. Was I bound to arrest this evidently hysterical girl, on the strength of a story which might, after all, be nothing but a tissue of cunning lies to save her lover?

I have not often been so puzzled. I have not often found the facts and probabilities, for and against, so equally poised in the balance.

Midday came and there had been no sign, or sound, of stirring in Miss Lewsome's bedroom. I sent in one of the servants and waited outside. Presently the maid screamed and ran out of the room, pale and speechless.

"What is it?" I asked, rather fearful myself. "What's up now, my girl?"

"Go to her, sir; go in to her quick! Oh, I don't know—I can't tell, but I'm afraid it's— Her hands are cold, stone cold, and her face is set. I can't waken her!"

She was dead—had been dead for hours—and on the dressing-table, propped against the pincushion, was a closed letter addressed to myself. I opened it, and read what follows:

"I, Maud Lewsome, make this dying confession. I, of my own will, no one knowing, no one advising, no one helping me, shot my friend, Mary Judson, at the orchard gate of Jex Farm. I had put on Mr. Jex's boots over my shoes in order that the crime might be shifted from my shoulders to his. I shot her across the orchard gate, in the dark, just at nightfall, when she could not see me. She was waiting for him. Perhaps I could not have done it, though I had resolved I would, but that as I came up, she said, 'Is that you, dearest?' Then I raised the gun and fired—seeing her only in outline against the little light still in the evening sky. She fell at once on the place where she stood and made no cry or groan.

"The gun gave no report hardly, but I was afraid they

might somehow guess indoors it was me, and I waited a long time, not daring to go in. Presently the gate from the road was opened. I knew it was Charles Jex coming from Bexton to her, and I was glad then that I had done it. I thought he would see me if I ran into the house, so I opened the orchard gate very softly and crouched down beside Mary's dead body. He came up to the gate and called 'Mary' twice, but he could see nothing and went away. Then I felt quite hard and callous, but my mind was very clear and active, and I thought I would take her watch, so that people might think she had been robbed. I took it and her chain, and, coming into the garden again, I buried them with my hands, two or three inches deep, in the flower-border, near the porch and smoothed the mould down over it. Then I was afraid he would hear me in the passage, and I took off the thick boots and carried them in my hand. I could hear him in his bedroom overhead, and I took the gun to the saddle-room and the boots I rubbed dry with a cloth and laid them in a row with the others. Then I felt I must see him, and I went up very lightly and knocked at his door and he came out in his shirt-sleeves and said, in a whisper, 'How pale you are, Maud,' and he kissed me, and I kept my hands behind me lest he should see the garden mould on them, but he did not notice that, and he said again:

"'How pale you look to-night! Have you seen a ghost?'

"And I ran back first to my room and washed my hands and looked at myself in the glass and thought, This is not the reflection of Maud Lewsome! This is the reflection of a murderess! And in my ears there is always the report of the gun as I fired it at Mary Judson, and in my nostrils the smell of the gunpowder smoke, and since then I have heard and smelt these two things day and night; but Mary's face, when I killed her, I did not see, and I am glad I did not. The doctor has given me chloral, and, presently, I shall take another double dose from a bottle of it I have, and before morning I shall be dead, for I cannot live after this thing that I have done. I thought I could forget it, but I cannot, and I must die. I tell the exact truth now in the hope that God may listen to my confession and my repentance, and forgive me for the awful wickedness that I have committed. I shot her with Charles's large gun; I had watched him loading it often, and I did as he did, and I put three little bullets in it that I took from the shot pouch that hangs third in the row on the wall."

The first thing I did after reading this was to call one of my men and bid him turn over the soil in the flower border close to the porch. He did so, and in my presence he found Mary Judson's watch and chain. Taking it in my hands, I carried it to Jex.

"We have found this, Mr. Jex."

"Where?"

I told him. He nodded, but said nothing.

"Will you, please, read this paper, Mr. Jex?" and I handed him that on which Miss Lewsome had written her confession. He read the first few lines and started up.

"Good God! Has she—?" I nodded.

"She took her own life last night."

He sank down on a chair and covered his face with his hands, but his emotion lasted for a moment only.

"Poor girl!" he said sadly, "I expected it"

"Then you knew she had done the murder?"

He made no answer, but read calmly through the confession he held in his hand, then he gave it back without comment.

"After this, Mr. Jex, you are, of course, at liberty. I have only to apologize to you for the inconvenience I have put you to, but the evidence against you was strong, you must admit."

"You could not do otherwise, Inspector Morgan, than you have done," and he held out his right hand to me.

I made some pretence of not seeing his action. I did not take Charles Jex by the hand.

Except for certain formalities that I need not give you, there is no more to interest you in the case. I need only add that with such evidence before us as Miss Lewsome's confession, it was, of course, impossible to charge Jex with any part in this murder; but, remembering all the circumstances since, I have sometimes asked myself, Was the girl alone guilty, was she a tool in the hands of a scheming villain, or was she perhaps only a victim and entirely innocent? Women are, to us men, often quite unaccountable beings.

The Border

BY HENRY C. ROWLAND

The Border

BY HENRY C. ROWLAND

"IT IS all very interesting," said Jones, "but a bit unsatisfying."

"The patients in my clinic of psycho-therapy do not find it so," answered Dr. Bayre. He turned to me. "You have followed some of my cases. Do you think that the wife of the *ouvrier* has found it unsatisfying? Formerly she received a beating, on an average, once a month, when her husband was drunk. Now he does not drink, and she is no longer beaten. There are many similar cases which I have seen." He lit a cigarette and frowned.

"I beg your pardon, Doctor," said Jones. "I don't mean to detract from the practical value of your science. I was speaking generally of the usual manifestations of spiritism: levitation and telepathy and messages from the dead and all the rest. In spite of the claims of mediums, I notice that none of them has taken up Le Bon's challenge in the *Matin* to shift a solid weight from one table to another before witnesses. And they must need the money, too."

"There are reasons. Also there are charlatans. Yet again, people needing money who could shift weights at will and without machinery would not be professional mediums. They would engage in the business of furniture moving."

"But can't you offer this Philistine something concrete from your own experience, Doctor?" asked I.

"What is the use? He would not believe."

Jones flushed. "I beg your pardon, Doctor. Your word is far more convincing than my doubts."

The psychologist turned to him with a smile.

"That is nicely put." His fine, broad-browed, highly intellectual face grew thoughtful. "Yes," he said, "I will show you something. I do not as a rule waste time convincing skeptics, but to you I feel that I owe something because I have so much enjoyed your tales. Excuse me for a moment."

He flicked his cigarette into the fire, rose lightly to his feet and left the room, to return a moment later with some leaves of paper held together in clips, and a newspaper.

"This is quite a long story, and as it proceeds you will recognize the characters and the events. But please do not interrupt—not even by an exclamation of surprise."

He laid the papers upon the table at his side, leaned back in his chair and brought the tips of his fingers together.

"One night," said he, "I felt myself to be unduly sensitive. As I have remarked before, my personal faculty lies almost wholly in producing or inducing what are known as mediumistic qualities in others. Myself, I have had very little of what is known as 'occult experience.' Take, for instance, the practice of crystal gazing; only twice have I ever seen anything in a crystal globe, although I have tried repeatedly.

"This night, as I have said, I felt myself to be highly sensitive, and it occurred to me to look into the ball, so I went into my study and turned down the lights and set myself to gaze. I do not know just how long I had been looking, when suddenly I observed the phenomenon so often described to me by my patients and others, but seen for the first time with my own eyes. The crystal clouded, became milky and opaque, then cleared, and I found myself looking into the face of a man. He was a handsome fellow, of somewhat over thirty, thoroughbred in type. The whole face was well known to me; I recognized it as one that I had frequently seen, and presently I recalled it as belonging to a gentleman whom I had often met when riding in the Bois.

"But what impressed me the most was the expression of earnest, almost agonized entreaty. The eyes looked straight into mine with an appeal which haunted me. However, knowing the irrelevance of pictures seen in this way, I tried to put the vision out of my mind and to congratulate myself that my efforts had finally met with success.

"Two nights later, I looked into the globe again, when to my amazement the same face appeared almost instantly; this time the expression of entreaty, the mute and agonized appeal, was even more intense, and I saw the lips move as if imploring aid. Then the picture vanished, leaving me shocked and startled.

"'This,' I said to myself, 'is more than coincidence.' I went to my telephone and called up a person with whom I had several times conducted experiments, and who was possessed of considerable mediumistic faculty. I requested her to come to my office at once.

"When she arrived I told what had occurred, and she agreed that it was undoubtedly an effort to communicate on the part of some entity who was in trouble. I suggested hypnotism, but she proposed that we first attempt communication by means of what is known as automatic writing.

"Before she had been sitting five minutes with the writing block on her knee, the pencil began to move. At the end of perhaps ten minutes I looked over her shoulder and found, to my disgust, the usual jumble of vulgar and meaningless sentences which is so often the result of this method of communication. Much disappointed, I put a stop to the writing, and asking her to wait, I went into my study and wrote a short note to another acquaintance with whom I have had many discussions on these matters. The note I gave to my servant, with instructions to jump into a motor cab and deliver it at once, bringing the gentleman back with him if possible. About twenty minutes later he arrived, when I explained the whole coincidence.

"'Yes,' said he, 'somebody is undoubtedly trying to communicate with you, but is unable to gain access to your medium. Perhaps we may be able to remedy that.'

"'Then go ahead and do so,' said I. 'We are quite at your command.'

"He went ahead then with a formulary which he had learned from his Oriental studies in occultism and Hindoo magic, and which I had always regarded as the mystic rubbish with which time and tradition have interlarded scientific truth. First he requested that I sit in the middle of the room facing my medium and at a distance of about three feet. Then he closed the doors and windows, and taking the fire shovel, proceeded to roast incense until we were nearly choked by the fumes. Thereafter, taking an ebony wand from his inner pocket, he drew a circle about us, and having ascertained the points of the compass, drew pentagrams at the four cardinal ones, accompanying each design with an invocation. All of this consumed some time, during which I sat there, half interested, half ashamed and wholly skeptical.

" 'This formula,' he remarked when he had finished, 'is one used by the Hindoos to keep out undesired entities when it is wished to communicate with some particular one. Now, Doctor, please invoke the presence of the person with whom you want to communicate, and request that he avail himself of the services of your medium.'

"Accordingly I did so. 'Will the entity whose face appeared to me in the crystal sphere please to come within the circle,' said I, 'and transmit his message through the pencil in the hands of the medium!'

"Several minutes passed without result; then suddenly the pencil began to move with great rapidity and apparent definite purpose. The sheets which I have here consist of a copy of the original, made by myself for reasons which I will presently relate. I will now read them. The narrative began abruptly, as you will see, and it was not until I had read for some length that I was able to recall certain instances."

Dr. Bayre adjusted his spectacles, and picking up the sheaf of pages read as follows:

"'. . . All that her kindness did for me remained imprinted upon a brain which she supposed to be stupefied from violence. For although my body was completely paralyzed for several days, my mind was active throughout—abnormally so, I think, as the impressions which remained were strong and detailed as though of a series of pictures I had painted.

"'Unlike my friend De Neuville and the *mécanicien,* I preserved the clearest recollection of the details of the accident itself. We were making over a hundred kilometers an hour, I shame to say, upon a greasy road, when that *char-à-banc* full of children shot out of the gate and across the track. At such a moment our actions are governed by some higher intelligence and we need take no credit for them to ourselves. A strength not of my body twisted the wheel in my hands and flung the big car over the edge of the bank. Why not? A nameless aristocrat, a *mécanicien* and a mediocre painter!

What did their lives weigh against those of a wagonload of children?

"'The crash itself is vague, but I remember the dreamlike journey on the swaying stretcher across the meadow, and down the cool, shady lane. It was here that De Neuville spread a scarf over my face, but it slipped off when they set me down in the antechamber of the chateau.

"'Through half-closed eyes I looked across the threshold of the somber hall and toward the great stairway. Everybody was watching the stair, and presently there was a subdued, expectant murmur. *"Voici madame qui descend—voici madame,"* I heard in whispers, which carried a note of relief, of confidence. Numb as I was, a tremor passed through me. And then I heard the tap-tap-tap of even steps, and a white-clad figure drifted down within my line of vision.

"'I find it difficult to tell how she appeared to me as I lay there, an all but disembodied consciousness. What most impressed me was her exquisite harmony with her surroundings. Strong and compassionate and undismayed, she crossed the hall to where I lay, and stood for a moment looking down upon me, her face tender with sympathy, her eyes very dark and deep. *"Quel malheur!"* I heard her say, beneath her breath.

"'For myself, there was the odd quality of utter detachment from it all. I could not realize myself that all this was being done for me. She followed me as they carried me up the stairs, and for many hours which followed it was only the delight I found in watching her which held my insecure soul to its heavy body. It would have been so easy to have gently loosed my hold and slipped out into the long, cool shadows. But because of the wish tc see her once more I lingered, at times reluctantly. In this desire to see her there was nothing personal, nothing of self. I could not speak, could not feel, could not even formulate an abstract thought. I could only look at my pictures, but as my mental power slowly grew these brought daily a deeper delight. It was then that I began to consider her not as a picture but as a person. I studied her features, her movements, gestures, expression, of which last there was never a woman's face so rich. I watched her. I will confess to my shame, through half-closed lids, when she thought me still wrapped in clouds. My speech was not yet articulate, but to myself I called her my "perfect chatelaine." "These gray walls and velvety lawns and old tapestries all love her," I thought, "because she has been wrought by them and their kind from many generations. No wonder that they enhance her and lend themselves a setting to her faultless grace! No wonder that she cannot strike a note to which they fail to vibrate! They belong to her and she to them, and they love her! Only France could have produced her," I told myself. "My Perfect Chatelaine!"

"'And so you can imagine my surprise when one evening she leaned from my window and called down softly to her little son, in English which carried the unmistakable accent of my native Virginia: "Your supper is waiting for you, dear!"

"'No wonder she found me with wide, staring eyes when she turned to leave the room! An American woman! She, my Perfect Chatelaine, whom it had taken centuries to perfect, and whom only France could ever have produced! The blood rushed to my head. I swear that it was more of a shock than the four-meter plunge in the racing car!

"'And this was the limit of my knowledge concerning her. I knew only that she was the widow of the late Count Etienne de Lancy-Chaumont, that she had a little son whom she adored and a mother-in-law who was jealous of her. This much I learned at Chateau Fontenaye.

"'As soon as my doctor would permit, after being taken back to Paris, I wrote to her, and received in answer a charming letter which went far toward hastening my convalescence. Thereafter we wrote frequently, and then one glorious day when I was sitting on the balcony of my studio at Dinard she came to me. She must have seen the soul pouring from my eyes, for her sweet face grew rich as the sunset, while her breath came quickly. I rose from my *chaise-longue* and took the small hand which she offered me.

"'"My Perfect Chatelaine!" was all that I could say.

"'This was the beginning of that brief epoch which comes in the earthly cycle of most of us to pay so royally for all of the pain and sorrow and discouragement which go to make a lifetime. Not long after, on the edge of the cliffs at Etretat, whither we had motored with a party, we found ourselves alone, looking out across the bright sunlit sea, the breeze on our faces and the hiss of the breakers on the cobbly beach below. There, her beautiful head against my shoulder and her hands in mine, she confessed to me a love such as I had never dared hope to gain.

"'Six weeks later we were quietly married in the little chapel of Chateau de Fontenaye, and the week following found us in Switzerland. Small need for us to make the ascent of mountains! We dwelt always on the heights, and the clouds formed our carpet. But because we were young and strong and thrilling with life, we must needs make the ascent. We were both experienced Alpinists and loved the sport, and so one day, as if to tempt the high gods who had favored us, we secured our guides—'"

Dr. Bayre stopped abruptly.

"At this point," said he, "the writing was interrupted for several minutes. When it recommenced I observed that the pencil was moving more slowly and in quite a different manner. Leaning forward to look on the pad, I saw to my disgust that the hand had changed its character, while the words themselves were random and foolish.

"'Some other intelligence has thrust itself in and got control of the medium,' said my friend. 'Let us see if we cannot oust him.'

"With that he proceeded to roast some more incense, then placed himself in front of the medium and deliverd what appeared to be an exorcism. After that he retraced his circle, wove his pentagrams, numbled his Sanskrit formula and then requested me to reinvoke the desired entity. This I did, feeling, I must say, rather like a fool, for although my own psychological work may seem dark and mysterious to the uninstructed, it is nevertheless all based on well established scientific knowledge and contains nothing of mummery and such hodge-podge as meaningless incantations and the like. Almost immediately the writing recommenced, and I saw to my gratification that it was in the same hand as the preceding narrative. But it appeared that some of the connecting passages had been lost, for the text began in this manner:

"'. . . looked over the tossing sea of distant snowpeaks,

when the pale beauty of the Alpine dawn burst into flame before the glory of the sunrise.

" 'Side by side in the doorway of the *cabane,* we stood and watched the majesty of day unfold itself upon a frozen world. Roseate rays shot to the zenith; the cold, hard rim of a distant icepeak melted and swam in the face of the jubilant sun. Then the blue and saffron of the snow mountains were scored by crimson bands, exultant tongues of living flame which leaped from glacier to lofty snow cornice and suffused with blushes the pale face of the virgin snow.

" 'I turned to look into the face of my bride. Her eyes were brimming, the rosy flush of the sunrise was on her cheeks and her sweet lips quivered. Her gaze met mine and she threw her arms about my neck.

" ' "It is so beautiful that it frightens me!" she whispered.

" ' "What, sweetheart?" I asked. "The Alpine sunrise?"

" ' "Yes," she murmured. "It is like my love for you—each moment growing fuller and more all-possessing."

" 'Our head guide, Perreton, came to the door of the *cabane* and pointed out to us our route.

" ' "We ascend on this side, madame," said he, "crossing the snow *couloir* you see above you, then following the *arête* to the other side of the *calotte* to the left, thence to the summit. That will take us the better part of the day, but we can *glissade* down very quickly on the other side. It should be easy going. There have been three days of the northeast wind and the snow is in good condition."

" 'Soon afterward we set out, proceeding in two parties, the first consisting of Perreton, my wife and Regier, while I followed, leading the porter.

" 'The ascent was safe and easy until, about halfway to the summit, we came to a broad ice traverse where it was decided to rope all together as the crossing was of considerable width, with anchorage here and there at long intervals where the smooth ice was broken by small patches of hard snow. Perreton, who was in the lead, cut the steps with skill and despatch, and we were about halfway across when we found ourselves in a position out of reach of any anchorage and where every member of the party was in danger at the same time. In such a place the rope, although of assistance in maintaining the balance and in giving confidence to the climber, is a deathtrap to the entire party should one member be guilty of a misstep. But mountain climbers are not supposed to make missteps, and it was decided not to unrope.

" 'Below us the slope descended steeply for perhaps one hundred meters, where it ended abruptly in a precipice. But to experienced climbers like ourselves, possessed of steady heads and with competent guides, the crossing presented the very slightest element of danger. So far was an idea of peril removed from our minds that my wife and I were chatting back and forth as we slowly proceeded.

" 'Perhaps it was this ill-advised relaxation on our part which led to Zeigler's fatal carelessness. He was the last man on the rope, and halfway over, all our backs being turned to him, he proceeded to light his pipe. As fate ordained, just as the unhappy man was holding the match to the bowl, all his attention centered on the act, I stepped forward. The slack of the rope was in his hands, and as it slightly tautened the pipe was knocked from his mouth and fell. I heard his exclamation, and, glancing over my shoulder, saw him grab for it with his free hand. As he did so his foot slipped, and the next instant he had lost his balance. His *piolet,* or ice axe, the spike of which was jammed into the ice, fell to one side. Realizing his danger, he snatched desperately for the shaft, but failed to grip it, and sent it spinning down the slope, he himself sprawling after it.

" 'Nothing is more helpless than a climber adrift on an ice slope without his axe, and, realizing the awful danger should the rope spring taut suddenly, I was obliged to let go the shaft of my own *piolet* in order to gather in the slack with both hands. Then I braced my feet to meet the strain. Below me swung Zeigler, quite powerless, and to the right and slightly above me Regier, who saw what had happened, quickly gathered in the slack between himself and me. Then the rope between Zeigler and myself straightened, and to ease the suddenness of the strain I let it slip slowly between my fingers until it had run its full length and the tug came upon the middleman's knot around my waist.

" 'And so we stood, Zeigler, glaring up from beneath with blanched face and wild, terror-stricken eyes; I myself, barely able to support his weight, wondered how long I could hold him there. Above me, sturdy Regier, his face frozen as rigid as the ice upon which we stood, glanced swiftly from one to the other of us in awful doubt and apprehension.

"'"Can you hold him?" he cried, and his voice boomed thick and muffled in my ear.

"'"Not for long," I answered breathlessly.

"'He glanced over his shoulder at my wife, and I knew well what was passing in his mind.

"'"Then cut!" he cried hoarsely. "It is death for all of us!"

"'I shook my head, not trusting myself to speak. Regier raised his voice.

"'"Zeigler!" he cried. "If you are a man—cut the rope!"

"'"God's mercy!" wailed the wretched porter. "I have no knife!"

"'"Then slip the bowline!" bellowed Perreton. "Monsieur cannot hold you, and if he falls madame will be dragged to her death!"

"'And then, in the awful tension, came the voice of my bride, sweet, tuneful and unafraid.

"'"Madame goes with her husband," she said.

"'Regier swung swiftly in his tracks, growling like a bear.

"'"Madame remains!" he shouted, and raising her ice axe with one powerful blow, he severed the rope between them, then came toward me, gathering the slack with his free hand.

"'But he was too late. Below me Zeigler, himself a brave man and eager to repair his fatal error at any cost, was struggling to loose the "endman's knot" around his waist. The vibration from his movements proved too great a strain for my insecure footing, and I felt the nails of my shoes grinding through the ice.

"'"Cut between us, Regier!" I cried.

"'"Never!" snarled Regier, plunging toward me. "Cut below you! Cut! Cut!"

"'"Cut, m'sieu'!" echoed Zeigler stranglingly. "I tell you to cut!"

"'Regier had almost reached me when my foothold was torn away and I felt myself going. "At least," I thought, "there is no need for Regier to die." Snatching the knife from my belt, I slashed through the rope above me, and as I did so I fell forward, slipping down upon Zeigler. But my knife was in my hand, and, throwing myself upon my face, I bore all of my weight upon the haft, driving the point into the ice. For a moment I thought that we might clutch it and arrest our course, but the next instant the blade snapped and I realized that hope was dead.

"'Downward we slipped, slowly at first, then with gathering speed. Looking back, I saw my wife, both hands clasped to her mouth, her face writhing in torture. She looked toward Perreton, and I knew as well as though she had spoken the words that had she not been roped to him she would have flung herself downward to join me. The guide himself, reading what was passing in her mind, drew in the slack of the rope between them, and none too soon, for all at once she screamed, and seizing the *piolet* by the head, began to saw impotently at the tough hemp. Perreton cried out, then walked quickly toward her and tore the axe from her hands, and this was the last I saw, my wife and the guide struggling and swaying on the steep, glittering icefield.

"'Down we shot, Zeigler and I, toward the fearful brink—and the moments were drawn out into an eternity. Down, on down, tearing our fingers, scraping with our heavy boots, yet speaking no word, writhing and twisting and with ever-gaining speed. Then Zeigler reached the brink—a cry burst from him as he disappeared—the rope tautened violently and I shot forward—forward and over, and saw beneath me the abyss yawning in shadows a thousand feet below. The cold air scorched my face—the soul within me leaped to meet the infinite—and then, oblivion.

"'I awoke as from a deep and restful sleep. There was no pain in my body, no sensation but that of dreamy peace and infinite well being.

"'Far overhead the stars glittered brightly in the cold, clear sky and the moon looked down directly on me as I lay.

"'Slowly consciousness and memory returned. I realized all that had occurred: the fearful accident, the swift gliding down the ice slope, the anguish on the face of my wife, the soaring plunge from the brink.

"'"A miracle," I thought. "A miracle of miracles. That

one can have such a fall and live! Truly, the high gods have worked for me!"

"'Awed and wondering, I cast my eyes about. It was a place of snow and stones, ragged bowlders and broken fragments of ice. A few feet distant lay the mangled body of Zeigler, and I shuddered while the wonder within me increased.

"'"How then," I thought, "can it be that I have escaped unhurt, unbruised and more at ease than ever in my life?" I raised myself with a lightness which astonished me, and saw that I lay on broken rocks, jagged and rough—and as I looked my soul was enveloped in a great and awful understanding. For there, grotesquely twisted, lay—*my own body*—and I saw that which told me that there was left in it no trace of what we mortals in our fatuous ignorance call "life."

"'Yet with this realization there came no shock, as we mortals know it, but a swift and fearful exhilaration.

"'"Then I am free—free!" was all that I could feel. "I am free of this heavy, senseless thing that lies mangled here—free to go to her whom I love!" And as if in answer to my thought came a swift and irresistible impulse.

"'Light as air, I rose from that dreadful spot and found myself flitting faster than the wind over snow and ice, glacier and moraine, until the lights of the village below me sparkled through the frosty air. Yonder was the Alpine hamlet where we had lodged before beginning our ascent; there the *auberge* where we had slept—and then I had reached it and drifted on the pale rays of the moon through the frosted window and found myself within the room.

"'Other things had passed me and surrounded me in my flight; things which you in your world could not understand and which I myself lack power to express even if I would, for there is no common language with which to interpret the conditions of these two worlds of ours, that of the living and that of the—more alive. As I entered the room all of my disembodied soul poured out to her whom I love.

"'Sobbing, sobbing, sobbing—the low, breathless grief of that sweet sufferer who needed only fuller understanding to raise her from the depths of her despair to joy ineffable. For a brief moment it seemed that this had been achieved.

From the foot of the bed I whispered her name, and she heard me and with a wild, rapturous cry sprang upright. She saw me standing there in the shimmering moonlight, and I moved to her side and gathered her in my arms, and the next instant her soul had torn its way from the body which enthralled it and we were together, happy beyond description in this new world of mine, while her human habitation fell back upon the pillows in what men call "unconsciousness."

" 'Yet our peace was not for long. Tied as she was to that earthly vehicle, she was forced to leave me and return, when, according to mortal laws, she carried with her no memory of that which had passed between us but awoke to a grief in which I shared from beyond. Ah, the needless misery of the dear bereaved! If only they knew! If only they knew!

" 'Since then she has come to me often. But in her waking state all recollection of these communions is swept away, nor have I ever again been able to communicate with her save sleep has loosed the bonds. Even then it happens frequently that her intelligence is dimmed and distorted by those fantastic discharges of the sleeping brain which men call "dreams," and my presence brings neither peace nor understanding. But waking and sleeping I am with her always, bound to this phase by her want for me, and sometimes she feels my nearness vaguely and it soothes her grief.

" 'Now I have learned that the strain and the hunger of her desire has nearly broken her resolute spirit, and I know that she has formed the determination to break from her earthly bonds by her own act. Should she do this our meeting must be long delayed, for in this place where I find myself there is no entry for those who with their own hands curtail the mortal span assigned to them. Let her but wait a little while and we shall be together, happy beyond mortal conception. But for the suicide there is still another phase, an intermediate plane, a road still to be traversed before . . .'

"At this point," said Dr. Bayre, "the writing was discontinued. It did not much matter, except in the interest of science, for the message had been delivered. Accordingly I brought the seance to a close.

"The next day I sent for a mutual friend, for of course I

recognized the identity of the intelligence who had delivered the message, as no doubt you have done. To this gentleman I showed the writing, without permitting him to do more than glance at the text.

"'Is this hand familiar to you?' I asked.

"He nodded, his face very grave.

"'Yes,' said he; 'that is the handwriting of poor Stanley Wetherill. He was killed, as you know, in a mountain accident while on his honeymoon.'

"'And his wife?' I asked.

"'She is a broken-hearted woman.'

"'Where is she now?' I asked.

"'At the Chateau Fontenaye, I believe. She was a widow when Stanley married her. He was badly hurt while automobiling and taken to the chateau. Perhaps you remember the incident; it seems that Stanley ditched his car to keep from hitting a *char-à-banc* full of children going to a *fête champêtre.*'

"I asked him then if he could get me a photograph of Mrs. Wetherill, which he kindly agreed to do.

"That night I made a verbatim copy of the communication and then mailed the original to Mrs. Wetherill with a note explaining the whole affair. Two days later, on opening my newspaper in the morning, I was startled to read the announcement of her sudden death. The notice said that she had been found dead in her *chaise-longue*. In the fire-place were discovered some burned fragments of paper covered with a handwriting which was recognized as that of her late husband. To my infinite relief the post-mortem examination showed that she had died from 'natural causes.'

"That same evening I sent for the medium who had assisted me in the investigation and requested her to look into the crystal ball. After gazing for some time, she saw the faces of a man and a woman. The expressions of both were described by the medium as 'radiant.' I then showed her a photograph of Mr. and Mrs. Wetherill, taken shortly after their marriage.

"'Are these the people whom you have just seen?' I asked.

"'Yes,' she answered, smiling. 'They are the same.'"

The Fenchurch Street Mystery

BY BARONESS ORCZY

The Fenchurch Street Mystery

BY BARONESS ORCZY

CHAPTER I

THE FENCHURCH STREET MYSTERY

THE man in the corner pushed aside his glass, and leant across the table.

"Mysteries!" he commented. "There is no such thing as a mystery in connection with any crime, provided intelligence is brought to bear upon its investigation."

Very much astonished Polly Burton looked over the top of her newspaper, and fixed a pair of very severe, coldly inquiring brown eyes upon him.

She had disapproved of the man from the instant when he shuffled across the shop and sat down opposite to her, at the same marble-topped table which already held her large coffee (3d.), her roll and butter (2d.), and plate of tongue (6d.).

Now this particular corner, this very same table, that special view of the magnificent marble hall—known as the Norfolk Street branch of the Aërated Bread Company's depôts—were Polly's own corner, table, and view. Here she had partaken of eleven pennyworth of luncheon and one pennyworth of daily information ever since that glorious never-to-be-forgotten day when she was enrolled on the staff of the *Evening Observer* (we'll call it that, if you please), and became a member of that illustrious and world-famed organization known as the British Press.

She was a personality, was Miss Burton of the *Evening Observer*. Her cards were printed thus:

MISS MARY J. BURTON
Evening Observer.

She had interviewed Miss Ellen Terry and the Bishop of Madagascar, Mr. Seymour Hicks and the Chief Commissioner of Police. She had been present at the last Marlborough House garden party—in the cloak-room, that is to say, where she caught sight of Lady Thingummy's hat, Miss What-you-may-call's sunshade, and of various other things modistical or fashionable, all of which were duly described under the heading "Royalty and Dress" in the early afternoon edition of the *Evening Observer.*

(The article itself is signed M. J. B., and is to be found in the files of that leading halfpenny-worth.)

For these reasons—and for various others, too—Polly felt irate with the man in the corner, and told him so with her eyes, as plainly as any pair of brown eyes can speak.

She had been reading an article in the *Daily Telegraph.* The article was palpitatingly interesting. Had Polly been commenting audibly upon it? Certain it is that the man over there had spoken in direct answer to her thoughts.

She looked at him and frowned; the next moment she smiled. Miss Burton (of the *Evening Observer*) had a keen sense of humor, which two years' association with the British Press had not succeeded in destroying, and the appearance of the man was sufficient to tickle the most ultra-morose fancy. Polly thought to herself that she had never seen anyone so pale, so thin, with such funny light-colored hair, brushed very smoothly across the top of a very obviously bald crown. He looked so timid and nervous as he fidgeted incessantly with a piece of string; his long, lean, and trembling fingers tying and untying it into knots of wonderful and complicated proportions.

Having carefully studied every detail of the quaint personality, Polly felt more amiable.

"And yet," she remarked kindly but authoritatively, "this article, in an otherwise well-informed journal, will tell you that, even within the last year, no fewer than six crimes have completely baffled the police, and the perpetrators of them are still at large."

"Pardon me," he said gently, "I never for a moment ventured to suggest that there were no mysteries to the *police;* I merely remarked that there were none where intelligence was brought to bear upon the investigation of crime."

STREET MYSTERY

"Not even in the Fenchurch Street *mystery,* I suppose," she asked sarcastically.

"Least of all in the so-called Fenchurch Street *mystery,*" he replied quietly.

Now the Fenchurch Street mystery, as that extraordinary crime had popularly been called, had puzzled—as Polly well knew—the brains of every thinking man and woman for the last twelve months. It had puzzled her not inconsiderably; she had been interested, fascinated; she had studied the case, formed her own theories, thought about it all often and often, had even written one or two letters to the Press on the subject—suggesting, arguing, hinting at possibilities and probabilities, adducing proofs which other amateur detectives were equally ready to refute. The attitude of that timid man in the corner, therefore, was peculiarly exasperating, and she retorted with sarcasm destined to completely annihilate her self-complacent interlocutor.

"What a pity it is, in that case, that you do not offer your priceless services to our misguided though well-meaning police."

"Isn't it?" he replied with perfect good-humor. "Well, you know, for one thing I doubt if they would accept them; and in the second place my inclinations and my duty would —were I to become an active member of the detective force —nearly always be in direct conflict. As often as not my sympathies go to the criminal who is clever and astute enough to lead our entire police force by the nose.

"I don't know how much of the case you remember," he went on quietly. "It certainly, at first, began even to puzzle me. On the 12th of last December a woman, poorly dressed, but with an unmistakable air of having seen better days, gave information at Scotland Yard of the disappearance of her husband, William Kershaw, of no occupation, and apparently of no fixed abode. She was accompanied by a friend—a fat, oily-looking German—and between them they told a tale which set the police immediately on the move.

"It appears that on the 10th of December, at about three o'clock in the afternoon, Karl Müller, the German, called on his friend, William Kershaw, for the purpose of collecting a small debt—some ten pounds or so—which the latter owed him. On arriving at the squalid lodging in Charlotte Street, Fitzroy Square, he found William Kershaw in a wild state of excitement, and his wife in tears. Müller attempted to state the object of his visit, but Kershaw, with wild gestures, waved him aside, and—in his own words—flabbergasted him by asking him point-blank for another loan of two pounds, which sum, he declared, would be the means of a speedy fortune for himself and the friend who would help him in his need.

"After a quarter of an hour spent in obscure hints, Kershaw, finding the cautious German obdurate, decided to let him into the secret plan, which, he averred, would place thousands into their hands."

Instinctively Polly had put down her paper; the mild stranger, with his nervous air and timid, watery eyes, had a peculiar way of telling his tale, which somehow fascinated her.

"I don't know," he resumed, "if you remember the story which the German told to the police, and which was corroborated in every detail by the wife or widow. Briefly it was this: Some thirty years previously, Kershaw, then twenty years of age, and a medical student at one of the London hospitals, had a chum named Barker, with whom he roomed, together with another.

"The latter, so it appears, brought home one evening a very considerable sum of money, which he had won on the turf, and the following morning he was found murdered in his bed. Kershaw, fortunately for himself, was able to prove a conclusive *alibi;* he had spent the night on duty at the hospital; as for Barker, he had disappeared, that is to say, as far as the police were concerned, but not as far as the watchful eyes of his friend Kershaw were able to spy—at least, so that latter said. Barker very cleverly contrived to get away out of the country, and, after sundry vicissitudes, finally settled down at Vladivostock, in Eastern Siberia, where, under the assumed name of Smethurst, he built up an enormous fortune by trading in furs.

"Now, mind you, every one knows Smethurst, the Siberian millionaire. Kershaw's story that he had once been called Barker, and had committed a murder thirty years ago was never proved, was it? I am merely telling you what Kershaw said to his friend the German and to his wife on that memorable afternoon of December the 10th.

"According to him Smethurst had made one gigantic mistake in his clever career—he had on four occasions written to his late friend, William Kershaw. Two of these letters had no bearing on the case, since they were written more than twenty-five years ago, and Kershaw, moreover, had lost them—so he said—long ago. According to him, however, the first of these letters was written when Smethurst, alias Barker, had spent all the money he had obtained from the crime, and found himself destitute in New York.

"Kershaw, then in fairly prosperous circumstances, sent him a £10 note for the sake of old times. The second, when the tables had turned, and Kershaw had begun to go downhill, Smethurst, as he then already called himself, sent his whilom friend £50. After that, as Müller gathered, Kershaw had made sundry demands on Smethurst's ever-increasing purse, and had accompanied these demands by various threats, which, considering the distant country in which the millionaire lived, were worse than futile.

"But now the climax had come, and Kershaw, after a final moment of hesitation, handed over to his German friend the two last letters purporting to have been written by Smethurst, and which, if you remember, played such an important part in the mysterious story of this extraordinary crime. I have a copy of both these letters here," added the man in the corner, as he took out a piece of paper from a very worn-out pocket-book, and, unfolding it very deliberately, he began to read—

" 'SIR—Your preposterous demands for money are wholly unwarrantable. I have already helped you quite as much as you deserve. However, for the sake of old times, and because you once helped me when I was in a terrible difficulty, I am willing to once more let you impose upon my good nature. A friend of mine here, a Russian merchant, to whom I have sold my business, starts in a few days for an extended tour to many European and Asiatic ports in his yacht, and has invited me to accompany him as far as England. Being tired of foreign parts, and desirous of seeing the old country once again after thirty years' absence, I have decided to accept his invitation. I don't know when we may actually be in Europe, but I promise you that as soon as we touch a suitable port I will write to you again, making an appointment for you to see me in London. But remember that if your demands are too preposterous I will not for a moment listen to them, and that I am the last man in the world to submit to persistent and unwarrantable blackmail.

"'I am, sir,

"'Yours truly,

"'FRANCIS SMETHURST.'

"The second letter was dated from Southampton," continued the man in the corner calmly, "and, curiously enough, was the only letter which Kershaw professed to have received from Smethurst of which he had kept the envelope, and which was dated. It was quite brief," he added, referring once more to his piece of paper.

"'DEAR SIR—Referring to my letter of a few weeks ago, I wish to inform you that the *Tsarskoe Selo* will touch at Tilbury on Tuesday next, the 10th. I shall land there, and immediately go up to London by the first train I can get. If you like, you may meet me at Fenchurch Street Station, in the first-class waiting-room, in the late afternoon. Since I surmise that after thirty years' absence my face may not be familiar to you, I may as well tell you that you will recognize me by a heavy Astrakhan fur coat, which I shall wear, together with a cap of the same. You may then introduce yourself to me, and I will personally listen to what you may have to say.

"'Yours faithfully,

"'FRANCIS SMETHURST.'

"It was this last letter which had caused William Kershaw's excitement and his wife's tears. In the German's own words, he was walking up and down the room like a wild beast, gesticulating wildly, and muttering sundry exclamations. Mrs. Kershaw, however, was full of apprehension. She mistrusted the man from foreign parts—who, according to her husband's story, had already one crime upon his conscience—who might, she feared, risk another, in order to be rid of a dangerous enemy. Woman-like, she thought the scheme a dishonorable one, for the law, she knew, is severe on the blackmailer.

"The assignation might be a cunning trap, in any case it was a curious one; why, she argued, did not Smethurst elect to see Kershaw at his hotel the following day? A thousand whys and wherefores made her anxious, but the fat German had been won over by Kershaw's visions of untold gold, held tantalizingly before his eyes. He had lent the necessary £2, with which his friend intended to tidy himself up a bit before he went to meet his friend the millionaire. Half an hour afterward Kershaw had left his lodgings, and that was the last the unfortunate woman saw of her husband, or Müller, the German, of his friend.

"Anxiously his wife waited that night, but he did not return; the next day she seems to have spent in making purposeless and futile inquiries about the neighborhood of Fenchurch Street; and on the 12th she went to Scotland Yard, gave what particulars she knew, and placed in the hands of the police the two letters written by Smethurst."

CHAPTER II

A MILLIONAIRE IN THE DOCK

The man in the corner had finished his glass of milk. His watery blue eyes looked across at Miss Polly Burton's eager little face, from which all traces of severity had now been chased away by an obvious and intense excitement.

"It was only on the 31st," he resumed after a while, "that a body, decomposed past all recognition, was found by two lightermen in the bottom of a disused barge. She had been moored at one time at the foot of one of those dark flights of steps which lead down between tall warehouses to the river in the East End of London. I have a photograph of the place here," he added, selecting one out of his pocket, and placing it before Polly.

"The actual barge, you see, had already been removed when I took this snapshot, but you will realize what a perfect place this alley is for the purpose of one man cutting another's throat in comfort, and without fear of detection. The body, as I said, was decomposed beyond all recognition; it had probably been there eleven days, but sundry articles, such as a silver ring and a tie pin, were recognizable, and were identified by Mrs. Kershaw as belonging to her husband.

"She, of course, was loud in denouncing Smethurst, and the police had no doubt a very strong case against him, for two days after the discovery of the body in the barge, the Siberian millionaire, as he was already popularly called by enterprising interviewers, was arrested in his luxurious suite of rooms at the Hotel Cecil.

"To confess the truth, at this point I was not a little puzzled. Mrs. Kershaw's story and Smethurst's letters had both found their way into the papers, and following my usual method—mind you, I am only an amateur, I try to reason out a case for the love of the thing—I sought about for a motive for the crime, which the police declared Smethurst had committed. To effectually get rid of a dangerous blackmailer was the generally accepted theory. Well! did it ever strike you how paltry that motive really was?"

Miss Polly had to confess, however, that it had never struck her in that light.

"Surely a man who had succeeded in building up an immense fortune by his own individual efforts, was not the sort of fool to believe that he had anything to fear from a man like Kershaw. He must have *known* that Kershaw held no damning proofs against him—not enough to hang him, anyway. Have you ever seen Smethurst?" he added, as he once more fumbled in his pocket-book.

Polly replied that she had seen Smethurst's picture in the illustrated papers at the time. Then he added, placing a small photograph before her:

"What strikes you most about the face?"

"Well, I think its strange, astonished expression due to the total absence of eyebrows, and the funny foreign cut of the hair."

"So close that it almost looks as if it had been shaved.

Exactly. That is what struck me most when I elbowed my way into the court that morning and first caught sight of the millionaire in the dock. He was a tall, soldierly-looking man, upright in stature, his face very bronzed and tanned. He wore neither moustache nor beard, his hair was cropped quite close to his head, like a Frenchman's; but, of course, what was so very remarkable about him was that total absence of eyebrows and even eyelashes, which gave the face such a peculiar appearance—as you say, a perpetually astonished look.

"He seemed, however, wonderfully calm; he had been accommodated with a chair in the dock—being a millionaire—and chatted pleasantly with his lawyer, Sir Arthur Inglewood, in the intervals between the calling of the several witnesses for the prosecution; whilst during the examination of these witnesses he sat quite placidly, with his head shaded by his hand.

"Müller and Mrs. Kershaw repeated the story which they had already told to the police. I think you said that you were not able, owing to pressure of work, to go to the court that day, and hear the case, so perhaps you have no recollection of Mrs. Kershaw. No? Ah, well! Here is a snapshot I managed to get of her once. That is her. Exactly as she stood in the box—over-dressed—in elaborate crape, with a bonnet which once had contained pink roses, and to which a remnant of pink petals still clung obtrusively amidst the deep black.

"She would not look at the prisoner, and turned her head resolutely toward the magistrate. I fancy she had been fond of that vagabond husband of hers: an enormous wedding-ring encircled her finger, and that, too, was swathed in black. She firmly believed that Kershaw's murderer sat there in the dock, and she literally flaunted her grief before him.

"I was indescribably sorry for her. As for Müller, he was just fat, oily, pompous, conscious of his own importance as a witness; his fat fingers, covered with brass rings, gripped the two incriminating letters, which he had identified. They were his passports, as it were, to a delightful land of importance and notoriety. Sir Arthur Inglewood, I think, disappointed him by stating that he had no questions to ask of him. Müller had been brimful of answers, ready with the most perfect indictment, the most elaborate accusations against the bloated millionaire who had destroyed his dear friend Kershaw, and murdered him in Heaven knows what an out-of-the-way corner of the East End.

"After this, however, the excitement grew apace. Müller had been dismissed, and had retired from the court altogether, leading away Mrs. Kershaw, who had completely broken down.

"Constable D 21 was giving evidence as to the arrest in the meanwhile. The prisoner, he said, had seemed completely taken by surprise, not understanding the cause or history of the accusation against him; however, when put in full possession of the facts, and realizing, no doubt, the absolute futility of any resistance, he had quietly enough followed the constable into the cab. No one at the fashionable and crowded Hotel Cecil had even suspected that anything unusual had occurred.

"Then a gigantic sigh of expectancy came from every one of the spectators. The 'fun' was about to begin. James Buckland, a porter at Fenchurch Street railway station, had just sworn to tell all the truth, etc. After all, it did not amount to much. He said that at six o'clock in the afternoon of December the 10th, in the midst of one of the densest fogs he ever remembers, the 5.05 from Tilbury steamed into the station, being just about an hour late. He was on the arrival platform, and was hailed by a passenger in a first-class carriage. He could see very little of him beyond an enormous black fur coat and a travelling cap of fur also.

"The passenger had a quantity of luggage, all marked F. S., and he directed James Buckland to place it all upon a four-wheeled cab, with the exception of a small hand-bag, which he carried himself. Having seen that all his luggage was safely bestowed, the stranger in the fur coat paid the porter, and, telling the cabman to wait until he returned, he walked away in the direction of the waiting-rooms, still carrying his small hand-bag.

"'I stayed for a bit,' added James Buckland, 'talking to the driver about the fog and that; then I went about my business, seein' that the local from Southend 'ad been signalled.'

"The prosecution insisted most strongly upon the hour when the stranger in the fur coat, having seen to his luggage, walked away toward the waiting-rooms. The porter was emphatic. 'It was not a minute later than 6.15,' he averred.

"Sir Arthur Inglewood still had no questions to ask, and the driver of the cab was called.

"He corroborated the evidence of James Buckland as to the hour when the gentleman in the fur coat had engaged him, and having filled his cab in and out with luggage, had told him to wait. And cabby did wait. He waited in the dense fog—until he was tired, until he seriously thought of depositing all the luggage in the lost property office, and of looking out for another fare—waited until at last, at a quarter before nine, whom should he see walking hurriedly toward his cab but the gentleman in the fur coat and cap, who got in quickly and told the driver to take him at once to the Hotel Cecil. This, cabby declared, had occurred at a quarter before nine. Still Sir Arthur Inglewood made no comment, and Mr. Francis Smethurst, in the crowded, stuffy court, had calmly dropped to sleep.

"The next witness, Constable Thomas Taylor, had noticed a shabbily-dressed individual, with shaggy hair and beard, loafing about the station and waiting-rooms in the afternoon of December the 10th. He seemed to be watching the arrival platform of the Tilbury and Southend trains.

"Two separate and independent witnesses, cleverly unearthed by the police, had seen this same shabbily-dressed individual stroll into the first-class waiting-room at about 6.15 on Tuesday, December the 10th, and go straight up to a gentleman in a heavy fur coat and cap, who had also just come into the room. The two talked together for a while; no one heard what they said, but presently they walked off together. No one seemed to know in which direction.

"Francis Smethurst was rousing himself from his apathy; he whispered to his lawyer, who nodded with a bland smile of encouragement. The employés of the Hotel Cecil gave evidence as to the arrival of Mr. Smethurst at about 9.30 p. m. on Tuesday, December the 10th, in a cab, with a quantity of luggage; and this closed the case for the prosecution.

"Everybody in that court already *saw* Smethurst mounting the gallows. It was uninterested curiosity which caused the elegant audience to wait and hear what Sir Arthur Inglewood had to say. He, of course, is the most fashionable man in the law at the present moment. His lolling attitudes, his drawling speech, are quite the rage, and imitated by the gilded youth of society.

"Even at this moment, when the Siberian millionaire's neck literally and metaphorically hung in the balance, an expectant titter went around the fair spectators as Sir Arthur stretched out his long loose limbs and lounged across the table. He waited to make his effect—Sir Arthur is a born actor—and there is no doubt that he made it, when in his slowest, most drawly tones he said quietly:

" 'With regard to this alleged murder of one William Kershaw, on Wednesday, December the 10th, between 6.15 and 8.45 p. m., your Honor, I now propose to call two witnesses, who saw this same William Kershaw alive on Tuesday afternoon, December the 16th, that is to say, six days after the supposed murder.'

"It was as if a bombshell had exploded in the court. Even his Honor was aghast, and I am sure the lady next to me only recovered from the shock of surprise in order to wonder whether she need put off her dinner party after all.

"As for me," added the man in the corner, with that strange mixture of nervousness and self-complacency which had set Miss Polly Burton wondering, "well, you see, *I* had made up my mind long ago where the hitch lay in this particular case, and I was not so surprised as some of the others.

"Perhaps you remember the wonderful development of the case, which so completely mystified the police—and in fact everybody except myself. Torriani and a waiter at his hotel in the Commercial Road both deposed that at about 3.30 p. m. on December the 10th a shabbily-dressed individual lolled into the coffee-room and ordered some tea. He was pleasant enough and talkative, told the waiter that his name was William Kershaw, that very soon all London would be talking about him, as he was about, through an unexpected stroke of good fortune, to become a very rich man, and so on, and so on, nonsense without end.

"When he had finished his tea he lolled out again, but no sooner had he disappeared down a turning of the road than the waiter discovered an old umbrella, left behind accidentally by the shabby, talkative individual. As is the custom in his highly respectable restaurant, Signor Torriani put the umbrella carefully away in his office, on the chance of his customer calling to claim it when he discovered his loss. And sure enough nearly a week later, on Tuesday, the 16th, at about 1 p. m., the same shabbily-dressed individual called and asked for his umbrella. He had some lunch, and chatted once again to the waiter. Signor Torriani and the waiter gave a description of William Kershaw, which coincided exactly with that given by Mrs. Kershaw of her husband.

"Oddly enough he seemed to be a very absent-minded sort of person, for on this second occasion, no sooner had he left than the waiter found a pocket-book in the coffee-room, underneath the table. It contained sundry letters and bills, all addressed to William Kershaw. This pocket-book was produced, and Karl Müller, who had returned to the court, easily identified it as having belonged to his dear and lamented friend 'Villiam.'

"This was the first blow to the case against the accused. It was a pretty stiff one, you will admit. Already it had begun to collapse like a house of cards. Still, there was the assignation, and the undisputed meeting between Smethurst and Kershaw, and those two and a half hours of a foggy evening to satisfactorily account for."

The man in the corner made a long pause, keeping the girl on tenterhooks. He had fidgeted with his bit of string till there was not an inch of it free from the most complicated and elaborate knots.

"I assure you," he resumed at last, "that at that very moment the whole mystery was, to me, as clear as daylight. I only marvelled how his Honor could waste his time and mine by putting what he thought were searching questions to the accused relating to his past. Francis Smethurst, who had quite shaken off his somnolence, spoke with a curious nasal twang, and with an almost imperceptible soupçon of foreign accent. He calmly denied Kershaw's version of his past; declared that he had never been called Barker, and had certainly never been mixed up in any murder case thirty years ago.

"'But you knew this man Kershaw,' persisted his Honor, 'since you wrote to him?'

"'Pardon me, your Honor,' said the accused quietly, 'I have never, to my knowledge, seen this man Kershaw, and I can swear that I never wrote to him.'

"'Never wrote to him?' retorted his Honor warningly. 'That is a strange assertion to make when I have two of your letters to him in my hands at the present moment.'

"'I never wrote those letters, your Honor,' persisted the accused quietly, 'they are not in my handwriting.'

"'Which we can easily prove,' came in Sir Arthur Inglewood's drawly tones as he handed up a packet to his Honor, 'here are a number of letters written by my client since he has landed in this country, and some of which were written under my very eyes.'

"As Sir Arthur Inglewood had said, this could be easily proved, and the prisoner, at his Honor's request, scribbled a few lines, together with his signature, several times upon a sheet of note-paper. It was easy to read upon the magistrate's astounded countenance, that there was not the slightest similarity in the two handwritings.

"A fresh mystery had cropped up. Who, then, had made the assignation with William Kershaw at Fenchurch Street railway station? The prisoner gave a satisfactory account of the employment of his time since his landing in England.

"'I came over on the *Tsarkoe Selo,*' he said, 'a yacht belonging to a friend of mine. When we arrived at the mouth of the Thames there was such a dense fog that it was twenty-four hours before it was thought safe for me to land. My friend, who is a Russian, would not land at all; he was regularly frightened at this land of fogs. He was going on to Madeira immediately.'

"'I actually landed on Tuesday, the 10th, and took a train at once for town. I did see to my luggage and a cab, as the porter and driver told your Honor; then I tried to find my way to a refreshment-room, where I could get a glass of wine. I drifted into the waiting-room, and there I was accosted by a shabbily-dressed individual, who began telling me a piteous tale. Who he was I do not know. He *said* he was an old soldier who had served his country faithfully, and then been left to starve. He begged of me to accompany him to his lodgings, where I could see his wife and starving children, and verify the truth and piteousness of his tale.'

"'Well, your Honor,' added the prisoner with noble frankness, 'it was my first day in the old country. I had come back after thirty years with my pockets full of gold, and this was the first sad tale I had heard; but I am a business man, and did not want to be exactly "done" in the eye. I followed my man through the fog, out into the streets. He walked silently by my side for a time. I had not a notion where I was.'

"'Suddenly I turned to him with some question, and realized in a moment that my gentleman had given me the slip. Finding, probably, that I would not part with my money till I *had* seen the starving wife and children, he left me to my fate, and went in search of more willing bait.'

"'The place where I found myself was dismal and deserted. I could see no trace of cab or omnibus. I retraced my steps and tried to find my way back to the station, only to find myself in worse and more deserted neighborhoods. I became hopelessly lost and fogged. I don't wonder that two and a half hours elapsed while I thus wandered on in the dark and deserted streets; my sole astonishment is that I ever found the station at all that night, or rather close to it a policeman, who showed me the way.'

"'But how do you account for Kershaw knowing all your movements?' still persisted his Honor, 'and his knowing the exact date of your arrival in England? How do you account for these two letters, in fact?'

"'I cannot account for it or them, your Honor,' replied the prisoner quietly. 'I have proved to you, have I not, that I never wrote those letters, and that the man—er—Kershaw is his name?—was not murdered by me?'

"'Can you tell me of anyone here or abroad who might have heard of your movements and date of your arrival?'

" 'My late employés at Vladivostock, of course, knew of my departure, but none of them could have written these letters, since none of them know a word of English.'

" 'Then you can throw no light upon these mysterious letters? You cannot help the police in any way toward the clearing up of this strange affair?'

" 'The affair is as mysterious to me as to your Honor, and to the police of this country.'

"Francis Smethurst was discharged, of course; there was no semblance of evidence against him sufficient to commit him for trial. The two overwhelming points of his defence which had completely routed the prosecution were, firstly, the proof that he had never written the letters making the assignation, and secondly, the fact that the man supposed to have been murdered on the 10th was seen to be alive and well on the 16th.. But then, who in the world was the mysterious individual who had apprised Kershaw of the movements of Smethurst, the millionaire?"

CHAPTER III

HIS DEDUCTION

The man in the corner cocked his funny thin head on one side and looked at Polly; then he took up his beloved bit of string and deliberately untied every knot he had made in it. When it was quite smooth he laid it out upon the table.

"I will take you, if you like, point by point along the line of reasoning which I followed myself, and which will inevitably lead you, as it led me, to the only possible solution of the mystery.

"First take this point," he said with nervous restlessness, once more taking up his bit of string, and forming with each point raised a series of knots which would have shamed a navigating instructor, "Obviously it was *impossible* for Kershaw not to have been acquainted with Smethurst, since he was fully apprised of the latter's arrival in England by two letters. Now it was clear to me from the first that *no one* could have written those two letters except Smethurst. You will argue that those letters were proved not to have been written by the man in the dock. Exactly. Remember, Kershaw was a careless man—he had lost both envelopes. To him they were insignificant. Now it was never *disproved* that those letters were written by Smethurst."

"But—" suggested Polly.

"Wait a minute," he interrupted, while knot number two appeared upon the scene; "it was proved that six days after the murder William Kershaw was alive, and visited the Torriani Hotel, where already he was known, and where he conveniently left a pocket-book behind, so that there should be no mistake as to his identity; but it was never questioned where Mr. Francis Smethurst, the millionaire, happened to spend that very same afternoon."

"Surely, you don't mean—?" gasped the girl.

"One moment, please," he added triumphantly. "How did it come about that the landlord of the Torriani Hotel was brought into court at all? How did Sir Arthur Inglewood, or rather his client, know that William Kershaw had on those two memorable occasions visited the hotel, and that its landlord could bring such convincing evidence forward that would forever exonerate the millionaire from the imputation of murder?"

"Surely," I argued, "the usual means, the police—"

"The police had kept the whole affair very dark until the arrest at the Hotel Cecil. They did not put into the papers the usual: 'If anyone happens to know of the whereabouts, etc., etc.' Had the landlord of that hotel heard of the disappearance of Kershaw through the usual channels, he would have put himself in communication with the police. Sir Arthur Inglewood produced him. How did Sir Arthur Inglewood come on his track?"

"Surely, you don't mean—?"

"Point number four," he resumed imperturbably, "Mrs. Kershaw was never requested to produce a specimen of her husband's handwriting. Why? Because the police, clever as you say they are, never started on the right tack. They believed William Kershaw to have been murdered; they looked for William Kershaw."

"On December the 31st, what was presumed to be the body

of William Kershaw was found by two lightermen: I have shown you a photograph of the place where it was found. Dark and deserted it is in all conscience, is it not? Just the place where a bully and a coward would decoy an unsuspecting stranger, murder him first, then rob him of his valuables, his papers, his very identity, and leave him there to rot. The body was found in a disused barge which had been moored some time against the wall, at the foot of these steps. It was in the last stages of decomposition, and, of course, could not be identified; but the police would have it that it was the body of William Kershaw.

"It never entered their heads that it was the body of *Francis Smethurst, and that William Kershaw was his murderer.*

"Ah! it was cleverly, artistically conceived! Kershaw is a genius. Think of it all! His disguise! Kershaw had a shaggy beard, hair, and moustache. He shaved up to his very eyebrows! No wonder that even his wife did not recognize him across the court; and remember she never saw much of his face while he stood in the dock. Kershaw was shabby, slouchy, he stooped. Smethurst, the millionaire, might have served in the Prussian Army.

"Then that lovely trait about going to revisit the Torriani Hotel. Just a few days' grace, in order to purchase moustache and beard and wig, exactly similar to what he had himself shaved off. Making up to look like himself! Splendid! Then leaving the pocket-book behind! He! he! he! Kershaw was not murdered! Of course not. He called at the Torriani Hotel six days after the murder, whilst Mr. Smethurst, the millionaire, hobnobbed in the park with duchesses! Hang such a man! Fie!"

He fumbled for his hat. With nervous, trembling fingers he held it deferentially in his hand whilst he rose from the table. Polly watched him as he strode up to the desk, and paid two-pence for his glass of milk and his bun. Soon he disappeared through the shop, whilst she still found herself hopelessly bewildered, with a number of snap-shot photographs before her, still staring at a long piece of string, smothered from end to end in a series of knots, as bewildering, as irritating, as puzzling as the man who had lately sat in the corner.

The Mystery of Seven Minutes

BY LOUIS JOSEPH VANCE

The Mystery of Seven Minutes

BY LOUIS JOSEPH VANCE

SCENE: One end of the main dining-room, the Cafe Plaisance, New York: a restaurant of the first class, handsomely appointed and decorated. The right-hand wall (from the view-point of the audience) is composed of wide windows heavily draped, which look out on Broadway. The left-hand wall is broken only by wide swing-doors, near the back, in front of which stands a permanent screen of carved wood and glass: this doorway opens upon the kitchen quarters. In the back wall, close to the right-hand corner, are huge swing-doors, closed; when open they show part of a dimly-lighted lobby. In the back wall, toward the left-hand corner, is a small, ordinary door which opens on a dark room.

The restaurant is lighted by means of wall-sconces and an ornate central chandelier of cut glass lustres. There are smaller lamps, resembling shaded candles, to each table; but of these only one is lighted—that which stands on the table in the center of the stage, next the footlights.

The stage (which shows less than half the restaurant) is crowded with tables of all sizes; but to the right these have been pushed back in confusion against the windows and the back wall, leaving a broad clear space. The table at center, down front, has two chairs, and is dressed with service for two persons; its candle-lamp illuminates the cold remains of a supper for two. A silver wine-tub stands to one side of this table, the neck of an opened champagne bottle projecting above the rim.

The rising of the CURTAIN *discovers several waiters and 'busses busily clearing the tables on the left-hand side of the stage, under the direction of* ANTON ZIRKER, *the maitre d'hotel; while* INSPECTOR WALTERS *of the New York Police*

Department, sits at one of the tables to the right; and a POLICEMAN *in uniform stands before the lobby doors.*

ZIRKER *is a handsome, well-conditioned man of about thirty-five; short of stature, and stout, but quick on his feet, he carries himself well, with the habit of efficient authority. His countenance is plum, of a darkish cast, and has alert, intelligent eyes. He speaks excellent English with a faint accent which becomes more noticeable in moments of excitement. He is dressed, of course, in admirably-tailored evening clothes.*

INSPECTOR WALTERS *is a man of some fifty years, of powerful build and a prime physical condition. His hair has begun to show gray at the temples. His face is of sanguine complexion, with an open expression, and he wears a heavy grayish moustache. He likewise wears evening dress, and he shows no insignia to betray his connection with the police force. . . . He sits sideways at a table well over to the right, resting an elbow on its bare top and chewing an unlighted cigar while he stares steadfastly, with a grave frown, at the table at center.*

One by one the waiters go off through the service-door, leaving WALTERS, ZIRKER *and the* POLICEMAN *alone on the stage.* ZIRKER, *standing to the left, pauses and glances inquiringly at* WALTERS, *who pays no attention. There is a sound, off-stage, to the right, as of people passing in the street, a wild blaring of tin horns, clattering of cow-bells, shouts, laughter. As this dies away,* ZIRKER *consults his watch.*

WALTERS (*who apparently hasn't been looking his way—sharply*). What time is it?

ZIRKER (*startled, stammers*). Half-past three.

WALTERS. Uh-huh . . . (*with this illegible grunt, relapses and gravely champs his cigar through another pause*).

ZIRKER (*nervously*). Beg pardon, Inspector—

WALTERS. Don't interrupt: I'm thinking.

ZIRKER. Pardon! I merely wished to inquire if you'd need me any longer.

WALTERS (*calmly*). I told you, shut up.

ZIRKER *shrugs and falls silent, but fidgets.* WALTERS *solemnly chews his cigar and frowns at the lighted table. The* POLICEMAN *yawns eloquently. Presently the pause is broken by a sound of voices in the lobby. All three men turn their heads toward the swing-doors: the* POLICEMAN *vigilantly,* WALTERS *expectantly,* ZIRKER *with a bored, wondering air. Immediately one wing of the doors is thrust open, and a young man comes hastily in, nodding in acknowledgment of a salute from the* POLICEMAN *and waving a cordial hand to* WALTERS. . . . *He's a good-looking, intelligent, well-bred youngster, in evening dress under a fur-lined coat; wears a silk hat and white gloves.*

WALTERS. Good morning, Mr. Alston—and Happy New Year!

ALSTON (*laughing*). Happy New Year yourself! Trust you to know the time of day, Walters! . . . You're in charge here, eh?

WALTERS. Yes: I happened to be here when the murder was committed.

ALSTON (*surprised*). You were? And let the murderer get away right under your nose!

WALTERS (*grimly*). No: I didn't let him get away. Did I, Zirker?

ZIRKER (*with a nervous start*). Yes—no—that is, I don't know. You arrested Ruffo, all right.

WALTERS. Yes: I arrested Ruffo all right . . . as you say.

ALSTON. Who's Ruffo?

WALTERS. The waiter nearest the table where the murder was committed.

ALSTON. And you think he—?

WALTERS. I don't know whether he did or not! But he was there, all right, by his own admission.

ALSTON. But couldn't you see—?

WALTERS. No: it was while the lights were out. Didn't you know that, Mr. Alston?

ALSTON. I don't know anything about the case: never heard a word of it until fifteen minutes ago, when a page called me to the telephone at the Astor—I was having supper there with some friends—and the Commissioner asked me to run down here, look the ground over, and report to him immediately.

WALTERS. Mr. Alston is the new Deputy Commissioner of Police, you know, Zirker.

ZIRKER (*bowing and smiling*). But yes: I know that very well. I've had the pleasure of serving Mr. Alston frequently.

ALSTON. But tell me: is it true, what I hear, that it was somebody connected with the Italian Embassy at Washington?

WALTERS (*heavily*). The murdered man—identified by papers in his pocket—was Count Umberto Bennetto, first secretary to the Italian Legation.

ALSTON (*whistles softly*). Whe-e-w! That makes it pretty serious, doesn't it? And you think this Ruffo . . .?

WALTERS. Well, he's an Eyetalian—Carlo Ruffo's his full name. I judged that was enough to hold him on, as a witness.

ALSTON. Nothing more incriminating than that?

WALTERS. No . . . Besides, he's an old man—Ruffo is—and I doubt if he had enough strength to strike the blow that killed this party. It was a quick, strong, sure thrust—right here—(*indicating spot on his own bosom*)—right through the heart. No fumbling about it: the blow of a practiced hand. This Bennetto party couldn't have known what killed him.

ALSTON. But if you don't think this waiter, Ruffo—

WALTERS. Well, we had to pinch somebody on general principles, didn't we?

ALSTON. Why not Zirker, then? (*jocularly.*) He looks able-bodied enough—Italian, too!

WALTERS (*seriously*). Well, I did think of it. But he was a good twelve feet from the table at the time: I know, because I happened to be trying to catch his eye when the lights went out; and when they went up again, he was right there in the same spot. Besides, he isn't Eyetalian.

ALSTON. He looks it . . .

ZIRKER (*smiling blandly*). But no: Swiss.

ALSTON. Of course: all good restaurateurs are Swiss . . .

WALTERS. So that let *him* out.

ALSTON. But come: tell me just how it happened. I take it, this was the table? (*crossing to table at C.*)

WALTERS. That's it, all right . . . It was this way: I'm sitting over here (*indicating table up back of that on which stands the shaded light*) and it's about half-past eleven when I see this party, Bennetto, come in, towed by one of the swellest dames I ever lay eyes on.

ALSTON. Just the two of them . . . alone, eh?

WALTERS. All alone, and glad of it, if I'm any judge.

ALSTON. Had they been celebrating a bit—perhaps?

WALTERS. Not so's anybody'd notice it. But then, these Eyetalians never show their loads.

ALSTON. So the woman was Italian, too?

WALTERS. I judged so, from her looks: a dark woman—black hair—cheeks like blush roses—and her lamps—O my! —headlights! Everybody turns around to pipe her off, the minute she comes through that door. They goes straight to this table—it's all ready for them—

ALSTON (*to Zirker*). Count Bennetto had reserved it in advance?

ZIRKER. Yes, sir: by letter, from the Legation, Washington, about a month ago.

WALTERS. And they sits down, and this Ruffo waiter rustles 'em a quart right away, and just before the lights goes out—at midnight, you know—he brings in their supper. And right there happens the first suspicious circumstance.

ZIRKER *shows surprise.*

ALSTON. How so?

WALTERS. It isn't the supper this Bennetto party ordered. I don't know what he did order, but I hears him speak sharply to this Ruffo waiter and say he didn't order steak, and to take it back and have the order filled properly.

ALSTON. Did what he said seem to make the waiter angry?

WALTERS. No: he just looks puzzled, and says he'll speak to the head waiter—Zirker, here—about it, and starts off to do it, and then it's all lights out, and everybody whooping and yelling and raising Cain generally.

ALSTON. But what's suspicious—?

WALTERS. Because—the way I figure it—if this Bennetto party had got what he ordered, there wouldn't have been a carving knife with it, like the kind that came with the steak —heavy enough to kill him.

ALSTON. Possibly . . .

ZIRKER. I never thought of that!

WALTERS. Well, you know, that's my job—thinking of those little things.

ALSTON. Well, and then . . .?

WALTERS. Then it's lights up again, and I hear a woman give a screech that isn't due to champagne, and I looks, and this Eyetalian party is slumped down sideways in his chair—

ALSTON. Which chair?

ZIRKER (*touching its back*). This was Count Umberto's chair, Mr. Alston.

WALTERS. And this knife is buried in his chest so deep none of the blade shows. He's just sitting there, dead and grinning, like he was defying us to guess what had become of his lady friend.

ALSTON. And what had become of her?

WALTERS (*nodding at Zirker*). I don't know any more than he does.

ZIRKER. But I know nothing whatever!

WALTERS. That's what I'm telling Mr. Alston: I don't know any more than you.

ALSTON. But—

WALTERS. She has disappeared—vanished completely—between the time the lights went out and the time they went up again. And how she managed it staggers me. I can see as far through a stone wall as anybody, but I'll be damned if I can see how that skirt managed to get out of this restaurant in pitch darkness, with these tables crowded so close together that even the waiters could hardly move around—and nobody know it or see her at any time. I've been over the ground a dozen times, and I just don't see how it could be done.

ZIRKER. It's impossible.

WALTERS. And yet it happened. She got away as slick as a whistle.

ALSTON (*reviewing the ground thoughtfully*). You've moved the tables, of course.

WALTERS. Had to, to take the body out. But I had sense enough to chalk their positions on the floor before I let them be moved. . . . Zirker, you help O'Halloran here put those tables back in place, will you? . . . Just to show Mr. Alston.

The POLICEMAN *comes down from the door and joins* ZIRKER *over to the right, and the two of them shift the tables back into place.*

ALSTON (*looking at the lobby doors*). If she went that way . . .

WALTERS. The only exit that way is to Broadway; and all the taxi chauffeurs outside swear nobody came out while the lights were down. Besides, the lights were on the lobby there, and the cloakroom boy and the guy that runs the newsstand both say nobody came out during the dark turn.

ALSTON (*turning toward the left; indicates smaller door up back*). And that?

WALTERS. That's the head waiter's office—Zirker's—and the door's locked and the key's in his pocket all the time.

ALSTON. Has it any communication with the street?

WALTERS. A door: but it was locked, too.

ALSTON (*gesture indicating doors in left wall*). And that's the way to the kitchen, I presume?

WALTERS. Right.

ALSTON. She might have . . .

WALTERS. Not unless you allow the whole staff of waiters here was in the plot to aid her escape. There's half a dozen of them waiting just outside for the lights to come up, so they can bring in their orders—and of course them lights over there: nobody could pass them without their seeing. Besides, as far as those two doors are concerned, they're twice as far from this Count's table, and would be three times as difficult to reach. You can see for yourself. . . .

By now the POLICEMAN *and* ZIRKER *have rearranged the tables, in a fashion that bears out Walters' contention as to the difficulty of reaching the lobby doors.*

ALSTON (*thoughtfully*). I see . . .

POLICEMAN. All right, Inspector?

WALTERS. All right, O'Halloran.

ZIRKER *makes his way toward the table at center.*

ALSTON. It's a pretty problem. . . . She simply couldn't have got away without bumping into somebody.

ZIRKER. Ruffo was standing squarely in the only clear way, and I only a few feet beyond him. Neither of us . . .

WALTERS. All the same, get away she did.

ALSTON. You, of course, questioned everybody?

WALTERS. You bet your life I did.

ALSTON. And nobody . . .?

WALTERS. There's this to be said: everybody was having too good a time to pay much attention. On the other hand, everybody that was seated along the lines of exit insists they'd have noticed anything as unusual as a woman feeling her way out in the dark.

ALSTON. In short, it's impossible.

WALTERS. *But* it happened! . . .

The lobby doors open and somebody outside whispers to the POLICEMAN.

WALTERS. What's that, O'Halloran?

POLICEMAN. You're wanted on the 'phone, Inspector.

WALTERS. Excuse me, Mr. Alston.

ALSTON (*abstractedly*). Yes . . . yes . . .

WALTERS *picks his way up to the lobby doors and goes out.*

ALSTON. I presume, Mr. Zirker, nobody knows who this woman was?

ZIRKER (*with a shrug*). If so, they refused to admit it, when Mr. Walters questioned them.

ALSTON. Had you ever seen her before?

ZIRKER. Never in my life.

ALSTON. She was not in the habit of going round in company with Count Bennetto, then—I fancy.

ZIRKER. I couldn't say, sir.

ALSTON. Then I infer that Count Bennetto wasn't one of your regular patrons?

ZIRKER. Not within my time; but then I've only been maitre d'hotel here for the last two months. I am new to this country. I never saw Count Umberto before to-night.

ALSTON. Yet you reserved a table for him—

ZIRKER. His letter was accompanied by a check.

Re-enter WALTERS *by the lobby doors.*

WALTERS (*cheerfully*). Well, that's better: we're on the trail of the woman, at least.

ZIRKER. But truly?

ALSTON. How so?

WALTERS. One of my men has been going round the hotels. They've found out that this Bennetto party was registered at the Metropole as "Antonio Zorzi and wife."

ALSTON. Oh!

ZIRKER. That would seem to indicate that Count Umberto feared something of this sort.

ALSTON. Why do you say that?

ZIRKER. Why else need Count Umberto and his wife adopt an incognito?

WALTERS. But she wasn't his wife . . .

ZIRKER. You are sure of that, eh?

WALTERS. Somebody else's wife, I guess. This Bennetto party was unmarried: or so the Italian Embassy tells Headquarters over the long distance.

ZIRKER. They . . . they couldn't tell you who the lady was?

WALTERS. Sure they could: her right name was Zorzi. She came on from Italy a couple of months ago, with Bennetto. He'd just been appointed to the Embassy, you see. Of course, I guess, they thought it would seem pretty coarse work for him to take her on to Washington; because she stopped here, and he ran back every week end. Oh, we know all about 'em, now.

ALSTON. All but how she got away . . .

ZIRKER. And where she is.

WALTERS. That's all we got to find out now.

ALSTON. It seems to me you've overlooked one direct inference, Mr. Walters.

WALTERS. Slip it to me: you couldn't do me a bigger favor, Mr. Alston.

ALSTON. You've demonstrated conclusively that she couldn't have left the restaurant while the lights were out.

WALTERS. Have I? I didn't mean to. Because, the facts are, she did.

ALSTON. But you say she couldn't . . .

WALTERS. I say, I don't know how she could—

ALSTON. But assuming for the sake of the argument that she couldn't—

WALTERS. Then she's still here.

ALSTON. Or—this is the bet you've overlooked—she left before the lights went out.

WALTERS. What do you mean?

ALSTON. If she couldn't and didn't go while it was dark, she must have gone before. In the noise and confusion of the jollification, it would have been easy enough for any woman to have left inconspicuously during the five minutes before the lights went down.

WALTERS. That's true. There's only one flaw in your theory: she didn't. I know she didn't because I was looking right past her—trying, as I say, to catch Zirker's eye and order more wine—when the lights did go out. And I know she hadn't left her seat. Don't go Sherlock-Holmesing. Mr,

Alston: police cases aren't solved on theories nowadays—never were, for that matter. Excuse me for speaking so bluntly—

ALSTON. That's all right. You were on the force when I was in knickerbockers. I'm here to learn.

WALTERS. If you want to know how a police detective gets to work, I'll give you a practical demonstration here and now.

ALSTON. How?

WALTERS. The first thing is to figure out how this girl makes her getaway, isn't it? . . . Well, I say she couldn't without attracting attention. But I'm wrong, for she did. Now how? Well, she either knew the way out or someone led her by the hand that did know. That's reasonable, aint it?

ALSTON. Perfectly . . . Isn't it, Mr. Zirker?

ZIRKER. But who would lead her by the hand?

WALTERS. Some guy who knew the ground very thoroughly.

ZIRKER. Myself, for instance.

WALTERS. Oh, I won't go so far as to say that . . .

ZIRKER. But why not? Let us reason it out as you suggest. You need to find somebody thoroughly acquainted with the arrangement of the tables, to fit your theory. Well, there was no such person.

ALSTON. Not even yourself?

ZIRKER. Not even myself, Mr. Alston. You see, we've got fifty extra tables in this room to-night. Our first intention was to put in only thirty-five, but the demand was so great—good customers coming at the last moment without reservation—that we made room for fifteen more. Hence the great congestion, and hence the fact that not even I was thoroughly conversant with the arrangement.

WALTERS. And yet . . . she got away! . . . The trouble with your contention, Zirker, is that you don't make any allowance for average human intelligence. Now I've been figuring on this lay-out ever since, and I think I see a way. I'll make you a little bet—a bottle of wine—anything you like—I can find my way out of this tangle in five minutes of darkness, and neither you nor Mr. Alston here will be able to tell how I did it. The only thing I ask is that you sit tight—you, Zirker, right where you were standing when the murder occurred, and Mr. Alston where I was sitting—and make no attempt to confuse me by talking. Is it a go?

ZIRKER. Why, certainly, Mr. Walters: I'll take that bet.

ALSTON (*after a brief pause, during which he has eyed Walters intently*). I'm in on it, too, Inspector.

WALTERS. Good enough. Now take your places. I'll sit here at the Count's table, in the chair the skirt sat in.

WALTERS, ALSTON *and* ZIRKER *take up the positions indicated.* And we'll have the lights out.

To POLICEMAN, O'Halloran, put all the lights out.

POLICEMAN. Yes, sir. *He turns to the switches beside the lobby doors and extinguishes first the wall-sconces, then the central chandelier, leaving the stage in total darkness but for the glimmer that penetrates the semi-opaque glass panels of the lobby door. Then, opening one of these, he thrusts his head out, and calls:* Hey, you—put them lights out, d'ye hear? Inspector's orders.

Immediately the lights are switched off in the lobby.

ALSTON. But Inspector—

ZIRKER. That's hardly fair, Mr. Walters. The lobby lights were going when the woman escaped.

WALTERS. You're right. O'Halloran, you bone-head, why the devil did you tell 'em to turn off those lobby lights?

POLICEMAN. I thought you wanted 'em out, sir.

WALTERS. Well, I don't.

POLICEMAN (*aggrieved tone*). But you told me—"O'Halloran," you says, "put *all* them lights out," says you.

WALTERS (*furiously*). Well, I tell you now, you born simp, to have the lobby lights turned on! Quick—d'you hear?

POLICEMAN (*sulkily*). Oh, *all* right!

The lobby doors creak as he thrusts them open. He continues in the same tone: Inspector Walters says he wants them lights out there turned on again. *A slight pause; then the lobby lights glow once more, through the glass panels.*

WALTERS. Now I'm starting. Remember, Zirker, if you catch me without moving, it means a bottle of wine for you.

ZIRKER (*with a confident laugh*). I'll win that bet.

WALTERS (*his voice sounding from the right of the stage*). Don't be too sure . . .

PAUSE. *A sound is heard of a table moving on the floor. A chair goes over with a crash. A moment later another topples.*

ZIRKER (*a sudden cry of triumph*). I've got you, Inspector!

WALTERS (*voice from the right*). Well, catch me then.

ZIRKER (*in a puzzled tone*). But you are here—and your voice there. What is this—a trick? (*A cry of fright.*) Ah-h-h, Madonna mia! What is this?

ALSTON (*alarmed—voice from left*). What's the matter?

ZIRKER. What devil's work—!

WALTERS. Lights, O'Halloran—light's up!

Instantly the central chandelier floods the stage with light. WALTERS *stands to the right, a revolver in his hand levelled at* ZIRKER. ALSTON *has just risen from his chair, where he sat when the stage was darkened.* ZIRKER *has jumped up from his and is cringing back in abject fright and horror from a* WOMAN *who stands within two feet of him. The latter has entered under cover of darkness, when the lobby lights were out, in company with a* PLAIN CLOTHES MAN *to whose left wrist her right is fastened by handcuffs. The* WOMAN *is the one described by* WALTERS *as Bennetto's companion; but she now wears a neat tailor-made gown, with a fur coat, etc.*

ZIRKER (*livid with terror—cowers and trembles*)—Elena!

WALTERS. Oh, you know this lady now, do you, Zirker?

ZIRKER (*attempting to recover*). I—I do not know her. Who is she? I—I have never—

WALTERS (*approaching the woman*). Madame, is your name Elena?

ZIRKER. Don't answer—

WALTERS (*savagely*). Shut up, you damned murderer! (ZIRKER *recoils from Walters' revolver.*) Madame—?

WOMAN (*with an effort*). My name is Elena Zorzi.

WALTERS. What relation are you to this man?

WOMAN. I am his wife.

WALTERS. His name.

WOMAN. Antonio Zorzi.

WALTERS. Which of you killed Count Umberto Bennetto?

ZIRKER. Elena, I command you not to answer!

WALTERS. Keep quiet . . . Here, O'Halloran—grab this guy before he does anything foolish.

The POLICEMAN *crosses to* ZIRKER, *rapidly searches him for weapons, finds none, and grasps him firmly by the arm.*

WALTERS (*to the* WOMAN). The only way you can save yourself is by downright confession . . .

WOMAN. Antonio killed Count Umberto. I was his wife, I left him for Count Umberto, he followed us to America for revenge. We didn't know . . . neither of us knew . . . he was here . . . Nor did I see him until just before the lights went out. Then I saw him standing there, grinning murder at me . . . I thought he meant me . . . and when in the darkness he seized my arm and told me to come with him I was too frightened not to obey. I did not then know he had killed Count Umberto. He did not tell me until he put me out of the side door, thrust a steamer ticket into my hand, and told me to leave the country if I wished to escape hanging for the murder.

WALTERS. How did he get you out of this crowded room?

WOMAN. I don't know . . . He warned me to keep quiet . . . and drew me very gently but swiftly away between the tables . . . twisting and turning . . . And then he opened that door—(*pointing to the door at back, toward the left*) and led me through the room to the street.

WALTERS. That will do . . . Well, Mr. Alston?

ALSTON. In Heaven's name, *how* did you do it?

WALTERS. Common-sense — every-day police detective methods. I promised you a demonstration. Now you have had it. If Zirker hadn't insisted that the woman couldn't possibly have escaped by way of his private office, I might have let him slip through my fingers. But it was just that—and the fact that he had the key in his pocket—that convicted him. It was clear enough the woman coudn't have left by way of either the lobby or the kitchen and pantries—without wholesale collusion, that is. Therefore, it was plain as day she must have beat it by the only other exit—Zirker's office. So I kept him here—stalling—until the men working outside found out what hotel Bennetto and this woman had put up at. They found out more—that she had returned to her room alone at twelve-fifteen, in great haste and distress, changed her dress, packed a bag hurriedly, and left the hotel. Then we traced her by taxicabs to the Cunard Line pier, which she reached just ten minutes before the *Mauretania* sailed at one A. M. The wireless got us in communication with the ship, and the captain held her in the Lower Bay until we could reach her with a police boat and take the woman off. Until that was accomplished, there was nothing certain—definite—to go on. I wasn't going to arrest this guy until I'd given him plenty of rope to hang himself with . . . But I've been watching him for three hours, and I felt pretty certain he'd cave and make some sort of a damaging admission if I could bring him unexpectedly face to face with the woman he believed to be safely out of the country. So I framed up this mild dose of the third degree—and it's worked!

ALSTON. I think it'll work out big for you, Inspector, when I tell the Commissioner.

The sound of a patrol wagon gong is heard off-stage.

WALTERS. Far be it from me to dodge anything in the line of official appreciation . . . Here comes the hurry-up cart. O'Halloran—Weil—hustle these people out before a crowd collects.

The PLAIN CLOTHES MAN *draws the* WOMAN *up-stage. The* POLICEMAN *is about to do the same with* ZIRKER *when* ALSTON *stops him.*

ALSTON. Here . . . wait a minute . . . I'm still perplexed about the way Zirker got the woman out of the room.

WALTERS. It's plain enough: he'd had a month's warning that this thing was going to happen—ever since Bennetto wrote on from Washington, ordering the table for to-night. He'd figured it down to the fine point of those five minutes of darkness to cover the murder and the disappearance of the woman. He had figured it out to the extent of picking a boat for her to escape on that left the country within an hour of the murder. Is it likely he hadn't figured it down to the point of having a complete floor plan of the room in his mind? Of course not. He knew his way in and out of those tables by counting his steps. Didn't you, Zirker?

ZIRKER *doesn't answer save by a scowl.*

ALSTON. Oh, come, be reasonable: I can make things easy for you in the Tombs if you'll satisfy us. It's no good being rusty about it. You can't escape the chair anyway you put it.

ZIRKER. You are right. I worked out the table plan a week ago.

[CURTAIN]

www.ingramcontent.com/pod-product-compliance
Lightning Source LLC
Chambersburg PA
CBHW032139010726
47494CB00002B/284

* 9 7 8 1 4 3 4 4 7 7 7 1 2 *